You

Don't

Love

This

Man

HARPER PERENNIAL

NEW YORK • LONDON • TORONTO • SYDNEY • NEW DELHI • AUCKLAND

You Don’t Love This Man

A NOVEL

Dan DeWeese

HARPER PERENNIAL

This book is a work of fiction. The characters, incidents, and dialogue are drawn from the author's imagination and are not to be construed as real. Any resemblance to actual events or persons, living or dead, is entirely coincidental.

HarperCollins books may be purchased for educational, business, or sales promotional use. For information please write: Special Markets Department, HarperCollins Publishers, 10 East 53rd Street, New York, NY 10022.

FIRST EDITION

Designed by Sunil Manchikanti

Library of Congress Cataloging-in-Publication Data

DeWeese, Dan.
You don't love this man : a novel / Dan DeWeese. — 1st ed.
p. cm.
ISBN 978-0-06-199232-2
I. Title.
PS3604.E9Y68 2011
813'.6—dc22

2010024949

---

11 12 13 14 15 OV/RRD 10 9 8 7 6 5 4 3 2 1

Morbius.

Something is

approaching from

the southwest.

It is now quite close.

Forbidden Planet

You

Don't

Love

This

Man

I

I LOST MY DAUGHTER ONCE. She was three. It was after dark on Halloween, and we were standing on the sidewalk in front of a house down the street from our own. She wore yellow rain boots and a fuzzy brown puppy dog costume that zipped from her feet to beneath her chin—black spots dotted the costume's body, and two black ears flopped atop the hood as she peered with undisguised suspicion at the cement walk that led to the door of this stranger's home. When I told her to go ahead, the door was right there, she shook her head and put her mittened hand in mine. "No," she said. "You go with me." I told her she was big now, she could do it herself—did she remember what to say? She mumbled the phrase, and I gave her a little pat to move her up the walk, but she turned back and hugged my leg, wordlessly holding on. "Miranda," I said, exasperated, "I'll be right here. You can do it." "No," she said, clutching even more tightly. "*No.*"

A group of six or seven ghosts, animals, and witches roughly her age or a bit older shuffled up behind us, bunched together in the dark. A few carried flashlights with orange plastic pumpkins over the bulbs, spheres that wobbled through the damp night air. A woman in charge of the group—in the dark it was just the shape of a woman, really—looked down at Miranda as the other kids moved past. "Did you want to go up, too?" she asked. And as if the words of a single stranger were all it took to hypnotize her, Miranda moved obediently up the walk with the others, the woman following. I watched them make their way up three stairs and congregate on a small concrete porch beneath the glow of a weak light above the door. A middle-aged woman in orange sweatpants and a black sweatshirt opened the door and asked with great astonishment who all these little creatures were, and the kids eagerly extended their bags. The homeowner distributed candy, the kids sang their ragged chorus of thanks, and the woman in charge herded the group laterally across the front yard toward the next house. Once beyond the reach of the porch light, only the orange glow of the flashlights betrayed their location, and when they passed behind a thick laurel and some rhododendrons that bordered the yards, even those lights disappeared from view.

My breath rose in a mist as I navigated the tilted and cracked sidewalk slabs toward the next house. It had rained earlier, and fallen leaves covered the concrete. They had formed a tapestry of rich browns and reds and golds during the day, but at night had become a slick material that slid easily beneath the pressure of a foot, so I chose my steps with care. I heard kids chattering nearby—whether it was the group I was following or just one of dozens of other groups nearby, I couldn't tell—but when I reached the head of the walk to the next house, I saw the little group of creatures and their trailing chaperone scramble up the four wide wooden steps that led to the next porch. The woman caught one stumbling little ghost by the arm, raising it up the steps to where it could join its fellows, and a brave lion pressed the bell next to the red front door. An old man in slacks and a cardigan appeared, dispensed treats into the pails and bags, and after another chorus of thank-yous, the woman herded the group off the porch and brought them out to where I stood on the sidewalk. "They seem to have the hang of this," I said, searching the group for my puppy. "It's the incentive," she said, laughing. I started to grab what I thought was a puppy, but realized it was a bear. Present also were the lion, a Darth Vader, a ladybug, witch, and ghost, and a gorilla. But no puppy.

"But she was right with us," the woman said.

I walked toward the house and checked the porch, but it was empty. I crossed into the dark area between houses then, calling Miranda's name, but all I heard was the woman telling the children in her group to wait, that everyone should stay together. The glare of porch lights pushed the space between houses into deeper darkness, and I could easily have tripped over any child dawdling there. I called Miranda's name into the void between the twisted rhododendrons, and called it again as I moved behind and around a laurel, but there was no response. Children's voices carried from multiple directions, their shouts and laughter bouncing through the cool night air. A car coasted slowly up the street, and I thought, But what if . . . , and found myself running toward the street, intending to head right onto the pavement to throw myself across the car's hood and bring everything to a halt. I stopped at the curb, though, and gazed breathlessly into the section of street illuminated by the vehicle's headlights while I shouted Miranda's name again, as if the sound of my voice would prevent her from appearing in their pale sweep. The car passed without incident, its taillights dissolving in the distance.

"I hear you're missing one," a voice behind me said. I turned and saw a man in blue jeans, a jacket, and a ball cap. It was the same outfit I myself wore, as did any number of other fathers in the neighborhood that night. Two boys stood silently beside him: the taller was a pirate with an eye patch, the other wore a bathrobe and held a sword.

"Yes," I said. "Somewhere between these houses."

"Could she have wandered home?"

"Not in the dark. She wouldn't find it."

"Which direction is it?" he said. "We can head that way."

I pointed down the street. "She's three. Dressed as a puppy."

The man patted his boys on the back and they headed off.

I walked again into the dark section of lawn between houses, calling her name. If she didn't make it across the lawn with that group, then where did she go? Did she double back and return to the house she'd just visited? Did she wander into a backyard? I shuddered at thoughts of dogs and chains and darkness, but decided a child wouldn't do that—she would follow the lights, the people, and the candy. I heard the approach of another car, but when I planted my foot to move toward the street, I slipped and fell in the wet grass. My knees hit, but I steadied myself, fingers in the sod, and pushed myself up, calling her name until the car passed and disappeared down another street.

I continued through lawns, past groups of parents and children who must have wondered why a lone figure was cutting through the darkness. Which way had the woman with the group of children gone? There was no way I would find them, or that they would find me. What had the man with the two boys looked like? I had hardly glanced at him.

I wondered how I was going to walk into the house and announce to Sandra, my wife, that I'd lost our three-year-old. It wasn't possible. Jack-o'-lanterns sat in windows and on porches, flames dancing behind their grins, while knots of adults and costumed children strolled the sidewalks. What would I say? That my only job had been to keep track of our child, and I had failed, and she was gone? Someone had probably stolen her, with the intention of doing unspeakable things? Sandra would run out the door and through the neighborhood, screaming. There would be police and questions and a massive search.

If I can just find her right this moment, I thought, then none of that needs to happen. So I will find her.

The sky, a sodden wash of clouds during the day, had become a great charcoal swath at night. Every breath clouded silver in the air and then vanished, and I jogged to the far end of the street so that I could turn and start slowly back. Miranda knew not to cross the street, and no adult would stand by and watch a three-year-old step alone onto the asphalt, so she couldn't have left the block. I tried to walk casually, while still examining every tree and bush and yard and adult and child I passed. From one lawn a whining motor powered a scarecrow that waved its arm and turned its head, and from elsewhere a stereo played a loop of creaking doors and demented cackling. I listened for her voice or cry or laugh, but there was nothing, and the closer I came to our house, the bolder I was about scouring other people's property: I circled cars, walked through side yards, and flattened bushes. By the time I reached the yard of the house next to my own, I felt as if I were floating, and walked through the grass in silence. A couple and a small boy in a vinyl skeleton costume walked past on the sidewalk. The couple nodded politely to me while the boy looked into his pail and talked excitedly about candy he had received at my own house. I was at the foot of the porch by then, and had a last, desperate thought: *Maybe she came home.*

The broken gate to the backyard stood ajar as always. I made my way through it and to the concrete pad behind the back door, where the dark sphere of the barbecue grill sat atop spindly aluminum legs. Miranda's tricycle lay on its side in the grass, as did her broken plastic lawn mower—in the weak glow of the back porch light, everything appeared bronzed. Beyond the light's reach, in the dark back corner of the yard, sat the little wooden playhouse I'd bought at the beginning of the summer. It had a little doorway without a door and a little window without a pane, and it was through the window that I saw movement—the shift of a shadow within shadows. I reached the house in a few quick strides, looked through the window, and my knees buckled: there was the puppy, sitting amid her scattered candy. I breathed, collecting myself, and knelt at the window. "What are you doing?" I said.

She looked up with an excited, guiltless smile. "Putting my candy away!"

"Come out of there. Right now."

I reached through the door and grabbed the scruff of the costume's neck. She struggled and cried, demanding to be released so she could gather her candy, but I was stronger, and pulled her kicking and wailing out the door. She watched anxiously as I swept the candy toward me, gathered it up, and dropped it into her bag. When she was satisfied that not a piece had been lost, she let me pick her up and carry her around to the front of the house. "What have you been doing?" I said.

She opened her mouth, displaying the contents.

"Eating candy?"

"Yes!"

"Well, that's enough now. Halloween is over."

"We can go again."

"No. You can only go once."

She twisted in the direction of the street, but I pressed her to my chest, and it was a crying and struggling Miranda that I ended up carrying through the front door. Sandra didn't question the tears—they were an expected part of Halloween, as well as a daily event in the life of a three-year-old. She pulled the costume off Miranda and threw the crumpled thing down the basement stairs to be washed, wondering aloud how it had gotten so filthy. I didn't answer.

Later, after Miranda was asleep and Sandra, too, had gone to bed, I stayed awake, manning the door for late-evening visitors. When I stepped out onto the porch at only ten-thirty, though, I found the neighborhood empty. Even the candle of our jack-o'-lantern had gone out, the monster turned to nothing but an empty gourd with a sinking lid. The woman with the children, the man with the boys: the absence of police cars or of anyone running through the neighborhood must have convinced them the situation had been resolved. As I locked the door and turned out the lights, I reminded myself that children are lost and found every day. A brief episode did not necessarily need to be mentioned.

TWENTY-TWO YEARS LATER, on the night before my daughter's wedding day, I dreamed of that Halloween. This wasn't a surprise, as by that point I'd been suffering the dream for months. I had never in my life had trouble sleeping until that year I turned forty-nine. A whirling of image and sound began to descend on me in the small hours, and I would find myself again in the dark, hearing children's voices and laughter as I marked the progress of those wobbling orange flashlights. Often it seemed I wasn't even dreaming, but was trapped instead in an undreaming and unthinking bewilderment. So before dawn on the morning of Miranda's wedding, exhausted by my mind's interminable running through darkened yards, I rose and stumbled down the hall, dread trailing me like a nightshirt's ragged hem.

It was cold in the house—strangely cold for what the forecasters had warned would be one of the hottest days of the summer—and outside it was raining. I squinted in the kitchen light's harsh fluorescence until I had successfully started the coffee, and then I turned the light off and stood in the dark, listening to the machine hiss and cough. On the microwave, a glowing digit flipped from one minute to the next—a relief—and I wondered if across town Sandra, too, was awake. If so, she would be stealing her own glances out a window, probably while ironing or folding or wrapping or arranging something—whatever she could to stay in perpetual movement. Though we had been divorced for almost a decade, the thought of her bustling created a sympathetic nervousness in me, as if we were still a team, and I, too, should have been doing something for the cause.

I had warned Sandra the previous evening that it would rain in the night, and that she shouldn't panic when it did. This was after the rehearsal dinner, when Miranda and her friends had led us to a bar where, despite its old-sounding Irish name, the bartenders were two college kids, Asian and Hispanic, respectively. A large adjoining room held a number of pool tables, and the whiplike snap that announced each game of eight ball was heard at regular intervals. Classic rock blared from a jukebox in the corner, forcing me to incline my head in Sandra's direction so I could hear her ask how I knew it was going to rain. When I told her I could just feel it, she laughed and said, "Feel it how? In your knees or in your nerves?"

"Neither," I said. "In the air."

She raised an eyebrow. "In the air? That seems suspicious."

"It's just a feeling. I'm telling you to reassure you. Any rain or clouds will burn off. Everything will be fine."

"I think it's cute that you're reassuring me," she said, patting me on the arm.

Sandra had remarried four years after our divorce, and her new husband, a genial insurance agent named Alan, was engaged in an earnest conversation with Sandra's sister and brother-in-law a couple tables from where we sat. It sometimes seemed that because I hadn't remarried, Sandra didn't quite know what to do with me. That was my guess, at least, as to why regardless of what I said, she often responded as if she found me mildly amusing. Before I could say more, though, an unfamiliar woman sitting to the other side of Sandra—the mother of a bridesmaid, perhaps—asked Sandra to identify the friends and family gathered in the bar. Sandra began by pointing out a few people at various tables, a spatial strategy that allowed her to point out "my husband, Alan" and then several other people before arriving at our own table and saying, "And this, of course, is Miranda's father, Paul."

"Oh," the woman said, brightening at my identification. "My daughter told me you gave quite a speech at dinner."

I thanked her for what I accepted as a compliment, though it troubled me. I had assumed that standing before family and friends to express some thoughts about my daughter and her marriage would be easy, so I hadn't bothered to prepare anything ahead of time. As a bank manager, I was perfectly used to speaking extemporaneously to customers and staff about accounts, cards, procedures, and regulations, and I didn't see any reason a few remarks at a dinner would be different. In the moments before I was to speak, though, I was surprised to find my hands trembling, and when I struck my spoon too hard against my glass, nearly knocking it over before I managed to control the force of my tapping, I realized I was in the grip of an anxiety whose intensity I hadn't seen coming. So though I did speak, afterward I retained no memory of what I had said. I remembered that clang of the spoon against the glass and could recall polite applause when I stopped, but the panic I suffered during the actual speech was such that, like film exposed to intense heat, my memory had been almost entirely fogged. So I couldn't help but note that, technically, the woman's comment that it had been "quite a speech" was not necessarily a compliment. "I hope I didn't go too long," I said.

"Well, you're the father of the bride, so you have every right to," the woman said. "But where is the groom I've heard so much about? Will he be here?"

"I don't know," Sandra said, and turned to me. "Do you?"

I shook my head. "I'm sure he's in charge of his own schedule."

"No guarantees, then," Sandra said.

"Oh well," the woman said, disappointed. "I guess I can wait."

Someone at a nearby table called Sandra over. She stood with what I suspected was relief, gave me a quick pat on the back as she apologized for having to leave us, and headed across the room.

"And what about you?" the woman asked. "Do you have a significant other somewhere here?"

"Do I have a significant other?" I repeated as if it were some kind of quiz. I actually looked around the bar as if one might appear. "No."

"Not even a date?"

She had already been at the bar when I arrived, and though it was an ungenerous evaluation—maybe she was just a friendly person—I noted that the drink in front of her was probably not her first. "I guess I forgot to ask someone."

"That's understandable," she said. "I'm sure it's stressful being the father of the bride. But listen." She placed her hand atop mine and leaned toward me. "If you need someone to dance with at the reception, I'll be happy to be your partner."

"Be careful," I said. "I'm afraid I have two left feet."

She glanced at my shoes. "Those feet look fine to me."

"All right," I said. "I have to mix right now, but I may come looking for you tomorrow."

"I'll make sure I'm easy to find," she said.

I made sure to shake a few hands and trade a few greetings, but it was only a few minutes later that I made my escape from the bar and headed home.

That next morning, though—as I stood there in my dark kitchen, arms crossed and shoulders hunched while I listened to the coffeepot—I felt like calling Sandra and asking that she acknowledge the correctness of my prediction. I was confident she was awake, and that she would have laughed. But there are times of day that one simply doesn't call.

WHEN I STEPPED OUTSIDE not much later, coffee in hand, it was to discover that the rain was really no more than a mist that hung ghostlike in the air before me, and only slightly fuzzed the surface of the courtyard lawn. The weather here often does this: it gives every appearance of rain, and then doesn't quite deliver. In summer especially, early threats made above are often false, and I could see that watery patches of sky to the east were already fading to a thin blue-gray. The ground-level mist disappeared as I walked through it, a diaphanous curtain endlessly parting, and in movement I took stock of myself. A click of cartilage dispensed its hurtful little jolt in my shoulder, a reminder that the ball caught in the socket there on occasion. A dull pain lay behind my right knee, the result of spending an entire day helping Alan move sofas and tables and beds in preparation for the arrival of Sandra's houseguests. My townhouse had two bedrooms, and I had offered the empty one as potential lodging for visitors, but Sandra hadn't taken me up on the offer. The visiting guests were from her side of the family—maybe she worried that placing someone with her ex-husband would be considered a slight. A pair of joggers, a man and a woman, announced they would be on my left, and then they were, two sets of nylon shorts whisking past as I continued my inventory. Eyesight? I trained my gaze on the lady jogger's round bottom, rejected that as an unscientific test, and squinted instead at the nearest street sign, pleased to find I could read it, though my already knowing the answer certainly helped. And hearing? The breeze in the firs, tisk of a sprinkler, hum of distant traffic, throb of my pulse in my ears: everything was there, present and accounted for. I was not old. I told myself.

The joggers continued down the street and into the mist while I kept my own pace, covering the route I took most mornings, a neighborhood walk that provided a good half hour in which my thoughts were my own. Satisfied I was in working order physically, I gave myself the mental challenge of recalling that speech. I'd believed I would be able to say something true and moving in two minutes, without preparation. Had I managed this? I knew I had started by dramatically clearing my throat, because immediately upon doing so I chastised myself for already having lapsed into cliché. I clasped my hands before me in order to quell their trembling, then decided I looked odd holding them that way, and shoved one hand into my pocket. The other found its way to my stomach, and I gave up the struggle there—if the pose was good enough for Napoleon, I thought, it was good enough for me. Throughout my search for a natural posture, though, I had been speaking. But about what? Nothing came back. It was a toast—had I raised my glass? Did people drink? I hadn't the slightest, and neither could I estimate how long I'd spoken. I just remembered Miranda, seated next to me, giving me a kiss on the cheek when I sat down. "It's okay," she had whispered to me. "Everything is fine." I didn't know what she meant, though. Had I apologized for speaking too long, or for the arc of my entire life? Drunk on the moment, the moment had escaped me.

A calico cat eyed me with suspicion from the edge of a shrub before it turned and disappeared within. A young man pressing a bundle of newspapers to his chest ran past and commenced firing the papers toward doorways. A seagull floated in for a wide-winged landing on the sidewalk not thirty feet ahead of me. There was something clumsy and ad hoc about its landing, but it had succeeded, and when it extended and refolded its brown and white wings I was surprised to note, even from a distance, the flick of a thin red tongue. The lizards are their cousins, I guess. The gull monitored my approach in the sidelong way birds have of turning parallel to their object of examination. A few desultory hops carried it into the street, but one wide blue eye remained trained on me. It opened its beak silently, again displaying that tongue, and then snapped it shut. Had the gesture been directed at me, or was it just the avian mechanism adjusting itself? I continued past the bird and onward, and when I looked back, it was to see the inscrutable creature twitch its head in another direction and hop off, pecking the asphalt every few steps—as if it expected to find something.

The morning walk was a new habit for me, adopted from the last woman I had dated, with whom I'd broken up six months earlier. Trish, a Realtor who had just moved into the city from the suburbs, began every morning—or every morning she awoke with me, at least—with a brisk walk through the neighborhood in one of her clean, pressed, nylon sweat suits. She owned these sweat suits, which she called "warm-ups," in a number of colors: baby blue with white piping, wine red with yellow stripes, and a neon green with electric blue trim were three of her more consistent choices. I've never particularly been one for athletic wear, and walked with her in my usual weekend-morning outfit of jeans and a jacket. That relationship had been over for a while, but I'd kept her ritual of the morning walk. I liked it.

IT WAS AT THE breakfast table in Sandra's house later that morning that I received the call. It was just after nine o'clock, and I had been listening to her brother, Bradshaw, read aloud from a sports Web site he was looking at on his laptop. He'd been noting various teams' victories and losses, pulling up detailed information on recent draft picks and trades, and estimating likelihoods of future success. I did my best to nod at appropriate intervals. I was supposed to be at Sandra's disposal that morning to run errands, pick up guests from the airport, or take care of any other pressing tasks, but I had been there almost half an hour and she had yet to come down from her room. Bradshaw's own wife and two teenage daughters were also upstairs, and though we heard occasional disputes among them over space in the bathroom, not one of them had shown her face yet, either. So I was trapped, drinking another cup of coffee while I watched Bradshaw take his own breakfast in what struck me as the ensemble of a teenager: oversized red nylon athletic shorts and a white T-shirt memorializing a "slo-pitch" softball tournament. Between installments of sports gossip, I asked him why the *w* had been deleted from *slo*, and Bradshaw pressed his chin to his chest to examine the usage. "It's a different word," he said.

"The pitching is slow," I said. "So why do they spell it that way?"

"The word is *slo-pitch*," he said. "It's a different word." He took an overlarge, tearing bite of his toasted bagel, the butter and cream cheese of which had gathered into points of glistening white at the corners of his mouth. Miranda once told me, rather gleefully, that Bradshaw had said he was surprised Sandra had ever married me in the first place, since I was such "a finicky guy." I don't think Bradshaw always understands the words he uses. And I was pleased when my cell phone produced its little trill and I was able to consider something other than his T-shirt.

"We were just robbed," my coworker Catherine said when I answered. "Everyone's fine, it's under control, but I thought you would want to know. It was silent, no weapon. Just a guy who pushed a misspelled note across the counter to Amber. The rest of us didn't even notice until it was over." She used the same disdainful tone she had when she had called me at home one Saturday morning to report that a stray, floppy-eared terrier was in the bank, had evaded capture for over twenty minutes, and was hiding behind the change machine in the back corner. I had driven to the bank, rattled the machine, and stamped my foot, but it was only after I told the staff to return to business as usual that the creature had emerged from his hiding place and loped out of the branch with a sad look in its eyes, as if disappointed we'd given up the game.

"I'll be there in a few minutes," I told her.

"You don't need to," she said.

I watched Bradshaw continue to work at the bagel—his movements were tense, relentless. "I have nothing else to do right now."

"I know that's not true. Oh, here they are, we're all saved now."

"Who?"

"The police. They just pulled up."

"What was misspelled?"

"It was a robbery," she said. "One *b*. I'll talk to you later."

I folded the phone in time to watch Bradshaw stuff the remainder of the bagel into his mouth and commence strenuous bovine chewing. He swallowed dramatically, and then again, and then a third time, tipping his head back to better reveal the contortions of his trachea as it convulsed beneath the slack skin and gray stubble of his neck. "There's a problem?" he said finally, feigning concern.

"Yes. Do you think Sandra will be down soon?"

He shrugged. "You can go up there."

Upstairs, someone was running the sink in the bathroom, a hair dryer roared from the master bedroom, and I sensed the press of footsteps within one of the smaller bedrooms. Miranda was staying in her old room here for the weekend, which meant there were, theoretically, at least five women trying to share the single upstairs bathroom. To my relief, though, all I was currently faced with was an empty hallway with four closed doors, so I knocked quickly on the door to the master bedroom and called Sandra's name. The hair dryer ceased, there was some shifting and rustling as she told me to come in, and then the hair dryer resumed. I found her seated at her dressing table bundled in a white terry-cloth robe, her head inclined toward the hand in which she held and waved the dryer while with her other hand she tugged at her long, blond hair. She has always kept her hair long, and in concert with her quick, dark eyes, her looks have held a slightly intimidating power over me. I waited for her to shift her gaze to mine before I told her, over the hair dryer's howling, that the bank had been robbed. She immediately killed the dryer, creating a portentous silence. "*Your* bank?" she said. "Was anyone hurt?"

"I don't think so."

"Can you get out of going?"

"No."

She restarted the hair dryer, waved it through her hair a few times, and turned it off again. "It's your daughter's wedding day."

"It will only take an hour. I'll talk to the police, fill out the forms, hand tissues to the tellers. And you don't need me this morning, anyway. There's nothing left to do."

She arched an eyebrow, just as she had the previous evening. "There's nothing left to do?"

"You're all going to the hotel. Why are you doing your hair when it's supposed to get done at the hotel?"

The hair dryer erupted, undead, and I made it out of the room and to the top of the stairs before the machine was strangled silent again.

"Have you heard from Miranda?" she called.

"No," I said toward her doorway. "Should I have?"

"Could you come here, please? And close the door."

Warily, I returned to the bedroom, and pressed the door until the latch clicked in place.

"Her bed hasn't been slept in," she said. "And I didn't hear her come in, so I don't think she came home last night." She continued ministering to her hair in the mirror, as if we were doing no more than chatting in a salon.

"Maybe she slept at her apartment," I said.

"Two of the bridesmaids are staying there. I called, and they said she's not there."

"She's with Grant."

"No. He doesn't know where she is, either."

I heard voices and laughter behind me in the hall—Bradshaw's wife and daughters. They had never particularly cared for me, and I waited for them to finish galloping down the stairs before I said, "Do you want me to look for her?"

Sandra turned on her little bench to examine me directly. When she was younger she had used this expression to convey anger, but the crow's feet and smile lines that now filigreed her features transformed the look into one of attractively wry disdain. Before she answered, though, something shifted—it was a relaxation of her eyebrows, perhaps, or a slight dilation of her pupils—and she asked, in her amused-by-me tone, "But where would you look for her?"

"I don't know," I said.

"You should go to the bank."

"I could keep trying her cell, or call the gallery. I could call the other bridesmaids. How many bridesmaids does she have again?"

"Nope. I'll do that. Go to the bank."

"Did she say anything to you last night? After I left?"

"I'm sure she's fine," she said. "Take care of what you have to take care of." She restarted the hair dryer, and I remained in place long enough for her continued silence to confirm that the discussion was truly closed.

It was. So I went to the bank.

I SUPPOSE THE PUBLIC'S romantic attachment to bank robbers—from Butch Cassidy and John Dillinger to Patty Hearst and local "gentlemen" bandits all across the country—stems from the belief that bank robbery is a noble act of defiance in the face of a corrupt social system. The persona of the bank robber isn't burdened with the repulsive deviance of the pedophile, the depraved insanity of the serial killer, or the arrested adolescence of the domestic abuser. Robbers of property seem empty-headedly compulsive—they steal the same make and model of car over and over, or snatch purses in the same way, or cut bicycle locks again and again. White-collar crime possesses the veneer of intelligence, but depends on deceits like counterfeit accounting or the cowardly resort to tax shelters, and often pays in stock options, debt financing, or other rewards too financially abstract to fire the imagination. What attracts the public to bank robbers is that bank robbers just want cash, and now. And so, the theory goes, we understand their motives.

This has not been my experience. And that experience began before I ever owned a suit, a car, a big-screen television, or any of the other trappings of my middle-class life. It began when the young woman with whom I had achieved the greatest pleasure of my life appeared one day at my teller window on the arm of another man.

It has always struck me as odd that I noticed Grant that day before I noticed Gina. It may have been a question of geometry: he walked slightly in front of her, perhaps, or I was stationed to the side. I remember the bank lobby suffused in the narcoleptic lemony haze of a summer afternoon as a Muzak version of an old standard played over the lobby speakers. A lilting flute carried the melody, and as I wondered at the choice of instrument, a young man stepped into the bank. On the street, the eyes of a stranger will occasionally fix on me and light up until, after a closer look, the person either averts his eyes as we pass, or else smiles and admits with a laugh that he's sorry, he thought I was someone else. The young man in the bank approached me with that same sense of familiarity: he executed a modest little duck of his head as he handed me his deposit, but his conspiratorial smile and bright eyes were those of someone who knew me well. He had the high cheekbones and clear complexion of a television actor, and his hair was trimmed short and neat, despite those having been the ragged Carter Administration years, when men visited their barbers less often. It was his suit, however, that struck me with the greatest force. I had never seen someone my own age wear a suit other than to a graduation, funeral, or wedding, but this young man wore his tan slacks and jacket over a white, open-necked dress shirt with the ease of someone who wore a suit every day. The terms *class* and *classy* were so poorly differentiated in my mind in those days as to be entirely conflated, so although I had previously thought I was quite professional and well turned out in my powder blue dress shirt and tie, after seeing that suit, I felt my shirts and ties were no more remarkable than the uniforms worn by employees of fast-food restaurants.

I had already set the growling dot matrix printer to producing his receipt by the time I noticed that the woman standing next to him was Gina. Her straight brown hair fell to the small of her back, and she wore a simple black skirt and royal blue blouse that revealed her figure without appearing immodest. It had been two years since I'd seen her, and her brown eyes, heavy-lidded and wide set, possessed a harder intelligence than I remembered, while her body seemed softer and more relaxed. The transformation in her—the way she carried herself and studied the room, and her smile when finally we made eye contact—was the beginning of my realization that women in their college years are coltish and ungainly to any man possessed of decent aesthetics. "This is Paul. He and I went to college together," she told the young man with her. Of him, she simply said, "And this is Grant." Though she left the exact nature of her relationship with each of us unspoken, it seemed clear enough, so I was surprised when Grant cheerfully said, "We should get a drink together sometime."

I said that would be nice, but before I could look to Gina for a hint as to how to proceed, he had turned her way as well, annihilating any chance of a private glance. "Where should we go?" he said, "Bristol's?"

She chewed her lip in feigned thoughtfulness. "That sounds good."

"Do you know it?" he asked me. "Bristol's, by the river?"

I said of course I knew it, by which I meant I knew that Bristol's was the bar where the city's local heroes and any real celebrities passing through town spent their evenings drinking scotch in leather armchairs. The last I'd heard, two Hollywood actors filming on location along the city's picturesque river for a few weeks had made it a habit to end their evenings in Bristol's. One of them, if the newspaper's gossip columnist was to be believed, had even gotten into some trouble over a woman there.

"Friday evening?" Grant said.

I found myself completely unable to recall whether I had plans, or even which day of the week Friday was, so I said it sounded fine. Grant nodded happily and thanked me twice for my service, the second thanks a subtle suggestion that I pass him the deposit receipt the printer had disgorged and which I held stupidly in my hand. I handed him the slip of paper, he and Gina walked out the door, and I helped the next customer. My mind spun. I helped perhaps twenty minutes' worth of customers without being at all conscious of what I was doing, so absorbed was I by thoughts of Gina as I had known her in the past and of Gina as she had walked into the bank that day, and how she had changed, and how I had changed. I speculated on Grant and who he might be, and on what kinds of activities he and Gina could possibly pursue together, and I thought of Bristol's, and of movie stars and scotch, and Grant and Gina, and of many things. And then I was pistol-whipped and robbed of roughly two thousand dollars.

My memory of the rest of that day is hazy—the images I carry were constructed primarily from the reports of coworkers. I remember standing at my teller station musing on my encounter with Gina and Grant and, in all honesty, attempting to discern the odds of my ever having sex with Gina again. This involved mentally rehearsing conversations in which I convinced her we should indulge ourselves one more time. I wasn't requesting that she break up with Grant—in my fantasy life I am always courteous—because the two of them seemed well matched, really. I was just talking about one more time, what did she think? And I was practicing this conversation not only between customers, but between each step of helping each customer, as in, Good afternoon, how can I help you? *I'd just like to withdraw fifty dollars, but you're out of withdrawal slips at the counter.* I'm sorry about that, let me get you one, there you go, because you have to admit that it was pretty good, wasn't it, I mean I think about it fairly often, I think we both enjoyed ourselves quite a bit. I'm not talking about getting back into the emotional depth of a full relationship, I'm just talking about finding out if that chemistry's still there, and if it is, enjoying it one more time from a different perspective, right? There you go. *Thank you.* How did you want that? *Could I get two twenties and a roll of quarters? It's laundry day.* You bet, and if you don't ever want to see me again after that, I think that's fine, I'd totally understand if you're uncomfortable, and I might be, too, so maybe we'll just have drinks this one time and then get together separately the one time for ourselves, and then we can go our separate ways. *Thanks.* You're welcome.

And so forth.

I recall three details of that day's final customer: eyes the pale blue of a frozen winter sky, dark stubble bristling from a pointed chin, and a black T-shirt featuring the image of a slobbering, monstrous creature beneath stylized gothic lettering that read "Mooncalf." I was fairly familiar with popular music in those years, and at least vaguely aware of the goofy "heavy metal" music characterized by satanic prancing and the miming of animal cruelty, but I had never heard of this "Mooncalf." So the mutant on the T-shirt's front, in concert with the pale blue eyes and dark stubble of the shirt's owner, served as the man's distinguishing characteristics when he looked into my own eyes and, speaking slowly and quietly, told me to give him all the money in my drawer. The words that had been running through my head before he spoke were something on the order of, *Now don't you think this was a good idea, don't you, don't you?*, so because the man's directive was completely irregular to my experience of transaction-opening sentences and, strangely, slipped fairly unobtrusively into the imaginative situation I was absorbed in, it failed to register with me. My response was simply to look up from my computer screen, apologize, and ask if he could repeat himself. He looked into my eyes and said even more quietly, "I want all of the money in your drawer, right now. This is a robbery."

That was when it finally stopped: the scene in my head, its soundtrack, and the autopilot consciousness that was completing transactions for me. I felt the muscles of my cheeks tighten as my vacuous work grin froze upon my face. What my coworkers told me happened next is that the man pulled out a pistol and, swinging it high in the air, brought it down on the crown of my head. I fell backward, the back of my head struck the floor—there was probably no pad at all beneath that thin carpet—and the world went out. The man leaped over the counter and, waving the gun in the general direction of the other employees, took the cash from my drawer, stuffed it into a canvas bag he pulled from the back of his pants, leaped back over the counter, and ran.

After he was gone, one of my coworkers attempted to rouse me. She told me she felt my hair was damp, and then noticed the scarlet corona of blood-soaked carpet expanding from beneath my skull. When I regained consciousness a few minutes before the police and medical personnel arrived, it was only in order to turn my head to the side and vomit.

CATHERINE WAS THE FIRST to greet me when I entered the bank. Her diminutive stature and boyishly short hair lent her a pixie quality enhanced that day by the immaculately pressed beige pantsuit she wore as she crossed the lobby to where I stood just inside the door. "You don't need to be here," she said in a stage whisper.

"But I don't need to be anywhere else," I said. "So tell me what happened."

"It was standard," she said, as if disappointed. "A middle-aged white guy in a gray suit came in right after we opened. He passed a note to Amber that said he wanted twenties and larger, no devices, so she gave him what was in her drawer. Then he apparently told her he wanted the cash in her safe, too, which she didn't even have to unlock, because she'd just come from the dispenser and was still putting her straps away."

I was surprised to note a healthy number of freckles scattered across Catherine's cheeks. She'd been working as a service manager in my branch for ten years, but that was the first I'd seen of freckles, and they further confirmed my belief that she was rarely more than a costume change away from Peter Pan. And had she really hidden her freckles beneath makeup every weekday for a decade? The thought was unsettling. "How much did he take?" I asked.

"A little over six thousand. Amber's still shaky, but she's toughing it out. Charlotte and Tina are thrilled, I think. They're telling their versions right now, but neither of them even has a hair out of place from the thing."

Across the branch, two uniformed police officers stood with Charlotte and Tina, the two other tellers who had been working that morning. The first officer listened as Tina gestured excitedly while Charlotte nodded in agreement. The second officer took notes on a small pad.

"Did you see it happen?" I asked.

"Not really," Catherine said. "I was sorting the mail. I just saw there was a man at Amber's window, and then he left and she started crying."

"Where is she?"

"In your office."

From the bank's front door to my office was a walk across a vast, yellow-carpeted space. The building was a rectangular box the size of a gymnasium, constructed in the golden banking days of the 1960s, when the location supported a staff of more than thirty. The vaulted ceiling was twenty feet overhead, and leafy trees outside brushed massive plate-glass windows that lined the upper half of the main wall. In the old days, smokers lit up at their desks without a second thought, and half of the managers, all of whom were men, ate lunch at the steakhouse down the street, trying to keep their ties clean while they enjoyed red meat and martinis before returning for the abbreviated banking afternoon. Those days are mere legend now, of course—the scrivening of daily credits and debits has shifted to centralized processing locations where documents and figures are run twenty-four hours a day by employees who have no contact with the public. The staff I managed in that building numbered only eight, more than half of whom were college students working less than twenty hours a week, and who didn't particularly care if their cash drawers balanced at the end of the day. If they lost their job at the bank, they could get a job that paid just as much at any number of mall stores. And banker's hours had disappeared years ago. Normal operating hours at my branch were nine to six Monday through Friday, and ten to three on Saturday. That the place was open at all on Saturdays struck me as absurd, an overt corporate strike against the sanctity of the weekend, but I never complained. Because to whom? These decisions are handed down from Valhalla.

When I stepped into my office, I found Amber seated on the cranberry-colored love seat against the wall. She straightened as if caught in some indiscretion. Her eyes were red and swollen, there were damp spots on the front of her navy blue company-issued polo shirt, and balled-up tissue lay next to her on the sofa. "I'm so, so sorry," she said, fighting the return of tears.

"Don't be," I said. "You haven't done anything wrong."

"No," she said, shaking her head miserably. "I screwed up. My safe wasn't locked. My straps shouldn't have been out, and I didn't hit the button. I didn't even look at the guy who did it. A guy robbed me, but I have no idea what he looked like, so now I can't even help the police."

Amber was an undergraduate pursuing a degree in psychology, and was the best natural cash handler I had ever employed. I assume she was aware of this talent, because she began painting her nails bright red not long after starting as a teller. We had a number of male customers who came into the branch even for simple transactions, apparently hoping to stand before Amber and her mane of blond corkscrew curls as she counted out their cash. I had heard odd denomination requests from these men, too—they asked for sixty dollars in fives, or twenty in ones, or anything, I suspected, that might increase the number of bills and thereby the glamour, cousin perhaps to the allures of Vegas, in Amber's fanning of the things across the counter. Once I even heard a customer, after Amber was done counting out his cash, say, "Can I touch the money now?"

I sat on the front edge of my desk. "Do you think you should have refused to give the guy the straps of hundreds from your safe?"

"No," she said. "But they shouldn't have been out."

"If your safe had been locked and he had asked you to open it and give him everything in it, should you have refused?"

"No. You're not supposed to get in a conversation with them."

"When he passed the note across the counter, should you have passed it back and told him he wasn't allowed to rob you, but you wouldn't be able to explain why, because you're not supposed to get in a conversation with him?"

"Are you making a joke?" she said angrily.

"No," I said. "I'm just reminding you that a teller's job is to give a robber whatever he wants so that he leaves the bank as quickly as possible. And it sounds like your guy couldn't have been here much more than a minute."

"But he got a lot."

"No."

"I'm not supposed to have more than two thousand out."

"The bank doesn't care about six thousand dollars," I said. "The bank spills more than six thousand dollars in the streets every day."

She looked suspiciously at me. "That's not really true," she said. "But fine. I still think I'm just going to try and forget the whole thing. I'm going to pretend it never happened."

"Do you think you can do that?" I asked, surprised.

"Repression can be a useful coping mechanism," she said, warming to a topic in her area of study. "I'll have to tell my mom, though. I won't be able to keep it from her."

"Won't she tell other people?"

"Yeah," she said, annoyed. "She'll probably tell my sisters right away, because my mom thinks everyone needs to know everything about everybody else. And I'm going out with my three best friends tonight, and I'll probably want to tell them, I guess."

"And the problem with talking about it in public is that other people might hear it, too," I said.

"Do I have to keep it a secret?" she said, alarmed. "It's not like some security deal or something, is it?"

"I just mean if you're trying to repress it."

"Oh, right," she said. "I have the order backwards. People repress first, then acknowledge later. I would have to not tell anybody about it right now, and then later remember it or whatever. I know this stuff, I'm just a little rattled right now is all. I'm kind of rambling. Look at my hand." She held it up so I could see she was still shaking. She didn't know what she was saying, and probably wouldn't remember any of it. She was actually smiling at the sight of her trembling hand, amazed by it.

"I think you should call your mom," I said. "You can use the phone right here."

"Is that okay?"

"Of course," I said.

I left the office as Amber dialed, and made sure to close the door behind me.

"THE POLICE want to talk to you," Catherine said. She had headed for me as soon as she saw me emerge from my office, and executed the little pirouette necessary to turn and fall in step with me as I continued across the branch.

"I'm surprised they know I'm here," I said. "They haven't so much as looked at me."

"Well you didn't exactly introduce yourself." A lapel pin she was wearing caught the light—it was a little golden bouquet no larger than a thumbnail, in which a few tiny gemstones sparkled in place of flowers. Catherine was a lover of nature, and kept little items of sylvan inspiration about her at all times. As we passed her desk, a photo of curled clouds floating across her computer screen dissolved into the image of a giant redwood, and I carefully avoided entanglement in a passel of willow branches stretching from the ceramic vase on her desk's corner. "I've already told them your daughter's getting married today and you can only stay a few minutes," she said.

"Did you tell them it's at six, or are they under the impression it's any minute?"

"I didn't tell them when. I just said 'today.'"

"Good. But you don't have to sacrifice yourself, either. Don't you have your own plans between now and then? Hiking, or communing with nature in some other way?" Catherine was invited to the wedding, of course, and knew many of the wedding plans and details because she had asked me about them over the months of planning, but I wanted to be clear that she didn't owe me anything beyond her time at the bank.

"Please," she said. "My day isn't even a concern."

As we continued across the lobby, I noticed a white-haired and slightly stooped older man standing before Amber's teller station. He wore a powder blue oxford tucked into navy blue slacks, and held in the palm of his left hand a flat tin tray, while in his right he wielded a black-bristled brush. The man lowered his brush to the tray, made a few deft back-and-forth swipes with it, and then raised it again so that he could address the countertop with painterly consideration. "Who is that?" I said.

"Fingerprints, I assume," Catherine said.

The uniformed officers headed toward us then. The badge of the first one read "Martinez," and the gray mixed within his closely cropped dark hair marked him as the senior member of the pair. His stocky build was furthered by the bulk of his uniform, and especially by the bulletproof vest he wore, which gave him the physique of a refrigerator box. He smiled widely and shook my hand with a formidable grip. "I know you've got bigger fish to fry today," he said. "I have a daughter myself, and I've married her off twice now, actually. And we should be happy here, since it looks like everyone's fine. I've seen plenty of robberies, and it's hard to find one as quick and clean as this one."

"We'll need to get a statement from you," the second officer told me, frowning down at a small notepad in his palm. He was taller, thinner, and younger than his partner, with ginger hair, red cheeks, and a badge that read "O'Brien."

"Statement about what?" Martinez said. "He wasn't present, so there's nothing for him to state. Miss L'Esprit has been very helpful." He nodded toward Catherine, and she ducked her head with a little dash of Gallic pride upon hearing her last name correctly pronounced to rhyme with *unfree*. "Everyone's statements agree, and we've got the description from your teller," Martinez continued. "Middle-aged men in suits don't rob banks on the spur of the moment, so we're probably dealing with a professional, which is good. Amateurs get nervous and hurt people, but pros are just passing through."

O'Brien peered at his notepad. "Too bad he took his note with him. It would be fun to see it. *This is a robery*. Hah. I'm impressed your teller noticed the mistake in such a stressful moment."

Martinez frowned, though it was unclear whether it was the

misspelling or O'Brien's delight in it that he disliked. "She didn't know it was a stressful moment until she'd already read the note, so you've got the cart before the horse there," he said. "No offense to the young lady."

"Analyzing the handwriting would have been nice, though," O'Brien said.

"So we could know if the guy was romantic or creative?" Martinez said. "Come on, we're just lucky his spelling wasn't worse, or she might not have understood the guy's intentions at all. I've seen that in other situations, and it can spin the whole incident in a bad direction."

The officers argued over whether spelling errors revealed anything significant about a robber, O'Brien claiming yes, Martinez, no. Some preexisting rift between them had clearly translated itself into aggressive conversational cross-checking, and though I could have shared my own robbery experience, it would only have been grist for the mill between them. There was something off-putting about the fact that they felt they were experts on an experience they had never actually had. I understood police officers investigated robberies, and had no doubt Officer Martinez had probably investigated hundreds of them. But cops themselves are not robbed, and I very much doubted whether either of these men had ever been held up off duty, either. And because I *had* been robbed before, I couldn't help but feel they were stepping on my toes when it came to theorizing about bank robbers. One thing I have noticed, however—and I will try to say this with as little self-pity as possible—is that no one particularly cares about the thoughts of bank managers. We are numbers men, people feel, and small-numbers men, at that. But I wished these cops would just, for the love of God, shut up. I maintained a neutral expression and said nothing, though, and it wasn't until Martinez said he'd rather read a man by his face than by his spelling that Catherine finally stopped their inanities by saying, "Oh! But we can. The photos should be e-mailed by now."

I had forgotten about the system the bank had installed that fall, brown plastic cylinders no more than eighteen inches tall that rose between each teller station. Designed to blend visually into the mahogany dividers and beige countertops, each cylinder had a small aperture at the top through which a camera snapped a photo every time a customer stepped to the counter. Every inch of the branch fell within the gaze of one camera or another, of course, but most were hidden behind tinted ceiling domes or tucked in corners, so these new lenses just two feet from customers' faces seemed especially bold. A few customers made halfhearted complaints, but there was really nothing to be done about it, and bank security boasted they would now be able to e-mail within an hour the image of any person who had seen a teller. After installation we heard neither whir, flutter, nor sigh from the cylinders, though, so I began approaching the customer side of the counter on purpose, hoping to provoke some observable effect in the things. On one slow afternoon I had even walked up and down the length of the counter, past all five teller stations, in a vain attempt to produce signs of life. The cameras remained silent. Catherine had called security, and they had assured her the system was working—the silence, it seemed, was intentional. In some climate-controlled warehouse, then, there hummed a server that stored among its digital mementos multiple five-image sequences of me walking. I liked to think a photo existed in which I was captured at a point of graceful, mid-stride levitation, but I also knew a large number of the images consisted of nothing but my face directly in front of the lens, peering in.

It was Catherine and the police who were watching me right then, though, and waiting for something—the officers in earnest, but Catherine as a bit of playacting.

"Right," I said. "Let's take a look."

Catherine headed to her desk, as she had obviously already intended to do. Catherine often hesitated in order for it to appear that I did not. I never asked it of her, and I don't know, really, why she did it. I suppose it amused her.

The gentleman collecting fingerprints abandoned Amber's teller station and moved toward the front doors, muttering crossly to himself. Martinez and O'Brien headed in his direction, and though I was only a handful of strides away from the counter and could see the Rorschach-like swirls and eddies left in the powder upon its surface, I resisted the temptation to examine them. Instead, I followed Catherine to her desk.

"I don't understand why you're still here when there are probably a thousand things you need to do," she said. "But here, if you're going to stay and bother me, you forgot to sign my transfer application, and it's due Monday." And without taking her eyes from her computer screen, she took a form from her in-box and put it in front of me on the desk.

What she had said was incorrect, though. I hadn't forgotten to sign the form that released Catherine to apply for other open positions with the bank. I had ignored it. "So you really do find me a pain," I said.

"Not true," she said. "We've had this discussion. I just want to advance like anyone else." On her screen, a tiny hourglass spun, emptying and refilling itself.

"It's not due until Monday. I'll sign it then."

"You're taking the day off on Monday."

She was right. I took the piece of paper in my hand and looked at it. It was just a form, bureaucratic and meaningless. "I sometimes wonder if you've forgotten the situation I got you out of."

She sighed. "I have not."

"You have, and now you feel like being a service manager is just treading water," I said. "You're sick of digging through paperwork and of the drive to the northern district for the monthly meeting and of all the business with keeping the tellers sharp."

"I don't mind any of that."

"You must, or you wouldn't want to be free of it. But remember Tony Sacco, how he had you trapped in his branch dealing with his insanity day after day until he made the mistake of letting you go to that managers' meeting for him so he could play golf? And so there you were, asking me if there was any chance I could get you transferred out. And I did. It took a ridiculous number of very artful phone calls, but he let you go."

"And I've always been thankful." She shook the mouse impatiently, and the hourglass veered back and forth on the screen. "As I've told you every time you've mentioned it over the last ten years."

"Oh? Do I mention it too often?"

"Not at all."

"Because if I mention it too often, I'll stop."

"I wouldn't want to forget," she said.

Though she hadn't looked away from her computer screen, I could see enough of her face to note the raised eyebrows and slightly flared nostrils that she adopts when trying to act calm—it's the only way I know I'm getting to her. I folded the form and put it in the inside pocket of my suit jacket. "I need your help today," I said. "And then I'll sign your transfer request and you'll be free to run your own show. And I won't forget, because the form will be right here in my pocket."

"What do you mean you need my help?" she said.

"The bride didn't come home last night."

She turned, surprised. "Did you call the police?"

"Christ, Catherine. We're not there yet."

The hourglass disappeared, and was replaced by a log-in box. "What should I do?" she asked as she typed in her password.

"Do you have the Kodak moment?" Martinez asked from across the lobby.

A small iridescent circle popped onto the screen and began to spin and pulse, as if it could see offstage and was greatly excited about what would happen next. "The system has been slow this morning," Catherine told Martinez. "But we should have it any minute."

The circle throbbed and spun, spun and throbbed. It should have been a stone a little man pushed up a hill and then watched roll back down. I stood there, motionless and watching it, for upward of a minute.

"I don't understand why this doesn't work," Catherine said.

I leaned down close to her. "Kill it," I whispered. "Fatal error, system down, whatever expression you want."

"Don't you want to see the guy?"

"We get photos every time it happens anywhere in the region, and they're on the local news all the time—it's not thrilling. It's banal. A person wanted money, so he came in and demanded some, and we gave it to him."

"Are you really that unaffected?"

"No, I'm just getting angry," I said. "All of this technology in the branch doesn't prevent *anything*. You and I have to go through exact, step-by-step procedures with all of these computer systems, but then when a guy walks in and asks for money, look at the computer—it doesn't help us. It's just a little machine that's confused and doesn't work well. The only people who are going to help Amber feel better are you and I. The guy is gone, and staring at the computer or filling out forms isn't going to change that."

"I understand what you're saying," she said. "But we don't really have a choice. We have to follow procedure, and the procedure is to pull the photos from the computer."

"And it doesn't work. And I have contempt for things that waste my time," I said. "What about our old stuff? The old video cameras are still running, aren't they? Can't we pull videotape?"

"Physical videotape? Only one of the cameras still records on actual videotape, and we're not allowed to pull the tape. We have to wait for bank security to do that. Everything else is digital."

"So we can't touch the videotape without Mom or Dad here, but we also can't see the photos, because their expensive computer system isn't actually working."

"Do you need to take a walk?" she said. "You seem incredibly upset."

At a regional managers' meeting a few weeks before, one of the other managers, chatting amiably about the big new house he and his wife had just bought, had joked that even though he'd worked for the bank for twenty years, his mortgage statement showed that he owed the bank money, rather than the other way around. "I guess just about every penny they ever paid me I gave right back to them," he'd said, and we had all laughed. But that sentence had stayed with me, repeating in my head. There was a condo down the street from my own—a unit exactly like mine—that had gone on the market two months earlier at a price below what I'd originally paid for mine, and it was still on the market. I did the mortgage on my condo through our bank, of course, so I, too, wrote a check to the mortgage division of my employer every month—a check made larger by the fact that I'd also taken out a home equity loan to finance the cost of Miranda's wedding. When I applied the list price of the condo down the street to what I owed on my unit and the equity loan, though, the number didn't cover the debt. On our weekend morning walks, my Realtor ex-girlfriend Trish used to urge me to sell my condo and buy something bigger. People's homes were their best investment, she told me more than once—the values only go up. I didn't recall her mentioning the scenario in which, via my home, I had somehow ended up owing my employer more than I could pay.

It grated. And Catherine was right: the more I spoke about the bank and the robbery that morning—about the police and their theories, about the computers that didn't work, about all the detailed procedures Catherine and I would be required to carry out—the angrier I was getting. I felt like I was seeing, with perfect clarity, the degree to which all these measures actually made it *easier* to rob a bank than in the past. I doubted there was a single person out on the street looking for the guy who had stolen our money—everyone was too busy either posing as an expert or looking at screens. It was crazy. And I wanted everyone *to see* that it was crazy. "I don't need to take a walk," I said. "Network problems, failing server, unable to connect—pick a term, it doesn't matter. Just announce it to everyone. I want to get going."

"Get going where?" she said. "Ten minutes ago you told me there was no hurry."

"That was before you got me going on this. I want out of here. What we're doing is pointless."

Martinez returned to us then with heavy, jingling strides—his keys, handcuffs, and other paraphernalia lent him the effect of a Clydesdale at Christmas. "Seizing up on you?" he said, stopping next to me. We waited together, our eyes on the screen. The computer whirred. Martinez was shoulder to shoulder with me, and I wanted to move, do something, but with him right there, I felt like I had paid for a seat to a show and now couldn't leave. Amber was in my office, O'Brien was across the branch laughing with Charlotte and Tina, and Fingerprints was bent before the front doors, brush in hand, dusting the panes.

Catherine had asked if Sandra and I had called the police. Why would we need the police? I checked my watch as if I would find the answer there, but discovered only that it was ten-thirty, which meant nothing in particular.

Another insanity: the bank relied on sophisticated computer systems to keep funds secure and accurate, but they did not feel that having top-of-the-line computers was a priority at the branch level. I knew from daily experience that the little circle on Catherine's computer could spin for any amount of time. "I'm sorry," I said. "But I have to make a phone call." It was a lie, but at that point I would have said my hair was on fire if I thought it would allow me to walk away.

"Go ahead," Martinez said, his eyes pinned to the screen, hypnotized. "We'll be here."

THERE WAS A SET of doors at the back of the branch, seldom used because they opened onto a less-traveled cross street. I unlocked them and pushed my way into the morning sunshine. Tall, thin trees lined the sidewalk, and a faint breeze sent the leaves aflutter, their papery rustle mingling with the muted roar of traffic from the freeway overpass a block away. Decades ago, when the branch had first been established, the neighborhood had been a thriving industrial area. Those businesses had moved north, though, to land that accommodated bigger warehouses with larger loading docks, and in the intervening years, our location had become marginal: we were six blocks from the nearest retail street, fifteen from the nearest chain grocery store. Two blocks south, the street between the back of a beer and wine distributor and the front of a wholesale tile showroom wasn't even paved—it was just gravel poured over the rusting, decommissioned rail line that used to snake through the entire neighborhood before World War II, when manufacturers loaded and unloaded their own rail cars. An elderly customer once told me that the last time he remembered the line being in use, Eisenhower was president. What was left in the twenty-first century were old apartment buildings, a handful of empty structures once home to small manufacturing concerns, and an art college two blocks west, which occupied just one restored warehouse, and outside of which unhappy-looking young people would smoke for ten minutes before casting their butts to the ground and heading back inside. I already had the business of every going concern in the neighborhood—none of the competition had a branch of their own in the area anymore—but our branch still missed our monthly sales goals fairly often. Upper management rarely bothered to complain, though, because they knew the deal: location, location, location.

Down the street, I could see a motley group of five or six figures gathered in the shade beneath the overpass, dwarfed by the massive concrete pillars that held the freeway in place seventy feet over their heads. Some sat upon the concrete embankment, others stood near shopping carts, and though they were a block away and in the shade, a few of the figures seemed familiar. Homeless people often brought cupfuls of change into the branch to be run through our coin machine. At a recent staff meeting, some of the tellers had complained that these people didn't have accounts, so why were we serving them? I'd asked if there had been any particular trouble, and the girls had exchanged uncertain glances until Charlotte had blurted, "One of them doesn't have a nose." "He has nostrils," Tina said. "But he doesn't have the top half. It's just a crusty hole, like a rat ate it or something." The girls had laughed—at times, they acted their age—and when Catherine confirmed that this person had visited a few times and was not lovely to look upon, the girls admitted it was his looks, really, that scared them, but still, could we make him go away? "But what if his fortunes change?" I had said. "What if he wins the lottery? Maybe then he'll buy roses every week for the tellers who treated him so well when things were rough." The girls had sighed, frustrated—they wanted better than roses, it seemed—but gave up on driving him out.

I wondered if this fellow was a member of the group I was peering at in the shadows beneath the overpass: the one leaning over his shopping cart with his ball cap pulled low, perhaps, or the one supine on the embankment with his arm over his face. When I looked down to dial my phone, a cackle of faint, disembodied laughter carried from that direction, and I looked up to find that one of them had turned and seemed to be looking toward the bank. I trained my eyes on the sidewalk and walked slowly along the back of the building, listening to the line ring, until I heard a woman's voice inform me that—Miranda cheerfully stated her name—was not currently available. Did that mean her phone was turned off, or just that she wasn't answering? "Miranda," I said at the tone, "it's Dad. I'm looking for you. Give me a call."

It's strange, the power of saying something aloud. It wasn't until I heard myself say, "I'm looking for you" that I realized that was what I was doing. And if I was looking for her, then at some level I believed she was missing. Sandra didn't know where she was; Catherine had asked about the police. Her absence was beginning to feel real.

When I reached the corner of the building, I paused to look back toward the overpass. The man with the ball cap had pushed his rattling cart out of the shade and was headed, tortoiselike, in the direction of the branch. Someone with longer hair—a woman?—trailed languidly behind him. I stepped around the corner of the building to where the high, unbroken brick wall that formed the bank's north side threw the sidewalk into shade. A chill rattled through me. Had I eaten yet? I couldn't remember. I dialed Grant as I walked toward the front of the building. The call went straight to voice mail, and I hung up without leaving a message. I couldn't ask him if he'd seen Miranda, because of course he hadn't, it was verboten on the wedding day. Unless they weren't observing that tradition—I hadn't thought to ask. I leaned against the wall, and was so startled when the phone began to buzz in my hand that I answered without even looking at who it was.

"So how is your bank?" Sandra said.

"It's fine," I said. "It wasn't that much money."

"Have you heard from Miranda?"

"I just called, but there was no answer."

"I've done that, too," she said. "More than once. What about Grant?"

"No answer."

I heard the sound of an exhalation from her end of the line, but couldn't tell if it signaled distress or was just regular breathing amplified by the device. "What if they eloped?" she said.

"We've made deposits we can't get back," I said. "He wouldn't waste our money that way. And you said you talked to him this morning."

"Maybe he was lying about where he was, so they could get away. He could pay the money back to us without any problem—it wouldn't be that much to him. They could be anywhere, wherever they wanted."

"They don't want to elope. And he wouldn't embarrass us in front of the guests."

"No?"

"Did she say anything to you last night? Anything that might give us a hint?"

"No."

"Nothing?"

"You were there," she said. "We had the dinner. We went to that loud bar and had drinks. When I left, she said she would see me in the morning. That's it. Why don't you get ahold of your friend and ask him?"

"Who? Grant?"

"Prove to me they haven't run off somewhere together."

"They haven't run off, Sandra."

"Prove it, dear," she said, and hung up.

The field of bricks that formed the broad, windowless side of the bank yawned overhead. Looking up, I felt momentarily dizzy and considered sitting down. The sidewalk was dirty, though, so I just leaned there and closed my eyes as the wall tilted on me, the bricks cold and damp against my hair. Keep moving, I thought, and bracing myself against the wall, I did, until I made my way to the front of the building and stepped into the sunlight. Approaching the front door, I saw Mr. Fingerprints still crouched behind it as he examined the lower pane, almost entirely covered in his dark dust. Looking at him there in the doorframe was like studying a photo whose surface had corroded with age. But he shifted, he moved—it was no photo, and struck by the effect, it took me a moment to realize that he was no longer examining the window, but instead looking through it at me. I raised my hand in acknowledgment.

"Could I talk to you?" he said, his voice flattened by the glass between us.

"Here?" I asked, though I mouthed the word rather than saying it.

He tipped his head toward the side of the building. "Come back in around the back."

So I headed back the way I'd come, walking briskly now that I'd been given a directive. I would talk to Fingerprints, check the photos, sign the police report, and move on, I thought. Then I turned the corner at the back of the building and nearly collided with the plastic grille of a shopping cart.

"Somethin' happen?" the man with the ball cap asked. Thinly bearded, he wore a flannel shirt and ragged jeans, and though at close range I could see he was older than I had expected, his gaze was not unintelligent.

"Yes. A little robbery," I said.

I looked past the man's shoulder to the long-haired person three steps behind him. It was not a woman, but a man, gazing resolutely down as if absorbed by the sidewalk. Then, without lifting his face, he peered at me through his eyebrows, and even with the hair hanging before him I could see the red, scabbed crater where his nose should have been.

"We saw the cops pull up, and then they didn't leave, so we figured," the man with the cart said.

"It was nothing major," I said, stepping around his cart. "I'm sorry, I have to get back inside."

"We didn't see anything," the second man said.

I stopped. "No?"

He shook his head slowly, his hair swaying. From the side, I couldn't see his wound—it had probably become second nature for him to orient himself to others at an oblique angle. But he said nothing more.

"You have a good day, sir," the man with the cart said, dismissing me.

He was protecting his friend from my scrutiny, it seemed, so I told them to do the same. Post-robbery procedure required that I lock the doors behind me after I reentered the branch. I did my best to lock them quietly.

AT THE TIME OF the Mooncalf robbery I had been dating Sandra for only six weeks, but she spent large parts of the following three days in my hospital room. She worked at her parents' small paint and wallpaper business and was able to take time off to stay with me while varying degrees of pain medication bounced my utterances from vaguely lucid to completely incoherent. Seventeen stitches sutured the wound on the top of my scalp, and eight more closed the gash where the back of my head had hit the floor. One or both of the blows had given me a concussion, and I floated in and out of shallow sleep from which I awoke muzzy, disoriented, and surrounded by an increasing number of flower arrangements: oversized yellow daffodils stood in one corner, spotted pink lilies gaped from another, and an ivy attempted to strangle a spherical wire frame on the bedside table. Sandra moved around the room at one point, reading the cards. "From Grant," she announced, "from the bank, from your coworkers, from Grant and Gina, from me"—she flashed a coquettish smile there—"from the bank again, from your grateful customers, from me again . . ." I can't recall her reaching the end of the list, probably because the memory is mixed with a dream I had that same day, in which Sandra circled the room again and again, intoning the same litany of names. Or was Sandra's reading of the cards only ever a dream, an entirely fraudulent item I've inserted into my memories? What I know for certain is that when I awoke Saturday afternoon from another uncomfortable doze, it was to discover a flock of irises clustered right next to the bed, not more than eighteen inches from my head. "Aren't they pretty?" Sandra asked when she saw I was awake. "And they smell wonderful."

The green stalks and purple flowers defied my attempts to resolve them into sensible focus—they were too close, or there were too many. And I couldn't smell a thing.

"Even the nurses have been admiring them," Sandra said. "You should find out where they got them."

"The nurses?" I said.

"Your friends Grant and Gina," she said. "They told me they knew you from college. Grant said he's a customer, too?"

Everything from the day of the robbery carried the quality of a fever dream for me, so I struggled to make sense of what Sandra was telling me. In the images I was able to conjure, Grant and Gina floated across the bank lobby in the manner of movie ghosts, I had a fevered and private conversation with Gina regarding the urgent necessity of our having sex, I began to demonstrate the utility of the suggestion, and then a man in a monster shirt hit me on the head with a gun. Not only did I believe the images belonged to dreams rather than waking life, but I was thankful they were dreams. To actually run into Gina with a new boyfriend would have been awkward, and nearly as unpleasant as being pistol-whipped and robbed. And yet it seemed clear that I *had* been robbed. And now Sandra claimed my encounter with Gina and Grant had also been real. Had the sex with Gina occurred, too, then? Had I been robbed *in flagrante delicto*? With a mixture of regret and relief, I decided it was unlikely.

Sandra seemed amused by my confusion. "You spent twenty minutes talking to them about Bristol's," she said. "How you wanted to take them there and buy them scotch and sit in leather chairs. You said you would buy them the leather chairs, too, if they were for sale, and you would introduce them to movie stars, because you weren't afraid of famous people. You said you would go right up to celebrities and talk to them, because you just have to treat them like normal people and bring them down off their pedestals. You said the pedestals thing at least seven or eight times—*Down off their pedestals, down off their pedestals!* And then you offered Grant your IV, and he said thank you, and you seemed really happy about it."

"So I completely embarrassed myself?" I said. "Wonderful."

"Oh, they knew you were on medication," she said. "But you were so chatty. Normally you're so self-consciously cool and reserved. It made watching you babble and offer to buy things for people and make crazy promises so much funnier. I think I like you better now. Even better than before, I mean."

Her appraisal irritated me. How could I be self-consciously cool when I wasn't conscious of being self-consciously anything, much less cool? How, therefore, could one be unconsciously self-conscious? And checkmate. I was too tired to press the issue, though, and resigned myself to asking how the visit had ended.

"Grant said we should all get together when you're better," she said. "He said he wants to make sure we go to Bristol's now that you've made all these promises."

"I won't be able to look him in the eye."

"There's nothing to be ashamed of," she said. "And there's nothing wrong with being nice to your friends, especially when you're on narcotics. And anyway, Grant has already sent three different flower arrangements. You really can't smell them?"

I could not.

AT THE FRONT DOORS to the branch, Mr. Fingerprints twisted the bristles of his brush over a grooved metal hand bar—a cloud of dust rose and then settled like ash upon the glass. "You're the boss?" he said without turning to look at me.

"The manager, yes."

"Your janitorial service, is it nightly?"

"Except Sundays."

"Well they're doing a good job," he said. "Because the customer side of the teller counter is clean. No new prints, no old prints."

"Nothing at all?"

"Oh, there are prints all over the girl's side of the counter," he said. "But I'm willing to bet those belong to her, so we'll have no problem tying *her* to the scene. The fella who visited, though, remains at this point what we call anecdotal."

"That's disappointing," I said.

"But not unusual. The largest part of planning a crime is planning covering up the crime. Smart guys cover up before, during, and after. Look at this door."

I bent to examine the glass, and saw in the dusted surface a tremendous number of egg-shaped reticulations, the whorls and lines of which interrupted or overlapped each other, or broke off as if they had reached some unseen border. A horror movie I'd seen as a boy came to mind, in which a mound of cockroaches had scurried wildly across and over one another's backs in a flesh-eating frenzy.

"It's good glass and there are plenty of prints," he said. "But do you think someone careful enough not to touch the counter would use his hands to open the glass door? And these prints are smaller and lower, probably women's. But look at this." He pointed to a spot higher on the door, where I could just make out a faint crescent in the dust. "Stand next to the door, but don't touch, please. You see how it's just below your shoulder? Someone roughly your height leaned into this door and pushed it open with his shoulder. Did you open this door with your shoulder when you got here?"

"No. I used my foot."

"Because you didn't want to leave any prints, either. Smart man. Good manager. And of course neither did I when I came in. We were being careful, just like this guy was being careful." He smiled. "We could rob a bank together someday, you and I. And if we invited the fella who visited earlier, we could all work as a team."

"We would just need to choose the right bank," I said.

"Oh, I think we should rob this one," he said, laughing. "It's pretty easy."

He seemed content to have shown me that there was nothing to see. I turned toward Catherine, who was at her desk, speaking to someone on her cell phone. She caught my eye and shook her head contemptuously while waving at her monitor, which I understood to mean the computer had still produced no images. "It hasn't been that long, really," she was saying into the phone. "I'm sure it will all get cleared up soon."

Charlotte, Tina, and Officer O'Brien weren't visible, but I could hear their voices in my office. Were they all in there with Amber? It seemed an odd place for people to congregate. Martinez paced a solitary circle a few yards off, hunched at the shoulders and speaking loudly in police jargon to no one. There was a microphone of some kind threaded into the lapel of his uniform, I assumed, though deranged people on the street argue with their invisible tormentors from the same posture. It seemed likely that at least some of Martinez's discussion was about our branch, but he spoke in an impenetrable code. At one point I heard him say the word *niner*, which struck me as ridiculous, and then I overheard something that made me pause.

"No, he's here," Catherine said into her phone, gazing impassively at me. "Absolutely, as soon as I can. You don't have to worry about that at all, Sandra. I'll talk to you soon." She closed her phone and set it on her desk.

Occasionally one stumbles upon a conspiracy of hidden forces that, working in concert, have concealed some essential fact of life. Deducing the world-market-level fraud regarding Santa Claus is an early instance, but one must also stumble upon the truth about sex, or discover that adults lie, you can't actually be whatever you want, crime pays, a tacitly condoned and perpetuated class system rules the population, love is a delusion far more often than a fact, capitalism is not the only way, death comes for everyone, recreational drug use is almost always harmless, and so on. I had felt no further revelations awaited me in life, but upon hearing Catherine say good-bye to Sandra, yet another seemingly solid boundary had disappeared: in addition to pro wrestling being rigged and innocent people being convicted, I now had to add that Catherine could use her cell phone to call my ex-wife. Sandra had most likely been speaking on *her* cell phone, too. They had each other's numbers. They carried them around in their little phones.

"I didn't know you and Sandra were friends," I said. "Much less that the two of you would be chatting today."

"Do you think I've spent the last ten years with my eyes and ears closed? That I've never written a number down and kept it in case of a situation exactly like this?" she said.

"Is it normal for you to call Sandra and discuss our family's personal crises with her? Do the two of you talk regularly?"

Absorbed in some occult activity involving rapid typing on her keyboard, Catherine shook her head impatiently, as if hurrying me through an argument whose opening moves were obvious. "Of course not," she said. "But I've answered occasional calls from Sandra for ten years, so I'd like to help her. And I can't help unless I ask what kind of help is needed."

"But you already asked me that. Was my answer not sufficient?"

"It's best to have as much information as possible."

"Best for whom?" I said.

In the instant in which I turned to walk away, Catherine actually glared at me. I turned back after a few steps, but her eyes were on her computer monitor by then, and she didn't bother to raise them. She leaned toward the screen as if increased intensity of focus might make the machine work faster, but I could see the color had risen in her cheeks. It was yet another benefit to seeing her without her makeup that day: her pulse was revealed immediately. My question had gotten its intended effect. "Please do not call Sandra any more today," I said.

"What do you mean?" she said.

"It undermines my authority. It means you don't respect my decision making."

She laughed, but that was fine, since it at least got her to lift her eyes from the computer. "It doesn't mean anything like that at all," she said.

"When you're printing out branch sales reports," I said, "do I call Tony Sacco and ask him what order he thinks we should do them in?"

"No."

"Let's say you were getting ready to do the reports, and I called Tony and chatted with him about how they do them over at his branch, and then I walked over to you and told you that I had just called your old boss and he said they do the reports in such and such an order. How would you feel?"

"What would it matter what Tony thinks? I haven't worked in his branch for years. He knows less about branch reports than I do, anyway."

"Right. So when I hear you calling my ex-wife, it's weird. Because what does it matter what she thinks?"

"No, that doesn't work," she said. "Because I know more about branch reports than Tony, but Sandra knows just as much about Miranda as you do. She probably knows *more* about Miranda than you do."

I tried to gauge the degree to which the anger Catherine was raising in me was intentional. She maintained an eyebrows-raised expression of innocence.

"Do you have kids, Catherine?" I asked. I knew perfectly well she didn't.

"No, Paul," she said. "I do not."

"Then listen. Never tell one parent that it's the other parent who truly knows their child."

"I didn't mean it the way you're making it sound."

"What I'm trying to tell you is that I am going to find my daughter, and I will be in charge of doing that. Not you. Not Sandra."

"And if I don't help you, you won't sign my transfer form," she said. Her tone was one of exhaustion. Did she believe I had invented the situation I was in solely to frustrate her attempts to complete paperwork?

"That's not true," I said. "The thing is two pages of small type and blank spaces that I don't have time to sit down and study right now is all. I promise you, Catherine, that when I have a moment at some point later today, I will take out your form and carefully fill it out and sign it. And then you will not have to work here anymore."

"It just means I'm allowed to apply for open positions," she said quietly. "It doesn't mean I'll get one."

"We both know you'll get one. Notice how I am having confidence in and supporting you, while you are busy questioning and doubting me."

"You are blowing this out of proportion on purpose," she said. "And I think you know that."

During the first few years Catherine worked for me, I sometimes worried whether she found me likable. Eventually, however, that concern faded—but not due to any evidence. It just seemed unlikely she would have continued working with me over the years if I were truly intolerable.

ON THE AFTERNOON I was to be discharged from the hospital, an older gentleman stepped into my room and asked Sandra if he could have what he called "another bit of time" with me. Shrugging, she said she would go out to get a sandwich. When she stepped out the door, I heard the man tell me his name was "Detective Buckle," and that we had spoken before. Sandra had told me a detective visited the day of the robbery, but I had no memory of it, and in my narcotic punchiness that afternoon a few days later, I heard myself tell the detective he had a funny name.

"I do?" he said.

"An interesting one, I mean."

"I suppose," he said, offering me his rough right hand while with his left he removed his badge from his shirt pocket, showed it to me, replaced it, and then from the same pocket extracted a loose cigarette. My eyes must have widened at the sight of the cigarette, because he laughed. "Don't worry," he said. "I won't smoke in the hospital. It's just the holding it that calms me."

He possessed a tremendous shock of white hair that stood straight out from his head, and the heavy fabrics he wore further enhanced his dramatic appearance: buttoned nearly to his chin, his flannel shirt was a shade of green so deep as to be almost black, and his dun-colored corduroy pants were fuzzed with age—a broken belt loop rose from one hip like an unruly cowlick. The clothes appeared to be a size too large, and this, in combination with the fact that he couldn't have stood more than five and a half feet tall, lent him a shrunken quality, as if life had at some point drowned and then roasted him, and though he had survived, it was in this reduced state. He stood near the bed at a point almost even with my head, and I had to crane my neck to look up at him when he asked how long I'd been working at the bank, what the routines were, who I'd been working with the day of the robbery—standard stuff—until he frowned down into his little notebook as if he'd just discovered an obscenity scrawled there in someone else's hand. "You mentioned the other day that just before the robbery you'd seen an old girlfriend for the first time in a couple years," he said. "I was wondering if you could tell me a bit more about that."

"About my girlfriend?"

"You said she was your *former* girlfriend."

"Sure," I said. "But why do you want to know about her? She's not the one who robbed me."

The detective had maintained a sophisticated though apparently unconscious bit of theatrical business while we talked, putting his cigarette through the standard paces—from fingers to lips and back, propped on the tabletop, and so forth—without ever actually lighting the thing. Now he held it thoughtfully against his temple while fixing me for some seconds with the impassive gaze a headmaster assumes when assessing the prospects of a student.

"If you want, I can get up, and we can walk outside to where you can smoke," I said.

"It's your comfort that's important, not mine," he said. "Memory works best when you're relaxed. A man sifts things over when he's in a porch swing, not when he's on the rack."

Skillfully crafted aphorisms have always appealed to me. "What do you want me to sift over?" I said.

"You're the victim of a crime, and what we've discovered is that things go better if we recognize you're a victim, and let you talk about what's happened to you—not just the crime, but the effects of the crime. Not just the criminal, as they say, but the personal."

"I'm just not sure what you mean by the personal."

He flipped through some pages in his notebook, and then read aloud in a rapid and strangely toneless voice: "*Jesus she was amazing in bed, I had no idea what that could be like, I was practically a virgin, I've never told anyone this, not even her, so please don't tell her if you talk to her, but Jesus, that kind of stuff—*"

"Stop!" I said. "Did I tell you that? Was Sandra here when I said that?"

"The girl who just left?"

"Yes."

"No."

"Good," I said. "And I was obviously saying crazy stuff. They've got me on drugs here. You shouldn't have talked to me when I was out of my head like that. And I don't see what this has to do with the robbery."

"But that's exactly what I'm wondering," he said. "I don't know you, and I don't know this girlfriend of yours whose name has already slipped my mind." He flipped through the notebook again.

"Gina," I said.

"I've written Sandra," he said.

"Yes, Sandra is my girlfriend," I said with mounting frustration. "But she wasn't there at all."

"Right, it was this Gina girl and the other fellow, what's-his-name." He flipped more pages. "Here. Grant. *The cool customer.*"

"The cool customer? Did I say that? Wait, it doesn't matter if I said it or not. I was obviously drunk on painkillers."

"Grant and Gina," he said. "They're in the bank, you're in

the bank, this Mooncalf fellow's in the bank—that's a lot of paths crossing."

"Well, we're open to the public," I said. "But only one person robbed the place."

"Calm down," he said, raising his hands in a gesture of self-defense that was preposterous, since I remained fully supine on the bed. "I'm not accusing anyone of anything. I know things are probably difficult for you right now, and it can't be easy having lost your parents at such a young age."

"What do you mean?" I said.

"Your parents. You said the other day that they've passed on."

"They haven't passed on," I said, exasperated by inaccuracies that, since the detective was relating them, seemed his own.

"You told me to look at all the cards on the flowers and tell you who was missing," he said. "You said it was family, because you didn't have any."

"I'm sorry," I said. "We're just not close. If I told you they passed on, I don't know why."

"So they're living?"

"As far as I know."

"Surely you would know if one of your parents had died."

If I hadn't been medicated, or maybe if I had just been older than twenty-three and not so quickly cowed by authority, I might have corrected him. My mother was in Florida, and yes, I spoke to her on the phone once every couple months. She had raised me in New Mexico, though, and the man she married when I was in high school—I never called him my stepfather—would certainly have called me if something happened to her. My father, on the other hand, had moved to Minnesota when I was in middle school. A self-taught cook who called himself a chef, he had never been married to or lived with my mother, and when a friend of his convinced him they were going to get rich taking over a failing restaurant in St. Paul, he went for it. The restaurant failed anyway, but he then picked up a job cooking somewhere in Wisconsin. After that he moved every year or two, usually after the restaurant in which he was working shut its doors. Never back to New Mexico, though. I saw him once a year, when he would come to town for a few days to see how much I'd grown, and to assure me that his was not the life he had planned, but the breaks had been bad. It had been almost a year since I had last spoken to him, and if he were to die, whether anyone presiding over the details of his death would know how to contact me—or would even know of my existence—was far from certain. But I was medicated and tired, and that all seemed too much to try and communicate. So what I ended up saying was "We're not completely out of touch. But they're thousands of years from here."

The detective tapped his pad thoughtfully. "I don't know what that means," he said.

"My mother is in Florida and my dad is somewhere else. I'm not sure."

"But you said they were thousands of *years* away. So you were being poetic?"

"No," I said. "I meant miles. I'm on medication and it's mixing up my words." I collected myself, and made sure to slowly and correctly say: "I'm just not in *regular contact* with them."

"Hmm. Estranged, then," the detective said, making a notation in his pad with all the care and attention of someone filling in a crossword puzzle. Did he really write *estranged*? I have, over the years, sometimes wondered if he actually wrote anything at all.

From beyond the room's closed door came the muffled, mellow

warning tones of the public address system followed by a woman's voice calmly announcing, *Dr. Murphy, code orange. Dr. Murphy, code orange.* I straightened my sheet and blanket, wondering if orange meant someone was dying. Buckle stood in front of the window, tapping his cigarette against his lips. Then, as if he'd settled on something, he jotted another note in his pad.

"Did you need to know anything about the robbery itself?" I said.

"No," he said. "You told me all of that the other day. You were generous and expansive. I think I have everything I need." He flipped his notepad closed then, and thanked me for my time and effort as he headed toward the door.

"The things I've told you are confidential, right?" I said.

He smiled, though whether out of benevolence or amusement, I couldn't tell. "Of course," he said. "Everything is strictly confidential. It's the only way."

He disappeared into the hall then, leaving me alone, and surrounded by my flowers. There were so many in that small room that I couldn't help but feel like the star attraction at a funeral.

I HAD SETTLED INTO one of the chairs in the customer waiting area and was pretending to read one of our procedures manuals—and pretending not to be growing more and more desperate and angry about being stuck there—when Catherine, at her desk, announced, "I have the photos."

Officers Martinez and O'Brien had been waiting, and were already standing behind her and trading enthusiastic comments about whatever image they were looking at as I crossed the lobby. I noticed Catherine open her cell phone and look thoughtfully at it, as if something interesting were happening there, too. She closed it and set it on her desk, though, as I stepped around and joined the officers in looking over her shoulder.

The camera had been to his right, and offered a semiprofile from mid-chest up. His gaze was directed down, probably at the cash he was putting in his bag, though in the absence of any visual context he appeared pensive and downcast, as if focused not on what was before him, but on some other, inward consideration. What I thought, though, was: How many people receive calls or messages from Catherine? When Catherine had called Sandra earlier, Sandra had obviously looked at her phone, saw the call was from Catherine, and decided to answer it.

"Look familiar?" Martinez said.

With a start, I realized that Catherine, Martinez, and O'Brien were all looking at me. "Oh," I said. "No, I don't think so."

"I'll pull up another one," Catherine said.

I looked at her cell phone, sitting there on her desk. "Can I borrow your phone for a minute, Catherine?" I said. "I need to make a call about the wedding."

"Sure."

I flipped the phone open, dialed, and listened to the little purr of the ringing line.

"He doesn't look like your usual bank robber," O'Brien said.

Catherine had pulled up a different photo now: the man was gazing straight ahead, probably at Amber. He had every appearance of a patient and somewhat bored customer going through a standard transaction. I gazed at the face on the screen while on the phone I heard a faint rustling, and then heard my daughter say, "Hello? Catherine?"

"No," I said. "I'm borrowing her phone, though."

There was a pulsing silence on the line—a faint, shifting hiss, like the closing of a sealed door. And as the hiss gave way to a clean silence, it was only because I was on the phone that I managed to resist saying something in surprise when I realized I recognized the eyes of the man on the screen.

"Why are you using Catherine's phone?" Miranda said.

I turned from the desk and walked away from the others. "Because it was sitting here. Where are you?"

There was another bout of static on the line as I looked back at Catherine's screen and studied the downcast eyes in the photo there. They were older now, and seemed more sad than angry. *Son of a bitch*, I thought. *Mooncalf.*

"You tricked me," Miranda said.

"Are you all right?"

"Oh," she said, drawing the sound into two syllables. "I suppose."

I was all the way across the branch by that point, but continued to speak quietly. "Could we meet somewhere?" I asked quietly, moving further across the branch. "To talk?"

I heard her breathe once, and then a second time. "I guess."

"Where?"

"I need to eat," she said. "And I left some things at the rehearsal dinner last night, so I need to go by the restaurant. Can we meet there? They open at eleven."

"Okay. I'll see you there at eleven."

"Wait," she said. "You're not going to bring anybody, are you?"

"I'll be alone," I said. "And no guns."

"What?" she said.

"It's a joke."

"Oh. Because of the not bringing anybody."

"Yes."

"That's good, Dad," she said. "I'll see you there." She hung up.

When I returned to Catherine's desk and set her phone down, Martinez looked at me. "Everything okay?" he asked.

"Sure," I said.

He nodded toward Catherine's screen. "Any recognition here? Friend of yours?"

It was in that moment, while I pretended to study the image, that I made an instinctive decision—more of a reflex, really—that would end up affecting the rest of the day. "Nope," I said. "I don't recognize him. Catherine?"

"Me neither," she said.

Martinez shrugged. "Well, we should be able to run these through our database pretty easily," he said. "He's done us a big favor here. The guy takes a good photo."

"We should frame it," I said.

And everyone laughed—which caught me by surprise, really. I hadn't been aware I was making a joke.

IT WAS ONLY A week after my release from the hospital that Grant, Gina, Sandra, and I made good on our plans to go out together. I recall preparing for the evening primarily by studying the skin of my face with closer scrutiny than I ever had before, as if perhaps success, class, and their attendant trappings were nothing more than a question of dermatology. I also checked the back of my head to make sure my hair was properly combed over the shaved spot where the doctors had stitched my wound closed. It wasn't as hard to cover the stitches as I had worried it would be—a single tug of the comb took care of it.

Sandra had purchased a new fuchsia flower-print dress specifically for that evening, and encouraged by her example, I had gone to a department store and bought a new blazer. By the time we approached the entrance to Bristol's, then, we had done everything we could to look the part of a sophisticated couple, and all that was left was to carry out our roles. I played my part by feigning boredom as the doorman looked over my identification, while Sandra chose to flutter her eyelids in a way I found unsettling. She also wore a sparkling necklace and earrings I hadn't seen before. She certainly never wore anything like that when she came into the bank to make weekly deposits for her parents' business, and neither had she on any of the dates we'd been on since I'd finally gotten up the courage to ask her out. I was pleased to see the gold buttons on my navy blue blazer shining in the muted light of the Bristol's entryway as we stepped into the club and, seeing neither Grant nor Gina, settled at the black marble bar that ran the length of one side of the room. The rest of the place was filled with small tables and leather furniture arrangements, the latter mostly the more decadent black leather in vogue at the time. The coffee and end tables were glass, their beveled edges a watery green, and it seemed patrons were encouraged to experience the place as a publicly situated living room. The bartender was tall, polite, and delivered our cocktails immediately, acknowledging my payment with a subtle nod. It was still early in the evening, but I noticed occasional wisps of smoke escaping the doorway of a closed back room, in and out of which flowed a steady traffic of husky middle-aged men in wool sweaters, pleated slacks, and tasseled loafers. Most of them exuded a boyish enthusiasm, and some approached the room already brandishing the cigars they would enjoy behind the door. When I wondered aloud if the cigar room was open to the public,

Sandra said I wouldn't fit in even if it was, because I was too young and thin. We were discussing how much weight I would need to gain to get into the room when I felt a hand on my shoulder, and turned to see Grant smiling at me.

"So you've survived," he said, leaning back to examine me. "And no worse for the wear." He wore a charcoal suit over a royal blue shirt open at the neck, and seemed perfectly relaxed and pleased as he shook my hand. Gina stood next to him, her smile somewhat less natural, though the simplicity of her khaki slacks and loose, long-sleeved white blouse, in concert with her long hair and deep brown eyes, was striking—she seemed equally prepared to sit for high tea or plunge into the bush with a rifle over her shoulder.

"I have a lingering hangover," I said. "But yes, I think I'll be all right."

"You've promised me a scotch," he said.

"I hear I promised a number of things," I said, my face growing warm.

"You were funny," Gina said. "And now I can only hope we run into someone famous."

They shared a laugh at my expense, and I joined them. I began to introduce Sandra, but was quickly reminded that introductions had been taken care of in the hospital, over my unconscious body. The bartender greeted Grant by name, they shared a few private words, and the man departed through a door behind the bar as Grant suggested we settle around one of the large coffee tables that had a love seat behind it and armchairs at either end. Grant said that as the guest of honor, I should take a chair at what he called the head of the table. Sandra sat at the end of the love seat closest to me, Grant sat next to her, and Gina took the armchair at the other end of the coffee table—in the geometry of tennis, Gina and I would have been playing singles while Grant and Sandra looked on. A waitress arrived with glasses and a bottle of wine that she opened expertly. She poured a luminous red swirl into Grant's glass, and I noted the simple way he inhaled and sipped without dramatizing the process, a skill I had yet to master. Every time a cork was placed before me back then, I felt as if a spotlight had swung in my direction, and I couldn't help but start communicating with wild shifts of my eyebrows. Grant nodded, the waitress filled our glasses, and Sandra and I now had two drinks in front of us, since we still had the ones we'd ordered at the bar. I could sense Sandra's discomfort, and watched as she instantly downed the remains of her cocktail and pushed the glass to the other side of the table. We chatted about the wine, which turned out to be something Grant and Gina had discovered on a trip they'd taken to "the wine country," which I took at first to mean France, though I realized my error soon enough. From the details they related of their trip, I was able to conclude they had been together maybe six months. It was hardly a long amount of time, but still made them seem a more established couple than Sandra and me. And though we were all getting along well—Grant's narration of their Northern California adventures was interrupted by frequent laughter and joking asides from the ladies—at a certain point I found myself struggling to follow the thread of the story, because even though she was at the other end of the table from me and the room was crowded, I had detected the scent of Gina's perfume. Not only was the return of my sense of smell, absent since Mooncalf had hit me, something of a momentary miracle, but the fragrance Gina wore that night was the same she had used when she and I had dated a few years before. The aroma instantly called up a whole array of sense memories, and I could picture her as she smiled up at me or down on me or back at me, could see the way she closed her eyes and tilted her head, the way her hair fell, the tones in which she whispered or moaned, the rhythm we fell into as we pressed against one another—

It was when my thoughts had reached that level of melodramatic ridiculousness that I looked down and realized that I, too, had finished my cocktail, as well as my first glass of wine. To avoid reactions with alcohol, I had intended not to take my pain medication before going out that evening. There in the bar, though, I couldn't recall whether I'd actually remembered to skip my pill, and the confusion caused by the convolution of failing to remember whether I'd remembered not to do something must have been evident on my face, because Grant looked at me with concern and asked if I was okay. When Gina and Sandra turned to look at me, too, I felt as if I'd been thrust suddenly on stage without any lines. But this, perhaps, is where I began to consider Grant a friend: he seemed to sense not only that I could use assistance, but exactly the kind of assistance I needed. "I know maybe it's not something you want to discuss, but I can't resist," he said. "I'd love to hear the story of the robbery."

If there was a single story I knew and was confident in, it was the story of the robbery. I felt as if Grant were setting me up—as if he and I had planned for him to warm up the audience so I could then move in to take center stage. And I did. I began the tale in its epic form, with unabridged internal monologues, background information on bank procedures, and detailed character descriptions including names and titles. Toward the beginning of the story I asked the waitress for another bottle of the wine Grant had chosen, and though it was delivered expediently and poured for all, it did nothing to ease my consciousness of Gina's perfume, of her eyes upon me, her smiles at my attempted jokes, everyone's laughter, Grant's enthusiastic responses to each part of the story, the men entering and leaving the cigar room, and the smell of cigar smoke insinuating itself among the aromas of leather and liquor that filled the main room. Grant provided thoughtful prompts where suitable, such as *You've got to be kidding!* or *So what were you thinking at that point?*, and the question of whether I'd skipped my medication began to fade from my mind as, like an actor who has hit his mark and now begins to ease into the rhythms of his climactic monologue, everything outside of my performance began to fall away. The perfume and wine and attention and energy in the room made me expansive as I moved confidently toward the story's climax. Here were Mooncalf's sinister narrowed eyes, the rasping growl of his voice, and my canny refusal to acknowledge his command. Here was the highly polished gun glinting in the light as he raised it overhead. I looked fearlessly into his animal eyes as he delivered the blow, which I took like a man. I staggered and struggled, I stumbled and fell, and by the time I finished the story and fielded questions regarding the ongoing denouements at the bank and with the police, I had indeed ordered scotch for Grant and myself. The ladies excused themselves to visit the powder room, Grant and I sipped our scotch, and for the first time since I'd started my story, I looked around. Bristol's was packed. Every table, chair, and sofa was occupied, the bar was full, and people stood in the gaps, leaning against walls or the backs of chairs or each other. There was a small jazz band playing with great animation in the back corner. They had spent the majority of the evening covering the Earth, Wind & Fire catalog, and the saxophone player in particular seemed to feel every burst of his instrument. The husky men continued to come and go from the back room, and each opening and closing of the door acted as a kind of bellows that pushed enough cigar smoke into the main room to lend the air the tobacco note I associated with good living.

Grant swirled the last of the scotch in his glass. "This is fun," he said. "We should get together again sometime."

I had to lean toward him and speak loudly in order to be heard over the crowd and music. "I might have gotten a little carried away," I said. "I hope I didn't talk too much."

"Not at all," he said. "You have a good story, so why not tell it?"

The women returned, and when the waitress brought the bill, Grant handed her his credit card. I couldn't see the total, but noticed Sandra glance at it and draw her lips into a tense smile. I suggested we split the tab, but Grant said, "Nonsense. We invited you out. We're your hosts tonight."

"It's too much," I said.

"Next time," he said.

"All right," I said. "Next time." Everyone smiled, both at the resolution of the bill and at the agreement that we would meet again.

That night, Sandra and I had the best sex we'd had yet. I had been excited by her as an inventory until then, thinking of the curve of her pale neck as one item, the back of her smooth thigh as another, and her small breasts, with their bruise-colored nipples, as a matched set next on the list. I had certainly paid attention to the items on this list, had given each its due of mental-anticipatory and physical-in-the-moment attention, but that night was the first on which I experienced Sandra's body as a singular, pulsing, integrated entity. This led also to a sense that our bodies were locations—sites of interest and possibility—rather than objects, and that we could become, together, a single location of investigated pleasure. We paid no mind to what we were doing or saying, and I'm sure that if Sandra's roommate was at home (I can't even recall the poor girl's name), she either laughed at what she heard through the wall, or else pulled a pillow over her head in a rage. Because does anything seem more ridiculous than the lusts of other people? To me, at least, they always seem delusions.

OFFICER MARTINEZ BROUGHT AMBER, Charlotte, and Tina by to take a look at the photos of Mooncalf, but when none of them recognized him, Martinez thanked them for their time, told them they were free to leave, and then very efficiently ushered them out of the branch. Mr. Fingerprints conferred briefly with O'Brien, and if I could trust my reading of the older man's bearing, the lack of evidence at our little robbery left him no more discouraged than someone who idly checks a pay phone for forgotten change but comes up empty. Fingerprints left without saying good-bye, and Catherine locked the door behind him. Though the photos of Mooncalf were automatically distributed to various law enforcement agencies, Catherine sat down and forwarded the photos to two other e-mail addresses O'Brien not only wrote down, but then, as if he were teaching elementary school, also spoke aloud to her, letter by letter. She did not betray even an ounce of annoyance with him, though I could see that her fingertips were well into composing the body of the e-mail while O'Brien was still spelling out the address. Once the photos were sent, the officers grew uncertain. I couldn't hear what they murmured to each other as they stood in conference several yards from Catherine's desk, but the equipment attached to their uniforms clanked and jingled as they shifted their feet impatiently. When they returned to where Catherine and I waited, Martinez said, "When do you expect that videotape from your security people?"

"I spoke to them a while ago, but their office is in the suburbs," Catherine said.

The officers nodded as if this were significant information. Not a person in the room was interested in remaining there, but no one wanted to appear derelict in his or her duties, either. "Security will pull the tape and forward it to these gentlemen as soon as they can, though, right?" I said.

"They're supposed to," Catherine said.

"Is there anything left for us to provide you, then?" I asked the officers.

"I think that's it," Martinez said. "Something about the guy seems familiar to me, but we've got computers these days that zip through and see if the photos match up with any other robberies, so there's not much to do right now."

"Well, we're sorry to have troubled you today. I can let you out, if you like," I said, and they followed as I headed toward the door. "It seems like there wasn't much evidence to collect," I added. "Almost like coming to the branch was a waste of time."

Martinez nodded. "With a car accident or a fight, the results are all right there in front of you. But this place looks normal. There's not really much evidence that anything ever happened here."

I thanked the officers for their work, shook hands with each of them, and closed the door behind them as they left. Returning to Catherine's desk, I could see that she remained busy. She had a large three-ring binder open on her desk, and looked alternately at the binder and then her computer monitor as she typed what I assumed was another procedurally necessary e-mail. "Bank security called before, while you were outside," she said. "They'll be here in half an hour. They probably expect that you'll be here, too. Will you?"

"Do I have a choice?"

She shrugged. "I don't know what they would do if you weren't here. What *could* they do? If you're not here, you're not here."

"I'm sure the procedures binder you have open there has a policy in it, right?"

She didn't even have to look at it—consulting the binder and moving step-by-step through the procedures was probably the first thing she did after the robbery. "It says you're supposed to be here if you can," she said. "But if you were out of town, of course you wouldn't be able to be in the branch, so they must be able to move things along without talking to you right away."

"Or ever," I said. "What if I were hit by a bus?"

"Let's not think that way," she said, flipping to the next page in her binder. The margins of the pages were filled with her own handwritten notes, and at first I tried to remember which training session she'd been to in which she would have written so many notes. When I watched her write a new note in the margin, though—*mgr absence?*—I realized she was taking notes *today*. She was keeping track of what happened, writing down questions, and listing topics not covered. *Catherine L'Esprit*, I thought. *The consummate professional.*

"So I heard your call," she said, turning back to her computer screen. "Is she okay? Where was she?"

"I don't know," I said. "I'm going to meet her for lunch. And then after that I'm supposed to be at the Quad, to get a bunch of chairs the rental company is dropping off."

"So you're not staying."

"No."

"You weren't even here when it happened, anyway," she said, typing furiously. "Charlotte and Tina did the cash counts with me, so I have all the information security needs. I'll tell them it's your daughter's wedding day. And if anything comes up that I don't know, I'll just give you a call."

"Thank you," I said.

She stopped typing. "And look, I'm sorry about what I said before, about Sandra knowing Miranda best. I just wanted to help."

"I know."

"I just don't like feeling like you're angry at me."

"And I don't like feeling that the things I say or the decisions I make are immediately discussed on the phone by a bunch of other people so that they can secretly manipulate me into doing what they want me to."

"That's not what was going on," she said.

"But how do I know that?" I said. "I've worked with you for ten years, but now I find out you chat on the phone with my ex-wife. It's like waking up and discovering there are a bunch of strings on me, because secretly I'm just a puppet, but I didn't know it."

"You're not a puppet," she said. "Though you mean marionette. The ones with strings are marionettes."

"It's suspicious that you know so much about the terminology," I said. "So am I a marionette, then? Are you and Sandra secretly pulling my strings?"

"No," she said. "You have no string. To hold you down."

"Do you and Sandra hang out?" I said. "Do you make plans and trade information?"

"We're women," she said, as if I had forgotten some fundamental rule about the way things worked. "If we like each other, we help each other. And I like Sandra. But no, we don't *hang out.*"

"Because you and I don't even hang out," I said. "And I know you a lot better than Sandra does. Or at least I thought I did."

She sighed one of her long, slow sighs of vexation as she sat there, staring ahead at nothing, her hands at rest on her keyboard. "We hang out all day, Paul," she said finally. "Every day. In this place."

"I guess that's true," I said, and made sure to shake my head ruefully before adding: "Though not for much longer. You can stop what you're doing right now, though? I need to leave." No one was ever to be left alone in the branch, which meant that if I was leaving, Catherine would have to wait somewhere else until security arrived.

She grabbed her phone and purse without bothering to answer my question, and studied her computer as she stood, clicking a last screen closed. "So are you done being angry?" she asked.

"I think I'm still a little angry," I said.

"When will you stop?"

"I don't know. Why don't you just not think about it?"

"Because it bothers me," she said in the neutral tone she often uses when referring to her feelings. Over the years, she has reported any number of other items—anger at an employee who walked off the job, alarm over a teller's large cash shortage at the end of the day, concern after a robbery at another branch—in the same dispassionate voice. It took me quite a few years to realize that the more carefully neutral Catherine's tone sounded, the more serious the situation.

"I'll probably get angry at someone else within the hour," I said as we stepped outside and I locked the doors. "And then you'll be off the hook. Does that work?"

"Fine."

"You're aware that I'm teasing you, right?"

"I'm aware that you're teasing me because that's what you do when you're angry," she said. "But I don't understand why you're angry, and I'm not in the mood for it right now."

"Fine," I said. "I'll stop. Where will you wait for them?"

"I don't know!" she said, finally properly angry. "Does it matter? Do you care?"

The intensity of her anger always thrilled me. And though I preferred to enjoy her anger when it was directed at a departed customer or absent teller, there were occasions, like that one, on which the absence of other targets meant I had to draw fire myself. "Of course it matters, Catherine," I said as I headed toward my car. "Of course I care." It was greatly satisfying to use the same condescending tone with her that she had just used with me a minute before. "It's just that I have to leave now. Call and let me know how things go, all right?"

She said nothing, and remained in the small area of shade outside the door even as I started my car and pulled out of my space. Because she was fishing around in her purse—or pretending to fish around in her purse—she didn't appear to see me wave as I drove past. But she probably saw me wave, I thought. Why else would she have been fishing around in her purse like that, if not to ignore me?

NOT TOO MANY WEEKS after that evening at Bristol's, Grant, Gina, Sandra, and I drove to Point Perdition, one of the many imaginatively named and determinedly picturesque little towns that dot the nooks and crannies of the coastline throughout the Pacific Northwest. It had rained the previous night, and the day remained cool and damp as we walked the beach in our cable-knit sweaters and blue jeans while a breeze that smelled of moss and sea salt sent grains of sand skittering past our feet. Gulls wheeled and cried overhead, and the point's lighthouse did stalwart scenic duty in the background, a whitewashed enchantment atop a rocky promontory a mile behind us. In town, images of the restored giant graced postcards, T-shirts, key chains, magnets, thermometers, and, in certain shops, suggestive boxer shorts and negligees. It looked smaller in life than on the postcards, but also nobler, perched there above the waves and spray. We walked away from rather than toward it, though—there were tide pools in the other directions, we'd been told. We tired before reaching those, though, and abandoned the beach by climbing a bluff-embedded staircase to the town's main street, where we found a little café, enjoyed a lunch of steaming clam chowder, bread, and apples, and then wandered past the small shops that lined the street. Point Perdition was smaller then than now, and many of the shops were housed in old two-story clapboard buildings whose wooden siding had gone gray and fibrous decades before. The whole town was either a firetrap or designed, in the interests of quaintness, to look like one, and I half expected to find a grizzled sailor in one of the thin alleys, singing drunkenly about how Brandy was a fine girl, what a good wife she would be. What happened instead, though, was that as we passed a bar that featured signs announcing the presence—with the same combination of all-caps type and suggestive photography found outside strip clubs—of a back deck with a view of the lighthouse, Grant suggested he and I rest there while the ladies shopped. Sandra and Gina looked at each other, shrugged, and said okay.

We found a table on the small cedar plank porch and, out of boldness, affectation, or both, ordered whiskey. A bored waitress brought us our drinks, and Grant studied the view of sea and sand as if it were an impressive painting. The waves did not curl gracefully to the sand, but fell as broad walls of water that hit the beach with heavy, thudding slaps, and as we watched the waves do their violence to the shore, Grant asked me about work. Had I studied banking, he wanted to know, or was the bank something new? I told him I had majored in business, but the bank was just a place I was working until I found something better. Did I have ideas, he asked, was it just a question of financing, that kind of thing? "I'm really just surveying my options right now," I remember saying, in place of admitting I had no particular plan or even sense of what I *could* do. Trying to shift the focus, I asked Grant about himself. Sandra and I had seen Grant and Gina a few times since Bristol's, but it had only been for drinks or dinner, and the conversation had been light. "I understand you do some kind of art," I said. "But I don't know enough about that kind of thing to even know what to ask."

He smiled, but in a pained way. "I got a degree in fine art—that's true. And I paint once in a while. But I just put the canvases in my dad's basement, or else throw them out."

"I'm sure it takes time to learn how to do something like that."

"It's also possible I'm not very good," he said, laughing. "But what I do for money is work at an ad agency one of my dad's friends owns."

He looked down into his whiskey as if he were looking into the ad firm itself, and when he raised his glass and finished his drink, I did the same. The whiskey tasted of smoke and heat. Dark clouds were gathering over the ocean and the breeze grew cool, but I felt fine—as though the drink had rendered me immune to conditions. A group of gulls on the glassy sand near the waves stood there as if at a loss about what to do next. When the next wave rolled in, they fluttered into the air long enough for the water to roll back, and then settled in the same spot as before. I couldn't tell if they were amusing themselves or were truly stupid and forgot, each time, that a new wave was on its way.

"The job I have is something my dad got me, and I'm lucky to have it," Grant said. "He told me how to do everything I needed to do. How to write my résumé, how to speak to the people who work there, how to dress, the whole thing."

"It sounds like a good deal," I said.

"What do your parents do?"

I sensed the degree to which he was particularly alert to this answer. And I suppose I was, too. I was hardly going to tell him I grew up in a small apartment across the street from the bowling alley where my mother worked. "My mom moved to Florida a few years ago," I said. "But I'm not sure what she and her husband are doing for money right now. My dad usually has restaurant jobs, so he moves around a lot. He was in Dallas the last time I talked to him."

Grant nodded, watching the gulls as if it were somehow his job to monitor them. "Well, maybe this will sound odd," he said. "But would you mind if I passed some suggestions on to you?"

I had no idea what he was talking about, and blurted the first thing that came to mind: "You mean about jobs? My résumé?"

"No," he said. "I just mean it seems like you could use some things I know."

I remember shifting uncomfortably, pained to hear him speak

so directly about something he wasn't naming and that I couldn't figure out.

"Look," he said, facing me. "You have to get rid of your blue blazer. The buttons make you look like you're headed to a yacht. And I don't have anything against yachts, but it's not a good look for you."

This stung more than I let on, not only because the blazer was a new purchase, but because I had liked and trusted the salesman who'd helped me pick it out.

"And you should get your hair cut more often," he said. "By a barber who knows what he's doing. I know I'm probably offending you, but these are the kinds of things I'm talking about. I feel like we're friends now, but I don't know you well enough yet to really know how to talk to you, so I'm doing this kind of clumsily. I'm probably coming off like an asshole, but I hope you understand I just want to help."

He didn't say anything more. We sat in silence, watching the gulls mill nervously about, and I wondered if I needed to revise my understanding of every previous interaction we'd had, keeping in mind that Grant had always been secretly amused by something I was wearing. All I could think to say, finally, was "Okay. I understand what you mean."

He nodded as another set of waves hit the beach and the gulls, screaming, took to the air. "Should we have another round?" he said. "Or would that be too much?"

"Another," I said. "On me."

The drinks were delivered, Grant moved the conversation to pro football, and the gulls flew off down the beach. When Sandra and Gina returned, they had a glass of wine with us while complaining at length about the cheapness of the trinkets and clothes in the shops. We made jokes about the town, and laughed, and had more wine, until neither Grant nor I was in any shape to drive. Someone suggested we stay the night in town, so we found rooms in a motel down the street—they had two right next to each other—and then walked to Point Perdition's nicest restaurant, an Italian place in the basement of one of the last buildings on Main, where we ate huge plates of pasta and drank more wine amid the flickering candlelight. When we finished and stumbled up the stairs to the street, Grant suggested we go back to the beach, so we wandered toward the sound of the surf. Crossing from the sidewalk into the sand, we passed beyond the muddy orange glow of the last streetlight and stepped into darkness.

The waves hissed against the sand, but the ocean beyond was silent, and extended to the horizon like an immense field of silver and black, above which the moon hung like a flattened coin. Sandra walked next to me, her face aglow in the moonlight, but when she smiled and said something, I didn't catch it. I asked her to repeat herself, but she shook her head, laughed, and said it was nothing. Grant and Gina were peering with great interest at something out over the water, and when I followed their gaze, I noticed a small but steady light on the horizon. We all stopped walking to study it. Gina said it must be a fishing boat, but Grant said it was too bright for that. I said it was a cruise ship or some other kind of ocean liner, while Sandra claimed it was a rich person's yacht, and the point of light was actually the whole boat lit up for a party. I stared at it as if I might discover further detail, but there was nothing to find—it remained a spot of light.

"Where are we?" Grant said, turning slowly around. Dark, tree-covered hills rose sharply at the back of the beach, with no houses visible. The only lights were at least half a mile inland, nestled up in the hills. He stared out to sea again. "It's not a boat. It's the lighthouse," he said.

He was right. We'd walked along a string of crescent-shaped beaches, but had forgotten that the series of beaches themselves, like the linked pieces of a necklace, comprised the coast of a large bay. At one tip of the bay was the lighthouse, and we had walked far enough that looking back involved gazing across the entire expanse of water, so that it appeared the lighthouse had floated to sea.

"How did we get so far?" Sandra asked. "And now we have to walk all the way back?"

We didn't, though. After ten minutes of trudging back the way we'd come, Grant spotted a gap in the trees that revealed itself to be a path. We followed it up to a two-lane road where a small market sat, its whitewashed walls phosphorescing in the moonlight. The store was dark, but the pay phone next to the door worked, and only five minutes after Grant made a call, a jovial cabdriver pulled up to take us back to the motel. Gina and Sandra thanked him effusively, and when we explained why we'd had to call him, he laughed. "It's always harder getting back, especially across the sand," he said. "But it sure beats swimming, don't it?"

After we wished Grant and Gina good night and made it to our room, Sandra kicked her shoes off and collapsed facedown on the bed. "God, they're exhausting," she said.

"Grant and Gina?" I said.

"It just goes on and on, drinking and eating and walking and walking and walking. Why are we even here? Why are we in this crappy motel in this crappy town?"

"It's a weekend trip," I said.

"I didn't sign up for a weekend trip. I signed up for a day."

"Sometimes you have to be spontaneous."

"Spontaneous? It wasn't spontaneous. You decided we were staying here the minute you started drinking whiskey with Grant. Whose idea was that?"

I was too surprised by Sandra's anger to remember. "I think it was mutual," I said.

"Making decisions for everyone else isn't spontaneous," Sandra said drowsily. "It's just taking control."

She seemed to drift into sleep then, and I turned off the light and sat in a chair by the window, looking at the gravel parking lot through a gap in the curtain. Had I made the decision to stay overnight, or had Grant? I couldn't remember, but neither did I work particularly hard to dredge from memory some singular, decisive moment. It had just made sense to stay.

I heard voices then, muffled and hollow: they were the tones of Grant and Gina in the room next to us. I couldn't make out any words, but there was an odd urgency to the pitch and rhythm that made me wonder if maybe they, too, were arguing. Then Gina's voice rose to where it was barely audible: "It's so good," she said. "It's so good." There was a growl of response, and then again, "Oh, it's so good." It felt unseemly for me to just sit there listening, but to go to sleep would have meant lying even closer to the wall between our rooms.

As I pulled Sandra's sweater off, she woke up enough to sit up and help me. I pulled her shirt up over her head and tugged her jeans off, too, and she may have thought I was helping her to bed, but when I unhooked her bra and pressed the center of my palm to her breast, she understood. "I'm pretty tired," she mumbled.

"Just lie down," I said, a command she seemed content to comply with. I pulled her panties off, and ran my tongue along the inside of her leg and thigh. At the first press of my tongue, she gave the little humming sigh I had hoped for. She was not one to talk during sex, but did employ the full array of feminine sighs, coos, and groans. I was not, at twenty-four, particularly experienced or skilled at what I was doing, but I had one thing going for me, which was insecurity. The insecure young man is eager to please, and I was happy to work my tongue between Sandra's legs, and to listen to her respond, for a long time. I don't think, at first, that she was aware of Grant and Gina in the next room—I had barely heard them even when our room had been silent, so it was the motel's thin walls that had created the situation more than any particular theatricality on their part. But at a certain point Sandra heard something, and though she didn't say anything, I think that was why she laughed a bit when I pressed my tongue against her more insistently. "Come here," she said, grabbing my arms and pulling me toward her. I slid easily inside, but because we hadn't planned on spending the night in town, I hadn't brought any condoms. Sandra wasn't on the pill—she said it made her feel sick—but when I told her I didn't have anything, she said, "It's okay, we're okay." She liked to keep her hand on the back of my neck when I was over her, and during orgasm would pull down as if she wanted the full length of my body directly on top of her. Did she pull me toward her that night, though? It would be nice to think so, but I don't remember. What I remember is that though I was fairly shy and usually silent during sex, I made sure to groan with pleasure that night. "Yes," Sandra whispered. "Yes, come, yes."

How embarrassing, these unsubtle competitions. Who will fuck more loudly in the motel? Who will cry more passionately, who will groan with more ferocity? How does one even decide a winner? At least we had the decency, when the four of us walked to breakfast the next morning, not to say anything.

WHEN A WAITRESS UNLOCKED the front door at precisely eleven o'clock, I was the only person waiting outside the restaurant. Miranda's rehearsal dinner had been held in a private room there the previous evening, and after dinner, when we walked past the main dining room on our way out, the place had been packed. All evidence of that evening had now been erased, of course. Trying to be as classy as a restaurant can be while still brewing beer on the premises, every heavily lacquered table in the dining room featured carefully folded white napkins and spotless place settings. The waitress—college-aged, with a full figure and long, frizzy hair—betrayed not an ounce of false enthusiasm as she escorted me to a table in the middle of the room and then departed to the kitchen, from where I could hear the scattered voices of the kitchen staff chatting and laughing as they finished their prep work for the day. I felt that if I could be the first person to locate Miranda, I would earn some kind of privilege or opportunity that others—Sandra, Grant, the rest of the world—would be denied. She would tell me she wanted to get out of the thing, probably, but that she didn't know how to go about it, and needed help. I would reassure her that people make mistakes, and walking out on a wedding was hardly the end of the world. She would certainly feel awful about all the money I had poured into the event, as well as the time and money many of the guests had spent on travel, and I would have to tell her that sometimes a person has to be strong enough to shrug off the pressures of a social context. If she didn't want to get married, she shouldn't get married. That was a simple fact, and plenty of people on the guest list were themselves the veterans of ill-conceived marriages, or were even currently in one. These people probably wouldn't blame Miranda one bit for changing her mind, and the ones who actually did feel put out about it would care much less after their second drink. Besides, her honesty would make for a far more interesting weekend than the same old mundane wedding procedure would, and everyone would go home with a dramatic story to share with friends. People would end up getting more out of the wedding if there wasn't a wedding, so there was really no social or financial pressure to worry about. She was free to do what she wanted.

When I actually saw Miranda, I realized what a fantasy all that was. She wore khaki shorts and a black T-shirt, a bit of purple elastic held her hair in a ponytail, and she walked toward me as casually as someone who was nothing more than slightly late for a picnic. Taller and more athletic than most of her peers from even a young age, she had been the captain of her high school tennis and volleyball teams, and still carried herself with the lazy ease of an athlete at rest, but prepared to join a game, should one spring up. I found myself thinking not only of her high school volleyball days, though, but also of a vaguely synchronous image: falling snow blanketing cars, sidewalks, and streetlights beyond a restaurant's windows as Miranda, seated across from Sandra and me, celebrated officially becoming a teenager by crossing her eyes in mock effort as she noisily sucked the last of a huge milk shake through a striped straw, and then laughed, coughing, at her gluttony—so a teenager, yes, but also still a child, cackling and mischievous. As she sat across from me on the day of her wedding, though, I realized she was nearly twice as old as she had been on that winter evening. She was not going to be outwardly trembling or in some kind of anguish she would lay bare, because when had she ever? She didn't operate that way.

"I hope you haven't been waiting long," she said. "It's so empty in here."

"They've only been open a few minutes."

People sometimes claimed they could see my features in Miranda, but tan, smiling, and offering the menu a cursory glance, she struck me as a variation primarily on the pattern of her mother. "So why were you with Catherine?" she asked.

"They needed my help with something. And what have you been up to?"

"Having a quiet morning. Trying to relax."

"And not answering your phone," I said. "Unless you think it's Catherine."

"That was so random, I thought something might be wrong," she said. "You know, it's a little like lying, Dad, calling with someone else's phone."

"It's not lying, it's deceit. And your mother is worried."

The waitress appeared from the back room, and when Miranda asked her what was good, it turned out that despite her dismissive treatment of me earlier, she did have enthusiastic beliefs about the sandwiches and chips. In the room's uneven midday light, I watched the two of them discuss the relative merits of rye versus sourdough for a turkey sandwich, and admired the way Miranda looked the waitress in the eye, negotiating their little exchange with a cheerfulness that did not seem false.

"So did your quiet morning help?" I said after the waitress left. "Have you been able to relax?"

"That's not going to happen," she said, the cheerfulness vanishing. "But there's nothing to be done about it."

"About what?"

She sighed in the same way she did when I used to ask what she had learned at school. "A lot of things. Or maybe just that I'm twenty-five, and that people seem to assume that means I'm naive, or that I don't know what I'm getting into, or whatever it is they say."

"Who has said that to you?"

"No one. But I know what people talk about when I'm not in the room."

"Which people?"

"Don't do the fake obtuse thing right now, Dad. You know what I'm talking about." She dropped her napkin into her lap with a disdainful little flip of the wrist. Those wrists, the taper of her fingers, the way she tapped them on the table while training a heavy-lidded look of impatience on me: those were her mother all over.

"So this is about what other people think?" I said. "Not about what you think?"

"I know what I think," she said. "I want to marry Grant. But he's older than me, so this marriage might not last forever. Maybe he'll die before me. Or he'll find out he doesn't like marriage. Or I'll find out I don't like marriage. Or maybe he'll leave me for some even younger woman, or maybe I'll leave him for some even older man." She gasped silently in mock horror, a gesture so filled with disdain that it took me aback. "I'm aware that people think I'm some kind of child, wandering into something I can't possibly understand, or that our age difference is some kind of scandal that no one should mention, or that they should treat with some kind of weird, desperately positive spin. Aunt Sheila actually tried to tell me I was smart to marry an older man, because I won't have to worry that he'll go after a younger woman, because I'll always *be* the younger woman. I didn't even know what to say to that."

"There's no point in trying to respond to her. You know that."

"But I keep getting all of these frozen smiles and courteous little handshakes from people who I can tell are just doing their best not to reveal their doubts about whether this will really provide me with *happiness and security for the rest of my life*—as if my goal is to be a little housewife, at home doing laundry for the next forty years. I don't know what our life will be like. And so what? What does it matter if I know what I'm doing or not? Does anyone know what they're doing? It just gets harder and harder for me not to scream, 'Look, this is what I'm doing! I want to be with this person right now!' It's nobody else's business, and if things change at some point, then they change. I don't think they're going to change, but even if they do, so what? There are more important things to worry about."

"Than what?" I said. "Than your life?"

She shook her head. "I know people think Grant is taking advantage of me," she said. "But he is not."

I was having a hard time following her. Was she trying to say she *was* happy, or that her happiness somehow didn't concern her? And I noticed that in her fervent naming of the supposedly unspoken issues, she had mentioned Grant's age, but had passed over the fact that Grant was—had been—a friend of mine. "That's all fine," I said. "But I don't think you should enter a marriage thinking of it as a short-term relationship."

"I'm not," she said. "But I'm also not sure how you can be all that worried about that, when you and Mom's marriage didn't last, right?"

Was her grievance with me personally? Or was I just in the

wrong place at the wrong time? "Your mother and I were headed in different directions," I said. "You know that."

"But how did you figure that out?"

"I don't know," I said. "It happened slowly. We each wanted control over our time, I guess, or over how we lived. And we didn't agree on how to do that, or we couldn't figure out how to do it, so we made a decision."

She nodded as if telling me it was all right to stop—as if it wasn't really the question she'd wanted to ask. "So what happens if Grant and I both want control?" she said.

The question was asked in earnest, and she waited for my response with an expression I knew well: she was a daughter challenging her father to explain how the world worked. And yet I could not help her there. "I guess I don't know the answer to that," I said.

"Well," she said, shrugging. "How could you, right? You and Mom split up."

If Miranda knew what other people thought about her and Grant, then surely she knew people assumed Grant was in charge. A successful businessman in his late forties doesn't marry a girl in her twenties so that the girl can tell him what to do. Did she really believe she and Grant were entering into a partnership in which each would have the same amount of power? He had money; she had none. He had traveled extensively; she had gone on a few childhood vacations to mid-level swimming-and-golf resorts, and a few ski trips. The question of what would happen if she and Grant both wanted control was off the mark, because the question didn't apply to him. Grant would certainly expect to have control over his work and home life, and the idea that Miranda would ever tell him how to go about his business seemed preposterous. "So are you worried about how people are talking to you, or about the fact that your mother and I got divorced?" I said.

"No," she said, "I know I'm talking about those things, but that's not it. Or it's not that simple. There's really nothing to resolve."

Except how to handle her feeling that people's enthusiasm for her wedding was false. And what would happen the first time she told Grant she didn't want him to go on a business trip, because he was traveling too much. Or maybe what would happen the first time she told him she didn't want to go on a business trip *with* him, because she was tired of tagging along. "You know, when you were a little girl and you threw a tantrum, you had this brain-rattling scream," I said. "The pitch was so high that the vibrations would basically stop everyone's brain from working. You would cry, throw things, spit—real *Exorcist* stuff—and then unleash this scream, and no one could talk to you. The only way to get you to talk was to sit on the floor and let you scream and hit me with your little fists, and whisper to you. And you wouldn't hear me at first, but you would know I'd said something. So I would whisper it again, and maybe again, until you stopped hitting me."

"And this worked?"

"Not really. You would still scream. But you would scream what was wrong, right into my ear, and then I could respond."

"That's why you keep the car radio so loud."

"Probably," I said, and then lowered my voice and whispered, "But Miranda? I can't understand you right now. You have to tell me what is wrong."

She laughed, but looked down, avoiding my eyes. "I don't think that's going to work this time, Dad. I've talked to you, and I've talked to Mom, and I've thought about it. I just have to make decisions for myself."

"What is this 'it'? What have you talked to your mother about?"

"Nothing. I'm just overthinking things. Or I'm thinking about too many different things. I have to—" she started, but then hesitated. "I have to use the bathroom." She stood, and laid her hand briefly on my shoulder as she passed. I heard her trade a word or two with the waitress, who asked if Miranda knew where she was going, and then her footsteps faded as she left the room.

So there had been no accident. She and Grant had not eloped. And rather than my imagined scene in which she would request permission to disappear, in person she had defended her resolve to do exactly what she was doing. She had expressed uncertainty about who she would become as a married woman, yes, but I wondered how much the marriage's role in that uncertainty was bit of a smokescreen, anyway. Miranda was only three years out of college, and was gamely trying to use her degree in arts and letters by working as an assistant in an art gallery. Most people her age, trying to find their way into careers and lives, were uncertain about who they might become, and what unforeseen people or powers would take part in their transformation. I realized that what she found most insulting, of course, was that exact conclusion: the belief that at twenty-five she was not yet a full-fledged adult, but still in some protean, pre-adult phase. Maybe this wasn't what she felt about herself—maybe she felt she was doing exactly what she wanted to do and being exactly who she wanted to be. If so, was it naive of her to believe that, or was it condescending of me to think she was wrong? How she and Grant spoke to each other when no one else was around, how they negotiated their time, how they chose who did what and when: these were things I couldn't know, and didn't want to. A series of images fluttered through my head. As I sat there in the restaurant dining room, watching condensation trickle down my glass, I was also adjusting Miranda's blankets during her afternoon nap when she was no more than a few years old. The room's white curtains stirred in the breeze as I placed my hand over hers, and was surprised by the heat of her little palm. I watched her let go of a playground swing as it reached its apogee, so that she could hang in the air, her hair suspended in a float of gravity-defying stillness, before she returned to the earth, landing on her feet with a happy thud. I heard her peal of laughter a few years later, her hat and false nose discarded as she sorted chocolates and candies beneath the glow of the kitchen table lamp one later Halloween night, a girl witch in dishabille, intoxicated with candy bar delight. Among the million images of my daughter that had passed through my eyes, why were these the ones that lingered? Asleep during a toddler nap, aloft above the playground, laughing at the table: each was of Miranda alone, I noticed. Or alone, save for the presence of the mind recording the moments, of course. Save for me.

How long had I been staring at my glass of soda? It seemed too long. A middle-aged couple had been seated across the room, and three young men stood at the entrance, waiting to be shown to a table. I stood, walked past the young men, and continued down the hall toward the restrooms. I stopped in front of the door to the women's room and thought, The only woman customer is at her table, so it's just the staff I have to consider here. I pushed the door a couple inches open with my foot. "Miranda? Is anyone in here?" I said. There was no response, so I pushed the door open, taking a half step into the room to do so. It was a standard bathroom: a tile floor, mirrors above each of two sinks set within a beige counter-top, and two stalls. From where I was standing, though, I couldn't see whether the stalls were occupied.

"Can I help you, sir?" the waitress said. She couldn't have done a better job of startling me if she'd been trying.

"My daughter," I said, stepping back and allowing the door to swing shut. "She said she was going to the bathroom a while ago, but she hasn't come back."

"You can't go in there, though."

"I understand. But I think it's empty."

"I'll check." She pushed the door open, stepped in exactly as I had, and said, "Is there anyone in here?" She walked in, letting the door close behind her, and a few seconds later stepped out again. "There's nobody in there," she said.

"Is there anywhere else she might have gone?" I said. "Are there other bathrooms?"

"This is it," she said. "But if you want to go back to your table, I can look around."

So not only was I not allowed to call Miranda's name into the women's restroom, but I wasn't allowed to walk around the restaurant, either. I was in trouble, it seemed. I told the waitress thanks, I would appreciate that, and headed back to my table while she went into the kitchen. From my table, I watched a young couple walk in the front door, look at me and the others in the dining room, share a quiet look, and then turn and leave.

"I asked the kitchen staff," the waitress said, returning. "They said they might have heard someone go out the back door, but I went out there, and I don't see anyone. I'm not sure where else she could be."

"Okay," I said. "I guess I'll try her phone. Thanks for checking."

I dialed Miranda's number, but there was no answer. I left a message saying I was in the restaurant wondering where she was, and then placed the phone in front of me on the table, studying it while I thought about how cell phones seem to exist primarily so that people can avoid ever actually having a telephone conversation. And then the phone buzzed in a way that was entirely new and confusing to me. I picked it up and said hello, but not only was there no answer, there wasn't even the sound of an empty line. What now? I thought. When I looked at the display, it indicated a message waiting for me. I dialed voice mail, but there were no new messages there, so I hit the menu button and found that there was, indeed, a menu titled "Messages," with an in-box that listed an item titled "can't talk now. h." When I opened the message, it read:

Can't talk now.
have to go. see you later.
sorry.

I understood what a text message was—the tellers at the bank were doing it all the time—but this was the first one I, personally, had ever received. I pressed the respond button and stared at a little blinking cursor. This was a form of communication for young people, I felt—it was ridiculous for me to try to take part. What could one even communicate by pressing numbers on a telephone? And this was a strategy, I thought: Miranda knew a text message would limit my ability to respond. With great concentration and the correction of some mistakes, then, I managed to type:

okay.

I stared at the ridiculous response, wanting to add to it. Communicating this way seemed laborious and pointless, though, so I gave up and hit send. A little animated envelope cartwheeled across the screen amid flashes of color, and then the standard display returned, as if nothing had happened. Had the message been successfully sent? I hadn't the slightest idea. When I looked up and saw the waitress walking toward the couple across the room, I briefly considered asking her the meaning of a cartwheeling envelope on a cell phone screen, but decided against it. Instead I said, "Is it too late to cancel our order?"

I didn't think it was necessary for her to slump as dramatically as she did—this was the worst news she had ever received, it seemed. But I left a five-dollar bill on the table anyway, which worked out to a twenty-five percent tip for her on the price of two drinks. And then I walked out of the restaurant and paused, blinking, in the midday sun. I wondered which direction Miranda had gone. There was no way to know.

ON A SATURDAY MORNING only a few weeks after our trip to the coast, I drove up to St. Joseph's, an older neighborhood on the north side of town. St. Joseph's, which had been its own city until being annexed in the 1920s, had maintained a thriving commercial district into the early 1970s. It had fallen on hard times then, however, and by the 1980s the words *St. Joe's* primarily evoked a sense of crime and disrepair. It had been a couple years since I'd had any reason to visit the neighborhood, but the two-story buildings, faded awnings, and stenciled lettering on the dusty shop windows that lined Petrus Avenue, the neighborhood's main drag, were exactly as I remembered them. When I parked, I examined the parking meter on the curb to confirm that it was even functioning. It appeared to be, so I fed it a few coins, walked past a hardware store that seemed open for business, an empty pet store that did not, and arrived at the address Grant had given me: a storefront which featured stenciled white letters on its window, spelling a single word: TAILOR.

Inside, there was a long, unmanned counter at the front—the place had maybe been a dry cleaner's at one point—and beyond it, a few racks of suit coats and trousers along one side of the room, and some dressing rooms and mirrors on the other. The only people present were Grant and a short, gaunt older man dressed in a three-piece wool suit, whom Grant, after beckoning me to join them, introduced as Mr. Anthony. When Grant had told me he needed a new suit for work and he wondered if I, too, might be interested in the experience of buying a tailored suit, I had been intrigued. Now, though, standing in the old store, in front of an actual Mr. Anthony, I was uncertain. Did I really need a tailored suit? A shirt and tie were required at the bank, but I had never seen a teller, at my branch or any other, wearing a suit. "You can just try some things, if you want," Mr. Anthony said quietly, reading my uncertainty. "You're not obliged to make any decisions today."

His tone surprised and reassured me, and it was only five minutes later that Grant and I stood next to one another on small pedestals, wearing white undershirts and unhemmed wool slacks as we studied ourselves in a mirror. Mr. Anthony knelt at our ankles, working quickly and methodically with pins and a measuring tape, a situation so foreign to me that just a few polite questions from Grant about how I was doing elicited a nervous chattiness from me, and I found myself going on about what a nice time Sandra and I had had at the beach, and how much we'd enjoyed spending time with Grant and Gina. I even mentioned how the more I thought about what Grant had said on the deck of the restaurant, the more I realized that this *was* a time in my life when I was entering new situations, and that I really did appreciate his willingness to talk to me about those things. "And then inviting me here today, to a place where I can learn about some of this stuff directly," I said, "I appreciate it, because I don't know anyone else who would invite me to do something like this, or who would even be able to tell me where I should go if I wanted to try and do it on my own."

Grant had no reaction to any of this other than to nod while studying himself in the mirror, as if the cut of his pants were a subject so consuming that it made responding to anything else impossible. And when Mr. Anthony, bustling about my ankles, accidentally stabbed me with a pin just above the heel and I cried out in an embarrassingly girlish fashion, Grant just smiled politely. Mr. Anthony quietly apologized to me, the four or five straight pins he held between his lips lending him the diction of a street tough in an old gangster movie, and then told us he had the measurements he needed.

It wasn't until we were slipping back into our own clothes that Grant spoke. "I'm glad you've enjoyed spending time with us," he said. "And I'm glad you're okay with what I said at the beach. I felt like I didn't do a very good job of explaining what I meant. I probably came off like the exact asshole I didn't want to be. But there's something I have to tell you that I guess is kind of regrettable now, which is that Gina and I have broken up."

I wasn't sure what to make of the entirely neutral expression on Grant's face as he watched himself tucking in his shirt in the mirror. "I'm sorry to hear that," I said, dismayed by the strangely modulated tone of voice I heard myself use.

"It's my problem, really," he said. "Because Gina is wonderful. It's just that sometimes things don't work out. I mean, if anyone knows what I mean, it's you, right?"

Did I? I had dated Gina for a couple months during my junior year of college, and our relationship had occurred primarily because she had just broken up with some kind of long-term, supposedly serious boyfriend, and I was a nice, unthreatening guy who happened to be doing a group project with her in a communications class. I suspect Gina asked if I wanted to see a movie with her mostly because she so outclassed me socially that she could feel completely in control—she could be confident she was signing up for nothing more than a movie, a confidence that was certainly confirmed when, after shocking me by asking if she could stay the night, she had gently made so many suggestions in bed that she was, for all practical purposes, taking on the role of instructor. I had perfect attendance to my college classes, delivered pizzas four nights a week, had been inside a bar no more than three or four times, had never done any drugs, and had had sex all of two times. After what was certainly fairly unsatisfying sex for her, Gina had told me it was good for her to be with "a nice guy, for once," a remark I naively took as a compliment. A couple months later, she thanked me for being so nice, but said she felt it would be better for her if she weren't in a relationship at all for a while, so maybe we could just be friends. Summer break started a few weeks later, and I never heard from her again.

If that's what Grant meant by "sometimes things don't work out," then yes, I suppose I understood that sometimes things didn't work out. I didn't think that was what he meant, though.

"I hope you and Sandra know that I really like both of you, and I'd like to stay friends with you," he said. "I know you've known Gina longer than you've known me, and that she's probably going to be pissed off and say all sorts of angry things about me. But I'm being serious when I say it's been fun to hang out, and I'd be disappointed if that had to end. Though I guess I would understand."

Ending my friendship with Grant because of something that had happened between him and Gina seemed preposterous. What would the point be? The reality of their breakup, and of how we would or wouldn't continue to know each other in the future, seemed entirely theoretical and irrelevant. "I can't say how Sandra will feel, but I'd definitely like to keep hanging out," I said, noticing again how often, when speaking to Grant, I found myself uttering sentences that embarrassed me.

He gave me a friendly pat on the shoulder. "Good," he said, and then headed to the front of the store to pay Mr. Anthony for the suit he'd picked out.

We said nothing more about Gina, but in an impulsive show of solidarity, I told Mr. Anthony I would go ahead and buy the suit he had measured me for, too. "It's a beautiful suit," he said, nodding. "And you'll be able to wear it to just about any kind of event, so you know you're going to get your money out of it. I think it's an excellent decision."

He was right. I wore that suit countless times over the years. And even though I stopped being able to fit into it a few years ago, it still hangs in the back of my closet.

I was not so assured of my decision at the time, though. The amount of money I'd just spent made the suit the single largest purchase I had ever made, eclipsing even the price of the used Dodge Dart I was driving in those days. I felt simultaneously dizzy and grown-up as I drove across town in that very vehicle, and a belated sense of financial prudence—or penance, probably—might have spurred me to cancel the round of golf I was heading toward, had Grant not already assured me the whole thing would be taken care of that day: we were going to play with his father, whose club membership allowed anyone in his party to golf for free.

So when I next parked my humbled Dart, it was in the lot of the Pheasant Valley Country Club. It was autumn by then, but the air at the course was heavy with the scents of damp soil and cut grass. Summer had been coaxed into lingering, it seemed, and though there had been scattered showers earlier in the day, the clouds had cleared by the time I arrived, leaving the place a carefully mowed, still-dripping Eden. Finches whirred among the trees and golf carts trilled in the distance. I found Grant at the driving range—he'd already spilled a bucket of red-striped range balls across the dark grass for me. I pulled a driver from my vinyl bag and squinted out toward the flagsticks set at short, intermediate, and long distance. The trio of flags lent the range exactly no resemblance to golf as actually played, but I sized them up as if they were of importance while I asked Grant when his father would join us.

"Oh, he doesn't believe in the driving range," Grant said. "He's probably having a drink right now."

A smattering of laughter carried from the direction of the first tee, among it a laugh that was deeper and louder than the others. I wondered if it might be the laugh of the source of Grant's career and fashion advice, and when Grant and I made our way to the first tee a few minutes later, I was happy to find that I was right: the foursome ahead of us was trading a few last quips with a tall, broad-shouldered man shouting rejoinders to them as they sped off in their carts. Grant introduced the man to me as his father. "It's nice to meet you, sir," I said.

"Don't bother with the mister or sir stuff," he said. "Call me Lon."

If I'd seen them together on the street, I wouldn't have guessed Grant and Lon were related at all. Grant had the compact build of a distance runner, but his father, a few inches taller than Grant and heavier by a good fifty or sixty pounds, looked like a retired football player gone comfortably soft. His wide face was dominated by an open smile, and he chatted unhurriedly, as if a round of golf were best undertaken as casually as a conversation over a backyard fence.

"Grant tells me you're a banker," Lon said. "That's a fine line of work to go into. Always a need for a good banker." When I told him I wasn't sure it would be a career I stuck with, but that it was fine for the short term, he shook his head. "Don't dismiss it. Markets can go down and businesses can go under, but banks are always there. There's nothing wrong with a small compromise in the direction of long-term stability."

"Or with using it as a short-term position before moving on to something else," Grant said.

Lon raised a brow as he tapped a divot back into the soil with the head of his driver. In his grasp, the club looked as if it were intended for a child. "I suppose," he said. "Though my first business was auto parts distribution, and I wasn't really interested in auto parts at all. But making that company work is how I bought the house your mom and I lived in. And it's how I clothed and fed you when you were just a kiddo. We had to buy you that little plastic suitcase so you could pretend it was a briefcase full of sales pamphlets and rate sheets like your old man's briefcase."

Lon laughed heartily, and though Grant forced a smile at what was clearly a familiar anecdote, the confidence I had come to expect from him seemed replaced that day by a moody remove. Grant examined the toes of his shoes, picked through a handful of tees he extracted from his pocket, and studied the trees that lined the fairway—he directed his gaze anywhere, it seemed, other than at his father. Meanwhile, Lon adjusted the fit of his golf glove, a worn leather item that made my own glove—new, soft, and glaringly white—look painfully effete. Addressing the ball, Lon peered down the fairway with the nonchalance of someone looking for a bus, then frowned down at the tee. Bringing his club slowly up and back, he exhaled as he uncoiled, striking the ball with a percussive note that carried through the afternoon air like the sound of a hatchet splitting wood. We watched the ball rise and hang against the blue sky, suspended and seemingly motionless, until it drifted slowly back to earth and bounded eagerly down the right side of the fairway. I told Lon it was a nice shot, and he nodded. "It'll play," he said.

Not only did that shot play, but so did his next, and the next after that. He moved around the course as if completely at home, and continued to indulge in every opportunity to release his booming laugh across the fairways. Everyone we crossed paths with seemed to know him. He called the teenage snack cart girl by name, and when he asked if she'd think less of him if he ordered another drink, she said, "I brought the pitcher of Bloody Marys out here because I knew you'd want one." He told her to give Grant and me whatever we wanted and put it on his account, and though Grant asked only for orange juice, I decided to try a Bloody Mary of my own. If it helped Lon's game, I thought, it might help mine. "We'll have a fresh pitcher waiting for you guys at the turn," the girl said brightly as she handed me my drink. Then she clicked the cart into gear and sped away.

Grant took one look at me after my first sip. "Have you ever had a Bloody Mary before?" he said.

"No," I admitted. "What's in it?"

"Tomato juice," he said. "And other things that I, personally, don't think belong in a drink. Enjoy."

I was just managing to finish the drink while we waited to tee off on a par three toward the end of the front nine when Lon, after finishing an anecdote about Grant throwing a club into a pond when he was a teenager, asked if I'd been taught to play by my own father. I felt the usual wariness rise in me as I admitted I'd mostly taught myself, though Grant had been giving me some pointers recently. "Your folks live here in town?" Lon asked.

"No," I said. "I'm from New Mexico. I came out here for college."

"You ever think about going back?" he asked. "Or are you here for good?"

Grant was standing nearby, apparently absorbed in the task of using a tee to clean mud from the grooves of one of his irons, though I could tell he was listening. "There's nothing to go back to," I said. "My parents are both gone from New Mexico now, too, so that's all over. My mom's in Florida, and my dad's in Texas."

Lon nodded sagely, glancing again at my cheap golf bag. I didn't quite have a complete set of clubs in those days—I had enough to be allowed on the course, but I was a little light. I knew Lon was appraising the situation, but one drink into a nice autumn afternoon, I didn't particularly care.

"They're just about done, Dad," Grant said. It was true that the last member of the foursome on the green ahead of us was putting out, but it also seemed that Grant was maybe less comfortable with his dad's questions than I was.

"Well, I can't say I have much knowledge about either Florida or Texas," Lon said, "but I've heard they have some nice spots.

Hurricane country, though, in both of them." He pulled an iron from his bag and stepped into the tee box. "We should make sure to get out on the course together a few times this summer, since it's free for you gentlemen when you're with me." He hit a clean drive that we watched drop onto the green one hundred eighty yards away. I again complimented him on the shot, and he laughed. "That one *was* pretty good, wasn't it?" he said.

Lon downed three more Bloody Marys, had one birdie, five pars, and triple-putted only twice over the rest of our eighteen holes. Two other snack cart girls knew him by name and beverage, and players traveling along parallel fairways continued calling out friendly hellos to him. Grant, on the other hand, seemed bored. The longer we walked the groomed fairways, and the more Lon spoke to me with amiable easiness, the more profound Grant's boredom seemed to become. I studied Lon's gestures—the trophy pose he held after completing his swing, the rhythms with which he spoke, the way he walked the course—but throughout the entire back nine, Grant hardly traded a word with us, and played largely on his own, as if completing a chore. I was baffled by his mood that day, but in recent years I've seen Miranda assume the same demeanor when I linger for any amount of time in a room in which she is with her friends—the presence of a parent can't help but flatten the child's carefully constructed façade of adult sophistication. So though I thought Grant's silence was the result of an uncharacteristically dark mood that day, I can see now that Grant was actually closer to being in no mood at all. It made no sense to think of him as possessing a mood, because it made no sense to think of him as even being himself that day. He was just his father's son, golfing for free.

When we finished and Grant added up the scores, I was surprised to learn that Lon had beaten Grant by only four strokes. Grant delivered the news as if it were a trivial detail, but Lon seemed pleased, and told us that even though he had to leave, Grant and I should have dinner at the club and charge it to his account. He shook my hand, thanked me for playing, and ambled toward the parking lot.

"I'm sorry if he was distracting," Grant said after his father was gone. "Half of what he says is just meant to mess with your focus, because he wants to win."

"He was messing with my focus?" I said. "I didn't realize it."

"Well," Grant said, "he may only have been messing with mine."

"Have you ever beaten him?"

"Once. He was less than thrilled. He didn't speak to me for two weeks."

Two weeks didn't strike me as a big deal, but I understood my expectations regarding communication with a father were set low. "Did you want to stay to get something to eat?" I asked.

Grant just shook his head. The idea was out of the question, it seemed—he and his father were involved in some ornate series of signifying gestures I wasn't going to catch the subtleties of. And I would never even get another chance to study them, because that October afternoon was the last I ever saw of Lon. Although I went golfing with Grant a handful of times every year, never again was it at the invitation of, or paid for by, his father.

I ended that day with Sandra. When I told her about the breakup, she seemed less surprised than I. Her roommate had gone out of town for the weekend, so it was one of the rare times she and I had her apartment to ourselves, and she had made dinner for the two of us, complete with candles on the table. She first asked whether Grant had said who broke up with whom, and when I told her I'd gotten the impression it was Grant who had ended things, she wanted to know how I'd gotten that impression, what Grant had said that gave me that impression, how he had said it, and so on, until eventually I just repeated the entire conversation to her.

"Well, I'm glad," she said as we ate our dinner amid candlelight.

"You're glad?"

"Because I don't have to keep pretending to be friends with her. She was your ex-girlfriend. It was weird."

"She was hardly a serious girlfriend, Sandra."

She shrugged. "Let's take Grant to Bristol's some evening. Gina can take care of herself, and besides, Grant's the person you're friends with now, right?"

I agreed, though I couldn't help but feel I was somehow betraying Gina. "I think it's cute that you're jealous," I said.

"I'm not jealous," Sandra said. "It's just that with her, I was having to be polite and friendly with someone that I didn't really care about. Grant, at least, gives you tips on new clothes and takes you golfing or whatever. The golf sounds like it's fun for you, and I like the new clothes. But what do we lose if we don't see Gina anymore?"

"It always thought the two of you were getting along."

"That's what women do," she said. "We pretend, to be nice."

"Did you think it was dangerous that we were all going out together?"

She smiled. "Dangerous? No. No offense, but I don't think she was after you. Were you after her?"

"No," I said. "I'm after you."

She raised her head defiantly. "Prove it."

I don't know whether Sandra ever considered it, but the sex life she and I were enjoying at the time had certainly been made possible, in part, by the two months of instruction Gina had given me a few years before. So though I wasn't allowed to say it, and though I understood Sandra's desire to be free of playing nice with Gina, I knew that Gina was someone who had contributed positively to our relationship. Because when I moved my fingers beneath Sandra's dress as we stood there kissing next to the table, I knew where and how to move my fingers once they reached their destination because Gina had shown me how. And one of the reasons Sandra was able to feel pleasure that evening in her apartment was because Gina had shown me how to make a woman feel pleasure. But I suppose that's usually true: the pleasure we find in another person is only possible because of the pleasure that person has already found, with others.

I HAD THOUGHT THE university district would be empty on a Saturday morning, but driving through it, I found the sidewalks filled with knots of people, all headed in the same direction. There was much chucking of shoulders and fake-wrestling among the college boys in the groups, and whatever they were anticipating, it was clearly a struggle for them to contain themselves. Driving past, I watched to make sure no one darted or was thrown into the street. The day's heat was gathering itself in earnest, and the college kids were dressed for it. The women wore shorts and bikini tops or spaghetti-strap halters, while the men favored baseball hats, baggy shorts, and slogan-emblazoned T-shirts—the more confident young men wore no shirts at all. I hadn't the slightest idea where everyone was headed, but it was obviously an event at which the sun would have ample opportunity to do damage to skin.

I pulled onto campus at the south end of the Quad, an immense rectangular lawn surrounded by the university's oldest buildings, and parked along the curb. Massive oaks bordered a concrete walk that ran lengthwise down the center of the area, their wreathed branches forming a vaulted arboreal hall the university featured in its marketing brochures each year, and I felt myself break into a sweat as I walked across the lawn toward the trees. The only other visible human was someone riding a bicycle along the opposite end of the Quad, two hundred yards from where I stood. When the rider steered his bike over the edge of the curb and onto the sidewalk, the clatter of wheel and frame arrived a quarter second after the act, and I was surprised, as always, at the phenomenon of sound lagging image. And then I was surprised again when I arrived at the walkway and found there was actually another person present, hidden within the trees and shade: Catherine.

"I thought you were talking with the security people," I said.

"It was a brief conversation," she said. "So I thought I'd stop by here just in case. How is Miranda?"

I was comfortable relying on Catherine at the bank, but this attention to my family life made me wary. We'd worked together for ten years, of course, so Catherine knew a bit about my life outside of work. But I wasn't a sharer of personal information, and had even done my best to keep private the fact that I was dating Trish. This proved impossible, since Trish banked at the branch, and changed her behavior toward me there after the first time we slept together. Being called "honey" was difficult enough for me, but being called that in front of Catherine was mortifying. So my instinct was to hide private struggles and uncertainties from Catherine. But when had her presence ever been anything but an advantage, really? And here she was. So I went ahead, cautiously. "I'm not sure," I said. "I sat down to lunch with her, but then she disappeared."

"What do you mean?"

"She said she was going to the bathroom, but then she sent a message to my phone saying she couldn't talk now. Or didn't want to, I guess. And she didn't come back." Intending to produce my phone so that Catherine could see the message, I discovered it wasn't in my pocket—I had taken it out to reread the message while driving, and must have left it on the passenger seat. I looked toward my car from where we stood. A hot breeze moved over the vast lawn, the blades of grass rippling in the sun. The shaded sidewalk felt like a protected port, and I was reluctant to move from it.

"Was she okay?" Catherine asked.

"I don't know. We only talked a few minutes."

"She must have been upset about something, if she left like that."

"Maybe," I said, "I should call Grant, but I left my phone in the car. You wouldn't happen to have his number, would you?"

"Oh, I don't know about that," she said, knitting her eyebrows as if taxed by a great mental effort. I'd been joking, but her response seemed suspicious. She pressed some buttons on her phone and squinted at it. "I guess I do," she said, handing it to me. There on the little screen was Grant's name and number.

"What a stroke of luck," I said.

"Yes," she said, nodding in placid agreement. She maintained such impressive discipline in her responses that at times, her stoicism approached the theatrical.

"Just how many numbers do you have in this phone?" I said.

"What do you mean?"

"You and Grant speak often enough that you keep his number in your phone?"

"He calls you at the branch, just like Sandra," she said. "You should be thanking me, not cross-examining."

"Thank you," I said.

"Is that the truck?"

At the opposite end of the Quad, a white delivery truck was trundling slowly around the corner, headed our way.

"Probably," I said. "But I don't think Grant calls me at the branch that often, and he's not a member of my family. Why would you have his phone number? Do you have a crush on him?"

"You're being a jerk. I have his number for the same reason I have Sandra's."

I pressed the dial button on her phone and listened as Grant's line rang. "You're blushing," I said.

"I am not," she said.

Grant didn't answer. I turned the phone off without leaving a message, and handed it back to her.

"Here I am trying to help you, and you're abusing me," she said, "trying to embarrass me because I keep the numbers of people who call the branch."

"What a monster I am."

"Yes," she said. "I can hardly make it through the days."

"I guess you won't have to much longer."

There it was again: her exasperated little sigh. I was just so tiresome, it seemed.

The white truck rolled to a stop nearby, and a college-aged kid in torn jeans and a blue company T-shirt jumped out, trotted toward us, and asked if we were expecting chairs. When I told him we were, he headed to the rear of the truck and, amid a tumult of metal-on-metal percussions, he unfastened latches, rolled the back door up, and leaped in. After further rattling of iron and shuffling of plastic, three white folding chairs came flying out the back of the truck. They crashed to clattering rest on the grass, and then more chairs flew out, and more, each group describing a graceful airborne arc before its members hit the lawn, seats and backrests issuing sharp plastic reports on impact. The deluge continued for some minutes until, seeing consecutive trios of green chairs heaved onto the grass, I stepped toward the truck.

"Excuse me," I called out. "But I think our chairs are all supposed to be white."

The boy poked his head out of the back of the truck, breathing heavily. "I know. But I'm out, sir."

"What do you mean?"

"I mean I gave you every white chair that's in here, but I counted, and it only came to a hundred thirty. You're supposed to have a hundred fifty. I have two other weddings to deliver to, but all the chairs left in here are green, so I'm giving you those."

"But they're meant for the other weddings, aren't they? Won't you just end up short down the line?"

He rubbed his buzz-cut thoughtfully. "Maybe they won't ask to count?"

I waited for him to laugh, but he didn't. "Have you ever heard of robbing Peter to pay Paul'?" I asked.

"I don't know, sir," he said. "Not really. I'm just taking it as it goes. I didn't load the truck."

I looked to Catherine. She shrugged. "Okay," I said. "We'll take the green chairs."

"Great," he said.

And five minutes later, Steffen was driving away while Catherine and I looked over one hundred and fifty chairs, twenty of which were green. And we had possibly damaged someone else's day.

I felt the setting up of the chairs was a task to be performed with expedience, but the sight of them flung across the lawn was daunting—it looked as if a violent storm had just swept through, and when Catherine asked how I wanted them arranged, I hesitated. Seventy-five should obviously be on one side of the concrete path that would serve as the aisle, I said, and seventy-five on the other, but my first inclination was that ten rows was a good number, which meant seven and a half chairs per row, and I was not in a position to begin sawing chairs in half. Five chairs was too few for a row, unless we wanted the feeling of a wedding on an airplane, I said, and of course it might be nice if the rows fanned out a bit, just got a bit longer as they got farther from the front, though that would change the math entirely. I had crunched only a few of those numbers when a flash of insight cleared my entire mental slate. "We should completely ignore the existence of the aisle," I said, excited. I expected this breakthrough would lead to new computations and numbers, but for some reason, I had no further thoughts.

"Are you all right?" Catherine asked, peering into my eyes. "Your face has gone white."

"I'm fine," I said. "Maybe a little warm, but fine."

"I think you should sit down," she said.

"Water is all I need, really. We have a lot to do."

"Let's rest while we think it over."

She pulled two chairs into a shaded area of the path, and we sat down. I was sweating profusely, I realized, so I loosened my tie and undid the top button of my shirt.

"I can't believe you're wearing that suit in this heat," Catherine said.

"It's not too bad," I said.

The breeze had disappeared, and the lawn suffered in stillness beneath the heat of the summer sun. It was pleasant in the shade, though, and it was only as I began to feel better that I realized I'd been feeling badly. My pulse stopped throbbing in my temples. I felt less of an urge to speak so quickly and loudly.

"Okay," Catherine said. "Yes, it's true I've had Grant's telephone number for a number of years now."

"I was just teasing," I said.

"No, you were right," she said, fixing her green eyes upon me as if seeking forgiveness. I had never seen her in that kind of anguish before. "Grant is obviously a good-looking guy. And I answer the phone pretty often, and he's very charming on the phone. And when he comes by to have lunch with you during the holidays each year, he brings me some little thing. This pin, for instance."

She turned to me, and as I had earlier in the morning, I examined her lapel. The little golden bouquet sparkled brightly, even in the shade. "You don't have to say another thing, Catherine."

"But I want you to know that I'm happy for you," she said. "For you and for Sandra and most of all for Miranda. It would bother me if there were any misunderstandings."

"It's nothing," I said. "I don't want you to worry about it."

She studied our scrabble of chairs as if it were their state, and not whatever it was she was trying to communicate to me, that had brought out these emotions in her. Without thinking, I took her hand in mine. It was warm, her hand, and though we focused on the chairs, she gently returned the pressure of my grasp.

"Well," she said. "I just wanted to tell you."

The line of shade wavered in the breeze. A bird dropped from a nearby tree and flew like a dart across the Quad. When it disappeared behind a nearby building, Catherine pulled her hand from mine to check her watch. "It's past noon," she said.

"That's less than six hours until the ceremony," I said. "I suppose we should get going."

So we stood and moved together toward the scattered chairs. And I was fairly certain that in the ten years I had worked with Catherine, taking her hand just then was the first time I had ever touched her.

IT WAS OVER A Sunday morning pancake breakfast that Sandra told me she had taken a pregnancy test and the result was positive. I had been sifting through the paper, looking at ads for stereos and television sets, but upon hearing her announcement, I pushed them away, nearly upsetting a glass of orange juice. "By positive, you mean pregnant," I said.

"I haven't been to the doctor yet, but yes," she said.

I felt empty. Or maybe the opposite, really—as if my body had disappeared while my mind remained in place, blinking. I'm not sure why I attempted to be witty just then, but the next thing I said was "And it's mine?"

To her credit, Sandra smiled. "It's hard to say," she said, trying to play along. Then she burst into tears.

I took her hands in mine and told her that everything would be okay, it wasn't the end of the world, we would be fine—all the things one says—and when she regained her composure, I asked her what she wanted to do. "What do you mean?" she said.

"I mean what's our next step?"

"We have a baby," she said. "Or *I* have a baby."

"*We* have a baby," I said. "And we should get married."

"You haven't asked."

"I will."

"Is this it? Are you asking?"

"Give me a few days," I said. "I want to do it right."

"I think we're too late for that," she said.

It was only a few weeks later that, walking to lunch, I noticed a trail of smoke threading its way through the margin of a barely opened window in a sedan parked down the street. Tracing the smoke to its source, I discovered none other than Detective Buckle in the driver's seat, pensively smoking a cigarette. He nodded toward me as he rolled his window down with a wince, as if the effort were somehow painful.

"Are you working?" I asked.

"Someone told me they always return to the scene of the crime," he said. "When your Mooncalf fellow does, I'll be waiting."

"Have you been sitting here every day?"

"No. I pick my moments. I thought I might see you around here, though. Still in touch with your friend?"

"My friend?"

"The Gina girl."

"Oh," I said. I wasn't on painkillers this time, but I still felt a step behind him. "We went out a few times, with our current people. Double dates, I guess."

"Double dates," he repeated slowly, as if it were the first time he'd heard the term. "How did it go?"

"Fine," I said. "I'm not clear on how this relates."

He laughed. "It probably doesn't. I'm prying. But you've definitely gotten a haircut, and that's a nice suit, too. Is it new?"

"Kind of," I said. "How did you know?"

He shrugged. He was the consummate shrugger, Buckle. I never heard him raise his voice, and never saw him angry. Just a slight tilt of the head and roll of the shoulders seemed to keep the whole world at bay for him—it was like Atlas in reverse. "Have you been following me?" I asked.

He shook his head. "I'm not that kind of cop," he said. "And if I were, you wouldn't be the kind of guy I'd be following. There's a price tag still inside the jacket there."

My jacket had fallen open as I leaned forward to speak to him, and a tag peeked just above the top of the inside pocket. I pushed it back down and looked around: two boys tried to elbow each other from the skateboards they rode side by side down the sidewalk; an old woman gazed at balls of yarn piled in a shop window. "Did you ever get any leads?" I asked him. "On the guy who robbed me?"

"No," he said, flicking his cigarette against the rearview mirror. "As far as we know, he's still out there."

"So should I assume that until you find him, you'll keep coming back to ask me questions about how much my ties cost or who I eat dinner with?"

"Oh, I didn't mean to make you paranoid," he said in a tone of melodramatic sympathy. "In the beginning, I thought this one would be simple. The guy drew a lot of attention to himself, and we had a dozen eyewitnesses. But it's clear now that the case isn't going to be wrapped up as quickly as I hoped."

"He gave you the slip," I said.

"He's lying low for now," Buckle said. "But he'll have to come up for air at some point. I can't know when that's going to happen, but it could happen today, or it could happen tomorrow—"

"Or soon," I interrupted, "and for the rest of your life."

He winced again. "I don't know what that means. All I'm saying is the case is still open, but I won't be coming around to give you updates."

"I won't be seeing you on the street like this?"

"We'll always have Paris."

"So you did get that reference," I said.

"Of course," he said. "And I can see I've hurt your feelings, and I'm sorry you're angry. I was joking. You're not under surveillance. But also, it's not unusual for robberies to be inside jobs. It's pretty routine for an investigating officer to want to get a sense of how the victim is responding."

"Well, you'll be glad to know I won't be buying any more new suits for a while. My girlfriend is pregnant, so the budget is going to get tight."

He seemed genuinely surprised by that. I was pleased to have caught him off guard. "Congratulations," he said.

"You've got kids of your own?"

"Two. In their teens now."

"That must be a busy time."

He shook his head. "Their mother and I split up a long time ago. She's somewhere in California with them now. It's been a couple years since I've seen them."

The revelation was awkward enough to render me mute, save for a ridiculously knowing nod—as if I, too, knew that pain. He shook my hand through the open window, and pulled a fresh cigarette from his shirt pocket. "I should be going," he said. I stepped back as he started his car, and he gave me a thumbs-up out the window as he drove off.

It wasn't until later that afternoon that I caught myself grinning. I was sitting alone in the little upstairs break room, at a plastic table covered in discarded newspaper sections and *People* magazines, and had just had an argument with a customer over his desire to cash a large check. His account had been overdrawn, and when I told him he would have to cover the insufficient funds in the account before I could give him cash, he had of course launched into a frenzy of outrage, including the usual suggestions that the area's banks were an organization of thieves colluding to persecute him, that it was obvious all of us were in bed with the government, the system was corrupt, and so on. The customer had carried his argument from me to Gene, our stout, Polish branch manager. Gene was professionally and personally conflict-averse, a disposition he enacted through forced, unchanging attempts at coming off as an avuncular boss who was just as much a victim of the insanity of bank policies as we were, and the customer had carried on with him for an additional fifteen minutes before leaving, still outraged. When the telephone behind the teller stations rang a few minutes later, I stepped back to answer it and discovered I was speaking to none other than Gene, who with a nervous chuckle told me that we—by which he meant me—should avoid ever telling a customer that something wasn't possible. Though we could easily have made eye contact while speaking, Gene resolutely studied a notepad on his desk, as if I were truly in some other location, and I had to turn away to prevent myself from being distracted by watching him as he told me that what *he* liked to do was discuss the options a customer had for addressing a situation. He and I both knew the amount of time it took a check to clear wasn't within our control, that I had spoken truthfully to a customer, and that the customer had vented his frustration on me. Now I was the one who needed to change my behavior? I told Gene I'd do my best in the future to discuss options with customers, he thanked me, and we hung up.

But it was afterward, as I sat in the break room thinking about how little I wanted to go back out for the last two hours of my shift, that I realized I was pleased. Beneath my hair, I could still feel the scar where Mooncalf had hit me. I should have been angry at him, should have wanted some kind of revenge, but instead I discovered that I was happy he was still out there. He was lying low, and my sense of relief at this was so exhilarating, in fact, that I remember almost laughing aloud when I recognized there was no way to deny it: a part of me had been rooting for Mooncalf all along.

CATHERINE AND I REQUIRED only ten minutes to unfold and set up all one hundred and fifty of those chairs. It turned out there was no math problem at all—Catherine suggested we decide where we wanted the first row, put ten chairs on each side of the walkway, do that for each following row, and then adjust the last rows however we wanted. The whole issue was solved painlessly, in practice, and when we were finished and retreated again to the shade to admire our work—the straight and even rows, the clean walkway down the middle—Catherine turned and, in a tone that implied nothing more than idle curiosity, said, "So what did you and Miranda talk about?"

I studied the granite columns and limestone façades of the university buildings, but the differences between what Miranda and I had talked about and what I had only thought about didn't immediately resolve themselves. "She mentioned control," I said. "And she asked about her mother and me—about our marriage."

"Do you think she's having cold feet?"

"I thought that just meant feeling nervous. Not disappearing entirely."

"She hasn't disappeared—you just saw her. I felt like running away on my wedding day. It's normal."

How she felt she could get away with relaying this news in a calm, reassuring tone was beyond me. "What are you talking about?" I said. "When were you married?"

"When I was nineteen," she said. "We were kids. It was stupid. He was my high school boyfriend and we thought we were in love."

She spoke as if summarizing the plot of a bad movie—as if the marriage had been nothing more than a couple hours' annoyance. "I've worked with you for ten years," I said. "I went through a divorce while you were working with me. And it's only now you tell me you're divorced, too?"

"Mine was hardly a real marriage. Or I don't count it, at least. It only lasted five months."

"Very efficient. And no one stopped you beforehand?"

"I didn't let anyone. I was nineteen and I knew everything. Or I did until the day of the wedding, when I suddenly realized I wanted to run in the opposite direction. But everything was already planned by then. And I was the one who'd planned it."

She looked at me as if watching me puzzle my way through the strategies of a game she knew better than I. "So what am I supposed to do?" I said.

"Well, if I ever tell you I ran into someone named Simon Tolliver and we're going to go camping together, don't let me go."

"I'm talking about Miranda."

"I know," she said. "But I don't know about Miranda. Did something happen last night?"

Did it? I'd made a speech I couldn't remember, after which Miranda had told me, "It's okay. Everything is fine." I had tried to reassure Sandra about the weather, and she had teased me about it. One of the bridesmaid's mothers hit on me—or didn't. I wasn't sure. Then I went home.

"Not that I know of," I said. "I'm supposed to see Sandra in a few minutes to check the reception site. Maybe I'll ask her. Again."

"That's where you're going next?" Catherine said, as if my plans were of significance.

"Yes. Why?"

"My conversation with the security people was so short because they wanted to talk to us after they've had a chance to look at the videotape and the photos. They're going to be unhappy if you don't show up."

"So I won't expect a birthday gift from them."

"I mean they might be *really* unhappy. They said they want to talk to both of us, because we have the most access to systems and approvals." Then, with the slightly widened eyes of someone alluding to something, she said, "And they always check staff accounts to see if there's anything unusual. They're probably looking at your accounts right now."

"There is nothing wrong with my accounts."

"I know. But they're going to go through all recent account activity." She enunciated the last four words as if naming an obscure disease or syndrome. I knew what she was getting at. Why didn't she just say it?

"You're saying they'll see I have no savings. And I've maxed out my line of credit."

"Yes."

"That's not unusual. Lines of credit have maximums to indicate the amount of money you are *allowed* to borrow."

"But they're going to be looking for things," she said. "And they'll consider that a red flag. All I'm saying is they want to talk to you, and after seeing those details, they're *really* going to want to talk to you."

Anyone looking for aberrations in my deposits or withdrawals, for large purchases, or for any financial details that would indicate a possible motive for stealing would probably see exactly what they were looking for when scanning my accounts. The home equity loan I had taken out was for twenty-five thousand dollars—I had deposited the money in my checking account and used it to cover every expense related to the wedding. But bank security could go back further than that. They could look at every financial transaction I'd made for the last decade, if they wanted. They could watch me pay thousands in lawyer fees while Sandra and I got divorced, could watch most of my remaining assets disappear when I purchased my townhouse—at what struck me as a ridiculously high price, though my Realtor assured me it was normal for the market, and that the value would only go up—and could watch me dispense with my remaining savings and then go into debt to cover the last two years of Miranda's college tuition. I had reduced, or, as I liked to think of it, *simplified* my lifestyle. But next had come the wedding, and anyone poking into my financial history would see it had all combined to flatten me. And my colleague at the managers' meeting who had joked that just about every penny the bank ever paid him, he had given right back? He'd been with the bank twenty years, and was talking about his purchase of a big new house. I'd been with the bank twenty-seven years, and what I had to show for it on the day of my daughter's wedding was no savings, a checking account I often checked the balance of before writing a check, the equity loan I was going to need to start paying on, and a mortgage on which I'd probably gone upside down. And now Catherine was saying I should go explain this to bank security—to total strangers who knew nothing about me at all, and cared even less.

"How many times are you going to make me angry today?" I asked her. "I thought you didn't like this feeling."

"I'm not the person you should be angry at," she said. "I'm just telling you I told them you'd be by soon."

"Then you'll be wrong about that. Because I have things I have to do, and if they're going to play detective by looking through my finances, then they can also play detective by tracking me down physically. Or you can just tell them where I am, if you want to."

"I feel like you're putting me in a weird position between you and the bank, as punishment for something I didn't even do. Can you at least call and tell them when you *will* stop by? I know it's awkward that I know about your finances, but I can't help that. Transactions show up on my reports. It's my job to look at them."

"I understand," I said. "That's fine. I'll call them. But not now." Seething, I started across the grass in the direction of my car. But something else occurred to me, and I had to turn and walk back. "Even if I find something out, how am I going to know if Miranda disappearing from the restaurant is the sign of a real problem, or if it's just jitters?" I said.

"You won't," Catherine said. "Because even when you *are* in over your head, you always think you can swim. I didn't know I was in trouble with the marriage I had until I was really in trouble. And I can't see how I would have known before."

"All right, then." I turned and headed across the grass again. And that time, I did not turn back.

THERE WAS NO BROKEN water, no alert in the night, and no panicked drive: Sandra and I simply awoke to the buzz of the alarm clock, ate our breakfast, and carried our bags to the car. There was nothing but wind that morning: trees bent and sprang and bent again, leaves tumbled by, and plastic garbage cans lay on their sides in the street. I drove a blue Ford station wagon purchased for the occasion and, unused to its length, pulled too far into a parking spot in the hospital's concrete parking structure—the car's front end hit the cement wall and we were jolted forward with a bang. Sandra shouted as if I had struck her personally. "Sorry," I said. "Here we are."

Obscure machines waited silently in the corners of the fourth-floor room we were shown to, where Sandra changed into a gown, climbed onto the mattress, and looked up at the wall-mounted television, whose dark screen reflected back a fish-eye image of the bed, herself, the chair, and me standing to the side, hands in pockets. The room's window offered a view of three buildings under construction across the street—their iron skeletons huddled beneath tarps that bulged and flapped in the wind, and some were already torn to tatters.

A nurse came in and, after some preparatory drama, inserted an IV into Sandra's arm, and pressed a button on a small black box attached to the IV stand. The box sighed, and its red light began to blink. It was dispensing the drug that would induce labor, the nurse said. After fitting an elastic strap around Sandra's belly, she flipped the switch of another machine, and the room filled with the sound of a galloping horse: it was the baby's pulse, rendered hooflike in the machine's cheap speakers. The nurse left, and afterward, whenever Sandra or the baby shifted, the pulse would distort into the sound of a grunting voice or the bellow of a frustrated beast, before shifting back again to galloping. Sandra expressed reservations about the name we had chosen, claiming I had chosen the name and then talked her into it. I calmly disagreed. She questioned the spelling of the name, and I reassured her the spelling was standard. Outside, the wind continued, buffeting a flock of a dozen small white birds as they flew past the buildings in unified darting swoops and vertiginous drops. Sandra wondered aloud how they managed to fly in the wind. When I told her I didn't know, that it seemed impossible, she bounced her leg and smiled. "I'm feeling something," she said.

The anesthesiologist—a grim, chubby man with pink cheeks—entered and launched into a businesslike preamble regarding what he would be doing, the technically possible but extremely unlikely risks, and so forth, and then rolled Sandra onto her side and inserted a huge needle into her back. I looked out the window, watching the tarps furl and snap, and when I looked back, the man was feeding a quivering filament through a tube that entered Sandra's back where the needle had been. The filament went in and in and in, the man taped everything down, rolled Sandra faceup, and gathered his tools and scrap lengths of filament into his bag, the same as any tradesman after a job. He told us it would take effect shortly, and walked out the door. When I looked back to Sandra, her expression had gone blank. She was submitting to forces larger than herself, it seemed. "Now," she said with a flat, strained little laugh, "I feel it again now." She bounced her leg on the mattress while beyond the window, we watched a windborne leaf levitate slowly upward and out of sight.

Sandra's obstetrician, a handsome young man who wore a white shirt and red paisley tie beneath his green scrubs, arrived and talked about how exciting it all was. He had Sandra raise her knees and, placing a sheet across them, bent to examine her beneath the little tent. They'd scheduled a tentative order to the day's births, he said—like airplanes lined up for takeoff. He remarked on my calmness, and instead of explaining that I was silent, not calm, I told him my demeanor was courtesy the fifth of vodka I'd had for breakfast. He laughed and left. The contractions began to arrive in earnest. Sandra said she felt pressure, but not pain. The creature galloped, then grunted and bellowed, and then galloped again, faster. A light rain began to fall, drops exploding in spidery bursts against the window as Sandra asked how long it had been since I'd gone down to the waiting room to give her parents an update. I wasn't sure, but when I asked if she meant I should go speak to them again, she said no, stay. The birds passed again, the whole flock darting and quivering and flitting as one, braving conditions. The wind pressed against the glass with a long sigh.

Then they all burst in together: the nurse, the doctor, a younger nurse, and a woman the doctor introduced as a resident who would assist. The nurse unfurled a machine printout as if it were a stock ticker and examined it, calling out numbers that seemed to please everyone. The doctor said he hoped to be holding the baby within an hour. "An hour?" Sandra said. The nurse pulled two levers beneath the bed and then struck the mattress with a balled fist, and the bottom half of the bed fell downward and away. Raising the back of the bed, she helped Sandra to sit up, legs dangling, as Sandra's entire body began to tremble uncontrollably. The younger nurse rolled a small table into the room, its surface lined with blankets and surrounded by short plastic walls, and the resident came in behind her pushing another table, but this one, holding a green plastic pan and a fantastic array of gleaming steel instruments, was rolled into the far corner, as if merely an idle threat. As Sandra gasped and wept, the doctor said to me, "Here, look." Just visible between Sandra's thighs was the crown, the slick dark hair covered in yellow mucus. The bones of the skull had collapsed to a dorsal ridge beneath the scalp, and I watched the ridge slip back within Sandra like a creature sinking beneath the surface of the sea. "I want the head this time," the doctor told Sandra. She tried to speak, but couldn't, and when I heard the doctor say, "Okay, let's turn her," I saw that there between his hands was the baby's head, the eyes shut tight and the silent mouth bent as if this creature, too, was in speechless agony. The child's shoulders were still pressed together and pinned within—it was a shock to realize that in the beginning, the frame is entirely collapsible. "Now!" the doctor shouted, and the child slipped free and fell wailing into his hands amid a rush of fluid. In one swift movement he wrapped the wailing baby in a blanket and placed her on Sandra's stomach, telling her she had done well. The nurses busied themselves with the cord while the doctor wiped the child's eyes and cleared her mouth.

"Do you see?" Sandra said to me, weeping. I nodded, unable to speak.

The doctor examined the baby's eyes and ears, ran his finger through her mouth, and took each of her limbs in his hand. He announced numbers that the nurse copied into a chart, and when he was satisfied, he stood back, smiled, and said, "This is all very good. But I'm afraid I don't know this young lady's name. Or have you decided yet?"

I looked at Sandra and she nodded, smiling, as she lowered her face to the child's and murmured in a tone I'd never heard from her before. Miranda's eyes remained tightly closed, as if she were concentrating intently upon that voice, in hopes of understanding it.

"We've known for a while," I said. "Her name is Miranda."

THE SYCORA PARK SUITES is a ten-story, atrium-style hotel located in the heart of Sycora Park, a vibrant neighborhood that features upscale shopping, many of the city's finest restaurants, and numerous popular coffeehouses and bars. Those, at least, were the claims made by the brochure Miranda had brought me eight months before the wedding, and which I had examined at my dining room table with the seriousness I bring to any business or legal document. I suppose I thought repeated examinations of the item might at some point reveal an inconsistency in its story, or uncover suppressed information: a broken vending machine beyond the cropped edge of the swimming pool photo, perhaps, or an overlooked sentence acknowledging that the fire alarm will go off inexplicably at three A.M., forcing disoriented guests into the parking lot in their pajamas. But there was nothing to find. And my review of the brochure was just a formality, really, because the decision had already been made: Miranda and Sandra had decided that the Sycora Park Suites would be the reception site, and I was to write my check, please. So I did.

When I entered the hotel on the day of the wedding, a black signboard on an easel announced in handwritten fluorescent script that one of the hotel's three ballrooms would host Miranda's reception, while the other two would be the site of a bar mitzvah and a thirtieth high school reunion, respectively. The news pleased me: I once attended a wedding reception in a hotel where those of us taking a break in the lobby late in the evening were treated to the sight of brides from adjacent receptions walking past each other on their way to and from the restroom. The sight had provoked a psychic shiver in me exactly like one I'd experienced upon seeing a publicity photo from a filmed version of the gospels, in which both the leading man and his stand-in were present and in full costume, attentively listening to their famous director. Two brides crossing paths in a Holiday Inn, two Jesuses taking orders from a man in blue jeans: images like these are best forgotten. The illusion of a wedding's uniqueness is probably as false as the illusion of a marriage's permanence, but still—one bride is enough.

The large oak door to our assigned ballroom stood wide open. I assumed that inside I would find a regiment of linen-covered tables standing in silent readiness, but instead I discovered not only that the room wasn't empty, but that one of those people was an altered version of my ex-wife. Sandra had hired a professional stylist—toiling away in a room somewhere among the dozen or so identical floors that rose overhead like stacked billiard racks—to charm the hair of each woman in the wedding party into exotic weaves and tangles, and Sandra's hair was now pulled up and held tightly against her head by what I could only assume was a hidden superstructure of clips or bands. A number of curls on top had been woven into a garland of tresses that seemed inspired by sylvan tales of giggling sprites or fairy princesses. The transformation, however, was not complete: beneath the imaginative fairy-tale locks, Sandra remained strictly middle-class in a white V-neck T-shirt, faded blue jeans, and sandals. She frowned at the other person present, a teenage boy pushing the heavy leaves of a fake-parquet dance floor into place at the front of the room. Sporting the khaki slacks and white dress shirt of someone trying to be promoted out of manual labor, the boy kicked at the edges of the floor as if they disgusted him, though I soon realized he was just tightening the gaps between the pieces. After a final, especially vicious kick, he raised his eyes, saw me standing in the doorway, and seemed about to address me—but Sandra beat him to it. "Do you think the ten-foot dance floor, or the fifteen?" she asked.

The boy returned to his task, grimacing as he pulled another slab of flooring from atop a stack balanced over a wheeled flatbed cart. The pieces were so long as to render the cart a mere fulcrum over which they bent, the ends touching the ground on either side like the drooping wings of an exhausted cartoon airplane. "If this doesn't look right, it's not too late to switch," he said, and then dropped, from waist-level, the next piece of flooring. It struck the carpet with a meaty thud, raising a faint plash of dust.

The Busby Berkeleyan imagination required to mentally transform the half-assembled dance floor into a fully realized and polished surface onto which I could project an estimated number of dancers was beyond my capacity. I had just left Catherine and the chairs behind at the Quad, and had no desire to enter a new story problem. Avoiding interminable indecision and speculation was one of the reasons I'd left the decisions to Miranda and Sandra in the first place, so all I said was "We're not big dancers."

"No, it's too small," Sandra said. "Let's go with the fifteen-foot."

The boy bent and began slowly to undo his work as the hotel's event coordinator walked briskly into the room. The sunny smile she wore to every interaction with us—along with her sober-colored pantsuits and designer glasses and immaculately painted red nails—decayed into a perplexed look as she noticed the boy engaged in a process the opposite of what she had expected. When she asked if everything was all right, though, and the boy told her Sandra wanted the fifteen-foot dance floor, she said, "Absolutely," and then moved swiftly into her intended business, a show-and-tell presentation meant to demonstrate how everything in the room was being set up in accord with the arrangements we had requested, and which were detailed in our contract. Her presentation was as polished as any that someone gives multiple times per week: the dais for members of the wedding party was a certain size and in a certain location; each of the guest tables featured an exact shade of off-white tablecloth, an exact number of place settings, an exact number of candles, and an exact arrangement of flowers; the deejay's area was clearly marked with yellow electrical tape, and the umbilicus of power-delivering cables that snaked from the wall to the taped area, she warned us, was "hot." In her business couture she looked thirty, but I assumed she was younger-playing-older, trying to do well. As she moved us through a door at the back of the room, I wondered if she might be younger, even, than Miranda. It was impossible to tell.

We entered the kitchen, a long galley of stainless steel counters and oversized ovens and industrial sinks and huge refrigerators and freezers that ran the full length of the three ballrooms. Somewhere from the far end of the room an unseen radio suffering incredibly fuzzed reception played a rap song whose melody had been lifted from another decade, though I couldn't immediately name the original. A handful of employees were present, unhurriedly chopping vegetables or pushing large rolling carts of covered trays or sorting dishes and silverware. Our coordinator, whom I felt confident was named Lisa, though it was also possible she was Laura, led us to a small counter where a number of already prepared dishes had been arranged. She picked up two of the plates and placed them in front of us: one featured a bloated piece of herbed chicken bounded by shiny slices of summer squash, and the other held a dry-looking piece of whitefish whose congealed cream sauce managed not to touch the glossy green beans and carrot slices to its side. Lisa explained that the two dishes represented the entrees we had chosen and which would be served to our guests. "And they'll look like this?" I asked, alarmed.

"Oh no," she said. "These aren't real, they're wax. They're just to show you how we're going to plate things."

Embarrassed by the stupidity of my question, I nodded with all the gravity I could muster, and when Lisa stepped away to ask someone about the location of the desserts, I reexamined the counterfeit food.

"I hope we're not signing off on a meal that's not going to be served," Sandra said as she looked down on the wax food with disdain. "Or even if Miranda doesn't show up, maybe we should invite everyone to come over here and sit down for a wax dinner. After dinner we can play music but not allow dancing. It will be a theme."

"It's probably too late to get a hundred and fifty wax chickens," I said. I considered not telling Sandra I'd spoken to Miranda, but it felt like a concealment that would take more energy to pull off than it was worth. So I said, "Besides, I talked to her. She said she'll be here soon."

"You spoke to her?"

"On the phone." There. That was the lie that felt right.

Sandra seemed stunned by this. So much so, in fact, that I'll admit it hurt my pride that she found it so unlikely my daughter would speak to me. "What did she tell you?" she asked.

"She's just taking some time to herself, and she'll be around soon," I said.

"So why doesn't she answer the phone when *I* call her?"

"Because she knows it's you. I called her with Catherine's phone, and she only answered because she thought it was Catherine."

"There is something wrong. She's completely out of touch on her wedding day."

"She's not completely out of touch," I said. "She said not to worry, she'll turn up. You should just go up to your room and have a glass of wine. Let the stylist finish your hair or do your nails."

She mimed surprise. "I should get tipsy and paint my nails? How chivalrous of you."

"If your plan is to wait here in the hotel and worry, then yes, I'm suggesting you get tipsy and paint your nails. Unless you know something I don't know."

"What do you mean?"

"She told me she's taking some time to herself, but she'll be here. Maybe you know something more about why she's taking this time to herself than I do, but I assume that means she'll be here."

"You're the one who's talked to her today, Paul," she said. "Not me."

Lisa returned then, telling us that though the wax desserts had been misplaced, their disappearance would in no way compromise the kitchen's ability to confect the actual items, and she was entirely confident that the staff understood the menu and our wishes, and that everything was in hand.

"I think Sandra and Miranda tried all of these things a few months ago," I said. "They drank the wine and ate the entrees and desserts and said it was all fine, right?"

"We did," Sandra said. "I'm sure everything is fine."

"So I doubt we need to worry about any of this," I said. "I, at least, am not worried."

Lisa smiled. "Some people just like to triple-check things," she said. "Overpreparation makes them feel secure. But as you can see, everything is swinging into motion here."

When we stepped from the kitchen and passed back through the ballroom, it was empty. It seemed like we had only been gone for a minute, but in that brief interval, the dance floor, and the boy who had been working on it, had somehow ceased to exist.

After Lisa wished us a wonderful ceremony and headed down an unmarked hallway to what I assumed was the safety of a hidden office, Sandra continued across the lobby, straight past the fountain, and toward the main doors. "I'm going out for some fresh air," she said. "Come with me."

When we moved through the doors and stepped outside, though, it began to rain. Clouds did not build or gather, thunder did not rumble, and no scalpels of lightning sliced the horizon. The sky appeared simply to have crumpled, wearily. A mist floated in under the concrete apron covering the drive outside the lobby entrance, and I watched it roll forward to where we stood. Brief showers visited regularly on summer afternoons—warm air moving eastward shed its moisture as it rose to cross the hills to the west of town, and that moisture would become a phalanx of impressively dark storm clouds. At some point on most summer afternoons, the clouds would break free of the hills and descend on the city to deliver what often appeared, from the dark wall of water overhead, to be a storm of serious consequences. The shower usually lasted no more than twenty minutes, though, before the clouds dissolved or moved on, and this pattern was precisely the reason Miranda had scheduled her ceremony for six o'clock. So the pinpricks of mist against my face, the scent of camphor and ozone in the air: a case could have been made that things were proceeding exactly according to plan.

"And now it's going to rain," Sandra said. "This wedding is going to kill me." She had told me she wanted some fresh air, but her true motivation became clear as soon as we exited the lobby: a portly, sunburned gentleman in khaki shorts and a wrinkled oxford was stepping from a white airport van, and Sandra, without the slightest bit of hesitation, asked him for a cigarette. He fumblingly responded in the manner of someone authentically stunned, working to extract a pack from his chest pocket. Having scored her cigarette and then a light from the man, she and I moved down the sidewalk and away from the valets and bellboys. She hugged herself with one arm while the other remained upright, the cigarette poised before her lips. The practiced manner with which she was holding her cigarette implied it wasn't the first she'd enjoyed recently.

"When did you start smoking again?" I asked.

"Five minutes ago," she said. "And I'm quitting again five minutes from now. Did you want one? I can ask the guy for another."

"That's all right. I've quit, too."

"You never started." She studied the rows of cars parked in the lot before us. Beads of mist were collecting on the windshields, but the scuffed and dusty bumpers were still dry. "So when you talked to Miranda, did she tell you where she was?"

"No. But I didn't just talk to her on the phone. I met her for lunch, too."

"What?" she said. "Why didn't you say that before?"

"Because she sat down at the restaurant for a few minutes, asked a few questions about our marriage, said she was going to the bathroom, and then snuck out the back door of the restaurant. She sent me a text message." I opened my phone, found the message, and showed it to Sandra. "What do you think that means? It doesn't sound good to me."

"I don't know," she said. "All text messages sound like that. What did she want to know about our marriage?"

"That wasn't clear," I said. "But look, this morning you said Miranda didn't come home last night, and you acted like it was something I should be taking care of. So I found her. But I still don't know what's going on."

At first Sandra looked at me without any expression at all, but then she shrugged. "You're right," she said, as if I'd made a point of such commonsensical persuasiveness that it had returned her to her senses. "It wasn't fair of me to ask you to spend your day tracking her down. Did you even get to eat lunch? The little bar at the back of the lobby has sandwiches and things. I'll talk to Miranda when she gets here. There's no need for you to worry about it anymore."

She was managing me. I thought I was managing her, and she thought she was managing me. And when Miranda had asked about control issues between married couples earlier in the day, I had responded using the past tense. "I might get lunch," I said. "But I don't think I'm going to stop worrying about Miranda. I'm having to call her with other people's phones, and she's disappearing out back doors. I'm not a stranger or some visiting cousin. I'm her father, and I'd like to know why she's so upset. I'm going to track Grant down so I can ask him what's going on, but if you can save me time by telling me what you know, that would be helpful."

"I'm the one who suggested you talk to Grant in the first place," she said. "This morning, on the phone. I've told you I don't know anything more than you do."

"At the restaurant, before she left, Miranda said she had talked to you about 'it.' She didn't say what 'it' was, but it seemed like it was something specific."

"I'm sure it was," she said angrily. "But I talk to Miranda every day, about all sorts of things. I'm sorry I don't know what she was thinking about when you saw her at lunch, but I wasn't in her mind then."

"I'm not accusing you of anything."

"Then why are you interrogating me? You're acting like I know what's bothering her, even though you're the one who has seen her, not me. I can't tell if you're acting this way because you're trying to help our daughter, or if you're just creating some kind of drama so that you can be the good guy in it."

"Miranda isn't worried about her relationship with us, Sandra. She's worried about Grant. And if we knew what was going on, we could help her, or at least know whether she needs us or not. I feel like there's a piece missing somewhere. And I don't like this feeling."

"I'm sorry you feel that way," she said. "But I don't think you have to investigate all of these things today, Paul. We're not prosecuting a case here. We're just trying to make sure she's okay. Have you talked to Grant?"

"No. He's been busy with his friends from out of town. They're guys he knows professionally, I think—people he's made money with."

"So if they're business types, try the country club. Or go by his condo. That's where he entertains, isn't it?" She tossed her cigarette to the sidewalk, and it rolled over the curb and into the gutter, from where it sent up a last, sad curl of smoke. "This is your friend, not mine."

I didn't know how to respond to that—there was more than one element in the statement that I felt like disputing. So I said nothing, while Sandra looked again at the sky, standing there alone in her jeans and T-shirt by the sliding glass entrance doors, her hair done and her face set. The breeze picked up, and it began to rain harder. I was close enough to the edge of the overhead roof that I felt some chilled drops hit my arms and neck.

"Call me if you find out anything," Sandra said. The lobby doors slid open as she walked toward and then through them. When they closed, she disappeared behind the wobbling, canted reflections in their glass: the cars in the lot, the trees swaying in the breeze, and behind and above them all, the sky gone gray and cold.

II

As the elevator in Grant's building carried me upward with a whir of motors and mechanics, I wondered if I was making a mistake. I had called him on my way over, at least, and had asked if he was at home, and whether I could stop by for a few minutes. "Of course," he had said. "Should I fix you a drink?"

"Just a beer would be fine," I told him.

"I'll leave the door open."

He lived in a tenth-floor condo in a neighborhood just north of downtown, which only a handful of years before had been blocks of run-down and forgotten five- and six-story warehouses. Developers had gotten hold of the warehouses, though, and remodeled them into expensive lofts with polished concrete floors, track lighting, marble countertops, and stainless steel appliances, and when they had run out of authentic warehouses, they bought up the adjacent square miles of abandoned rail yards and open land that stretched down to the river. Eighty years earlier, stables had housed hundreds of draft horses on the land, but now the developers had put in new buildings designed to look as if they, too, were rehabbed warehouses, and in the space of a few short years had created a whole new section of city from almost nothing, complete with parks and fountains, restaurants, banks, upscale clothing and gardening stores, designer eyeglass shops, and at least one business that provided nothing but specially designed stalls in which residents washed and dried and kissed their dogs.

But it had been on an evening almost two years earlier—I had been happily anticipating the arrival of a vodka tonic I had ordered at Prosperity, a new restaurant in Grant's neighborhood that featured a lone orchid in a white bud vase at the center of each linen-covered table, and a wine list that ran to fifteen pages—when I felt a pair of hands settle on my shoulders. Sandra has a weary tight-lipped smile she gives to only one person and when I saw that look on her face, I knew who the hands belonged to even before I turned to look up.

"Always a pleasure to run into old friends," Grant said. His khaki pants and knit polo shirt suggested a just-completed round of golf, and although Labor Day was a fading memory—through the restaurant's tall windows, I saw an occasional yellow-orange leaf flutter to the ground from the maples along the street—Grant was as tan as if it were midsummer. I asked if he'd been traveling, and he admitted he'd just spent four days alone on a beach on Maui. It was a reward he'd given himself for finishing a big project, he said.

"Alone on Maui?" Sandra said. "Have you run out of places to chase women in our own state?"

Grant's smile didn't falter, but neither did he manage to respond before Sandra, who seemed as surprised by the comment as any of us, said: "That didn't come out the way I meant it."

"Is there an event of some sort this evening?" Grant asked. I'm sure he was wondering why he should encounter Sandra and me sitting together in a restaurant. When I told him it was Miranda's twenty-third birthday, and that she was supposed to arrive any minute, he seemed stunned. "She's twenty-three? Are you sure?"

"Fairly sure," Sandra said.

"This is a family occasion, then."

"But you qualify," I said. "Sit down with us."

"No, no," he said, "but wish her a happy birthday. I'll catch up with you another time." And still smiling, he wished us a good evening and headed back across the room and behind the wall that divided the dining room from the bar.

"I didn't think what I said was *that* bad," Sandra said.

"I don't think he cared," I said.

"Then why didn't he sit down?"

"He probably thought we were just being courteous."

Sandra raised her eyebrows. "Finicky, finicky," she said.

Miranda arrived a few minutes later. I was facing the entrance when she did, and watched her step through the front door and peer into the room with an expression of bemusement, as if playing a game of hide-and-seek. When she caught sight of my raised hand, she smiled, as if pleased that she had won the game. As she crossed the room at a brisk pace, I noticed a number of people—men and women alike—look up at this young woman in loose black slacks and a red silk Chinese blouse. Her cheeks were flushed nearly as crimson as her blouse, and she sighed dramatically as she leaned down to hug her mother and kiss me on the cheek. "I'm sorry I'm late," she said, shaking her head as if dazed. "It's been a weird day. I just got a new job."

Only a year removed from finishing her undergraduate

degree in liberal studies, she had spent the previous six months as a filing clerk at a law firm whose senior partner, Eli Bernhardt, was an account holder at my branch. When I told him my daughter was out of college and looking for a job, he had offered to take her on without so much as an interview, but Miranda had quickly assured me the work was dull—"soul-sucking," she called it. So there in the restaurant, while carefully adjusting the two black enamel sticks she was using to keep her hair up, she told us how a woman had come into the firm that morning, and that unlike most clients, who were fidgety and anxious while waiting, this woman had been well dressed, relaxed, and composed, and had actually had a conversation with Miranda instead of just chatting in her direction. It turned out the woman owned an art gallery, and used the law firm to help her write contracts with artists and collectors. While she spent a few minutes in the reception area waiting for her lawyer, she told Miranda she was looking for a "gallerina" for her gallery—a hostess who would welcome people when they came in the door, answer their questions, handle the telephone, and do some general office work. "I thought about it for a couple hours, and it sounded a lot more fun than working at the law firm," Miranda said, "so I called her this afternoon and asked if I could interview, and she said I should stop by after work. And then she offered me the job as soon as we finished the interview."

"But do you even know anything about art?" Sandra said.

"She said I would pick everything up soon enough. And now, here I am."

Sandra looked at me as if it were my turn to say something. "I assume you've given Mr. Bernhardt two weeks' notice," I said.

"I've never seen Mr. Bernhardt in the office, Dad. I asked my actual supervisor if he wanted two weeks, but he said Gina had already talked to him about it on the phone, and they have temps and assistants who can cover. So I start tomorrow."

"What's the name of the gallery?" Sandra said.

"That's the other thing. As soon as she saw my full name on my résumé, she asked if you were my parents, and when I said yes, she said she knew you. Her name is Gina Crivelli."

I tried to recall any occasion during the years I had known her on which Gina had expressed an interest in art or owning a gallery, but I came up with nothing. Sandra laughed with what sounded, to my surprise, like genuine pleasure.

"Why are you laughing?" Miranda said.

"I'm just surprised," Sandra said. "Gina is an old girlfriend of your father's. And of Grant's, too."

"She was a girlfriend of yours *and* of Grant's?"

"You should see if she's still single," Sandra said to me. She had taken to making occasional comments like that over the years, as if we were buddies. I could never tell if her tone signaled earnest encouragement, though, or if it was closer to the tone police use when making jokes over a homicide.

"He's here tonight, too," I said.

"Who?" Miranda said. "Grant? For my birthday?"

"It's a coincidence," I said. "He's in the bar."

No sooner had I completed the statement than Miranda stood and headed in that direction. And a minute later, she emerged from the bar leading Grant by the elbow through the maze of tables, while he did his best not to spill his drink. "He tried to resist, but I wouldn't let him," she said as she pulled out the fourth chair at our table and pushed Grant into it. I saw Grant no more than once every five or six months in those years—at the occasional birthday gathering, holiday party, or similar social event—and I had never once seen Miranda handle him that way. "If the birthday girl gives the command, I guess you have to follow it," he said.

"I just got some gossip on you and Dad," Miranda said. "And I want to grill you about it. Do you remember Gina Crivelli?"

The same puzzled look passed over Grant's face that had appeared when he heard about Miranda's birthday. "This city gets smaller every year," he said.

"She hired me to work at her gallery. And Mom says Gina went out with each of you at some point."

"That was a long time ago," Grant said.

"Did she break up with one of you to go out with the other?" Miranda said, pressing her palm to her cheek in an expression of mock horror. She may have felt she was allowed more leeway on her birthday than usual, or maybe she was still energized from getting a new job in just one day, but either way, she seemed perfectly comfortable and greatly entertained by her aggressive questioning. When I assured her that I dated Gina in college and Grant dated her a couple years later, and that regardless, these things had happened almost a quarter century ago, in a past so distant as to be almost prehistory, she laughed. "Oh, Dad," she said. "She broke up with you, didn't she?"

"Why do you say that?"

"I can tell from your explanation. And what about you?" she asked Grant. "Who broke up with whom?"

His expression went blank. "I'm sure I don't remember."

She studied him. "You broke up with her."

"You don't know that," he said.

"You guys give yourselves away," she said.

"Miranda, this is not particularly elegant," Sandra said.

"Should we ask about *your* personal life? Are you seeing anyone lately? Any interesting dates?"

Whether Sandra was stopping Miranda out of dinner-conversation politeness or due to some other motivation was unclear, but the question was effective: Miranda's face clouded, and her shoulders dropped in annoyance. "Not really, Mother, no."

"No dates at all? No one we should know about?"

"No. No one you should know about. And I get it. You can stop any time."

"Then I'm done, darling." Sandra refilled Miranda's wineglass, and as often happens when I watch them speak to each other, I sensed that they were communicating through a series of tones and gestures too subtle for me to fully understand. I also knew that if I were to ask either of them about it later, they would profess to have no idea what I was talking about.

"And what has our old girlfriend hired you to do?" Grant asked.

"I'm a host. I say hello when you walk in the door, and I ask if you have questions, and I answer the phone when it rings."

"But will you still be able to read novels on the clock, like you do at the law firm?" he said. He suggested she was underestimating the importance of that perk, and as we were served our appetizers and the meal proceeded, he continued controlling the conversation until he had guided it into breezier territory. The warm, day's-end light that had suffused the room at the beginning of the meal slowly dimmed, and we found ourselves a little party of four at a candlelit table. We had a bottle of wine, and then another, and then ordered a third as Sandra complained about eccentric clients at the interior design firm she worked at, and Miranda pretended to help by suggesting ridiculous room themes: she described a bedroom of nothing but leopard prints, a dusty reading room presided over by a mannequin dressed as a spinster librarian, a kitchen with a variety of microwaves but no oven, and a handful of other fantasy propositions. I expected Grant to play along, but he seemed content to do little more than smile and listen until dinner was finished, at which time he placed his napkin on the table, thanked us for inviting him, and wished Miranda a happy birthday. When I told him we were planning on dessert, too, and he should stay, he shook his head. "I've enjoyed this, but I should go," he said. He shook my hand, patted Miranda and Sandra on the shoulder, and then returned to the bar. It was only a few minutes later that we saw him through the restaurant's windows as he moved down the sidewalk and then passed out of view. It wasn't until after dessert, when I asked for the check, that the waiter informed me the bill had been taken care of.

Sandra shook her head angrily. "He shouldn't have done that."

"He was being nice," Miranda said. "For my birthday."

"I know," Sandra said. "But he shouldn't have done that."

And now, less than two years later, I had driven through that same neighborhood—and right past that very restaurant—on my way to Grant's building. I had expected the streets to be lively, but the lingering storm clouds and the overriding sense of clean and seamless functionality in the neighborhood had combined to produce a surprising degree of order and quiet. Grant hadn't asked why I was stopping by, or what I needed, or how long I would be there, but that didn't surprise me—he wasn't inquisitive in that way, and especially not on the phone. He was used to people—employees and clients especially, but probably just about anyone who knew him—coming to him with problems. The exquisite courtesy he had developed over the years, in fact, was probably not only a way of being respectful toward people, but also a defense against them. Grant certainly believed that it was more productive to speak about a problem face-to-face—he had said that to me more than once over the years—but he also seemed the type who not only hates emotional phone conversations, but dislikes the phone in general. And here I was, on the day of his wedding, calling him on the phone with a problem. Did he have a tight schedule that I was intruding on? I had no idea. And I also knew that even if the answer to that question was yes, he would tell me it was no.

A part of me wondered if it was a mistake to even involve him at all.

My telephone rang. The elevator doors had opened onto the tenth floor by then, and I could see Grant's door open at the end of the hall. The phone's screen showed the call was coming from Catherine's extension at the bank, which meant it was either Catherine herself, or the bank security people. I closed the phone without answering, though, and stepped through the open door to find Grant standing in front of the floor-to-ceiling windows across the room, holding a glass of ice water while he gazed down at the streets below. In a gray T-shirt, worn jeans, and barefoot, he seemed entirely at ease.

"You probably just watched me park and walk up here," I said.

"I didn't notice," he said.

"I hope I'm not screwing up your schedule."

"Not at all. I just got back from letting Alex Massoud beat me at golf, but he still hasn't agreed to extend our contract with him. So now I'm wondering if things would have gone better if I'd just gone ahead and beaten him. But I'm glad to get away from them for a while." He retrieved a beer from the large refrigerator that dominated his otherwise compact, gleaming kitchen.

Dark clouds still blanketed the city, and everything in Grant's kitchen—the marble countertops, chrome faucet, and stainless steel refrigerator and dishwasher; the bright yellow label on the beer he was opening; the earth-colored liquid that swirled inside the bottle—glowed as if lit from within. A glance overhead revealed the actual source of illumination: bulbs within the concrete ceiling created the pools of light that Grant moved through as he handed me my beer. If there had been a third person in the room with us, watching Grant stand by the counter in his jeans and T-shirt, the person would certainly have guessed him to be a full decade younger than he was. I knew he spent an hour in a health club most weekdays, which made it possible for him to keep fitting into his slim T-shirts and jeans, and to shop on the men's side of the same fashionable clothing stores where Miranda bought her own clothes. His tan was even, his close-cropped hair as dark as it had ever been. Had Grant been dying his hair, lying in the sun, performing exotic variations of sit-ups, keeping his nails carefully manicured and his hands moisturized, and observing any number of other personal-care details not only out of standard vanity, but also out of a desire to minimize the visual dissonance of what people tended to refer to—when in my presence, at least—as an "interesting" age difference between him and Miranda? I was a bit soft in the middle, as is every middle-aged man's right, and my thinning hair contained a liberal mix of gray. I bought my clothing from department stores, in the usual sections for men our age—or the sections for men our age who didn't make time for the gym.

I picked up my beer and asked if he would be joining me, but he shook his head. "I already had a couple on the course. Good speech at dinner last night, by the way."

"Passable."

"More than passable. It was honest. And heartfelt. You did a good job."

I shrugged. The beer tasted shockingly good. I wondered if it was due to the fact that I hadn't had anything to eat since breakfast.

"Sandra called me this morning," Grant said. "Asking if I knew where Miranda was. Is that why you stopped by?"

"I managed to track her down," I said. "I sat with her for a few minutes at lunch. But then she left again."

"What do you mean?"

I summarized the lunch I'd had with Miranda the same way I'd summarized it for Sandra, and finished by saying, "And I guess I assume she'll show up at the hotel sometime soon. Though it's still true that I don't know exactly where she is or what's going on."

He nodded. "But you think something *is* going on."

"Yes. Nothing happened between the two of you, did it?"

"No. But have you talked to Sandra?"

"She doesn't know where Miranda is, either. But if she's feeling nervous or anxious, I guess I assumed it might have something to do with you. You *are* the one she's marrying today."

"Maybe." He seemed to turn something over in his mind before he added, "It's a big thing, what she's signing on to."

"But she hasn't said anything to you, has she?"

"No. But she's had boyfriends in the past, and I assume she knows she could have boyfriends in the future. There's a whole alternate future still available to her, but all of those options are about to close down."

"The two of you will be opening up a lot of new options together, though."

He smiled, but seemed tired. "Probably not as many as it seems. Not to her."

Was I overestimating Grant's career success? His wealth? I didn't think so. "At dinner last night she said she adored you," I said. "She seemed perfectly confident and happy."

"You mean her speech? That was something she said in front of a group of people. I don't think she actually adores me in the true sense of that word, or I hope she doesn't, since that seems dangerous. She and I have talked about these things over the last couple years, and I think we understand each other. Nothing I said or did last night would suddenly have upset her. I know she's your daughter and you'll always think of her as a girl, but she has a pretty solid sense of herself as an adult."

"I still think she's upset about something. I trust my sense of that."

"I just think you're overestimating my role. If Miranda wanted out of what she's in, she could still get out of it and be fine. What she's signing on to now is big. It seems perfectly understandable to me that she would think about escaping it."

"But for what?"

"For freedom," he said, as if it were obvious. "The guys I was playing golf with this morning are friends, but they're friends I've made through the course of business, and other than you, those are pretty much the only kind of friends I have. My life these days is about running the firm. I don't draw product designs anymore—I look at other people's designs and say how they should be modified. I live what is probably a vaguely *corporate* existence, if I correctly understand what people mean when they say that word with a sneer. Miranda knows this. And she knows it's not how the painters who show in the gallery live their lives, and it's not how her musician friends live, and it's not how she has thought about her own life. But the direction she's headed in with me is away from those freedoms. Why wouldn't she second-guess that?"

He had said he felt I was overestimating his role, and then described a scenario in which Miranda's disquiet was probably the result of his role. So what was behind the contradiction? It seemed he was saying it was his *existence* that was the problem—not anything he'd actually said or done. And was he mentioning painters and musicians because there actually was some painter or musician who was a rival for Miranda's affections? The idea that there was a third person involved seemed impossible. Miranda had never, at any time, mentioned another man. "When did you see her last?" I asked.

"Last night, toward midnight. At Jo's."

"Who is Jo?"

"It's a cocktail bar downtown. You've been there."

He said this as if it somehow resolved the situation—or as if there *were* no situation, other than my inability to immediately place the name of this particular bar. "I'm sorry," I said. "I don't remember the name of every place I've ever been."

"I'm not—"

"There are days that I feel like every person I know is talking down to me," I said. "And maybe you're not. Maybe it's in my head. I don't care. I'm not asking to take a quiz on bar names. I'm asking you what happened when you saw her last."

"I'm not talking down to you."

"I don't care. It doesn't matter. What happened?"

I had never been that aggressive with Grant, but he seemed to accept it. Or his response, at least, was to accede to my questioning with nothing more than a slight shrug. "We only ended up there by coincidence," he said. "Or not a coincidence, really, since we've been there a number of times together—but we picked the same place. She was with her bridesmaids and some other friends, and I was having a drink with some people I know who didn't make the invite list."

If it had been anyone else, I would have found it odd to spend the evening before your wedding with people who weren't invited. But Grant's parents were both dead, and I knew his only sibling, a half sister, had manufactured a vague story about pressing business that would prevent her from leaving her home in Minneapolis to attend the wedding. So Grant was friendly, and well-off, and unencumbered by family. And if people, for whatever reason, like to collect things, then it was probably true that what Grant liked to collect was people. Even if he claimed the only friendships he had were business-related, that was still twenty-five years of friendships. It was a rare occasion that I walked into a restaurant or bar with Grant and one or two people didn't immediately wave, or call his name, or walk up to him. And though many of these friends were people currently involved in his professional life, I'd had a sense on more than one occasion that Grant also kept in touch with people who were no longer active in his professional sphere, and that he maintained those friendships not because it was professionally useful, but because he actually did like people. Between all these professional and semiprofessional relationships, Grant could have easily filled three hundred chairs on his side of the ceremony alone, so it didn't necessarily surprise me that he wanted to do something for the people he couldn't invite. And I was probably a little embarrassed about it, too, since I'd been insistent on paying for the wedding myself—an insistence that had necessitated a budget, and a budget that had included a guest limit. And Grant had never once complained about this. He had acceded to my budgetary limits in every detail.

"Did you notice anything unusual?" I asked. "Was she upset?"

"Not that I know of," he said. "She didn't stay very long, because she said she didn't want me to see her on the day of the wedding. She left just before midnight."

"And you haven't talked to her since then."

"No," he said, frowning. "But you have. What did she say that has you so rattled?"

"She was asking about control. About Sandra and me, and our marriage. It seemed like she was worried she's going to lose some kind of control. Like she's going to drown."

"Drown how?"

"She didn't say drown—that's just the word I'm using. There was something about marriage that had her worried she was going to lose herself."

His face tightened, almost as if he were in pain, but I couldn't figure out what I had said that had caused the reaction. "I don't think you should be telling me this," he said.

"Why?"

"Because she was sharing that with *you*. Not with me."

"She hasn't spoken that way to you?"

"No." He shook his head slightly, as if confused. "She could be at the hotel right now, getting ready and feeling fine. This could all be idle speculation."

"Maybe. I don't know what's speculation and what's not."

"Look," he said, "you don't need to be subtle with me. I know what people think about me. And maybe you think it, too. I haven't been married before. I've traveled a lot, and I've had my share of girlfriends, but I don't have some super-complicated life or dangerous power. I feel like there's a perception out there that I'm some kind of playboy who's been jet-setting around the world at my leisure. But I actually find life as difficult as anyone does. I've succeeded at what I do, and I have the money I have, because I worked harder than anyone else I know. I took risks and worked to succeed. And then when I hit my forties, I realized there were other things I wanted, and I realized I was lucky—damn lucky—that I hadn't been married before. Because I meet guys all the time who have just plowed through marriage after marriage, creating all of this carnage behind them that they joke about. And they baffle me. I don't understand them. And I avoided it until in my forties I thought, Here I am, I'm lucky to have what I have, but I'm ready to try and get to know another person, and to learn to share myself. And now that turns out to be the hardest thing I've ever tried to do. And if Miranda is having doubts, they don't have to do with something that happened between the two of us last night. If she's worried about something, it's just whether she wants to do all of this. Because she can still get out. And maybe she wants to. And maybe I wouldn't blame her." He looked silently down into his glass of water, which was empty. I realized then that my beer was gone, too, though I couldn't remember drinking it. "Did you want another?" he asked.

"No," I said. "I should go. I have things I'm supposed to do. And I'm sorry. Maybe I'm worrying you about nothing."

He gave me an earnest look, as if desperate to have me understand something. "I don't want Miranda to drown," he said. "I never wanted that. But I'm not going to bother her today. She said she didn't want us to see or talk to each other today. If she wanted to talk, she would have called me." And then he smiled, as if we had just launched a little conspiracy. "So if there's something wrong, it's in your hands."

"I'll do my best," I said.

He nodded. "I know you will," he said.

By the time I made my way back down to the street, the rain was falling harder, soaking the now-empty streets. To the west, though, I could see the dark back edge of the storm coming over the hills like the edge of a curtain being drawn slowly back. The storm would make its way out over the plains to the east next, where it would give the farmers some rain, and then probably break up and evaporate. Once or twice each summer, though, these seemingly innocuous clouds turned black and, with little or no warning, hammered the earth with a maelstrom of hail. A storm like that could break windows, total cars, and destroy an entire summer's crop in the space of ten pounding minutes.

That day's storm didn't look unusual. But it's also true that one never knows.

AFTER MOONCALF, I was robbed only once more. It happened the summer before Miranda turned sixteen, which was also the summer during which I was forced to remove a boyfriend of hers. She hurt herself, and I removed him. And I would do it again.

The trouble started when I sat on the lowest bench of a set of aluminum bleachers next to a solitary tennis court in one of the city's quieter parks. The day's heat had decayed into a lazy warmth that hung heavy and still as I loosened my tie, waiting for Miranda, a member of a junior tennis team that summer, to face a counterpart from a suburban team. A cheerful man and woman were seated above me on the bleachers, and I assumed they belonged to the gangly teen standing on the court, a girl who flashed them nervous, braces-filled smiles as she gathered her red hair into a ponytail and twirled her racket. I anticipated watching Miranda and her opponent bounce the ball and play their points, adjust their ponytails and call the score, shriek in frustration or satisfaction, win or lose a set, lose or win another, and at some point leave the court wearing similarly weak smiles. When I asked the girl on the court if she knew where her opponent was through, she said, "Nope. I haven't seen anyone." After a few more minutes passed without any sign of Miranda, the girl's father rolled up the sleeves of his powder blue dress shirt, climbed down from the bleachers, and shuffled around the court in his penny loafers, hitting ground strokes to his daughter and gamely chasing her errant replies, the soles of his shoes scuffing chalky half-moons onto the court's surface.

"Creepy-crawly on your shoulder," the woman on the bleachers said. I looked over in time to watch a tiny, dust-colored creature scuttle along my collarbone. The local news had done its best to frighten everyone with multiple stories covering the plaguelike number of spiders that had appeared that summer, but a mere flick of my finger sent this one spinning into oblivion. "Is the girl we're waiting for your daughter?" the woman asked.

"Yes," I said, looking up to where she sat four rows above me. She was petite, blond, middle-aged, and beaming down at me from an angle that made it difficult not to examine the place where her pale white thigh flattened against the bleachers.

"These teenagers and their sense of time," she said. "Cassie spent half an hour trying to choose a skirt."

Children screeched happily from a nearby playground. A brown station wagon purred along the narrow park road. "That's the way, really hit it!" the father called to his daughter as her forehand sailed out of bounds.

"Do you play?" the woman asked.

It wasn't merely that her thigh was pale, but that the surface of the aluminum bleachers had pressed an exotic pattern of lines into the surface of her skin. The terrain seemed a provocation. "I used to," I said. "But I've left it to my wife now."

"Is she on a team, too?"

Sandra was not only on a team, but was playing a match of her own at one of the main complexes in town that evening, a fact that, as soon as I related it, set in motion a chain of narrowing questions which revealed not only that this arachnid-spotting woman was herself a member of a team, but that she played in the same league as Sandra. It wasn't a surprising coincidence, considering our setting, but it nevertheless filled the woman with a delight that only increased when I described some of the members of Sandra's team. "I think I know exactly who your wife is!" she said excitedly. "She played mixed doubles against me just two weeks ago. Her partner was a man named Grant."

"Yes. He's a friend of ours."

"This is just so funny," the woman said, "because my girlfriends and I had an argument later about whether or not they were together. Nothing unusual happened, mind you, it was just that they seemed to have so much fun playing together, and neither of them was wearing a ring."

"My wife says the ring gives her blisters."

"Wonderful! I told my friends those two were having too much fun to be married. So I win the bet."

"I'm sorry my daughter isn't here," I said. "I don't know where she could be. I suppose I should forfeit in her name."

The woman gasped as if I had sadly unsheathed a razor-sharp sword while suggesting a ritual suicide could restore my family's honor. “I’m sure it’s just a misunderstanding,” she said. “And it’s such a gorgeous evening anyway. I just hope she’s all right.”

I did, too, but by the time I gave up waiting and headed back to my car, the sky was shifting into dusk. As I drove home, warm evening air rushed past the open sunroof, and trees along the streets pressed their silhouettes against the plum-colored sky. Stopped at a light, I watched people wander into a retro ice cream parlor playing hits of the fifties, file into a fast-food place that reeked of fried hamburgers and potatoes, stand in line outside the air-conditioned movie theater, or wander with no destination in mind at all, on the street simply to be on the street, amid the pulsing and twisting chaos of shorts and T-shirts and sandals, of ragged hats and churning limbs and flapping mouths. Groups in conversation spilled past the edge of the sidewalk and stood laughing and chatting along the margin of the street, while an army of people passed in the crosswalk before me, talking and laughing only a few feet from where I sat behind the wheel. Not a person acknowledged my presence, of course, until two groups traveling in opposite directions failed to successfully negotiate each other, sending a young woman in a magenta halter top off balance. She pressed her palm to the hood of my car to steady herself and she met my eyes through the windshield just as her top slipped down enough to reveal the healthy brown nipple of her left breast. I offered her a weak smile. She laughed, righted herself, corrected her top, and moved on.

By the time I drifted the car to a space in front of my home, the evening’s first stars shone clearly in the sky. Our Japanese maple lowered its head in a shadowy corner of the yard, the cherry tree at the side of the house rose in a column of darkness, and light from the living room window revealed a robust constellation of spider silk entwined within the tangled rhododendrons beneath the front window. Climbing the creaking stairs to the porch, I spotted in the branches of the nearest bush one of the web's dark architects—he scrambled away from me, silver filaments swaying beneath his fluid weight.

At my first touch, the front door swung inward. It had been left slightly open, I realized as I stepped into the entryway and found three pairs of shoes in a line against the side of the staircase: the tongues of my grass-stained yard shoes yawned boredly, the waxy soles of Miranda's tennis shoes shone in the bright entryway light, and the frayed Velcro straps of a pair of large black sandals that I had never seen before rose stiffly skyward like something vegetal. I heard a faint cry from the back of the house then—a strained, vaguely animal bleat that stopped almost as soon as it began. As I moved down the hall and through the kitchen, I heard the cry again and knew, though it wasn't a sound I'd heard from her before, that it was Miranda. I opened the back door and stepped into the glaring incandescence of the porch light, where I found her standing there in the white skirt and T-shirt of her tennis uniform, her hair pulled into the ponytail she wore when playing. The bleat, apparently, had been an odd new laugh she had offered to a shirtless young man who reclined on a deck chair nearby, casually grinding a cigarette into an empty plastic planter tray as if he'd been smoking on our back porch all summer long. His thin, nearly hairless torso glowed burnt orange beneath the outdoor bulb, and his shirt, if he owned one, wasn't in sight. He had a large Roman nose, its prominence accentuated by his decision to shave his hairline an inch higher than his ears, and the balancing act of reaching across himself to his plastic cup had caused his bare feet to rise from the surface of the porch in a way that struck me as canine. "Hi Daddy," Miranda said. "This is Ira."

The boy jumped to his feet and shook my hand with an exacting precision. Though his eyes met mine, his focus seemed that of someone looking through rather than at me as he said, "Pleased to meet you, sir. I hope you don't mind my spending some time with your daughter this evening. We've just met, but I think she's a fine young woman."

"She certainly is," I said. "But she was supposed to have been playing tennis tonight."

"I twisted my ankle," Miranda said. "During practice. It's not serious, but I'm not supposed to play on it."

"I haven't noticed you limping," I said.

"I said it's not serious," she said in a tone meant for the obtuse. "I just don't want it to get worse. I tried to call Coach, but nobody answered."

"Did you try to call me?"

"I didn't know you were coming to the match, or I would have. I'm sorry."

It wasn't normal for Miranda to lie to me, and the transparent falsity of her statements, combined with her shirtless friend's grating pseudo-formality, annoyed me. Returning to the kitchen, I filled a glass with ice and tipped a generous amount of vodka into it, watching the liquid trickle down. I took two healthy sips on the way to my office, and felt a welcome warmth spread across the base of my skull.

When I reached my office, I thought to open the window and catch some floating bits of conversation, but the room was on the north side of the house, and I couldn't recall if I'd ever actually opened that window. A casual upward push had no effect, and it was only when I got my shoulders down beneath the sash and pressed with my full weight that that it gave way, rocketing upward with a squeal before jamming crookedly, halfway. The move had not been expertly accomplished, but I did detect the faint tones of Miranda and her friend: their rising pitch and staccato cadences betrayed a nervous energy, and I felt an instant and intense animosity toward the boy—I wanted to throw him bodily from my property while telling him never to come within ten miles of my daughter again. I realized my anger was out of proportion to anything he had actually done and that it was reasonable to keep open the possibility that he was unaware of the degree to which smoking shirtless on my patio would antagonize me, but something in me also felt greatly confident the boy was perfectly aware of his behavior. I filled my glass again, and when I stood a few minutes later, the room wobbled a bit as I wandered out of the office and through the dining room, whose walls confronted me with so many framed images: me with Miranda, Sandra with Miranda, Sandra and me together with Miranda, and, in one photo, Miranda by herself. I could hear her and the boy through the back kitchen window, and then I saw them through it, lit up like goblins in the orange porch light as the boy added another stubbed cigarette to the pile he'd formed in the planter tray. "Miranda," I sighed tiredly through the screen, "it's time for your friend to leave."

"Okay, Daddy," she said.

Miranda had called me any number of things over the years—from loving nicknames to ironic formal addresses to angry insults—but she hadn't called me "Daddy" since she was five. When Sandra got home, I thought, we would all of us have a talk, review some rules, and put a stop to this "Daddy" business. I wandered the house straightening things, was briefly cheered when I heard the bathroom door close—I thought it meant the boy had finally left—and was then disappointed to hear the hollow, thunderous plash whose source could only be male. The sound's suggestion of liquid disorder disgusted me, especially when the noise continued well beyond the period of physiological modesty until, when it finally ceased, the toilet's flush was followed much too quickly by the sound of the door opening, and then here came the boy toward me through the dining room, casting in my direction a glassy and unblinking gaze as he asked, again with that grating formality, if he could speak with me. A person of intelligence would have blunted or concealed the naked aggression that rang out from this boy as he pretended to need to catch his breath while saying, "I know this is fast, sir, but I like Miranda a lot, and I wanted to know if you'd mind if I took her out on a date—with her consent, of course." When I told him her mother and I wouldn't let her date until she was sixteen, he didn't miss a beat before asking if maybe he could just take her for coffee or ice cream, then, because she was *almost* sixteen, wasn't she? I told him the type of date didn't affect the policy, and he nodded while affecting a thoughtful contemplation so extreme that I almost laughed. Could they spend time in a group, he wanted to know, or maybe with friends at the mall? "The number of people or location or time of day doesn't matter," I said. "She's simply not to date."

His face clouded into a tight-jawed expression of contempt so clear that I knew he couldn't be aware of it. A second later he had replaced it with a mime's version of hurt feelings, though, as with a self-pitying shrug he said, "Okay, so maybe you just don't like me."

"It has nothing to do with you," I said. "I don't know you at all."

He sighed, lips pursed in frustration. "All right," he said, "I understand. And believe me, I really respect that you're protecting your daughter. I wish my own dad had half the commitment to being a parent that you have. But maybe I'll see you again sometime."

"Maybe," I said.

He returned to the porch. I returned to my office, where I spent the next half hour pretending to go through financial files while I waited for him to leave. But he did not leave. I continued hearing their wordless voices and staccato laughter through the open window as my anger spun restlessly, and I realized that though I had no memory of it, at some point I had brought the actual bottle of vodka into the office with me. Finally I wandered to the back door and asked Miranda if she could please come inside and speak with me. She sighed as if incredibly put out by this, and I walked back to my office telling myself that certainly I was my usual, composed self. Except, of course: part of me was not. But that angry self seemed separate from me, like an animal that had climbed into my lap and was content to sit there, purring, until a whispered command from me would send it bounding off toward a creature into which it could sink its teeth.

"What is wrong with you?" Miranda demanded when she stepped into the office.

"Send the boy home," I said.

"We're just talking."

"I'm asking you to politely tell him to leave. You can blame it on me if you want."

"He won't go home."

"He's refusing to leave his pile of cigarette butts?"

"I mean he won't go *home*. He'll drive around or go somewhere else, because his stepfather's a jerk and they don't get along, so he doesn't like it where he lives."

"So you want him to move in with us?"

She narrowed her eyes. "Have you been drinking?"

"Not much," I said. "But the better question is why you're acting like this is the first boy you've ever seen."

Her jaw tightened. "You don't have to be an asshole about it," she said thickly.

"And when did you start talking to me that way?"

"Since you started acting like this. If he were one of your stupid banking friends' sons, you wouldn't say anything."

"One of my stupid banking friends' sons wouldn't be so dumb as to chain-smoke on my back porch before even meeting me."

"Oh my God," she said, laughing. "You don't like that he smokes? You know Mom smokes, right?"

"Rarely."

"Every day. Ask her."

"It's late. Please send your friend home."

"I'm not a child anymore, Dad."

"I never said you were."

"You're treating me like one."

"You're free to think that and to complain to me about it—tomorrow morning. We can take it up then."

"Whatever," she said as she turned and stomped from the room. Her steps retreated through the house, the back door slammed, and the indistinct voices from the backyard resumed.

I stared at a large, muscular black spider spinning a web across the outside of my window. His body was dark, save for white markings that formed a segmented cross on his belly, and he moved quickly from one side of the frame to the other, binding strands in a series of decisions that appeared haphazard at first, but which revealed a method soon enough. The creature continued its work as I listened to Miranda and her friend move through the house and out the front door, it spun out more silk as I heard a car start and drive away, and it tugged fitfully at its strands as I heard Miranda reenter the house and close the front door behind her. By the time she had thumped her way upstairs and slammed the door to her room, the outer crescent of what would clearly be a grand arachnid construction was complete. I was reluctant to move my attention from the spider even when I heard the front door again, followed this time by the familiar cadence of Sandra's steps. "I just saw two cars drive away from the front of the house. Were we having a party?" she asked as she appeared in the office doorway. Her black tennis skirt and white collared shirt were so clean and unwrinkled that it was hard to believe she'd come from an evening of physical activity.

"There's been a boy here," I said. "And Miranda skipped her match because she claims she's injured, though I didn't see any evidence of the injury."

"Who was the boy?"

"She said his name was Ira. They were talking on the back porch when I got home. The boy was shirtless."

"It's summer. And I know who he is. He works at the park, and I've seen Miranda talking to him before. You didn't get uptight about it, did you?"

"Only if it's uptight to wish visitors would wear clothing and not fill our porch with cigarette butts."

"So he's not the most cultured kid in the world. There are going to be boys now. It's not like she's going to date one of the sons of your banker friends." I gazed impassively at her while she crossed her arms and blew a few strands of hair from her face. "There's a spider watching you."

"I'm aware."

"Aren't you going to ask if we won?"

It was obvious they *had* won, though when I dutifully inquired, Sandra gave me an excited summary of the entire thing before confirming the victory. I knew their win meant she and Grant had qualified for some kind of regional tournament, but when she told me where the tournament was held, I was surprised to hear the name of a city over a day's drive away. "It's a road trip, then," I said.

"Yes."

"You and Grant and who else?"

"One of the singles players. That's all that made it."

I asked if she wanted Miranda and me to go along, and she said it was up to me, but Miranda would have her own match here in town next weekend, so that was a problem, unless she was still hurt and wouldn't be playing anymore anyway, and then of course she and Grant could lose right away. "So who knows what will happen," she said.

Was she talking so fast because they'd won the tennis match, or because the victory meant she had a chance to spend a weekend alone with Grant? It could have been both, or neither. Did I trust Sandra alone with Grant? Did I trust Grant alone with Sandra? Did I trust Miranda alone with boys, and did I trust boys alone with Miranda? I was tired. The questions made me more so. How had I become the house's ill-tempered chaperone? I found no joy in being officially suspicious of everyone, and yet there I was, asking myself these questions.

The phone on my desk rang. I glanced at the clock—it was after eleven.

"You're not going to answer it?" Sandra asked.

"Who would be calling me?" The second ring stopped midway.

I studied the handiwork of my friend in the window—he was making impressive progress.

"Miranda!" Sandra called upstairs. My desk clock ticked off two seconds before we heard a muffled, aggrieved tone from Miranda's room, at which point Sandra and Miranda began a shouted conversation between floors: Sandra asked who was on the phone, Miranda yelled down that it was no one, Sandra shouted that she should come down, Miranda asked why, and Sandra shouted even more loudly for her to *just come down here!*

"I'm sure the neighbors appreciate this," I said.

"Now remember that if you make a big deal out of this, it will only make things worse," she said sternly.

"He just asked if he could date her, and I told him our rule."

A pained expression crossed her face. "*Our* rule?"

"We all agreed upon the rule."

"She's allowed to have fun, you know," she whispered as footsteps approached.

Miranda appeared at the door in wrinkled pink cotton pajamas with large, jersey-type numbers on the front and back. The first time I'd seen them I'd said I couldn't think of a single sport in which people wore pajamas, and Miranda had laughed in a way I'd found disconcerting. "Who was on the phone?" Sandra asked.

"No one," Miranda said. "They hung up without saying anything."

"The boy from the park was over tonight?"

"Yes."

"How is he?"

"He's super-great. Can I go now?"

"What did you guys do?"

"We talked. What's with the third degree?"

“This is only the first degree,” I said.

Sandra shot me a dark look. “When did he leave?” she asked.

“A little while ago. Dad scared him away because he doesn’t like him.”

“I did nothing of the sort,” I said.

“Well, your father apologizes.”

The phone rang again. That time I picked it up quickly and said hello, but there was only a whispery static at the other end of the line. “Hello?” I repeated. “Who is this?” The static felt live, as if there was indeed someone on the line, listening. I hung up, somewhat forcefully. “No one,” I said.

“Can I go to bed?” Miranda asked.

I looked to Sandra, who shrugged. “Sure,” she said. “I’m tired, too.”

And then they were gone, headed up the stairs together, Sandra inquiring in sympathetic tones about Miranda’s ankle. My friend in the window had finished his outer two rings, and though that had taken him some time, I knew his progress would quicken as he worked inward, each ring becoming smaller and tighter, the spokes and ratchets more refined. He dropped from the top of the window to the bottom, suspended on a glistening strand, and I wondered at the phenomenon. How strange to think that out there in the night, there were thousands, maybe millions more of these creatures, spinning away at their exotic traps.

Somehow, I fell asleep there at my desk for what must have been an hour or two. I woke to gaze confusedly at the bent shadow of myself cast upon the wall by the jaundiced light of my old desk lamp, and then stood, straightening painfully. My glass lay on its side on the carpet, a wet stain spreading from its mouth. I restored it to the desk, and had almost left the office to head upstairs when

I caught sight of the window: there, shifting in the breeze like a living membrane, was the completed web. Its maker was nowhere in sight.

I ENTERED THE BANK to the sound of laughter. A young woman was seated at Catherine's desk, and I heard a male voice within my office, both of them laughing at something that must have been said before I entered. The police had left yellow tape around the teller area, but the woman at Catherine's desk seemed unconcerned by the site's designation as a CRIME SCENE CRIME SCENE as she stood to greet me, while at the same time a young man shot out of my office like an eager puppy. "Thanks so much for coming in," he said as if I'd had a choice. "I understand today's an important day for you."

"Yes," I said. "If we could get through this as quickly as possible, I'd appreciate it."

"Absolutely," he said, shaking my hand with the earnestness of a car salesman. He was John, he said, and his partner was Annie, and he assured me that they wanted to move quickly, too. Annie gave me a similarly energetic handshake, and they both stood there smiling, attired in stylish business casual clothing and possessing designer spectacles and flawless complexions and assertive speech patterns. I couldn't help but find their aggressive competence off-putting. Perhaps it was sentimental, but I felt one should bring a sense of humility to the question of a robbery, some deference to the inscrutable convergences necessary for an event of that nature to occur. Something in John and Annie's bearing made it seem they found the situation humdrum, a bit of a goof. I didn't appreciate having my bank robbed—and I had no desire to get tangled up in it—but I appreciated less the attitude that the robbery was of no particular interest. The thief, at least, was probably taking it seriously, I thought. And John and Annie were supposed to, as well.

John extended his arm as if inviting me into a drawing room. "If we could go back into your office," he said.

"Where is Catherine?" I asked.

"We've already spoken to her. She left a little while ago."

Rain trickled silently down the outside of the branch's windows as we tromped quietly through the dim, empty branch and into my office, where I discovered that John had already found the branch's old combination television/VCR and had placed it on the corner of my desk, facing the room. The procedure manuals and incentive guides I'd previously had on my desk were piled sloppily on the floor in the corner.

"We've seen the images. They're excellent," Annie said.

"First, though, the video," John said dramatically, pushing a button on the VCR. A gray image of our teller counter flashed onto the screen. The camera was overhead and slightly behind the counter, so that we were looking down on Amber's long, corkscrew-curled hair as she counted cash and placed it in her tray. Something about the angle—watching from above is a deity's point of view, I suppose—along with the low-quality black-and-white image made me feel we were watching events not from that morning, but from a more distant past, and a slight disorientation settled over me as I watched Amber quietly organize money. "It's just a second here," John said without taking his eyes from the screen. "It's hard not to concentrate on your teller since you know her, but do your best to keep your eyes on the customer." Mooncalf entered the frame then, in his suit, and making no attempt to hide his identity. His hair was trimmed short, he was clean-shaven, and he offered Amber a tight-lipped smile as he placed a torn sheet of paper on the counter and slid it toward her. His bearing struck me as familiar—I knew countless middle-aged men who wore suits and whose smiles were cursory or distracted, and I wondered if maybe Mooncalf had, indeed, kept an account with us over the years, and had moved quietly through the branch from time to time, making sure to keep himself inconspicuous. "Your teller placed him in his forties," John said. "The angle makes height tough to estimate, but he's probably a bit under average." On the screen, Amber had the piece of paper in her hand, but wasn't moving. The man tipped his head forward in a gesture meant to indicate the cash drawer she'd just finished preparing, though from the angle we were watching, the gesture seemed aggressive and vulgar, as if directed toward her person. She pulled money from her drawer and pushed it across the counter while the man pulled what appeared to be a tightly folded canvas bag from his back pocket, unfolded it with a few quick flips, and then, his fingertips touching nothing but the money and the note, slid all of it past his edge of the counter, where everything fell into the waiting bag. Amber's movements were nervous and uncertain; Mooncalf's were smooth. Amber paused, and the man pointed at Amber's side of the counter, indicating the safe he clearly knew was hidden below. The branch I'd been at twenty-five years ago hadn't had individual safes below the counter, but Mooncalf clearly knew not only when it might be easiest to hit my current branch, but also how things were arranged behind teller stands these days. Because the camera was behind Amber, we could see that her safe's door wasn't even closed—she had been moving cash from the safe to her drawer when the man walked up. She knelt, pushed the safe's door the rest of the way open, and then stood and placed several paper-banded stacks of cash on the counter. The man slid them into his bag as she knelt to get more stacks, placed them on the counter, knelt again to get the last stacks, and then placed those, too, on the counter. The safe was empty. "She gave him the marked money and the dye packs," I said. "Just like she's supposed to."

"He probably knows," John said.

"That's not the point," I said, not quite managing to hide my irritation, but John just shrugged. On the screen, the man swept the last of the cash into his bag, turned, and walked away. Amber stood rigidly still, her arms on the counter, until five or six seconds had passed, and then she slowly lowered her head to the counter and covered it with her arms.

"He didn't care the slightest bit about the cameras," John said as he stopped the tape. "He let us watch him every step of the way."

"Any recognition?" Annie said. "He almost certainly cased the branch beforehand. Can you think of any day you might have seen someone like him in the branch? Or any time someone came and left without doing anything?"

"No, I can't remember anything like that."

"There are better pictures from the post camera," she said. "They're on your service manager's computer."

"I saw them this morning," I said.

"Maybe take another look, though," John said. "As long as you're here."

I followed them out of my office and toward Catherine's desk, where I could already see yet another image of a massive redwood floating slowly across her screen—she must have had hundreds, if not thousands, of similarly arresting images of those forest titans locked away in her computer's files. John said something about how nice it must be for me to have my office at such a distance from everyone else, but I didn't respond. I had obviously decided not to mention that I recognized the man on the videotape. Certainly that was in part because I was afraid it would mean having to spend more time with John and Annie than I wanted to, but I also felt that what had happened between Mooncalf and me twenty-five years ago wasn't particularly any of their business. What information would I have been able to give them, anyway? *This man robbed me twenty-five years ago. I know nothing about him, though, he was never caught, and it was all forgotten.* They could figure that out on their own. It would be a good little test of their abilities, I thought.

As soon as Annie touched the keyboard, the redwood on Catherine's screen vanished, and in its place appeared one of the images of Mooncalf—the semiprofile from the right, in which his downward-directed gaze lent him a thoughtful appearance. "He doesn't look like the usual bank robber," she said. "I'll just click through them quickly here."

I sensed John's eyes on me as Annie pulled up two similar photos of Mooncalf looking straight ahead, after which she displayed one I hadn't seen before: a blurry shot of his back that must have been taken as he turned to leave.

"Anything?" John asked.

"No. They're good photos, but I don't recognize him."

"You're sure? Guys usually walk through a few times to case a place before they rob it. It's likely he's been in the branch before."

"If he has, I was probably in my office," I said. "I don't see as many customers as the rest of the staff."

John nodded, though there was something solicitous in his bearing that I didn't like. Catherine had told me these two would have gone through my accounts by now and would ask me about them, but neither of them had mentioned it. What were they waiting for?

"Okey-doke," John said. "I think that's all we need right now."

"That's it?"

"We'll probably have some follow-up stuff soon, but a look at the videotape is what we really needed from you. We'll let you get back to your family."

"And congratulations," Annie added brightly. "I'm sure it's an exciting day."

"Yes," I said, "but do I need to let you out? Or to lock up after you?"

"Oh, we have our own keys," John said. He held up a ring thick with them, and jingled it as if taunting me—or maybe that was just my perception. How many branches did that ring of keys allow him access to? It didn't seem like a particularly good idea to even have a ring of keys like that in existence, I thought—though probably I was just jealous of the degree to which the bank trusted these two young people, while Catherine and I were still following the letter of every security guideline, signing and countersigning forms every time we moved a bit of cash, spun a combination lock, or turned a lever. If young John and Annie were allowed to let themselves into and out of any branch they pleased, then what was the point of the care I had been taking to follow the rules all these years? It made me look ridiculous, I thought. Even if only to myself.

BY THE TIME I left the bank, the clouds had rolled east and the rain had moved on. Silver drops of rain hung from the trees, dripping at intervals onto the damp sidewalks below. Finches flitted and chirped somewhere overhead. A huge, leashed poodle pulled a middle-aged woman down the sidewalk, while the engine whine and warning beeps of heavy equipment a few blocks away were perfectly audible. John and Annie were behind me in the bank, and I was pleased to leave the investigation of Mooncalf's escapade in their hands.

Two sedans were parked near the bank door: mine, and one I assumed belonged to Annie and John. At the far end of the lot, though, I noticed another vehicle: a beat-up white pickup a decade or two old, its body spotted with mud and rusted dents. More than one sign in the lot warned that parking was for bank customers only and violators would be towed, but those signs dated to the old days, when it was conceivable that the thirty spaces in our lot might actually be used. Computers and ATMs had long ago rendered our parking lot's size an anachronism, and it wasn't unusual for us to find mysterious vehicles parked there. I, personally, had never called a towing service—I didn't even know which one we were supposed to alert—but something compelled me that day to walk out to the truck and take a look. Through the driver's side window I saw a red vinyl bench seat cracked at various stress points, and the only things upon it a badly folded city map and a worn pair of leather work gloves. A metal toolbox ran the full width of the truck's bed against the back of the cab, and two extension ladders filled most of the rest of the bed. All these things—the toolbox, the ladders, and the bed itself—were spattered with various-colored drips of paint, and though the truck seemed in no way related to anything I was involved in that day, I pulled a pen and a scrap of paper from my pocket and copied the vehicle's license plate number anyway. I had just made it back to my own car when I heard someone say: "He took off about five minutes ago. Walking south." My eye caught a bit of movement at the front corner of the bank, maybe thirty feet from me, and I realized a man was sitting there, his back against the side of the building. The sun was behind me, and the man was just far enough around the corner to be within the shade the front wall cast across the sidewalk. The movement I had noticed was his left hand wandering past the line of shade and into the light as he absentmindedly tapped a pebble against the sidewalk.

"Is that right?" I said.

"He parked and sat there for a while, then just got out and walked off. You find anything inside the truck? I saw you looking in there." He lifted his face from the sidewalk in order to cast me an accusatory little glance—or maybe it was merely curious—and even though he was at a distance and in the shade, I could see the dark, wet crater above his mouth: This was our noseless gentleman, with whom I had already chatted once that day.

"Nothing unusual," I said.

He returned his attention to the pebble. "Too bad. Thought maybe you'd find some kind of clue."

"A clue?"

"About the robbery. Or did you already catch that guy?" He looked at me again, holding my gaze a bit longer that time. I suppose I thought he might be embarrassed of his wound, but there was actually something austere and almost cold about his glance.

"No," I said. "I just looked at some video of it, and there are other people inside looking at it some more."

"I hope you catch him. The ladies who work in there have always treated me nice. It's too bad someone had to go and do that to them."

"I think everyone's okay. Though I'm glad to hear my staff treats you well."

He seemed surprised. "You're the boss?"

"Yes. The manager."

"I thought it was the woman. Have you ever been robbed before?"

"A couple times." There was a fair amount of the schoolyard in his maneuvers with the stone, as if he'd gotten in trouble and was passing time against the wall now, waiting for the teacher to let him back into the fray. "You were here earlier today," I said. "Did you need anything?"

"Oh no," he said, returning his attention to the pebble and his scraping of it against the sidewalk. "I'm in the shade here. I'm fine."

"Have you had that wound looked at recently. It seems like it shouldn't be exposed."

"It doesn't give me any trouble. The air's good for it."

"When was the last time a doctor looked at it? If you walk into an emergency room, they have to help you, you know. Even if you don't have insurance."

"The doctors can't do anything," he responded, and with a backhand motion tossed the pebble into the street. "Once it's gone, all you can do is keep it clean. You probably need to work on catching that guy that robbed you, so you have a good day, now." The pebble was still bounding erratically toward the opposite curb as he stood and moved along the side of the building, beyond my line of sight. And without thinking—it was a move as simple as any reflex—I stepped toward the sidewalk, so that I was able to look down the side of the bank and watch the man. Almost as soon as I had reached the point where I could see him, though, he turned and caught me. "Did you need something?" he said.

I shook my head.

"Then what are you looking at?" he yelled.

Even before I turned and moved back toward my car, I could see that he had reversed course and was heading back to the front of the bank. He came around the corner as I got into my car and closed the door, bellowing something indecipherable at me as I put the car in gear and backed away from him. And he continued to yell and gesture, even as I drove out of the lot and into the neighborhood.

My pulse was racing as I wondered bitterly why I even tried to interact with other people. It was a courtesy that I even let that man come into the bank to turn in his change, I told myself—I could just as easily bar him from the branch and tell him he had to go somewhere else. And yet I also knew I would do no such thing. Why had I provoked him, anyway? It was while considering that question that I realized with a start that I was driving in the direction of Sandra's house, when I actually needed to be headed in the opposite direction. A single individual had yelled at me, and I was as flustered as if I had been chased by an entire gang of thugs. I pulled into a driveway, backed out, and headed in the opposite direction, passing on the way a mustachioed man in dirty, paint-spattered coveralls, who stood on the sidewalk, studying a piece of paper and then looking up to the house before him. After only that brief glimpse, he slipped behind me, out of range, but immediately I thought: And that is the owner of the truck.

When I drove back past the bank, John and Annie were in front of the main doors, from where they appeared to be addressing the noseless man. He stood in the parking spot my car had occupied, still gesturing angrily. Of the three of them, only Annie turned as my car passed. I thought about how every minute the two of them spent arguing there with the man, or returning to the branch to enter the tellers' statements into the bank security database, to gaze again into the photos of Mooncalf's eyes and speculate about his identity, to make telephone calls to the public relations department to coordinate the release of information and photos to the media—while they were busy with all that, Mooncalf could only be getting further away.

ONLY A FEW DAYS after the evening on which I first met Miranda's friend Ira, Sandra and I hosted a barbecue for her tennis team. Most of the team members had suffered their final losses of the season, of course, so rather than being a sendoff for the three players going on, the occasion actually felt as if it were a celebration of the end of things: another summer tennis season, the regular gatherings the season had provided, and, at some level, the end of summer itself. The tournament-qualifying singles player—his name escapes me, but I recall that he was younger, and had a propensity for swearing audibly during his matches—floated around the party displaying an ostentatious modesty that only underscored the pride he took in his achievement. Grant and Sandra had played two practice sets against another doubles team just before the party, and Grant had showered at our house afterward so that he didn't have to go home and then return—the result was that he now wandered the party in a pair of my old jeans and one of my bank T-shirts emblazoned with a pithy slogan regarding interest and convenience. He made polite but brief conversation when approached by fellow teammates or their family members, but seemed not particularly invested in the occasion. He spent considerable time fascinating a guest's schnauzer by hiding, throwing, and hiding again a short length of knotted rope. Sandra, however, seemed in her social element. She responded with a smile and laugh to almost anything said to her, and listened to others with her head tilted in an attitude of enthusiastic interest. I was impressed by the degree of mastery and even lightheartedness she brought to these social interactions, since in our private life we were already moving through what I would later recognize as the final stages of our marriage.

It had been just a few months earlier that she had walked into my office one evening with a look on her face that made me think she had just gotten awful news. "I don't know how to say this," she had said. "But I'm unhappy. And I want to talk about it. About our life." I knew that by "our life," Sandra couldn't have been referring to anything about Miranda, a bright and funny girl who earned excellent grades and seemed to have plenty of friends. And I knew Sandra wasn't unhappy with her work life, either—the interior decorators she had started working for back when we were first married had switched to calling themselves an interior design firm. Sandra, after taking classes on evenings and weekends for a couple years, had earned a professional certification in interior design, and shifted from the front desk to a position as one of the company's design consultants. She carried fabric swatches, picture books, and paint samples from work to home and back every week, and seemed entirely absorbed in solving the problems of placement and decor—it was "decor," she had taught me, not "decoration"—for the firm's clients. When expressing unhappiness with our life, then, Sandra could only have meant with me, a fact it took her only a few minutes to acknowledge as she sat perched on the arm of a chair in the opposite corner of the room. When I asked her what she wanted that I wasn't providing, though, she couldn't give a definitive answer. She said but hadn't I ever felt like there were other things to do in life, and that spending our whole lives just doing the same thing over and over wasn't a good idea, that it was a waste of us as people? There were other potentials out there, she said, other things we could do. When I tried to argue that we weren't doing the same things over and over—Miranda was in high school now, for instance, and I had just become a branch manager, and Sandra was working with new clients all the time—her face fell. "That's not what I'm talking about," she said.

"Obviously not," I said. "You're talking about me, and being tired of being married to me." "I just think we've become different people over the years. Don't you think we've become different people?" Though I wasn't, at the time, sure what she was working toward, I knew enough to realize I needed to dispute her narrative. "We've gotten older," I said, "But I think we've grown in ways that are good." "But are we still in love?" she said, "Do you still love me? Are you still *in* love with me?" "Of course," I said—though yes, it felt like a lie. Because what, after all, did it mean to be *in love*? That I couldn't bear to be away from her? That I counted the hours until I could see her again, shuddering through paroxysms of anticipatory anxiety? I felt nothing like that, and doubted that any adult actually did. Why would anyone even want to? We were married. Sandra was my wife. I loved her. These were simple facts. They had been well established. I thought. "Do you still love *me*?" I asked. "I'll always love you," she said, "I'm just not sure that I'm *in* love with you anymore." "I don't know what that means. What does that mean?" "I don't know how to explain it, but you know what I'm talking about." Though lost in thought, she held her hands demurely in her lap, as if at a formal occasion. "It's the difference between a brother and a lover—that's what it is," she said. "So you're not attracted to me anymore." "We've been together since we were in our early twenties! How could things not grow stale after sixteen years?" "So you're leaving. Is that what you're saying?" "I'm just trying to tell you what I'm feeling." "But how am I supposed to take this? You're telling me you're unhappy, and unhappy with me, specifically, and there's nothing I can do about it—because you're just not in love with me anymore." "I'm trying to sort through some things—things about myself and my life. And I want to be able to talk to you about them." "And when you were planning on talking to me about this, how did you imagine I would react?" "I don't know. I guess I hoped we would have an honest conversation." She looked at me as if I were some kind of captor she was imploring for mercy. And I hated that look. I had no intention of being her captor. I was not her captor. "We never seem to talk about anything anymore," she said, "I feel like it's been years since we've had any kind of heart-to-heart talk at all." "But how can we have a heart-to-heart talk when you're telling me you're leaving me because you're bored with me? It's like you're saying you're dumping me, but you were hoping it would be a really touching moment between us." "I'm not saying that!" she said angrily, and then, in a controlled tone: "I haven't said that. But maybe you're right. Maybe this was a bad idea." "So what are you going to do? Am I on some kind of probation now? You're going to be evaluating me to see if you can stand being a part of this marriage anymore?" "I'm not going to be evaluating you. I'm going to be evaluating myself." "I see," I said, "Well, let me know when you've finished your evaluation." She shook her head in apparent anguish. "My inability to talk to you about this in any kind of productive way is part of the entire problem." "But it sounds like in your mind, you hoped you could deliver a monologue to me, and I wouldn't respond. Maybe you even thought I would be moved by it? But the reality of talking, if that's what you feel like you can't do, is that I am allowed to talk back. Which I guess ruins your fantasy." "Yes," she said quietly, "I guess it does." And then she stood and walked out of the room.

And then for the next three months, Sandra did not raise the subject of our marriage even once. The conversation just hung there, coloring every interaction between us. When she'd said she hoped I hadn't been uptight about Ira smoking cigarettes on our porch, for instance, what had she meant? Had I lost points with her, and was I moving ever closer, with my *uptightness*, to being disqualified from being her husband? It seemed clear she was, in some secret part of herself, mulling over whether she could continue to stand to be with me. If she was evaluating me, then, I felt it was only fair to let her see my truest self.

Which was, to be honest, fairly liberating.

And so at our little tennis team party, I felt no compunction to be outgoing and social, and neither did I try to hide the fact that I cared nothing about the adults at the party, and that my attention was directed primarily toward my daughter—because not more than half an hour into the event, I had noticed that her friend Ira had shown up. He and Miranda had walked to where Sandra stood on the opposite side of the yard, but I could see him match Sandra's social effervescence by smiling widely as he greeted her, and I saw Sandra gesture toward the rest of the yard—probably telling Ira to feel free to get some food from the grill I was tending—and then trade a laugh with the two of them before turning back to the guests she had been chatting with before. Miranda and Ira remained at that end of the yard, though, and I was still trying to monitor them when Grant, who had wandered past more than once, finally stepped behind the grill with me and said, apropos of nothing: "So I want you to go to Los Angeles with me."

"What are you talking about?" I said.

"We'll go out Wednesday morning and stay the night. I'll have you back home by noon on Thursday."

I had never been to Los Angeles, and the city's name elicited only vague images: circling klieg lights, starlets in fur stoles, popping flashbulbs, and red carpets. I automatically and without taking my eyes from the other end of the yard told Grant I didn't think I could do something like that on short notice, and he responded by taking the metal spatula from my hand and, through a series of artful manipulations, pushing hot dogs to the edges of the grill, sliding hamburgers toward the middle, and continually prodding or flipping the other items while he told me he knew it was short notice, but that it was a business trip, so everything would be paid for and I would receive an appropriate consulting fee. A big opportunity had come up without warning, he suspected there would be financial discussions slightly beyond his depth, and he didn't have time to interview accountants or financial advisors before the meeting.

"As a branch manager, I don't think I'm allowed to do outside consulting," I told him.

"But surely you're allowed to go on a trip with a friend," he said.

The confusion I suffered as he switched between characterizing the offer first as a business trip and then as a personal vacation must have registered on my face, because he began to tell me how he wasn't asking me to become a full-time advisor, he just

Grant introduced himself and, as he and Ira shook hands, said, "So did you play on Miranda's team this summer?"

"Oh, I don't play," Ira said in a tone that seemed to imply that summer tennis was for children. "I work for the city. I manage the park with the tennis complex in it, so I kind of help make sure everything is in good shape so everyone can have a good season."

Grant raised an eyebrow. "I wasn't aware the city allowed high schoolers to manage parks."

"I already graduated," Ira said. "Last year."

"You're twenty, then?" Grant said. "Miranda's only going to be a sophomore."

Ira's expression clouded. "But it's normal for men to date younger women. I bet your wife's younger, right?"

"I'm not married," Grant said. "But the women I go out with are quite a bit older than Miranda, actually."

"I meant younger than you, not her," Ira said, frustrated by Grant's deliberate misunderstanding. When I asked if Ira wanted something to eat, he chose a bratwurst, thanked me quietly, and headed back across the yard.

"That wasn't normal," Grant said. He left the grill himself then, joining a group that included Sandra. The group cheered upon his arrival, and Grant smiled when one of the men punched him playfully on the arm, while across the yard I saw Ira, jaw tight and eyes ablaze, lead Miranda away by the hand. When the two of them disappeared around the side of the house, I passed an anxious five minutes flipping and reflipping sizzling burgers until I saw Miranda return alone. She wandered to her mother's side, and when Sandra, without pausing in her conversation and laughter, put her arm around Miranda and pulled her close, I felt that everything was again where it belonged.

needed help from someone he trusted, and he didn't have anyone on call for something like this. "And also," he said, looking, as I was, across the yard, "why does that boy with Miranda look like someone poisoned his food?"

Ira was sitting on a lawn chair in the shade of a tree a few feet behind Miranda, taking occasional sips from a can of soda and doing nothing to mask the look of boredom on his face. "That's Ira," I said. "I guess he's Miranda's boyfriend."

Grant shook his head, aghast. "Why?"

"I'm not allowed to ask. Sandra told me to leave it alone. She said she'll handle it."

"Well. I'm not a parent, but I don't necessarily believe in women handling men. Even young men."

Miranda was doing her best to make enthusiastic conversation with Margo Talbot, holder of the team's second women's singles position, and coowner of the interior design firm that employed Sandra. Even at a distance and peering into the shade, I could see Ira on the chair behind them, glowering. "Unfortunately, in our house it's two against one," I said.

Grant started to say something about the limits of democracy, but stopped when Ira stood and began walking toward us. The boy's gaze ranged everywhere but in the direction he was heading, and an excessive spring in his stride seemed designed to portray a relaxation so coolly extreme that it resembled drunkenness. "Good evening, sir," he said, shaking my hand when he reached us. "I thought we might see each other again. I hope you don't mind that I'm here. I know you're not crazy about me."

"I have nothing against you, Ira," I said.

"It's okay," he said. "I know you're just looking out for your daughter."

That feeling remained throughout the following two hours, until the last of our guests had departed and I was able to settle into a chair at the table on our back deck and gaze up at the sky. Drifts of cloud bloomed pink in the day's last light, and it seemed to me that the sky behind them was slightly spinning—the sense was something like the gravitational pull one feels while coasting downhill on a bicycle, which rendered even more strange the announcement I thought I heard Grant make: "I have some good news. I've designed a toaster."

I sat up, and was startled to discover that everyone was there at the table with me. But no one responded. Sandra regarded Grant as if his announcement were some sort of ruse, Miranda's face went blank, and I was dumbfounded. Over the previous years, Grant had occasionally chatted with me about business, but the last thing he'd told me was that he'd been forced to lay off the three young designers just out of college who had comprised his staff, and that he was back to working by himself. Never had he mentioned toasters. But he had entered a design competition sponsored by one of the nation's larger discount retailers, he explained, and his toaster had won, and now was going to be sold in the company's stores all over the country. If it sold well, he said, they might let him design an entire line of kitchen products.

It was then that the flurry began.

"What does it look like?" Miranda said.

"We should have champagne," Sandra said.

"I thought you were into chairs, desks, and furniture," I said.

Grant assured me that he was interested in furniture, but that this was an opportunity that had come up. I heard Miranda ask again what it looked like while I wondered aloud if this would solve Grant's staffing problems. There followed rapid and simultaneous conversations between Grant and Sandra and me regarding which brand of champagne to serve, how this would change things, and how Grant's firm would now be expanding or hiring or adjusting its financial structure and attendant accounts. Miranda had stood and, glass of lemonade in hand, walked out into the backyard grass during our discussion. I probably thought she was taking a little stroll, or getting some air, or probably I didn't think anything particular at all as I idly watched her make her way to the barbecue and look down into it. And then, in one unhesitating motion, she placed the palm of her hand on the grill.

For an incredible second, she said and did nothing. Then she threw her head back like a startled colt and cried out, dropping her glass to the lawn as her face contorted in pain. I jogged across the yard, angrily demanding to know what she had done, and when I arrived at her side, she held her burned hand in the palm of the other as if it were some kind of gift. Four parallel red lines were already blistering across her palm, and she looked at me as if she had been betrayed by some natural phenomenon—stung by a bee, or struck by a falling branch. "I didn't know it was hot. It didn't look hot," she cried.

Sandra wanted us to go to the emergency room, but Miranda shook her head so forcefully that Sandra relented, and instead filled a bowl with ice and told Miranda to sit at the table. Seated between me and Grant, Miranda didn't seem particularly uncomfortable once she was settled with her hand on the ice, and she even smiled when Grant told her he had ordered medium, not rare. "Grant," she said as if his name were a perfectly familiar command: "What does the toaster look like?"

He studied her with the same look I had seen him use on the

golf course when trying to estimate his distance to the pin. "Like a block of slightly melted ice cream."

Miranda nodded, satisfied. Sandra brought out a bottle of champagne and three glasses, and the evening resumed. When the phone rang a bit later, Miranda hopped up and ran into the house to answer it as if there were nothing wrong with her hand at all—and she didn't return to the porch.

"Do you think she'll be okay?" Grant asked. "Those burns looked pretty bad."

"We'll look at them tomorrow," Sandra said, waving her hand as if shooing a fly. "Sometimes I don't know where her head is these days. It's just her age, I guess. It's all about boys now. And she acts like I'm an evil stepmother."

"I met the boyfriend," Grant said.

"You did? I'm surprised. He seems shy around people. But very polite."

"Polite, yes," Grant said. "But I didn't sense the shyness."

Sandra shrugged. She seemed tired, and it was only a few minutes later that, citing exhaustion, she disappeared into the house herself. Night had descended by then, but neither Grant nor I moved from our chairs. "It must be hard to be the father of a teenage girl," he said.

"She's in a strange place these days," I admitted.

"Though I suppose locking her in the house wouldn't work any better."

"That's what I'm told."

We sat in the dark listening to the chirping crickets and the bubbling aspiration of the champagne until those sounds disappeared beneath the hiss of rushing water when Sandra turned on the shower in the master bathroom, which was directly above the porch.

"You know, maybe I will go on that trip," I said.

"Of course you will," Grant said. "Why wouldn't you?"

I hadn't really been thinking about the trip, and was surprised to hear myself agree to it. It felt as if some obscure part of myself was daring me to do it, though it was also unclear to me why taking a simple two-day trip would require a dare.

"Did you see her put her hand on the grill?" Grant asked quietly.

"Yes."

"She didn't even hesitate."

I watched it happen again in my mind—the way she had studied the thing before it happened. "I don't think she realized it was still so hot."

"Maybe," Grant said, unpersuaded. "Maybe."

ON THE AFTERNOON OF Miranda's wedding, I found Gina in the back office of her gallery, propping open the door of a miniature refrigerator with her shin while she poured water into two tall glasses of ice. Upon seeing me, she dropped her jaw in a theatrical expression of shock, though when she spoke it was barely above a whisper. "I didn't expect to see you here today," she said. "Aren't you getting married tonight?"

I had just walked past an older couple out in the gallery's main room, both of them thin, white-haired, and examining paintings through the bottom halves of their bifocals. I assumed it was their presence that necessitated a lowered voice, so I played along. "Close. You're one generation off."

"Your mother is getting married tonight?"

"Still off."

Grabbing her brown linen dress at either thigh, she wiggled her hips while tugging downward, then smoothed the front with a quick sweep of her palms. "Well, don't get married yet. I'll be back in a minute." She carried the glasses of water around the corner and out into the gallery. I heard the older couple thank her, after which the three of them began trading comments about the beauty of a particular piece.

When Miranda started working at Gina's gallery, it had been over twenty years since I'd seen Gina. Miranda passed along bits of information she gleaned while working: Gina had lived in New York for a few years, Miranda said, and had also lived in Los Angeles. She had been running the gallery for less than a year, and before that had worked as some kind of counselor or administrator at the city's school of art. Gina had said that starting the gallery had been her big leap, Miranda told me—the thing she had been thinking about doing for years, but had never done until she inherited money after the death of her father and decided to use it to make the gallery dream a reality. She had been married twice, was twice divorced, and had some kind of current boyfriend Miranda had said hello to on the phone, but hadn't yet seen in person. I was intrigued by this information, of course, but the more I learned, the more I also felt reluctant to see Gina myself. She had known me in my mid-twenties, and I felt confident that my mid-forties self could only be a disappointment. My male-pattern baldness was advanced, I was fifteen pounds overweight, and if I wanted to see Gina clearly I would need to wear my glasses, despite my fear that they produced a grandfatherly effect. And when it came to the positive aspects of age, to stories of life and experience, what would

I have to offer? Gina had gone places and done things. I was still at the bank.

Months passed this way: Miranda worked for Gina, and I made sure never to appear there. The situation felt like a school reunion that I had the power to delay while I held out for some kind of personal transformation that was never actually going to occur. And eventually it was only circumstance that forced my hand, because although Miranda had answered my questions about Gina, there came a point when I needed to ask Gina a question about Miranda. So after closing the bank one evening, I drove to the gallery.

Its name—IDÉE FIXE—was emblazoned in large block letters across a picture window that fronted the sidewalk, and the large, open room I stepped into featured olive-colored industrial carpet and the bright white walls of any typical gallery. I had been hoping to find Gina there alone, but the first person I noticed was a stocky, middle-aged man in blue jeans and a denim shirt. Though he didn't strike me as the type of man to be pacing the orderly confines of an art gallery, he was patiently following a woman in gray wool slacks and a collared white dress shirt as she walked slowly along the opposite side of the gallery. Gesturing toward the wall, she told him how a certain arrangement would accentuate the depth of a composition, but it wasn't until he looked doubtfully at the wall she indicated that I realized she wasn't referring to the canvases currently in the room, but to some speculative, future arrangement. When she turned briefly in my direction and told me I was welcome to look around, but that the gallery would be open for only a few more minutes, I said, "Actually, I was hoping to chat with you."

She looked at me again, trying to divine why I would need to chat with her, and I watched the recognition hit her. "My God," she said.

"You didn't recognize me."

"It's been a while." As she walked toward me, I realized she was taller than I recalled, and also thinner. Her hair, as long and dark as ever, was gathered loosely at the back of her neck, and though she may have intended to give me a hug, by the time she reached me I had turned my attention to one of the paintings on the wall—a field of gray marked by a single slash of deep, brilliant blue. "I would ask how you've been, but the others have already told me," she said, examining me through her oval glasses.

"Which others?"

"Sandra. Grant. Your daughter. She works here, you know."

"I heard something about that."

She introduced the man with her as "Gregory, a very talented gentleman I'm happy to represent," and explained to him that I was "an old friend." When Gregory stepped forward to shake my hand, his large, worn work boots made my shoes appear dainty. I noticed, though, that his nails were bitten to the quick. "I'll head over and get us a table?" he said. Gina told him that sounded good, and after telling me it was nice to meet me, he lumbered out into the night, leaving us alone in the gallery. Recorded music—a female singer with an accent that compounded the oddness of the music's electronic burbles—came from somewhere behind the gallery's back wall, which didn't quite extend the full width of the room. There was a second, smaller space behind the wall, though I couldn't see into it.

"So of course I know you and Sandra aren't together anymore," Gina said. "And when I asked Grant about you, he said that if I knew you before, then I know you now."

It occurred to me that once, briefly and long ago, I had been a project of hers. A bracelet of small green stones circled her left wrist, and she wore a silver ring on her right hand, but the fingers of her left hand were unadorned. "Miranda told me you're divorced, too," I said.

"Yes," she said, smiling. "Twice."

"I'm sorry to hear that."

"I'm not," she said.

When the light struck her hair, a dark red tint revealed itself in the highlights. I wondered which salon had earned the trust of the city's aesthetically demanding gallery owners. "I'm sorry it's taken me so long to make it in to see you," I said. "I guess I was trying to get in better shape."

"I'm flattered," she said. "Did you?"

"No. This is the me I thought I might get into better shape."

She laughed. "You look fine. I don't think you need to get in better shape."

"You're being kind. But I've wanted to see what your place looks like. When Miranda said she was going to work here, I realized I didn't know how galleries work, or what she would do, or who her coworkers would be—anything about it at all."

"Her coworkers are me," she said. "And this is a pretty local gallery—local artists, local buyers, nothing exotic. I'm sure she's told you that there's nothing complex about the place. And greeting people and answering the phone probably isn't particularly stimulating for someone as intelligent as she is. I imagine she'd like to do more than that at some point."

"Do you have more for her to do?"

"I have as much as she has time to do. In fact, I wish she had a sister. I've never been able to trust anyone with the details here before, but Miranda seems to be able to do everything exactly the way I would have done it. You're not hiding another one, are you?"

"No. Sandra wanted to get back into the workforce. I didn't disagree."

"I'm sure it's difficult," she said. "But I've forgotten my drink. Would you like one?"

I told her I would, and she headed to the back room, leaving me to contemplate the paintings. There was a fuzzy blue canvas that called to mind headlights in fog, and next to it a pinkish-rose one that, upon closer inspection, was colored by a fine scarlet spray. A short but extremely wide canvas appeared at first to be a uniform light blue, but when I looked closer, I realized that the intensity of the blue wavered slightly along the length of the canvas, defeating my sense of depth. One second it was a painting against the wall, but the next, my eye decided maybe we were looking through a window at a distant sky. The involuntary refocusing was dizzying, and when I tried to resolve it by staring fixedly at the canvas, the visual stuttering only worsened, until eventually I had to step away and look elsewhere.

Gina returned and handed me a glass of white wine. "What do you think?"

"They're skillful. What's the artist like?"

"A mess." She stepped past me to straighten the painting on the wall behind me. It was the blue one that had bothered me, so I didn't turn to watch. I waited until she stepped back from it, apparently satisfied. "So is this just a social call?" she asked.

"I did have something a bit awkward that I wanted to ask you," I admitted.

"What?"

"Do you think Grant and Miranda are dating?"

Though she maintained a level façade, I sensed gears turning. "Why do you ask that?"

"A number of reasons. But mostly because I took Miranda out to dinner the other night and she ate almost nothing. And I know she stops eating whenever she falls for someone new."

"Why do you think it's Grant? She could be spending time with any number of people, couldn't she? Do you really know that much about her social life?"

"No. That's why I'm asking you."

"I don't know," she said, looking around the gallery as if she had just realized every painting was in the wrong place. "It's true that Grant has been around lately. He stops by, semiregularly."

"To take Miranda out?"

"No, just to say hello. Though now I don't know."

"Do they leave together?"

"We've all left together, more than once. And then we go our separate ways. But if he was dating Miranda, he wouldn't let me know about it any more than he would let you know about it."

"I'd like to think he would ask me before doing something like that."

"If he were *a boy*," she said, amused by my logic. "Miranda wouldn't want him to ask you, anyway. And it's also true that this is exactly the kind of thing that appeals to him."

"What do you mean?"

"There's an energy around him when he's going after something. He gets sharper. It's like he starts playing a game, and you're in it, but he doesn't tell you about it, because not mentioning the game is part of the game."

"And you think that's what he's doing? That they're having a grand and secret affair?"

"I don't know what he's doing any more than you do. But it's true that I've had that feeling around him this last month—that sense that he's playing." She laughed then, covering her face with her hand. When she dropped the hand, though, it was to reveal a smile of pained, comically melodramatic heartbreak, so that her actual emotions were concealed behind her parody of them. "Would you believe I thought it was me?"

"You thought he was interested in you?"

"I thought—" she started, but didn't finish the sentence. Instead, she drew herself up into a posture of formal composure. "I don't know what I thought. I haven't seen you in twenty years, and maybe I'm just babbling. It's good to see you. I'm glad you came in to say hello, but I don't really know whether Grant is going out with Miranda. And Gregory is probably waiting for me, so can we chat again sometime soon? And can I at least give you a hug?"

I allowed her the hug, but in the couple of years that had passed after that evening, we shared no particularly deep or personal conversation. When, on occasion, I stopped by the gallery to take Miranda to dinner, Gina joked with me about the pieces she had on the wall, or about the artist who had made them, or about the people who had looked at them. This gallery running was all a lark, her manner suggested, an eccentric goof. Her lightness about the place was so charming, as was the easy and knowing way in which she touched my elbow before relating an anecdote, or the way in which she sometimes exclaimed, upon my walking through the door, that here, finally, was a person she could actually *talk to*, that I sometimes had to remind myself that her flirting was just a part of her professional persona. And despite not earning much, Miranda enjoyed her job there immensely, and it was clear she viewed Gina as something of a model in how to be a successful and stylish professional, an attitude that, quite frankly, cheered me. Miranda was young, intelligent, and responsible. There would be plenty of time for her to worry about money when she was older, I felt.

Gina never spoke about money, either, and I suspected she joked with me about the place as a kind of placation, probably assuming that I didn't take her endeavor seriously. The result was that I didn't truly realize the depth of her commitment to the gallery until a day that Miranda, in a state of awe, told me how Gina had spent most of a half-hour phone call one afternoon screaming at a patron who had tried to back out of a purchase. She'd told the man he had stolen money from an artist by reserving a piece and then later trying to change his mind, and that she would not let someone rip off one of her artists that way. She would not let some "spoiled, upper-class twat," Miranda told me Gina had called the man, cause her artist to starve. After bullying the man into paying for his purchase, though, Miranda said Gina had hung up the phone and burst into tears, admitting to Miranda that though what she'd said about the artist getting ripped off was true, it was also true that if she hadn't sold the piece, she wouldn't have been able to pay her next month's rent on the gallery space.

But Gina spoke not a word of this to me, ever. I got only laughter and light flirting from her—only jokes. Gregory faded away, replaced by a new boyfriend, someone well connected in the city's art scene. When I saw him wearing a navy sport coat with gold buttons at a recent opening, though, I decided he couldn't be someone Gina was serious about. In fact, it didn't seem that Gina was interested in being "serious" about any man. Whatever had happened—whether it was one or both of her marriages, or something else entirely—sharing her life with a man in some traditional way didn't seem to interest her. There had been only that one, brief admission—"Would you believe I thought it was me?"—before that voice had been silenced, and in its place had appeared: composure.

And it was that professionalism and composure that I heard Gina use on the afternoon of Miranda's wedding as she spoke to the older couple out in the gallery. I had glanced only briefly at the pieces on my way in—they appeared to be large pieces of wood, each of which featured a surface spattered with layers of red or green or yellow paint, and then scratched or hacked at with some kind of rough implement—but I could hear the man and woman murmuring quietly to one another about them. The man was concerned that this wasn't art, while the woman said they would be striking in the foyer. In a tone of cheerful contemplation, Gina validated both responses by saying that one of the interesting things about the pieces, to her, was the very way in which they were both striking and thought-provoking. "They don't just fade into the background," I heard her say, "when you see them, you look at them. And when you look at them, you think about them. That's what drew me to them." She told the couple to take as much time as they wanted, and then came back into the office and propped herself against her desk as if doing nothing more than waiting for a bus. "So what was it you were doing here, again?" she said. "When you should be any number of places other than here?"

"I wanted to find out if you've talked to Miranda today. I tried to call, but you didn't answer."

"I'm sorry, I didn't look. I was with customers," she said, and whispered: "*And I need this sale.*"

"I don't want to bother you," I said. "It's just that Miranda didn't come home last night. And I saw her today for a few minutes, and she seemed upset."

"About what?"

"She didn't say. And she's supposed to be at the hotel now, getting ready, but she's not. And no one seems to know where she is."

Gina looked quickly into my eyes—like a doctor reading the dilation of my pupils it seemed. "She's fine," she said.

"What do you mean? You've seen her?"

"She stayed at my place last night. And she was here a little while ago."

"She stayed with you last night?"

"She said her friends and the guests and all of the demands on her were too much, and she needed a quiet place to sleep. She asked if she could stay with me, and I said yes."

I was dumbfounded by this. Gina hadn't been at the rehearsal dinner. She hadn't even been at the bar we went to after the rehearsal dinner. So Miranda had called her late at night, asking for a place to hide? "What's going on?" I said. "She's acting like someone having doubts."

"Oh, everyone has doubts," Gina said, as if the question were irrelevant. "I've had doubts about everything, my whole life. And it's easy to get swept off your feet and fall in love, but the actual day is different."

"I don't remember doubts. I remember thinking it was the natural next move."

"And yet we're both divorced," she said, flashing me a sympathetic little smile as she crossed the room to pull two glasses from the cabinet.

"Well, there's more than one road to Rome."

She turned, surprised. "Did you say there's more than one road to ruin?"

"To *Rome*."

"I thought you said *ruin*!" she said, laughing. "The expression is 'All roads lead to Rome.' I like your version better, though."

"Sorry. I don't know my expressions. I'm just trying to figure out what's going on with my daughter."

She filled the glasses with ice and water, exactly as she had for her customers not three minutes earlier, and handed me one. "I feel like I'm in a privileged position here," she said. "Though not necessarily in a good way."

"What do you mean?"

"Well, I've dated both the groom and the father of the bride, for starters."

"A lifetime ago."

"Thank you. I always enjoy hearing how ancient I am."

"That's not what I meant."

"Maybe yes, maybe no. But I've spent most of the last two years working with Miranda, and I consider her a friend of mine, too. So I'm happy to tell you that she stayed with me last night, and she was here earlier today. And she's fine. But the rest of it is between you and her."

"The rest of what? If she has doubts about getting married, she didn't have to agree to it."

"Why do you keep asking about doubts? Is someone smarter, better-looking, and with more money than Grant really going to come along?"

The woman who had been out in the gallery stepped past the back wall then, her lips pressed into a polite smile as she asked if

Gina could answer a few questions. Gina said of course, and then, as she stepped past me on her way out to the gallery, she whispered: "It seems to me like you're the one with the doubts."

As she disappeared around the wall, I stared at the glass of water she had poured for me. The imprint of a lip was visible beneath the rim, and I set it down without drinking. Two years earlier, Gina had covered her face in embarrassment over having thought Grant had been pursuing her, but now I was supposed to believe she was fine with things, and I was the emotional slowpoke? Did she really think she was helping me uncover some hidden emotional life I was unaware of? She felt I had doubts about the fact that my daughter was marrying a man almost a quarter century older than her, who had known her since she was a child? Of course I had doubts. That should have gone without saying. Did she expect me to run through the streets screaming about it? I could hear her chatting with the old couple in her voice of quiet enthusiasm, confirming each hesitant opinion they put forth, validating the soundness of their aesthetics and the wisdom of their responses, trying to make her sale while I thought: Miranda is a grown woman. She and Grant went to get a drink one evening, and then went to get a drink another evening. Things proceeded from there. There was nothing to be done about it.

The building's back door stood halfway open, offering a view of the alley's potholed asphalt, and of the weeds growing up from the base of the building opposite. The upper half of that building's cinder-block wall was so intensely ablaze with the heat of the afternoon sun that it appeared almost white, and I noticed, sitting on the corner of one of the desks, a pair of black sunglasses I knew were Miranda's. In their lenses, I could see a reflection of the room: a little warped image in which I was nothing but a stretched shadow.

When Gina returned, she raised her eyebrows in a way that suggested the couple in the gallery was serious. "Maybe," she whispered. "Maybe, maybe."

"So you think my concerns are just in my head," I said. "And I shouldn't worry."

Again I got the level gaze from her. Did a shift in countenance really allow her to see something in my head? "She's going to be fine. But you should keep in mind that your daughter thinks you're Superman."

"What do you mean?"

"I mean you don't seem to care about the opinions of other people. Or maybe you do, but you hide it."

"And Superman is like this how?"

She sighed. "Fine. Maybe not Superman. You know what I mean."

"How much is a person supposed to care about the opinions of other people?" I asked. "What's the norm?"

"That's what I mean," she said. And she smiled then in a way that unnerved me, because as I looked into her eyes, I felt that the person smiling at me was not the joking gallery owner, but the Gina I had known long ago, who had been kind to me in school. I hadn't seen that person in years and years. "I worry about you," she said.

"I don't think so."

"I do. Though I don't know why, since I know nothing about you. Do you have anything else going on in your life right now other than this wedding? Even as just a distraction? What about that woman you work with? The little one. What's her name?"

Gina knew Catherine's name. "You're saying that if I sleep with my coworker, maybe it will distract me from being concerned about whether my daughter is going to be okay in her marriage?"

"I'm saying that if you had other relationships in your life, maybe you wouldn't be so fixated on this one."

So she had dropped her persona and come back from the past in order to fix me. It was charity. "I can't remember," I said. "How many children was it that you have?"

She laughed, but it was forced now, and her eyes had gone flat. The Gina who had reappeared for an instant had vanished again. It was in her usual, ironic tone that she said, "Has anyone ever told you that you don't take advice well?"

"That might be because I feel like I'm trying to get permission from you in order to speak to my own daughter. Which seems odd to me."

"Miranda chose to come to me. Not the other way around."

"And what did she say to you?" I asked—and loudly enough that the couple in the gallery could hear.

She glared at me for a fraction of a second, but with a sigh, the anger faded from her expression. "One thing she asked was if I would do it if I were her."

"Do what?"

"Marry Grant."

"And what did you say?"

She fluttered her eyelids, supremely annoyed. "I said if I loved him, then yes." Then, with a defiant look, she whispered: "And you. Are being. An asshole. Darling."

"Only because I was asked to," I said, my voice again at an appropriate level. "Sandra doesn't know where our daughter is, and she asked me to try and find her. And I think you know where she is."

"I don't. She was here earlier today, but I don't know where she is now. And you need to talk to *her.* Not me."

I looked at my watch. "Her wedding is supposed to start in three hours. But at some point between now and then, she's going to call you, isn't she?"

"Maybe."

"And you'll tell me when she does?"

She shrugged—so tiredly, though, that it was clear she was conceding only because I had worn her down. "Fine. Yes. I'll call you."

I stood to leave. "Thank you. Sorry about raising my voice."

She nodded toward the alley. "Back door, please."

Fair enough, I thought. And that was how I left.

CALIFORNIA. AND I FLEW THERE, with Grant, on only three days' notice. We drove along a patchwork street of grooved concrete and crumbling asphalt. Small stucco houses held space between tired apartment complexes, and the signs above the businesses in the strip malls were paragons of simplicity: ZAPATOS, said one, or TELEFONOS, and CARNICERIA. There were palm trees and bus benches and graffitied billboards, and all of it—every surface, it seemed—had been stained a dull, rusted brown by whatever pollutants or smog filled the air. Grant had offered me the window seat on our morning flight, and I had tried to smile while I gripped the armrests and watched the earth tilt away. By the time we leveled off, the cabin pressure had stopped my ears every bit as effectively as if they were filled with cotton, and I had to ask Grant to speak louder when he told me he had just been in Los Angeles a few weeks before to meet with potential clients, tour an injection molding plant, and visit a former stepmother—or maybe, he said, he should just say she was a nice older lady who had been part of his family for a few years when he was a kid. I knew Grant's father had been married a few times, but Grant had never spoken about the specifics, and because what I knew of Los Angeles was derived entirely from television and movies, it seemed odd that a person would have a stepparent there or, for that matter, would go there to visit factories.

Once we retrieved our bags and picked up our rental car—a BMW, because it was "the easiest way to blend in," Grant said—he moved smoothly in and out of various lanes on the freeway while I unfolded the rental company's map, a bewildering latticework of freeways both named and numbered, and which bent toward or twisted into each other seemingly at random. Only a few minutes after we'd exited the freeway and passed the strip malls, though, he pulled to the curb in front of a crisp glass box of a building, six stories tall. Grant handed his keys to a valet in black slacks and a tight black polo shirt while I tried to look up through the immense plate-glass windows that fronted the building. The sun's reflection in the glass was blinding, though, and I was still seeing spots as I stepped into a large, air-conditioned lobby, where sofas and chairs draped in white fabric sat on a white-planked wood floor. Pale candles—the source of the room's jasmine scent, no doubt—burned in glass jars on birch shelves, and an Asian man and a white woman sat quietly behind the front desk, both of them young, with short, dark hair, perfect complexions, and the same outfits as the valets. Grant spoke to the man behind the desk, but I moved slowly around the lobby, examining various pieces of what appeared to be nothing more than large swatches of wrinkled white fabric that had been framed beneath glass and hung on the wall. Sandra would love this, I thought.

She and I were barely on speaking terms by that point, though. The previous day I had ignored a call on my line at the bank as I worked through lunch, trying to get as many things as possible taken care of before my trip. But my phone had rung again, with the insistent chirp that indicated a call from within the bank, so I picked it up. "Your wife is here to see you," Catherine had said at the other end of the line.

"No," I said.

"Yes," she said.

By the time I opened my office door, Sandra had already made her way across the lobby and, as she stepped past me and into my office, said she hoped she wasn't interrupting me. I looked to where Catherine sat at her desk. A chubby-faced young man in a crew cut and camouflage pants anxiously bounced his leg as he sat across from her. The young man wore an expression of outraged disbelief I had seen from so many customers over the years that I needed no other information to know that he was overdrawn, had probably written a few checks without realizing he had no funds, and then, when the checks bounced, the whole situation emerged as a nasty and baffling surprise to him. Catherine had joined the branch only a few weeks previously, and we were still on formal terms. So when she turned from the man and raised her hand in a shy, abbreviated wave, I nodded politely before closing the door. She was, from what I could tell, working comfortably in the face of the man's anger.

"She seems nice," Sandra said. "Before I told her I was your wife, she even made an excuse for you. She said you were on a conference call."

"I told her I wanted to get some work done, and I didn't want to get bogged down in going over elderly customers' statements with them."

"You don't do that anymore? Too bad. I thought it was sweet."

Sandra had visited me at work only a few times in the two years since I'd moved to a new branch to become a branch manager. On each visit, her presence had struck me as awkward. My spousal self diminished my managerial self, it seemed, and I could only return to being the branch manager after Sandra left. Now she was opening up the shopping bag she had carried into my office. "I bought you something for your trip, to wear with your beige suit. I think it looks like something a financial advisor would wear, don't you?" She laid a silk tie across my desk: a pattern of small red ovals against a field of black.

"Unless the ovals represent zeroes," I said.

"The ovals represent sensitivity. Financial advisors are sensitive. That's why they're able to advise."

"I see."

She wandered the small space of my office, idly examining shelves filled with procedure manuals. "I also came by to tell you something that I don't want you to respond to right away," she said, "because your first response will probably be emotional, and that's not what's important right now."

"What do you mean?"

She stole a glance at me as she plucked a withered leaf from a dead plant on my filing cabinet. "I just came from taking Miranda to the doctor's office. She's going on birth control."

So this visit wasn't about clothes for my trip. It wasn't about me at all. "When am I allowed to respond?" I said.

"You can respond."

"Then I don't agree to this. She's fifteen."

Sandra was prepared. "She's almost sixteen," she said. "And she's starting to go out with boys, and they're not going to go away."

"No," I said, feeling an anger more elemental than any I had felt before.

"What do you mean, no? You don't have the slightest idea what it's like to be a teenage girl."

"You should have talked to me. I would have told you I don't want this."

"Well, it's already done."

"We could not do it."

"No. Emotionally, no, that doesn't work. She and I have already talked about it."

"So you're just going to allow this creepy Ira kid to have sex with her."

"You're about a week behind," she said tersely. "I'm trying to prevent something horrible from happening."

"You're not preventing, you're encouraging."

"It's easy to criticize when you haven't done a thing yourself."

"You asked me not to. You told me not to be uptight. Now I see it was so you could just go ahead and screw everything up."

"You don't want our daughter to grow up, so you're burying your head in the sand. You don't understand what she's dealing with."

"What is my role in this family?"

"What do you mean?"

"If you're going to raise Miranda from here on out, then what is my role? Should I just be satisfied with the closeness of *our* relationship?" As with my agreement to go to Los Angeles with Grant, the comment seemed to have been spoken by someone else.

"I understand that we are not on great terms with each other," Sandra said quietly, "but that doesn't mean you're allowed to attack me."

"I'm not attacking you," I said. "What I do is go to work and come home, and I don't bother you at all. I stay out of your way. And now you're telling me to stay out of your way even further when it comes to Miranda. So how is it that I'm attacking anyone?"

"If you want to talk about our marriage, this is not the time to do it."

"And if you want to talk about Miranda and birth control, you shouldn't have come to my workplace to tell me about it. You did this because you thought I wouldn't get angry here."

"I was obviously wrong about that."

"Have I thrown things? Have I cursed or insulted you? I'm expressing my feelings. Isn't this the emotional honesty that's supposedly so good for people?"

"Not when it's so ugly."

"So who's attacking now?" I said. "Take this tie away. I know how to dress myself."

She took the tie off my desk and dropped it back into her bag. "Boy, you're a piece of work today."

"What does that matter?"

"Please stop," she said so quietly it was almost a whisper. "Treat me with some respect."

"You mean you don't like being treated like a subordinate? You don't enjoy having someone talk down to you as if you're stupid?"

She rose. "I'm going to leave now. Maybe this little vacation of yours with Grant will be good. And maybe it's a good idea if we just avoid each other until you get back."

"That sounds fine."

She paused in the doorway. "Do you want the door open or closed?"

"Closed, please."

She closed it quietly behind her and became, through the door's frosted glass, a blotch of wavering color that bobbed a bit, grew smaller, and then disappeared. When I reopened the door five minutes later, I was surprised to find the same beefy young man still sitting across from Catherine. His cheeks were flushed and his forehead shone with the sweat of what I assumed was restrained frustration, but he was following along and nodding as Catherine went carefully over a list of each and every one of his transactions. Intent on their study of his account, neither of them raised their eyes or took note of me in any way.

Sandra and I hadn't spoken since then. So while looking at swatches of fabric in a lobby that seemed more fit for a spa than a hotel, while the little monochrome nirvana and its attractive, black-clad staff exuded a decadence pitched so low it felt almost stoic, I thought of Sandra, and how she would love the place. But I also knew I would never even tell her about it.

I was interrupted in my examination then by a Hispanic bellboy—also young, immaculate, and in the same black uniform as the others—who asked if he could show me to my room. Grant seemed intently involved in conversation with the young woman behind the desk, so I followed the bellboy into a small elevator at the back of the lobby. The level of fitness present in these employees was daunting. The bellboy held my hanging bag over his shoulder, and carried my suitcase with just the three outside fingers of his opposite hand so that his index finger was free to operate the elevator. Faced with the same task, I would have leaned or hobbled my way through it, but he moved swiftly and gracefully through the entire procedure, and even, after the door closed, politely asked whether I was visiting Los Angeles on business or pleasure.

"Business," I said.

"The movie business?"

"No. Home appliances."

"For real?"

"Yep."

"Like washers and dryers and shit?"

"Toasters, actually."

He nodded. "Hmm."

When the elevator opened, he showed me to a small room that contained a bed with a white birch headboard and white comforter, a small white desk with a white chair, and in the corner, a white bureau upon which sat a small television. When the bellboy asked if everything was all right, I told him I wasn't sure what else I could possibly need, handed him five dollars, and then he was gone. And I was alone in a boutique hotel room in Los Angeles.

I turned on the television, flipped through the channels with dissatisfaction, and turned it off. I skimmed the magazines and information left in the hotel's fake leather binder on the desk, thinking there should probably have been some bit of preparatory business for me to take care of, though I couldn't think of what. I could call Sandra and tell her I'd made it, but that seemed pointless. It was just a flight and a drive, and I felt there was a mutual understanding that we wouldn't be talking to one another while I was there. It occurred to me then that Miranda had recently left a message on our home phone's voice mail system without my ever having heard the phone ring. When I'd naively complained that it seemed like sometimes the phone didn't work, she had smiled at my lack of telephone sophistication while explaining that a person could leave a message without actually calling. And so there in Los Angeles, I resorted to the strategy I'd been taught by a teen: I dialed the number of our voice mail system, worked my way through the options, and left a message saying I had arrived, was fine, and would call sometime soon. And then I hung up with—like a teen—no actual intention of calling.

I put my hanging bag on the rod near the door and removed and hung each item of clothing: a tie, a polo shirt, two dress shirts, and, as per Grant's suggestion, a simple navy blue suit. I elaborately laid my razor and toothpaste and toothbrush in a line on the counter next to the sink, and was in the middle of reading the back of the tiny, complimentary bottle of shampoo when there was a knock on the door, and I opened it to find Grant there, changed now into a tan suit over a white dress shirt open at the neck. "Ready to go?" he said.

"I didn't know I was supposed to be ready," I said. "I thought we were going to discuss things first."

"Right." He stepped into the room, examined the place idly—was his room not exactly the same?—and sat down at the desk. "I guess I just meant ready existentially."

"How do you want me to act?" I said. "I'm a bank manager, but here I'm supposed to be your CFO?"

"Aren't those close to the same thing?"

When I explained to him that I didn't work with big businesses, and that there were certainly plenty of people in Los Angeles who were actual CFOs, and who would possess much greater sophistication than me, he rubbed his forehead and looked out the window into the hazy sunshine. "I think I just want you to be yourself," he said. "You can act however you think is appropriate."

That meant nothing to me. "I'll do my best," I said.

I slipped the pants and jacket on and looked at myself in the full-length mirror, trying to decide what knot the financial consultant of an industrial designer would use. Full Windsor, I decided. Grant was writing something on the hotel stationery—notes to himself, probably—while I looked at myself in the mirror and wondered why I was finding it so difficult to imagine being a suit-wearing financial advisor when I actually was a man who wore suits and advised people on their finances. And I was about to laugh at the idea of Grant dressing me as a prop when I suffered a brief temporal collapse. I was standing in a suit, in front of a mirror, and Grant was speaking to me. This was all just as it had been when he had helped me choose my very first suit at his tailor's, years ago. I had somehow completely forgotten about that.

Later, while he again negotiated the streets of Los Angeles, Grant drummed his fingers anxiously on the steering wheel and told me a bit more. "I just have a sense that I'm on the edge of things," he said. "I've been working hard, and I feel like I have what it takes to work with these people, but I'm operating on a mix of intuition and bluffing. So all I can do is walk into a room and know that you're the financial guy wearing a dark suit and tie, and I'm the creative guy wearing a light suit open at the neck. It's a calculated effect, but that's just because effects are all I know how to calculate right now."

"But that's what I meant before," I said. "You don't want me to be me. You need me to be a certain kind of character. And this is like a job interview for you, right?"

"Yes," he said, "but only to the degree that *every* social interaction is a job interview. I don't want you to be a character, I want you to play a role. And you already are that role. You don't have to do anything more."

After we parked in the lot of a large, square, glass building in Culver City half an hour later, Grant pulled something from his briefcase: a miniature bottle of Maker's Mark, no more than a couple ounces. He broke the seal on the plastic lid, closed his eyes, and drank the contents in one gulp. "That'll be good for the nerves," he said.

"Do you have one for me?" I said.

"Sorry," he said, "but listen, remember that you don't need to do or say anything in there. Just follow my lead and use one rule: never say more than one sentence at a time. If there are documents you need to say something about, keeping it to a sentence will make everything easier."

"But what if things are more complex than one sentence?"

"We can talk about complexity later."

We entered a lobby of highly polished marble, where a receptionist directed us to the seventh floor. Grant said nothing as an elevator paneled in honey-colored wood carried us upward, and I sensed that having prepared me, he was now preparing himself. I wondered what rules for himself he might be going over as the elevator doors slid open and another receptionist showed us to a conference room with a long, black glass table, upon which sat a silver tray with a crystal pitcher of ice water, and five glasses. Grant sat at the head of the table, propping his large black portfolio case against the side of his chair. I sat to his left, from where I could look out a wall of windows that gave on to the parking lot, where hundreds of BMWs and Mercedes and SUVs glistened in the afternoon sunshine. These were the boom years of aggressive financing and acquisition, and I couldn't help but think how much interest was accruing on the car loans represented in that lot. As Grant wrote another little note on a pad of paper he had pulled from his portfolio, I wondered how aggressively he was financed. I knew he was living in an unfinished warehouse loft in a low-rent district, but I had always assumed that was by choice, for aesthetic rather than financial reasons. But here in Los Angeles, we were staying at a chic Sunset Boulevard hotel and driving a BMW. Was it usual for Grant to make these leaps from city to city and life to life? And how much did they cost him? I had, at some level, assumed that the way Grant lived was standard for his means. The idea that some—or many?—of his flourishes were achieved on credit hadn't occurred to me before.

"Any last questions?" he asked.

"No."

He nodded. "We're going to do well," he said. He didn't sound like himself when he said it, though. Or maybe I'd just never heard him speak that way: nervously.

Two people entered the conference room then: a man with a shaved head, who wore a sport coat and designer blue jeans, and a woman whose khakis and crisp white dress blouse seemed pulled straight from the company's catalog. The man introduced himself as Jeffrey and the woman as Lynn—her title indicated she was his superior. Grant introduced me as his financial manager, and then, as a series of seemingly benign comments about fax machines and freeways moved seamlessly into remarks about Grant's toaster, Lynn began to reference industry details and design terms I had only a hazy understanding of, and I realized that the meeting was under way. Grant delivered some of his remarks directly to me, as if I were the appropriate audience for certain pieces of info, and each time he did this, he nodded as if what he was saying had ramifications between the two of us that didn't involve Lynn and Jeffrey. I tried to respond by nodding in an appropriately knowing way, which felt mechanical at first, but then the oddest thing happened: I found myself responding to a conversation the content of which was almost entirely meaningless to me. I noticed that although they were dressed more casually than Grant and me, both Jeffrey and Lynn were perhaps a decade older than us, and I began to feel that there actually were two distinct teams present here, and that though we weren't doing something as simple as playing a game, that was only because something real was at stake. When Jeffrey slid paperwork across the table to Grant at one point, Grant passed the copies to me without even a glancing at them, and I thought: Yes. Good move. And from then on, whenever a new piece of paperwork appeared, Jeffrey passed the paperwork to me while explaining aloud to Grant what it was. There were pages filled with statistical information regarding tensile strength, specifications for materials, for units of production, for manufacturing windows and production and distribution scenarios dependent on product sizes and availability dates. Organizing and studying this stack of paperwork gave me something to do, and I began to feel as if my role in the conversation was becoming more than ceremonial. Grant opened his portfolio and slid two large sheets of paper across to Jeffrey and Lynn, and I understood from the explanations between them that the figures and statistics I had in front of me referred to whatever it was Jeffrey and Lynn were looking at. Grant seemed possessed by an earnestness I had never seen in him before. When listening, he did so with an abundance of attention, elbows on the table and knuckles laced beneath his chin. When speaking, he gazed thoughtfully out the window, or ran his hand through his hair, or grimaced as he chewed on his thumb—actions that made it seem his every response was requiring intense thought and introspection. At one point he turned to me and said, "Not all of this involves you, but you'll want to keep the paperwork anyway, because it's all related."

"He's just here to look at the numbers that represent money, right?" Jeffrey said. There were smiles all around at that.

"Those are the only ones that will make sense to me," I said.

Everyone laughed.

We moved on. And I was so taken with the way in which Grant was soliciting Lynn and Jeffrey's attention through the manner of his delivery that I didn't even realize Grant had begun talking about Sandra until well after he'd already started. She wasn't a housewife, he was telling Lynn and Jeffrey, but neither did she reject the role of the housewife, and it was important to remember we were designing for a consumer who played multiple roles, and where, for instance, did Sandra get her thrills?

It was only when Grant didn't answer the question himself that I realized he was actually asking me. "What?" I said.

"Where does she transgress?" he said. "Where does she rebel? What makes her feel guilty in a way she enjoys?"

I was baffled. No one seemed to be breathing. "She only mentions guilt about shopping."

"For what kinds of things? Not the groceries, right?"

"No. She says she buys bedding too often." I was about to explain that we had seasonal bedding now in our home, and that I didn't understand why we needed a different comforter every three months, but hemmed in by Grant's one-sentence rule, I bit my tongue.

"Is it *our* bedding?" Jeffrey asked.

"Sometimes," I said.

"If sometimes means less than thirty percent of the time, then there's work we need to do," Lynn said.

"Exactly," Grant said, and then went on to tell Lynn and Jeffrey that he knew they found his work a bit extreme, but that people wanted something extreme in their lives, because having or doing something extreme is what made them feel like individuals. But most people didn't want their extreme experience to be financial or emotional, he explained—they would rather scream at a football game on television, or listen to loud music in their car, or try a spicy new recipe in their nice kitchen, or whatever it took to make an extreme experience perfectly safe and normal. As Grant continued to make what I knew was a perfectly coherent and standard analysis of the company's demographic, though, I lost my feeling of relaxation, and found it replaced by a strange sense of terror. My mouth dried up; the room seemed to recede. I wasn't frightened by anyone there, or by anything in particular that was happening, but I felt the urge to leave, immediately. I did not want them talking about Sandra. It wasn't making me angry, so much as confused. Because how—there, on that day, in that conference room—had Sandra become a standard example? She was not a test case, or I didn't want her to be. And she and I were not typical examples of predictable behavior. Or I did not want us to be.

"So by making basic products a bit extreme, your customers can have that sense of transgression," Grant was saying. "The products will be mass-produced, of course, but extreme appearance comes across as uniqueness to most people, and because these products are also inexpensive and functional, they're the very products you should start with. You'll be giving your customers an opportunity to overpay and luxuriate in the sense of having made a decadent decision, but at a price below ten dollars, which is incredibly low for the privilege of feeling that they've not only indulged in the crazy impracticality of art, but then also got to feel pleasantly guilty about having supported the insanity of it all."

"I understand that," Lynn said, "and of course our customers want nice-looking things. But I don't know that they're interested in design theory to that extent."

"Your *company*, though, needs to have a coherent design theory," Grant said, "or else you'll continue to fill your shelves with products whose design is just dumbed-down or absent, and that won't work. Because even though your customers might not think about design theory overtly, their instincts are sharp, and they know cheapness and emptiness when they see it. Just think of all the products you've put out that end up in the dollar bin."

It seemed to me that Grant had just insulted the very people he was talking to, and yet his tone was energetic and upbeat. Trying to escape my own state, I tried to study Lynn and Jeffrey, but I didn't detect any change in their demeanor. And when Lynn agreed that no, the customers weren't dumb, Grant stood and began pacing at the front of the room, gazing at the carpet or out the windows while he continued speaking about how manufacturing advances meant that even cheap products could be perfectly durable and wouldn't necessarily break any time soon, and so their company could probably only differentiate themselves from other companies either ethically or aesthetically. If they wanted to differentiate ethically, he said, they would have to be willing to try to prove that their company was somehow ethically clean.

"We're not at all interested in that kind of positioning," Lynn said. "Not just because in an industry that relies on mass production it's pretty much impossible, but also because it's an ugly stance, and quite frankly, kind of boring."

"Right," Grant said. "It's Pollyanna-ish, so neither fun nor sexy. And that's not what people go to the store for. What you really want to do is differentiate aesthetically, and the way you do that is to have products that work just as well as anything carried at Wal-Mart, but that look completely different."

"So our toasters look like melting butter," Jeffrey said.

Grant smiled. "I've been saying ice cream, but I like that. So yes, like butter."

"But this has been done," Jeffrey said. "The competition just copies our designs. Jesus, we copy *other people's* designs. You can't differentiate for more than a month."

"Sure," Grant said, "but we want to set the terms. When they copy us, we'll change. And when they copy us again, we'll change again. And in that dynamic, where they're mimicking us, we'll be in control of each change. And therefore in control of the market."

Jeffrey smiled as if Grant had delivered an amusing but predictable punch line, while Lynn looked again at the pieces of paper Grant had given her. "Well, we're obviously interested in what you've shown us here," she said, "and you're right that I find it a bit extreme. But you're also right that it doesn't look like Wal-Mart."

"And so this aesthetic differentiation that you're after," Jeffrey said, "you feel it can be delivered in something like this?"

He held up one of the drawings Grant had given them, and I was finally able to see what we were talking about: it was a mechanical drawing, complete with exact dimensions and material specifications, of a spatula. "Yes," Grant said. "If I design it."

After the meeting, Grant and I went to dinner. We were seated at the restaurant's bar and having our first drink, in fact, before I even realized that the light coming up from beneath the glass sections of the floor not only illuminated the entryway and bar, but also an entire sub-floor environment in which immense koi and waving green plants rippled through water lit a white so blinding that it was almost heavenly. Surrounded by a crowd of incredibly attractive and mostly younger people, I mentioned being surprised by how friendly the young women were about apologizing when they reached past me to get a drink from the bartender. Grant laughed. "We're wearing suits in a city of unemployed actors and writers," he said. "They're wondering whether we might be studio executives." It wasn't until we were seated and had our dinners in front of us, though, that Grant mentioned he'd been meaning to ask me about Miranda's boyfriend, because Sandra had told him we were having problems with him. This surprised and angered me. Sandra had told me I had limited input on these decisions, but she apparently chatted about things with Grant between sets? "The situation isn't completely clear," I said. "Miranda's full of secrets and privacy these days."

"You know, every time I watch TV shows or movies, I feel like the relationships presented as normal are actually either completely preposterous or outright abusive," Grant said, looking around the restaurant as if the surrounding tables held the writers of the very shows he was referring to. "And I think a lot of young people's first relationships or even marriages are just attempts to copy the crap they've seen on television. And the problem is that when these relationships go wrong and people become unhappy or scared, that unhappiness and fear makes everything seem dramatic and adult and serious in a way they kind of like, but only because the people who make these shows present serious and mature adulthood as a state of fear or dread or unhappiness, in which people just hurt or cripple each other over and over again. And I guess I think that's mostly just a bunch of bullshit."

"You think that's what's happening with Miranda?"

"That kid she's hanging around with seemed like a liar, and also kind of crazy. I can't for the life of me figure out why she would give him the time of day, except for the fact that crazy lies told by an older guy might seem sophisticated to her. But you and I know that crazy lies are just crazy lies. It's the opposite of sophistication."

"Sandra says we shouldn't intervene. That we have to let this run its course."

"I'll be blunt with you. And I know I'm probably just riding this whole speechifying energy I started using in that meeting this afternoon, but what I'm going to say isn't something I've mentioned to Sandra, and I'd suggest you not mention it to her, either. I don't want to see Miranda get hurt. And it seems to me that the fact that you and Sandra are her parents is the very thing that's preventing you from protecting her right now."

"What do you mean?"

His elbows were on the table, his chin propped on his fists—just as he had done during the meeting earlier—and he spoke to me as if I were the only other person in the restaurant. "I understand you're trying to treat her with respect, and you're hoping she'll make some of her own decisions and learn something from her relationship with this kid—I get that whole line of approach. But I have to tell you that I think what you're really doing is asking her at age sixteen to understand things about life that a sixteen-year-old can't understand, and you're not keeping in mind that kids are perfectly capable of hurting each other very badly, in very real ways. Because that Ira guy isn't a kid. And I know you know what I mean, because I could tell how tense you got when he was talking to us at that party in your yard the other day."

"It's just that it's all new territory for me," I said. "I've never had a teenage daughter before. I don't know how much freedom she's supposed to have."

"But why should it be new territory? If you've defended your daughter from dangerous situations before, why stop now? In this very city, right now, kids are hurting or killing other kids. And I'm not suggesting this Ira kid is a murderer, but neither do I see why you and Sandra shouldn't take steps to keep him away from your daughter."

"It just doesn't seem like he's done anything wrong. It's hard to sell the idea of doing something about it when there hasn't been something to do something about."

"Why do you need to sell the idea? If you and Sandra disagree and are going to argue about it anyway, why not just do what you want to do, so that you're arguing about the way *you* handled it, instead of complaining about the way *she's* handling it? I think you're asking for permission to do something you don't need permission to do. And he's not going to do anything wrong in front of you, you know. He uses that bizarre fake courtesy in front of adults. It sounds like you're waiting for an event that will give you an excuse to do something, but I'm saying that you should act now, before that event occurs. You don't want that event to happen at all."

"Of course I don't want anything bad to happen. It's just tough to see how to get there."

He shrugged, as if what I was saying was difficult was actually perfectly simple. "Look, if things go like I hope they'll go, I'll be opening a small office in Los Angeles. Not much will happen there, but I'll need an assistant, and a job in Los Angeles, largely unsupervised, would be a pretty hard thing for a kid to turn down. And even a super-low, entry-level salary would probably seem like a fortune to this Ira kid."

Confused by the rapidity with which Grant was moving between scenarios, the last sentence seemed a non sequitur. When I realized the connection Grant was suggesting, though, I laughed. "Moving Ira to Los Angeles is an attractive idea, but I don't think it's the kind of thing people actually do."

"Of course it's the kind of thing people actually do," he said. "In the business world, if someone isn't working out in one place, they find themselves either out of a job, or transferred somewhere else. And I don't see why you wouldn't protect your daughter with at least as much care as a business shows its employees. And though a kid Ira's age might not follow money directly yet, he'll follow sex, and selling him on the idea that money plus Los Angeles will equal starlets taking their clothes off for him can be done very easily."

I felt as if I were being given the hard sell on a product I knew almost nothing about. "It's too much money," I said. "Not to mention that it feels like playing God with the kid's life."

"He wants to play God with Miranda's life. I can assure you of that. You can see it in his eyes. And I know all this might sound extreme, but I'm telling you, there are a hundred thousand young men exactly like Ira in Southern California, and it's very normal for them to prowl around and attack each other and live out their generally fucked-up lives with great satisfaction and brutality. I'm more familiar with it than I'd like to admit, and the fact that it's not normal in your family, and that this kind of fucked-up stuff doesn't exist in your life, is why your family is important to me.

So sleep on it, but let's decide soon. Because I think we need to act quickly."

When we returned to the hotel after dinner, Grant thanked me for my help, and then apologized for being too tired to show me any more of the city. "I think I'm not only tired, but I'm even tired of myself at this point. I'm tired of hearing my own voice," he said. So I returned to my room, took off my shoes and, sitting on the edge of the bed, turned on the television. Neither Sandra nor Miranda had called, and I couldn't help but think, as I moved through the channels without finding a single interesting program, that they were each probably happy to be rid of me for a day. Casting the television remote aside, I stood and went to the window. The traffic below, the chattering television behind me, the contents of my suitcase open on the bed: these all seemed items to be considered idly, from a remove. It was still early, and I still had my suit on, but I had nowhere to go and nothing to do, and the question of how to get through life—how to kill all that time, really—seemed pressing. I stretched out on the bed and searched the texture of the ceiling for recognizable images, until what seemed only a few minutes later, when I was startled by the ringing phone, and discovered that I was wrapped in the bed's comforter, though still in my suit, and that sunlight was coming through the window. It was morning, and Grant was calling to make sure I was up, because our flight home was an early one. I told him I would be ready shortly, and as I washed my face, brushed my teeth, and straightened the suitcase I had brought but had hardly touched, I tried to figure out how I'd slept through the night in my suit and shoes. I hadn't the slightest idea what time we had returned to the hotel, though, so it was impossible for me to know if I'd been asleep a long time or hardly at all.

It was after our flight back, upon climbing the porch steps, that I discovered the front door of our home had been damaged. Stupefied by the injury, I knelt to examine the point where the bottom corner of the door should have met the jamb. The splintered wood that remained testified to some kind of blast, and the resulting hole was large enough for any small animal to wriggle through. The door was locked, at least, though after I turned my key, I had to use my shoulder to pop the thing out of the jamb, and then had to do the same from the inside to press it closed.

I found Sandra in the kitchen, working at a counter covered in slices of bread, tomatoes, cucumbers, cream cheese, and various lunch meats. A huge platter sat nearby, half filled with sandwiches. "You're not at work today?" I said.

"It's my turn to provide lunch for the staff meeting, but I forgot," she said, too busy spreading cream cheese to even look at me.

"Why is the door broken?"

"Ask your daughter."

"Just tell me."

She shrugged as if the whole thing were mystifying. "She says her boyfriend broke it."

"How?"

"I don't know. I wasn't here."

"But what did she say, Sandra?"

"She said he kicked it."

"He kicked our door hard enough to break it?"

"I really have to get this done," she said, slicing a sandwich into triangles. The providing of the staff meeting meal was obviously a competition Sandra did not want to lose. Stray locks of hair had come loose from her headband and hung in her face. Her forehead shone with perspiration as she focused on stacking the sandwiches just so. There was a quickness to her in those days, a confident flutter of fingers and a surety of movements, especially in the house. The making of little sandwiches or salads or snacks, the selection of a picture frame and the photo that went in it, the placement of pillows on a couch or the angle of an armchair: she knew these tasks and made sound choices without thinking. When she pulled her hair back into a ponytail, she could spin her energy and bounce into a youthful vivacity that still carried something of the ingénue about it. Tennis, yard work, and the hustle of professional and social life had been good to her. She was in excellent shape, and I'm sure there were male developers or vendors or customers she worked with who were quite taken with the way she looked in a pair of slacks and the serious-business glasses she often wore at work, though the prescription was weak enough that her optometrist, who didn't want to be seen as a pusher of lenses, had mentioned more than once that her use of them was entirely optional. And yet the idea that I would reach out and touch her myself had somehow come to seem an impropriety. It was like we were children again, really, and there were lines one did not cross. When she had placed the sandwiches on her platter and arranged them to her satisfaction, she paused to look at me. "So how was Los Angeles? Did Grant's meeting go well?"

"It went fine. Grant has interesting ideas."

"Good for him," she said, and returned to stacking the sandwiches at breakneck speed.

"Yes. Good for him."

I returned to the front door. Stepping back through it and onto the porch, I closed it as well as I could, so that I could study it again. The ability to see the wood of our entryway floor from outside seemed vaguely obscene. And though I knew it was paranoid, I couldn't help but feel as if the hole would somehow, through the simple fact of its existence, elicit the appearance of a person deranged enough to attempt to use it.

Neither Sandra nor Miranda knew how to fix a door, of course. That was a problem I knew I would have to deal with myself.

I WAS NO MORE than twenty steps out the door of Gina's gallery when my phone rang. The display indicated it was Catherine's line at the bank, so I took the call, but it wasn't Catherine. It was "John with security," as he called himself, and he was calling to tell me that he and Annie were still in the branch, and could I come back by for a few minutes to look at a couple things?

"I don't have time right now, John, but I'm happy to talk on the phone."

Two college-aged guys loped past on the sidewalk, their faces sunburned, their movements loose. Laughing, they were so filled with exuberance that they were almost shouting their conversation, though they were right next to one another. They went past as if I wasn't even there.

"It will only take a few minutes," John said. "But it's really something that needs to be done in person."

"What are you talking about?" I said. "What is this thing that can only be done in person?"

"There are some more photos we'd like you to look at."

"I've looked at the photos two times now, John. Nothing new is going to come of looking at photos."

"These are different photos."

"Of what?"

A breathy emptiness occupied his end of the line. I sensed the conversation wasn't going the way he wanted it to, and that he was now casting about for a way to move it back in the direction he wanted. "They're of a different robbery. A robbery of you, from twenty-five years ago. There was a note about it in your employee file, so I had someone look up the old incident report and e-mail the frames we have from the security camera that day. And I think the guy who robbed you today might be the same guy that robbed you back then."

"He didn't rob me. He robbed Amber."

"I meant your branch."

"And why do you think this?"

"The guy in the old security photos has the same build. But most importantly, the faces look really similar. And there's the fact that this is the same city. And you're the same you."

"Twenty-five years apart, and the photos look the same? That doesn't seem right."

"I can show you. That's why I want you to come in and take a look at them. It won't take long."

I could hear music in the distance—a ragged, distorted bass line. There were still other people coming and going, on both sides of the street. They seemed happy. What were they doing, I wondered.

"I'm sorry, John, but I can't. As I've told you, this is a busy day for me, and I'm headed to an errand I can't skip. I have about one more minute right now, but after that I won't be able to talk to you any more today."

"I'm just talking about ten, fifteen minutes, tops. If you're already out and taking care of things, this would just be one more very short errand."

"I understand that you have information that excites you, and that proving this is the same man who robbed me twenty-five years ago seems like a breakthrough of some kind. That's all clear to me, and it sounds very interesting. But another thing that is clear to me is that I don't have time to talk to you about this today."

"But if you were delayed in one of your errands for ten or fifteen minutes longer than you thought it would take, you would have time for that."

"Of course."

"So then you do have ten or fifteen minutes in your schedule."

"For something related to my daughter, on her wedding day. Not for you."

"I feel like you're being difficult on purpose. To be honest, I feel like you're avoiding talking about this for some other reason—something that has nothing to do with your schedule."

I probably should have been angry at John, but for some reason, I was merely amused. "Those are very interesting feelings," I said. "It sounds like you're a person who feels a great many things. But I'm not going to talk to you again today."

"I'm trying to make things easier on you," he said. "Spending a few minutes looking at these photos today could be a whole lot easier than other ways of doing it."

"And I'm trying to be honest with you. I'm not going to talk to you today. And I'm almost out of time for this very conversation."

"I think you have more time than you're pretending."

"Do you want to know what I'm doing, John?"

"What do you mean? What are you doing?"

"I'm using something called authoritative listening, and here's how it works: I have decided that I do not have time to talk to you today. And yet I know that you are going to try various ways of arguing with me about that. You will plead, threaten, bargain, cajole, use guilt or shame, any number of things. And what I have already decided to do, when you argue with me, is, first, to acknowledge that I understand what you're telling me, and second, to reiterate that your argument in no way changes my position. Here's an example. You've said you think I have more free time than I've claimed. So what I will say is this: I realize that you can't know where I am or what I'm doing, and that you feel that maybe I'm not being honest about my schedule. That must be very difficult for you. It sounds like you have a very difficult job today. Unfortunately, my own schedule today is such that I don't have time to talk to you. And I won't be coming by."

"You're not really being cooperative. Can we at least agree on that? That you're not cooperating with me?"

He sounded as if he were reading off of a sheet of paper that said something about what bank security is allowed to do when an employee is being uncooperative, so I had no choice but to be uncooperative about being uncooperative. "No," I said, "I don't think we can agree on that. I feel like I am cooperating with you. I've visited with you already once today, and I'm talking to you now. I understand what you've said to me, and I've answered your questions. Unfortunately, my schedule today is such that I don't have time to talk to you, so I won't be coming by."

"Could we step out of the authoritarian listening thing or whatever? Could you stop doing that for a second and just talk to me? Man to man?"

"I am talking to you man to man, John. I'm being very honest with you."

"Okay, so I'm going to be honest with *you*, and tell you that I really don't want to escalate this investigation, and if you can just come in and look at these photos and answer some questions, then I don't think I'll have to. But the fact of the matter is that you don't appear to have any savings, you've maxed out a home equity loan, and it looks like you're living month-to-month right now. I'm sorry to be speaking so directly about this stuff, but that's what it looks like."

"Apology not accepted," I said. "You're being incredibly presumptuous. You're looking into my personal finances because you have the power to, but not because it's right. You're a snoop. You're a Peeping Tom."

"This is my job," he said. "I have to investigate these things. On the one hand I see the state of your personal finances, and on the other I see your branch get robbed by someone who robbed you before, but who never got caught. You have to appreciate how many red flags that raises for me."

"Red flags?" I said, almost sputtering at the ridiculousness of the expression. I, probably one of the least extravagant, most risk-averse people in the entire city, if not the whole region, was in this kid's analysis *raising red flags*? "Can you not see how ridiculous that seems to me? We are only talking to each other on the phone right now because of a coincidence. The same person who robbed that branch I worked at a lifetime ago robbed the branch I work at today. They aren't the same branch. And I wasn't actually there this morning. But you've used this as an excuse to pry into the details of my personal financial life, which is completely irrelevant to the fact that my branch was robbed this morning. It's an incredible and reckless invasion of my privacy, but you've done it anyway, and now that you have access to all of my personal information, you're desperate for it to somehow reveal only the things you already wanted to see. But your little red flags are not actually there,

John. You really think that because I have a home equity loan, I should be under suspicion for some kind of paltry bank robbery designed to net all of something like five thousand dollars? This is your theory?"

"But that's why I'd like you to come in and look at these photos and chat for a few minutes—so I can rule this out and reassure the company that this isn't something we need to investigate further. So I can reassure them exactly what you're saying, which is that this is just a coincidence."

"But what you don't to understand, John—and maybe this is what's really setting you off—is how deeply I don't care about reassuring you. I didn't have anything to do with this, so if I don't talk to you today, and that causes the bank to launch some kind of paranoid-delusional full-scale investigation of me, the bank will still find nothing. The outcome is the same either way. But if I ignore you, I can go about my business today."

"But surely you understand that your response to this is something that will be in your employee file. I mean, this doesn't have anything to do with me or what I do for the company, but if you want to advance someday, the company is going to look at this incident in your file. And they're going to see that you didn't cooperate."

That made me laugh. The stupidity of this kid was actually making me happy. "You say 'the company' as if you're referring to the all-powerful Oz or something. I can assure you that there is no 'the company.' There are people you work for, and people who work for you. That's it. You've looked at my file. You know I've worked for this company for twenty-five years. I've never done anything wrong, and I even got robbed and hit on the head once, and took stitches on my scalp for it. And here's where my relationship with the company is: after all of these years of working for them, they've sent a boy to snoop through my finances and harass me on my daughter's wedding day. That's the quality of the relationship I have with the company."

"But don't you think your attitude has something to do with that? If you've spoken to other people the way you've spoken to me, you can't exactly blame the company for not being your best friend."

"Today is the first day I've spoken this way, John. This is it. This is me getting fucking fed up. So tell 'the company,' or write in my file, or put down wherever you put things down, that I don't care that this guy robbed me twenty-five years ago, and I don't care that the bank lost some money in a robbery today. It's not my money, and no one was hurt, so I'm over it. I am moving on."

"But I can't do that," he said. "I have a job to do. There are procedures I have to move through."

"And I will be happy to talk to you about all of it on Monday. But this is Saturday. I took today off. So I won't be coming by."

He didn't immediately respond. What was he doing? Consulting a manual? Squeezing a stress ball? Cruising through my personal account transactions? "I just think your . . . *orientation* toward the situation is unfortunate," he said eventually. "I hope you understand I've done everything I can to make this convenient for you."

"Now you're speaking like a banker."

"I'm going to let you think about this for a bit," he said, unfazed. "And then I'm going to call you back. I want you to think this over, and then I'll give you one last opportunity to come in and talk."

"Sounds real good," I said in my professionally cheerful manager voice. "Good-bye, John. I have to be going."

"I think you should really—"

I hung up on him. It was mid-afternoon, and I was standing on the sidewalk on a day whose temperature, at that point, had to have been close to triple digits. But I felt good.

A group of young women—laughing, chattering, their arms playfully linked—came down the sidewalk then. "Excuse me," I said as they passed, "but what's the big event everyone's headed toward down here today?"

"Brewfest!" two of the three sang enthusiastically.

"You should go!" the third said over her shoulder as they continued down the sidewalk, never having broken stride. They laughed again, obviously already having taken advantage of the event. To be young and carefree, I thought—to be young and drunk and carefree and laughing. I crossed the street mid-block, in front of oncoming traffic, and drivers were forced to slow while I thought about John, and how strangely satisfying it had been to deny him. And if all the traffic was about nothing more than getting to cheap beer, I decided, then my business was more important than theirs.

THE MORNING AFTER I discovered Ira had broken the front door of our home, I noticed two suitcases stacked in the entryway when I came down for breakfast. Hunting around a bit, I found Sandra in the basement, feverishly ironing a blouse, and when I asked about the suitcases and she told me she wouldn't be coming home from work, for a split second—there in the dim, unfinished basement, beneath the glare of a naked bulb only inches overhead—I thought she was telling me she was leaving me. And I felt an inward part of myself begin to nod, as if to say: *Yes, of course.* But then she added that her "rackets were already in the car," and I realized that she was just talking about her big tennis tournament. Which I had completely forgotten about.

I made some polite inquiries about when her first match was and how she was feeling about it, and then returned upstairs to my office, the better to watch my spider friend continue to filigree his elaborate construction in my window—the work he had done that first night, which had seemed complicated enough at the time, had turned out to be mere scaffolding upon which he had now latticed any number of fiendish little fascinations. So Sandra ironed in the basement rather than in our bedroom, and I ate breakfast in my office rather than at the dining table. It's painfully amusing to think of how carefully we arranged our schedules in order to minimize the possibility of having to speak to one another. I felt she found me annoying, and I was annoyed by her annoyance. She would later claim she felt I found her boring, and that she was just tired of being around someone so bored by her. So we were both right, really: she *was* annoyed with me. And I *was* bored by what I felt was her constant annoyance. We had, at some point, turned each other into walking, talking confirmations of our gloomiest suspicions.

And we were in that state when Sandra stepped into my office that morning to announce that she was leaving. The blouse she had been ironing was the very one she was now wearing. She looked crisp, clean, and confident. "And do you think you can talk to this kid?" she said.

"Which kid?"

"Ira."

"No. Because I told him not to date her in the first place, but then he was allowed to. So now he's not going to respect anything I say."

She looked hard at me—she already had her tournament game face on, it seemed. "I'm aware that you and I disagree on things. But now is not the time for you to sit around sulking, and blaming things on me because I said something that upset you. The person you're punishing by acting this way is your own daughter, and it's selfish and stupid."

"Can I tell you something?" I said.

"Yes."

"Are you listening?"

"Yes."

"But are you listening for real?"

"Say what you want to say," she said angrily—exactly the state I had been hoping to produce in her.

"You do not understand what it's like to be an insecure and angry young man."

"I know that."

"No, you don't. You've acted like you understand exactly what's going on here and how to handle it, but you don't. You've told me I don't understand what it's like to be a teenage girl, so now I'm telling you that you don't know what it's like to be that boy. And what you need to understand is that that boy will not be spoken to."

"You can't talk to him at all?"

"He won't be spoken to. He will pretend to listen, and he will nod, and then he will ignore everything that was said. So I don't even intend to try. And just so we're clear, I'm not sulking. I'm angry at you."

"And you're throwing a big tantrum."

"Right. Because no matter what I do, you characterize it as immature. When I tried to keep Miranda out of the relationship, I was being stupid. And now that I'm refusing to try and help you get her out of the relationship, I'm again being stupid. Either way, it doesn't matter, I'm being stupid."

"You are obsessed with being right!" she said. "And you think that the only way you can be right is if I'm wrong. It's incredibly frustrating to try and talk to you when you're this way. I feel like you're still nine years old and following the rules your mom gave you for when she was gone in the evening, like as long as you don't answer the door and don't speak to anyone, you're allowed to watch as much television as you want, and you'll be praised for it."

I laughed. I felt I had finally decoded her, and everything was clear. "Again, you're saying I'm immature," I said. "This is your stock response, and psychologizing my childhood, which you weren't there for and know nothing about, is just a variation of the same thing. I'll be going to work today, then I'll come home and measure that doorway, and I'll go out tomorrow and buy a new door. I'll bring it home and spend my weekend working on fixing the whole thing, while also keeping an eye on our daughter. What a child I am, right? How immature. You have a good time at your little tournament."

The issue of whether my rhetorical analysis was correct or not seems hardly important now—or less important, at least, than recalling when and why I began to think Sandra was a code I needed to break in the first place. But of course that was the shift that had been occurring so slowly and consistently that it had acquired the feel of seismic inevitability. Continents shift because they ride on plates. Why do the plates shift? I don't know. I have never known.

Sandra's response was simply to leave the room. I stayed there, listening to her take her bags out to her car, and then return for a few more things, and take those to the car. I listened to her walk upstairs, and heard the muffled tones of her saying good-bye to Miranda, who was still asleep. When I heard her come back downstairs, I thought she might come back into the office one more time, so I sat there, staring at the empty web, and wondering where the spider went when he wasn't there. But then I heard the front door rattle shut, followed by the sound of Sandra's car starting. She hadn't come back to say anything more to me. She just left.

So when I pulled into the bank's parking lot less than an hour later, I was glad to find Grant already there, waiting. It was still early, and the streets were empty, but the sun was already high and bright, which is, I assume, why Grant was wearing sunglasses in addition to his jeans and black T-shirt, though the sunglasses made me feel a bit paranoid. I didn't even have a chance to say good morning and ease into the discussion, before he said, "So you want to go ahead with it."

"How do you know?" I said.

"It's the only reason you would ask me to meet you in person."

"Okay, so I'm not subtle. How long do you think it would take?"

"To get him out of town? Not long. I already met with him last week, for an interview." On seeing my surprise, he laughed. "I was going to do it even if you weren't okay with it," he said.

"I thought it depended on whether you got that job."

"I got it. They called me yesterday. I'll do most of the line I proposed, but not the blender. They won't let me do the blender, for some reason."

"Congratulations, then."

"Thanks. And so I can hire the kid and have him down there

almost immediately. I'll send him for a weekend to scout things out, then extend the trip so he can set up the office down there for me, and then I'll offer to ship all his stuff down and get him set up in an apartment, and that'll be it."

A long-legged dog—thin, ragged, and panting—loped past alone, without casting us so much as a glance. Part of me expected a police car to roll up, and an officer to step out and ask us what we thought we were doing. "How much money do you need?" I asked.

"None," he said. "I'm hiring the kid, and he's going to work for me. That's all there is to it."

"But it's going to cost you a lot."

"It's one flight and a few nights in a hotel. That's nothing, and I can write it off. I'm telling you, the kid is going to do actual work, and a lot of it."

"Do you even trust him to do actual work?"

"Not really. And especially not when I'm not there watching him. But whatever he doesn't do, or whatever he does wrong, or steals, or lies about, it will give me the reasons I need to let him go six months from now. And really, he'll probably quit on his own before we even get that far. A lot of people exactly like this kid move to Los Angeles and within a few weeks decide that they're actually an actor or a director. And I'll be happy to encourage him in that."

I couldn't think of anything else to ask. It seemed Grant was right—everything was taken care of. "Is this what you meant when you told me I shouldn't ask for permission?" I said. "That I should do what I want, and argue with people about it after it's already done?"

He laughed. "I suppose. Are you angry at me?"

"No. And at least you pretended to ask me about it. That's something."

"A show of respect," he said.

He drove out of the lot just as Catherine pulled in—they traded a wave through windshields, I think. And after Catherine parked and joined me at the front door while I unlocked it, she said, "So you're doing business in the parking lot now?"

"Only for friends."

"The manager meets you in the lot," she said, eyebrows raised. "It's even better than the drive-through."

I RECALL A SENSE of calm settling over me—a serenity that colored that entire weekend that Sandra was away. Miranda and I ordered pizza Friday night. She didn't mention Ira, I didn't mention the broken door, and the two of us ate while happily making fun of an entertainment gossip show on television. Miranda didn't mention going out, and fearful of breaking the spell, I didn't ask. After dinner, she disappeared up into her room. She was lying low, it seemed. Was she hiding from Ira, though, or was her sudden presence an effort to appease me? Two birds with one stone, I decided, which was fine with me. He had scared her, and she had probably scared herself a little, and if she was going to use the need to mollify me as the motivation to remain safe at home for a few evenings, well—go on mollifying, I thought.

Later in the evening, I climbed the stairs and knocked on her door. There was a bit of shuffling before she told me to come in, and I found her on her bed, a book in her hands and multiple sheaves of notebook paper spread around her. She was apparently so absorbed in her book, in fact, that when I told her the two of us would have to fix the front door in the morning, she didn't even raise her eyes from the page as she mumbled that that sounded fine. The mood of lighthearted laughter we had enjoyed while watching television earlier had disappeared, it seemed. And when I asked her, for the first time, what had actually happened to the door, she just shrugged, her eyes still on the book. "It was just an accident," she said. "I'll pay for it."

"I don't care who pays for it," I said. "I just want to know what happened."

"He broke it accidentally. He said to tell you he's sorry, and he'll help pay for it, too." With a dramatic excess of wrist, she flipped a page.

"Could you put the book down and talk to me? I want to know what's going on."

She carefully closed the book, a torn paper bookmark in place, and adjusted the wrap on her palm. "Nothing's going on."

"A front door doesn't get broken on accident."

She rolled onto her back and sighed, contemplating the ceiling. "We were having an argument."

"About what?"

"Stuff."

"And where was your mother?"

"At a movie. With Margo Talbot."

"So you were here by yourself while this guy was breaking down the door?"

She finally looked me in the eye then, and with a complete and utter lack of intonation said: "Yes."

Was she hoping I would investigate? That I would keep asking questions, so that she could reluctantly give up the information that some code was preventing her from giving voluntarily? "You don't have to tell me what you were arguing about," I said. "But I can't fix the door unless I know how it was broken."

"He kicked it. I was mad at him and I wanted him to leave, so I pushed him out the door and locked it."

"And he kicked the door hard enough to break it?"

"Yes. He got upset and kicked a door. That's all that happened. And he didn't think it was going to break, and he's sorry."

There was no way he could have kicked it only once. It had to have been a sustained attack. But Miranda continued to offer me a look of opaque blankness that matched her tone of voice.

"Were you scared?"

"I was angry. But it's normal for people to argue."

"Why do you like this guy? You don't seem to have a good time with him."

"He's a good person. He's just had a hard time in life."

"It's not your job to help people."

"It was an accident, Dad." She returned to reading—or pretending to read—as if the conversation were over.

"Tomorrow," I said.

"Tomorrow what?"

"We fix the door."

"Okay." She turned another page in her book, though she couldn't possibly have read that much while we'd been talking.

"I want to show you how to do it."

"What do you mean?" she said, looking up.

"I want to show you how to fix the door. How to use the tools. You need to learn how to do it."

"How to fix a door?"

"You're old enough now. You need to understand how to do some simple things."

She looked at me as if I were speaking in a foreign language. "Okay," she said.

I thought: She's safe here, in her room, with her books and notebooks, and her clothes draped and stacked in various spots, with her little stereo and clock radio and posters of Paris and Rome. She is okay here. "What are you reading?" I asked.

She actually turned the book over to check the cover. "*Crime and Punishment*," she said. "Did you have to read it when you were in school?"

"I don't remember. Would I like it?"

She chuckled in the little amused way I understood was at my expense, though maybe not maliciously. "I don't think so."

After breakfast Saturday morning, we headed to the hardware store, where the jingle of the entry bell followed by the aroma of solvents and cleansers announced the commencement of the spell that never failed to work its power on me. The aluminum bins of carefully sorted nails and nuts and bolts and staples, the waxed aisles of tools, the rows of pipes and wires and buckets and rags, the cans of paint and their attendant brushes, the sandpapers and push brooms and saw blades, and the yard out back, where the scent of freshly hewn lumber filled the air: there was no problem here that couldn't be solved. Miranda and I walked past shelves filled with loose windows of all shapes and sizes, and then turned into an aisle where a seemingly endless queue of front doors hung along a wall, so that not one of the doors opened onto anything but the next door. "They're like dominoes," Miranda said happily. "If we swing the first one hard enough, it will open all the others." When she reached for the first door, though, I quickly put my hand on her arm and said, "Don't try." She laughed. And after choosing a door similar to the damaged one we already had, we headed home to make our repairs.

The afternoon was hot and nearly silent. My red aluminum toolbox lay open on the porch, tools scattered about, while I led the project and Miranda made notations in pencil on a small pad of paper: the height of the door, the width, the depth of the jamb, the placement of the hinges and strike plate. Our glasses of iced tea sweated on the porch railing, the ice cubes glinting in the sunlight. When I suggested you couldn't just break solid wood and I was surprised Ira's foot wasn't broken, Miranda reminded me there had already been a crack in the door large enough that you could see light through it during the day—Sandra had complained about it more than once, and that's where the door had split. "Well, this one will be able to take whatever Ira can dish out," I said.

Miranda shook her head—not angrily—and said, "You need to stop. Why do you hate him so much?"

Pretending not to understand why I disliked Ira could only have been an emotional affectation at that point, pretend bafflement at a reaction she actually understood perfectly well. But her thoughts on people and the world seemed entirely in play, as if she had decided not only to discard her childhood identity, but also to open up to inquiry every system of sane thinking and every scrap of common sense. Everything that had once been proven would now have to be proven again. "You're my daughter," I said. "So if you're going to have a boyfriend, I want it to be someone nice. Not someone who smashes doors in a rage."

"Did Grandma Carrie act this way when you were a teenager? Was she this super-critical of everyone?"

"I'm not being super-critical. And Carrie didn't have to worry about who I was dating, because I didn't date anyone in high school."

"Why do you call her Carrie? Didn't you ever call her Mom?"

"Not really. Maybe once in a while, as a joke. Most of the time we just called each other by our names."

"And you didn't date anyone at all? Ever?"

"There were only about fifty people in my whole graduating class, Miranda." Miranda knew my mother had been seventeen and unmarried when she had me, and that my father, only eighteen himself at the time, never lived with us. In her youth, Miranda had asked me more than once to describe the two-bedroom apartment Carrie and I lived in across the street from the bowling alley—she referred to it as if it were one of the wonders of the ancient world. I did my best not to use the modest means of my own childhood as something to hold over Miranda, and I suspect she avoided asking much about it for the same reason: when she was making a demand, there was no way her own situation could look anything but fine in comparison to the years in which my mother would slip over from the bowling alley on her evening break, make me dinner, and then walk back across the street to finish her shift. I was allowed—encouraged, in fact—to watch television until I fell asleep on the couch, and I still have fond memories of the little independent station that showed, in my memory, almost nothing but *Star Trek* episodes and sci-fi films from the 1950s. My favorite of these was *Forbidden Planet*, not just because of the film's otherworldly soundtrack, but also because it was about a single parent and child marooned on a distant planet. Over the course of my childhood I probably saw that movie twenty or thirty times on that station, identifying every time with the father—as if *I* were the parent, and Carrie my daughter. How I had flattered myself into believing that I, a boy watching television, was actually taking care my mother, who was working night after night in the run-down bowling alley to provide for us, is beyond me. But I sustained this belief throughout my childhood. It's hard to know if it was simply the relative economic poverty of my childhood that made Miranda bashful about her own demands, or if she also sensed the little self-flattering narrative I had invented for myself in that childhood, and felt sorry for me on that account, too. She didn't need to feel sorry for me at all, but I always sensed a shift in her demeanor when the subject of those years came up.

"But still," she said, "I'm sure people went out. I didn't grow up there, but I know that even in small towns, people have boyfriends and girlfriends."

"I'm sorry, but I didn't," I said. "I worked at the bowling alley on the weekends when I was a teenager. And Carrie always knew where I was, because she was working there, too."

"I still think guys that work at bowling alleys can date, Dad. It's the perfect situation, really."

"Well. Maybe the boys in our class outnumbered the girls."

Miranda's attempts to retroactively bolster the self-esteem of my sixteen-year-old self were cute, but I could also sense—especially as she hesitated there in the conversation, as if picking her next move—that she was trying to make some kind of deeper point. "But don't you see that Ira isn't that different?" she said. "He's always had to work, too. And maybe he's not always good around people, but that's just because he hasn't had good role models."

Did I sigh aloud, or just inwardly? "He has to work because he's not in high school anymore, Miranda. And I'm sure his problems have a source, but he's not the only person in the world who has problems. And also, I don't see how you can already know him well enough to be coming to these conclusions about him."

"But if a lot of people in the world have problems, and if a lot of people need help, then why are you against him?"

As she stood there waiting for an answer, a pencil behind her ear and a hammer hanging idly from her bandaged hand, I felt for the first time in a very long time that she was actually listening. She was studying me intently, as if alert to the possibility of unlocking some bit of new or important information not about Ira, but about me. It felt almost mathematical: Why was *I* against *him*? Why did *x* not equal *y*?

"Because not everyone breaks down doors," I said. "And I don't see how you can expect me to be okay with him when you won't even tell me what happened. I understand that a young man was so angry that he actually destroyed the front door of our home. I don't respect that kind of person."

She tapped the handle of the hammer thoughtfully against the side of the house. "He was just being jealous. It was stupid."

"What do you mean?"

"It's ridiculous."

"What is?"

"He said he knows I don't really like him, because he thinks I want a boyfriend who's rich. He said I probably want a rich, fancy person like Grant." Her eyes darted quickly toward and away from mine before she laughed, and resumed tapping the siding.

"Did you tell him Grant is your father's age?"

"He said it doesn't matter. He said you and Grant don't like him because he's not from a rich family."

"You're not from a rich family, either. And I still don't understand how this turns into smashing the door."

"He was saying stupid things, so I told him to leave. And then he said that proved he was right."

"What kind of stupid things?"

"He was just trying to shock me. It doesn't matter. He just needs to learn to trust people."

She was so invested in this idea that people could be good on the inside, regardless of their actual behavior, that I could see direct argument would get me nowhere. It was a marvelous consolation to know that the situation was already on its way to being resolved. "Hand me the drill," I said.

Her eyes actually widened in alarm. "Why?"

"Because I need to put this hinge on."

"Right!" she said, and jumped to retrieve it.

We didn't get that door in until almost eleven o'clock that night. It took that long primarily because I slowed the pace of the project to make sure Miranda would have to be at my side for the entirety of the evening. When we were done, I opened the new door a few inches and then closed it, listening to the crisp sound of the latch. Miranda asked if she could try, and when I moved aside, she opened the door wide, shifted her grip, and then swung it with enthusiasm. It slammed shut with a clean, two-note strike: latch against plate, door against jamb. "Good work," she said, nodding with satisfaction.

"I hope so," I said.

THE SECOND TIME I entered campus on Miranda's wedding day, it was from the side opposite where I had earlier in the day. I passed a row of squat, utilitarian buildings that in previous years I had considered little more than glorified tin sheds, but on the day of the wedding, I was struck by how clean and solid the places now seemed to me. Armed with the knowledge that somewhere within each structure's dim, oil-stained concrete interior lay a glassy little office, fluorescently aglow Monday through Friday, I felt a wave of gratitude for the invisible number of hands that had indeed cleared the Quad that day, that had mowed its grass and silenced its sprinklers and completed the other unseen tasks that, together, created the sufficient conditions for my daughter's wedding. I knew—had been warned repeatedly, in fact—that the buildings were empty and locked that day, and should there be a problem, there would be no one to appeal to. But that was fine, I thought. It was as it should be.

When I turned into the Quad, I saw Catherine and a man I assumed was our photographer standing beneath the trees. Earlier in the day I had felt uneasy about accepting her help, but I also found her presence comforting. I suppose I felt uneasy *because* I felt her presence comforting, and I knew well that comforts could not be relied on. And yet there she was, a protective spirit watching over the careful rows of plastic chairs that lent the area the charged aura that precedes any piece of theater. *If she wants to help, she wants to help*, I told myself, and with a tautology no more complicated than that, I sailed forward. The grass was still slick and wet from the rain, and I could see, even from the edge of the Quad, that the chairs were beaded with water, too. We were scheduled to take the wedding photos there at four o'clock, only half an hour away, and my solitary march across the grass felt like a formal movement, the true beginning of things. The silence with which Catherine and the photographer watched me only added to the sense of ceremony, and I was glad to reach them there beneath the trees and, by speaking, to break the spell.

The photographer, a short fellow with dark eyes whom I hadn't had occasion to meet before, introduced himself as Kurt. The anxiousness with which he raked his fingers through the sand-colored hair that fell perfectly across his forehead, and the enthusiasm he showed for his spearmint chewing gum (its odor fully detectable and identifiable from ten paces) reminded me of any number of male customers in early middle age I had helped over the years, men whose financial lives were in tatters due to bad divorce settlements or amateur investment strategies, and who tended as a result to focus their attention almost exclusively on matters of health and personal appearance: they drank bottled water and chased it with breath mints, gelled their hair rigidly in place, and shaved so closely and with the use of such bracing aftershaves that the tight skin of their ruddy cheeks shone with an unhealthy plasticity. Radically uncertain of where they stood with the fairer sex, these men often ended up worshipping at the feet of Catherine. Her dual backgrounds in finance and femininity placed her in a position to take them by the hand, it seemed. And something about the way Catherine was standing under the trees there in the Quad—she was a bit farther from Kurt than seemed necessary, and wasn't looking at him—made me wonder if perhaps the opening exchange of some transaction had already occurred between them. But Kurt seemed perfectly at ease. He shook my hand with great earnestness, leaning forward as if he had reached the end of a diving board and was prepared to jump, and then punctuated his words with staccato chomps of his gum and with what struck me as an excess of eye contact as he assured me his equipment was in his van, and if I let him know what I might like as the background, he would begin setting up. "The buildings here are great," he said, "and I've done a lot of weddings where we take pictures in front of them, or on the steps or by the columns, but the trees are great, too, of course, so we could use those just as easily. It's all up to you."

"Why do you still have your suit on?" Catherine asked. "Shouldn't you be in your tuxedo?"

"I've been busy," I said.

"It's fine," Kurt said. "You have plenty of time."

"We had a plan for inclement weather, didn't we?" I said. "We would take the photos after the ceremony?"

"Sure. It looks like it's going to be clear, though, doesn't it?" He looked up into the trees, though from where we were standing, their canopy blocked any view of the sky.

"It's not the weather," I said. "We've had a change of plans. The bride has decided she doesn't want to be seen before the ceremony."

Kurt nodded not only with his head, but with his shoulders, too. He followed a band around the country for a while when he was younger, I thought—it was that kind of nodding. "That's cool," he said. "Like you said, we can do them after. It'll work fine."

"Good. I was hoping that would be true."

"Did you find that person you were looking for?" Catherine asked.

"Someone flake on you?" Kurt said. "Not the groom, I hope!"

For his benefit, I smiled. It wasn't necessary for him to be there any longer, and I didn't want to discuss Miranda's disappearance in his presence. Some irrational part of me probably feared he would set about shooting photos of me standing there without her, and that the images would appear in the city newspaper, fronting some inside section devoted to tales of local trouble. "Just a minor detail," I said.

"But minor details aren't the father's job," he said jovially. "The dad's just supposed to be the money man."

I assured Kurt that I had never been anything other than a

money man, and hinted that if he were looking for cues on how to prepare for our new plan for the wedding photos, I would get back to him about that in just a little while. But he persisted in making what he clearly believed were helpful comments. He had a prediction for how long it would take him to set up after the ceremony, suggestions for how to quickly hustle the guests off to the reception so we would have the Quad to ourselves, and thoughts on how he would streamline the process, which, he told us in the lowered voice of a magician revealing one of his tricks, would involve him moving back and forth between two cameras. Eventually I was forced to tell him that it all sounded very good, I trusted him implicitly, was glad we were in his experienced hands—but could he please allow me a moment or two with Miss L'Esprit?

"Absolutely," he said. "So Cathy, I'll catch you at the reception, then?"

I almost laughed as Catherine admitted she would indeed be at the reception, news which sent Kurt marching happily across the grass, almost but not quite at a trot. I waited until he was safely out of earshot to say, "If you're Cathy now, we should probably change the nameplate on your desk."

"Catherine is fine," she said. "What have you heard from Miranda?"

"Nothing."

"And how did things go at the bank?"

"Fine. Though after I left, John called and asked if I would come back. He looked in my employee file and found out I was robbed once back when I was a teller, and he thinks that's something he should talk to me about."

"Why does he want to talk about that?"

"He wants a promotion, I think. He wants to be super-thorough and tough as nails. So when I told him one conversation was enough and I couldn't talk to him again today, he got upset and told me things would be easier if I came in to talk to him. I think we don't like each other."

"What did he mean by 'easier'?"

"I think he was just practicing making empty threats."

Catherine knew as well as I did, though, that in their company-sponsored zeal, bank security had been known to pester employees for months about the details of even standard robberies. "I imagine they'll be calling me again, too, then," she said doubtfully. "And now we can be sure that they're really combing through all of our personal accounts."

"Well, when they call you in, don't let them break you, Cathy."

She shot me a warning look. "Don't call me that."

"Sorry, Cathy."

We stepped from under the trees and headed across the Quad. Little crystalline globes of rain clung to the grass blades, and when I looked behind us, I could see that we were leaving dark, wet footprints in the grass.

"You've been looking for her?" she said.

"Yes."

"And no one has been able to help? No one knows where she is?"

"No. But I'm starting to think she's doing exactly what she wants to do today."

"What do you mean?"

I shrugged. "She knows where she is. And she knows my phone number. So wherever she is, it must be where she wants to be."

Catherine nodded, reserving comment. I watched as she pulled something from her pocket and dropped it into her purse. "What was that?" I said.

"Oh. You can have it," she said, pulling it back out and handing it to me.

It was Kurt's business card. I flipped it over and found a handwritten number on the back. "I believe they call these 'the digits,'" I said. "Is this his home number on the back?"

"I don't know."

"Did you give him yours?"

"No."

"He seems nice. He said he'll catch you at the reception."

"I hope not."

"You should have a good time at the reception. I don't want you continually acting as our family servant."

She looked at me with a frightening lack of expression. "I guess I didn't realize I was a servant."

"That's what I'm saying. I'm telling you you're free to enjoy the party."

"And you're seriously suggesting I hit on your photographer?"

"I'm just saying."

She had acquired the tightened jaw and deliberate gait of someone genuinely angry. "He's not my type."

We had reached her car by then and stood next to it in the street. Catherine had never, in the decade that I had known her, given me any clear impression of her personal life. She dated. I knew that. But how often, I did not know. And the gentlemen were not allowed to come by the bank, it seemed. I had tried to joke with her once about it a few years before, saying that if she were really serious about someone I assumed she would bring him by, and her response had been to immediately assure me that would never happen. "No one needs to visit me at work," she had said. "I had an issue once with a person who bothered me at work, and there's no reason for that to happen. It's off-limits." I pressed her for details, but she said it wasn't important, all that was important was that people respected her boundaries. So the next time I had an excuse to do so, I of course scoured her employee file for any reference to an incident. There was none. It was a mystery episode not in the books, so all I could know was that Catherine had boundaries, and that I was on one side of them, and her personal life was on the other. Which, I will admit, was exactly in line with how human resources suggested we manage our personal lives in the workplace, so I was hardly in a position to complain, or even to ask further questions. The manager is not to ask questions about the staff's private lives.

And yet. "But I have no idea what your type *is*," I said to her as we stood there by her car.

"It's not that guy," she said. "And there are other things to think about right now, anyway."

"You always say there are other things to think about."

She fixed me with another warning look, as if outraged by my behavior.

"What?" I said.

"Stop."

"Stop what?"

"Just stop. Not today."

"Not what today?"

She studied me, shaking her head. "I hate that I can never tell what you're aware that you're doing, and what you're not aware that you're doing."

"I don't know what you mean by that," I said.

But I knew what she meant.

IT WASN'T MORE THAN two or three days after Miranda and I fixed the front door that Catherine stepped into the doorway of my office and said, "You have a visitor." And then in walked Miranda, in the worn khaki shorts and wrinkled T-shirt she wore around the house in the mornings. Her eyes were red-rimmed and puffy, as if she'd been crying, but she seemed calm as she took a seat across the desk from me. "You're up early," I said.

Her lips twisted toward what might have been an attempt at a smile, but then she abandoned it. "Something happened," she said.

"What do you mean?"

"Grant didn't like Ira. He made fun of him. And Ira didn't like Grant, but now he thinks he's great."

"What are you talking about?"

"Ira just told me he wants me to fly down to Los Angeles with him. He's going there to do some kind of work for Grant. I told him there was no way you would let me go."

"Not remotely."

She went on to tell me that Ira had called and told her he was going to make some quick money doing some work for Grant, and might be gone for a few weeks. It was easy money, he said, just making copies and deliveries and buying furniture and supplies for an office, and buying things for an apartment Grant had rented there, too. "Which I don't understand," Miranda said, "because it sounds like he's doing something that's kind of a job, but more like just being a gofer. And why wouldn't Grant just have someone who lived there work for him?"

"I'm sure he wanted someone he knew," I said. "He has to be able to trust the person."

"But nobody trusts Ira. You said he had negative energy, and Grant made fun of him."

"And I still think that. But Grant makes his own decisions."

"Grant didn't talk to you about this? He didn't mention it to you?"

"Grant doesn't ask me how to run his business. And maybe he's doing it as a favor. It sounds like Ira's going to make some money. Are you upset about it?"

"All I was doing was dating someone. It doesn't need to be a big deal."

"I agree with you."

She slowly pushed her hair back from her face, a common-enough gesture. This time, though, it seemed an expression of sadness. "You used to take me everywhere," she said. "You used to answer every question."

"I still do."

"No. I think there are things you don't tell me now."

"And there are things you don't tell me. Should we really be telling each other everything?"

"I guess it depends on what you mean by everything."

"I could hear more, if you want. I'm a good listener."

She smiled—though again, it seemed sad. "I guess you know enough. Maybe another time."

I was about to suggest that there was no time like the present, but our conversation was interrupted by the sound of shouting from out in the lobby. Stepping quickly from my office, I saw that the source of the noise was two men wrestling on the tile floor near the teller stands. I recognized the one having the better part of the fight, since he was wearing the same camouflage pants he had worn each time I had seen him at Catherine's desk, patiently listening to her explain why he was overdrawn. But now he stood over the second man, twisting the man's arm and then, awkwardly and from an odd angle, kicking the man in the ribs. When the victim fell, curled in pain, the man in the camouflage pants leaned down and punched him in the face. It was not anything resembling a knockout blow—the victim had been rolling onto his side, and the man in camouflage seemed unable to figure out how best to punch someone from the angle he was at—but the victim of this barrage groaned, writhing in pain. His blue jeans were brown with dirt, and when he raised his face, which he was covering with his hand, one could see that the armpits of his worn white T-shirt were stained a healthy yellow. As he began slowly to crawl toward the bank's rear exit, his hand still over his face, I saw Catherine repeatedly pressing the alarm button beneath her desk. The man in camouflage said, "Where the fuck do you think you're going?" before he grabbed the man on the floor by his ragged blond hair and pulled his head back, revealing a face covered in blood, and then punched him again, this time solidly, high up on the cheek, near the outside of the man's eye. Again the man fell to the floor, emitting a wordless wail, and then dragged himself to his knees and resumed crawling—dragging himself, really—toward the door. Blood dripped from between the fingers of the hand over his face. When the man in camouflage moved toward him again, I heard myself yell, "Let him go!"

The man in camouflage spun and looked at me in outrage, his face flushed. "He was robbing the place! He had a knife!"

"Just let him go."

It took several seconds for the would-be robber to make his way to the glass doors at the back of the branch, and no one—none of the employees, none of the stunned customers—made a move. The man used the door's black metal push bar to pull himself to his feet, and then shouldered the door open and staggered out of the bank. I looked back to where Miranda stood outside my office. Her hand was over her open mouth, her eyes wide. "Is everyone all right?" I said, but no one responded. People stared at me dumbly, as if I had spoken in a foreign tongue. As if the question were nonsense.

By the time I got home that day—over an hour later than usual, due to all the procedures and paperwork Catherine and I had to do in order to have the branch ready to open again the next morning—I expected to find an empty house. Sandra and Miranda were both waiting right there in the living room, though. The television was on, but they seemed to have been ignoring it in favor of paging through glossy magazines. "Did they find the guy?" Miranda asked.

She had tried to stay at the branch after the robbery, but the police had plenty of witnesses, and had asked everyone not on staff to leave. "Yes," I said. "He was only a few blocks away, stumbling down the street. And easy to spot, I guess, since his face was covered in blood."

"It looks like you have some on your shoes, too," Sandra said.

I looked down and saw that she was right. The toes of both of my shoes had dark spots dried on the leather.

"That poor man," Miranda said. "He got so beat up. Was his nose broken? Or his face?"

"I don't know. They took care of him a bit before they brought him by the branch for us to identify him, but he was only back for a minute before they took him away."

They nodded. I felt awkward standing there in front of my wife and daughter, giving an account of an event that, for the most part, hadn't involved me. And a part of me was also thinking: *Why didn't you call, Sandra?* I knew Miranda had told Sandra about the robbery, and had told her I was fine, too. So she hadn't needed information. I understood that. And yet.

I wandered toward my office, thinking maybe things would be quiet there. As soon as I sat down behind my desk, though, I felt something was off. And then I noticed the window. "What happened to the spiderweb? And the spider it belonged to?" I asked toward the living room, trying to sound casual.

"I killed it," Sandra answered. "With a rolled newspaper. And then I cleaned the web out of the window. That thing was scary. It took a bunch of whacks."

Somehow, that news was more upsetting than anything else that had happened that day. The living creature I had spent the last few weeks admiring—the being who had created something beautiful right there in my window—had been killed. Its death struck me as incredibly senseless and cruel, and yet also, I knew, a perfectly standard act of housecleaning. I couldn't stay in the office with the window empty like that, though, and neither did I want to join the women in the living room. In fact, I couldn't think of a single space inside the house where I would feel comfortable at that point, so I wandered out to the back deck and fell into an armchair, wondering why I was so upset. Why did she have to kill it? I thought. Yes, I knew: anyone would have killed it. So why, when Sandra had only done something that any normal person would also have done, was I so angry at her? And now that the spider was dead, why did I feel so raw and unprotected myself?

The back door opened a few minutes later, and Sandra stepped out. As she took a seat in a chair on the other side of the deck, I had that sense I often have of someone studying me, and I realized I had been conscious of this—of her eyes upon me, searching for something—for years. "Miranda says Ira's leaving town for a while," she said. "She says he's going down to Los Angeles to work for Grant."

"That's what I heard."

"He didn't tell you about this ahead of time?"

"No. Did he tell you?"

When she had returned home from her tennis tournament the previous afternoon, Sandra had told me she and Grant lost their first match, waited most of a day to play another match, and then lost that one, too, and that was it. Instead of being disappointed, though, she had seemed vaguely embarrassed about the whole thing. I wondered if Grant hadn't lost those matches on purpose so that he could get back to town, and back to work on getting Ira out of town. "He didn't mention it at all," she said. "Which I find odd."

"He told me he was going to open an office in Los Angeles, but not that he was going to hire locally."

"Well. She's pretty upset about it."

"It doesn't seem like it to me."

She looked at me again. "Did I do something to you?" she asked.

"It's just clear to me that I'm the lesser person in this relationship."

I was surprised to see that she had placed a pack of cigarettes on the arm of the chair. She fished one out and—slowly, deliberately—lit it. "What do you mean?" she said. "What does 'the lesser person' mean?"

"It means I can't talk to you anymore, because you disagree with everything I think and feel," I said. And finally I began to speak. In an unstopping rush of bitterness, I told Sandra I no longer knew if she disagreed with everything I thought or felt, or if she had disagreed with me on so many things that I now simply assumed the disagreement was complete and total. And likewise, it seemed hardly to matter whether she was entirely bored with me, or if I was just assuming her boredom had become entire. I no longer had a desire to speak to her, because it felt like the only feelings left for me to learn about from her had to do with how high, exactly, her levels of disagreement and boredom and frustration with me had risen. I told her I understood she enjoyed her job and the tennis team and other social groups or functions that we took part in, or that she took part in without me, but that the fact of the matter was that I didn't enjoy a single one of them, because they had nothing to do with me. I was being pulled through a life I didn't care about, I told her, and I knew she was just as tired of dragging me around as I was of being dragged around. "And somehow the person I am, or wish I could just be allowed to be, has become indefensible," I said. "Because how can I argue against all of our success? How can I argue against having all of our friends and parties? I realize it's what people do. It's how people have fun. But the fact of the matter is that I don't like it, and I don't know why, and I'm sorry, but I don't. And I don't like being in this house, knowing that you're frustrated with me, and knowing that I'm angry about the fact that you're frustrated with me, and knowing that Miranda can tell we're frustrated, and I can tell she feels uncomfortable any time the two of us are in the room together, and now she's starting to get frustrated with us, just like we're frustrated with each other. And so this is just spiraling into some weird place, and I'm tired of it, and I'm exhausted by my own frustration and anger, and it has to stop. I need to get out of here, to go somewhere where I can think about things. I have to get out of this house and whatever is happening inside it. And I don't know how you feel about that, but I know that what I'm feeling right now is that no one here needs me like this, the way I am in this house. I can't keep fighting with you about how to live, because quite frankly, you'll just crush me. I understand that. You are much stronger and faster than me. I get it. And I don't know how to explain or argue for my right to not take part in all of the nice and good and social things that you enjoy, but I don't want to. I'm sure that's very clear to you by this point, and I'm sure that's what you were talking about when you came to me a few months ago and told me you were unhappy. The fact is that I want to be left alone. And I can't change that. And I understand that means I need to find a new place for myself, somewhere that isn't here. So I'm going to do that." I wasn't bold enough to look at Sandra when I was finished. I stared out across the backyard instead, embarrassed. I didn't understand why I couldn't just keep going, or change myself somehow so that the parts of me that were a problem would just no longer be parts of me. But I felt I had tried those things, and I had failed.

I didn't sense any movement from her. Was she looking at me? Or was she, like me, looking away, toward the horizon? I didn't check, because I didn't want to risk accidentally meeting her eyes. But when she spoke, she didn't dispute a word of what I'd said. She just said, "So do you want to see someone? Should we get counseling?"

"You didn't mention counseling a few months ago."

"No. But I would do it."

"As an exercise, so that we could say we did it. And I'll just attack the counselor, you know."

She laughed. And because I hadn't been looking at her, the hoarseness of her laugh was the first I realized that she was crying. "You would. I can hear it."

"I wonder why," I said. "Why is it so obvious that I would attack the counselor?" I may as well have asked: *Who am I?*

"Because you don't respect experts."

"It's because I can't stand it when someone who doesn't know me tries to tell me who I am. Or how the world works."

"*I* know you," she said. I finally looked at her then, and I could see in her eyes, and in the openness of her entire expression, that what she had said wasn't a statement, but a true-or-false question. And she wanted me to give her the answer.

"No," I said. "Not lately."

"No. Not lately," she repeated softly.

The trees waved gently in the breeze. Somewhere down the block, wind chimes produced their glistening little tones. It was a perfectly beautiful summer evening, and I remember wishing I could just remain there—in that warm breeze that was neither the confused past nor the uncertain future—and somehow stop time.

But that is not the way the world works. Sandra shifted. Seconds passed. "So what are we doing?" she said. "Do you have some kind of plan?"

I didn't. All that I held in my mind was the image of an empty room. And it had been so long since I'd made a decision that wasn't just a reaction to something someone else had done, that I struggled even to hit upon a tone of voice appropriate for speaking. So I just whispered. "I'll move out. Somewhere small."

"What about the house? It's too big for me to take care of by myself. And how will we tell Miranda?"

"We'll figure it out. But not right now."

She nodded. "Okay," she said. "Okay." We seemed to be in agreement, but I think we were both in shock, too. Though when Sandra headed quietly back into the house, I can also remember thinking: She can't be too upset. This is what she wanted.

Later, I went back into my office and sat at my desk, by the window. It had been just one spider out of millions, I reminded myself—it was just as well that he was dead. I hadn't been there long, though, before I heard Sandra's voice again. "I forgot to say thank you," she said. "For fixing the door. It looks good." Because I was facing the window, I was turned partially away from where Sandra was standing in the doorway, and all I did to acknowledge her was silently raise my hand, as if to suggest the whole thing was nothing. But the reality was that I didn't speak because I couldn't. And I didn't turn toward Sandra because I didn't want her to see me crying. Though I'm sure she could tell.

Long after I had heard Sandra's footsteps recede down the hall, I continued to gaze out the window: at the patch of ground that was our neglected side yard, and at the blistered and peeling paint on the side of the neighbor's house beyond. Without the web there, though, the window felt like an empty square—just a framed view of nothing.

WHEN THE MAN AT the Sycora Park Suites front desk told me Sandra's room was on the eighth floor, my first thought was that no one should ever be given a room on the eighth floor of an atrium hotel. To my mind, anything above the third floor was cruel. Are there really people who enjoy the precipice? Who want to stand up against the abyss so that they might peer past the edge, and fantasize a fall down into the stunted trees and churning fountain? But my second thought was: I bet she *requested* a high room. It's classier. It's quieter. It's more private. The abyss offers an element of drama, but the railing makes it safe. Gazing down at the people milling, antlike, below—while sipping a glass of wine, probably—would be relaxing for Sandra. She had never had a fear of heights.

The glass elevator ride eight stories up was enough for me. It was not only the height, but the fact that behind the machine's glass panels, and then while treading the open hall that circumscribed the building's gaping center, I felt exposed. I walked next to the wall, as far from the open side as possible, until I found Sandra's room. And though I rapped solidly on the door, it seemed to make almost no sound at all.

"There you are. I've been calling you. How are you?" she said upon opening the door only as much as was necessary for her to peer out. With her hair and makeup immaculately done and only her head visible, I felt as if the bust of an ancient Greek goddess was peering at me.

"I'm fine," I said, surprised by her concern.

"Are you hungry? There are snacks in the room. You can't come in, but I can get one if you want—sandwiches and popcorn and things."

"Is Miranda here?"

"No."

"But all of you are getting ready. So have you talked to her?"

She turned and told someone in the room that she would be

right back, and then slipped around the door and out into the hallway, letting the door swing shut behind her. Still in her jeans, black T-shirt, and flimsy pedicure sandals, she seemed now like the goddess caught on her day off. "No," she said. "But we have the photos"—she looked at her watch—"at the Quad, in fifteen minutes. I don't know what else to do but assume things will happen. You need to be in your tux."

What had happened since I'd last seen her? Earlier, she'd been telling me about how this wedding wasn't going to happen and it was all going to be a disaster, but now she seemed to have changed her mind. She was not given, in my experience, to magical thinking, and neither was optimism her mode. And yet she was speaking to me now in the matter-of-fact tone of simple wisdom, and the anxiety she should have been working out on me had disappeared.

"I just talked to the photographer," I told her. "I said we had some scheduling issues, and we'd do the photos after the ceremony. He said that was fine."

She seemed stunned by this. "Why didn't you tell me? You should have discussed it with me before making that decision."

"I wasn't aware it was a decision. We haven't heard from Miranda. Without her, there are no photos to be taken."

"Have you told anyone else?"

"This is that. This is me asking you how to best go about doing that."

Her shoulders dropped. She closed her eyes and sighed. It seemed I had committed some kind of colossal blunder.

I'd had enough. "My phone is dead," I said. "Can I borrow yours for a second?"

She pulled it from her pocket and handed it to me. "Who are you calling?"

"Gina."

"Why?"

When she gave me the phone, I flipped it open and, before dialing, glanced at the list of incoming calls: there was Gina's name, more than once. And so, while looking at Sandra, I dialed Gina.

"Hello, Sandra," Gina answered.

"Nope. Not Sandra."

"Certainly not," she said upon hearing my voice. "I hope you haven't done something with her."

"She's right here. She's been bringing me up to speed."

"Would you believe that couple bought not only the piece they were looking at when you were here, but two more? They wanted one for each of their houses. Who knew, right?"

"Not I," I said. "But listen, Sandra's busy getting ready for the photos, and she wants to know if Miranda has come back by the gallery yet."

"In the five minutes since we talked? No."

"Since who talked? You and Miranda, or you and Sandra?"

"Me and Sandra. She must really be nervous."

"Yes, I think so. But did Miranda say how long it was going to be? Everyone is dressed, and the photographer is getting a bit antsy is all."

"She didn't say. She just said she would be back soon."

So it was just as I had expected: I was on the outside. "Didn't you tell me you weren't sure if she would be coming by or not, and that you would call me if she was?"

"I'm sorry. I was asked not to say anything."

"It doesn't seem fair," I said. "I knew you first, after all."

"I don't think that applies here, darling. Keeping track of who has known whom the longest seems beside the point."

I heard the sentence, but it didn't register as meaning anything—my mind could not make it fit the situation. It sounded as if Gina was arguing that expecting to be able to trust people you've known for years was childish. "I can't think of what other point there would be," I said, which, though it sounded like I was disagreeing with her, was actually just me reporting my immediate mental state.

"Do you want me to call you when we're on our way?" she asked.

"On your way where?"

"To the hotel. Sandra asked me to drive Miranda over."

"Right," I said. "Yes, that sounds fine."

When I closed the phone and handed it back to Sandra, she appeared genuinely confused. "Why did you do that?" she said.

It is always the same between her and me. It's not that I doubt her confusion—Sandra only playacts in the direction of certainty, never the opposite—but that I cannot comprehend how she could possibly be confused or, often, almost offended by my responses. "Because you've talked to Gina more than once today," I said. "The two of you have been trading information."

"What's wrong with that?"

"What's wrong is that you know where Miranda is, but you're pretending you don't."

"What are you talking about?"

"Come on," I said. "You told me you hadn't heard anything from anyone, but your name was on Gina's cell phone multiple times, and I just saw her name on yours. You said you didn't know where Miranda was last night, but it only took me a couple minutes to get Gina to tell me Miranda stayed with her, so I'm sure Gina had already told you the same thing. You've known where

Miranda was last night, and you know where she is right now, and yet you've told me none of it. So I want you to tell me what's going on. You told me you wanted me to find her, but now it seems like you're keeping me away from her on purpose."

"You are completely paranoid. This is a bizarre theory that only makes sense in your mind. I never commanded you to find Miranda."

"You're only denying this to try and embarrass me, so that I won't recognize what's obvious. Miranda is upset, and she's not sure she wants to go through with getting married. You're convinced I want to be some kind of hero today, and you think I'll jump in and try and convince Miranda not to get married, so you're keeping me away from her. You want to talk her into just going through with things, because you can't stand the social embarrassment of something going wrong. Right? You can just tell me if I'm right."

Her lips pressed into the angry line I knew well. Any confusion she had felt was gone. "You are not right," she said. "You have dreamed this up in your head."

"Then where is Miranda? And don't lie again and tell me you don't know anything, and then send me running off so you can laugh as soon as I'm gone. I told you earlier I felt like everyone knew something I didn't, and you said I was being paranoid. But did I dream up the fact that Gina just told me you asked her not to tell me where Miranda was?"

"Enough!" Sandra said, raising her hands as if she wanted to grab me by the neck. "Enough! You always have to press everyone, on every little thing! You can't ever just let something go! So fine, I'll tell you what's going on, if it will stop you from running on like this."

"So where is she?"

"On her way to the gallery, I guess. Though she was supposed to be there by now. She is supposed to be on her way *here* by now."

"I've figured that much out myself. I'm asking where she has been today."

"When I told you earlier that I didn't know where she was, I actually didn't know where she was. There is no big conspiracy."

"So then why aren't you answering my question? And I don't want a minute-by-minute analysis of when you were lying and when you were telling the truth today. I don't care about that. I care about what's going on with *her*."

"She doesn't want to tell you that."

"Doesn't want to tell me what?"

She shook her head, as if changing her mind about having the conversation. "You should really talk to her about this. On any day other than today. This is—"

"Just tell me, Sandra!" I shouted, loud enough for my voice to carry out into the atrium's open middle. The sound of my voice echoing back at me surprised and upset me, though. The walkway that surrounded the void was hexagonal, and the sonic ricochets of my voice sounded hollow and empty in that space. "We're her parents, for Christ's sake," I said, under better control of myself. "Tell me what is going on with our daughter."

Sandra searched my eyes, but unlike Gina, it wasn't in order to guess at something. The aptitudes I had or didn't have, the faculties I did or did not possess: she knew. She only watched me that way—silently, with an almost dreadful patience—when she found herself in the position of the cat standing over the exhausted mouse, waiting to see if the little creature might thrash, or be made to thrash, once more. But finally she sighed, and seemed finished.

"Our daughter is pregnant," she said. "She's pregnant, and she doesn't want to tell you. And she didn't want *me* to tell you. She doesn't want you to know."

The door to Sandra's room opened then, the percussive snap of the latch ringing out like a gunshot. One of Miranda's bridesmaids stood there in her pale green dress, silent and barefoot. I hadn't been able to keep track of all Miranda's friends in those years—she never brought any of them along when visiting me, which meant that to me, these girls were just names Miranda occasionally referred to. I hadn't the slightest idea who this girl studying us was. "Are you guys okay?" she asked.

"We're fine, Jennifer," Sandra said. "I'll be back in a minute."

The girl actually glared at me as she closed the door.

"Why wouldn't she want me to know?" I said.

"Because you'll be disappointed," Sandra said. "She's supposed to tour the world now with Grant, or whatever it was you said in your big speech last night. You've spent the last ten years talking about how beautiful and smart she is, and how she's going to find out what she wants to do in life, and it will be great, and she'll do all sorts of big, huge, amazing things. But she's not going to be flying around and changing the world now. She's going to have a baby. And I doubt that you've ever listed being a mother among all of those wonderful and amazing things she might do. You're her knight in shining armor, and she thinks she's let you down."

Sandra was looking at me as if I'd put some awful weight on Miranda's shoulders, and I knew I had. I was confused. I had done something wrong, it seemed. But I could not fathom what. "Grant knows?"

"Of course."

"And Gina?"

"Yes."

I wondered if my trembling was visible. It was difficult to speak. "Does Alan know?"

"Of course," Sandra said. "And he's been great about it. Very supportive."

Alan was not Miranda's father. And yet he knew everything. I thought of Sandra and Alan and Miranda working through things, sharing their thoughts and feelings with each other—around the dinner table? in the living room?—and never telling me any of it. A wave of shame engulfed me. What was so wrong with me that these people did not trust me with their thoughts and feelings? And now they had decided, for some reason, to lock me out of my own life. I looked at Sandra, baffled. "Why didn't you tell me?"

She spoke softly. "It wasn't just about you. She kept it from everyone for a while. She said she thought she might not keep it, so she didn't want to tell anyone. But then she told Grant, and he was happy about it. And they decided this is something they want. They want to do this."

What was there to say? Everything had happened without me. These discussions of love and marriage and children—of life—had occurred in other rooms, with other people. And now everything was taken care of. Gina would deliver Miranda to the hotel, Sandra would receive her in the room behind the door across the hall, the bridesmaids and the stylist would attend to her, and everything would proceed. Not only did my presence no longer seem necessary, but it seemed maybe it had never been necessary at all. Sandra claimed she had never asked me to find our daughter, and it was all a misunderstanding. Or, to be exact, it was all *my* misunderstanding. Everyone else seemed to understand things perfectly.

I don't remember what I said to Sandra before I walked away.

And I was too stunned, standing there in the glass elevator like a little figurine on display, to think very clearly about anything at all. In all honesty, I probably said nothing. Walking away without saying good-bye is the kind of thing people tell me I often do when my mind is elsewhere.

I REMEMBER RETURNING TO the present after I stepped out of the elevator, though. Because as I tried to head through the lobby, a young man stepped directly in front of me, blocking my path. I did not, at first, even recognize him as he said, "I'm sorry I had to do this, but I'm going to have to ask that you not leave the hotel right now. There are some people on their way who want to talk to you."

It was young John. "With security," he probably would have liked me to add. I was baffled as to how he had tracked me down—I knew I hadn't told him what hotel the reception was at. Was a person able to look up wedding reception bookings? It seemed like the kind of thing that should be private, and yet it's not rare for me to find out that things I think should be private are not at all. And then I thought: My credit card statements. That son of a bitch saw it on my statements. And now he's come running to ruin everything. "I've already told you I don't have time for this. I have to go."

He shook his head like a scolding parent. "No, you'll need to wait a few minutes. You'll get to move on with your day in a little bit."

It had been no more than five seconds, but already I found him insufferable. "You're not my supervisor," I said. "What are you going to do, tackle me?"

"I don't need to be your supervisor. And I don't need to tackle you, because I've called the police, and they're coming here to meet us. They're the people you'll need to speak to."

"What are you talking about?" I said, but even as I turned to look out the glass lobby doors, I noticed a squad car in the first row of spots in front of the hotel, and a second car—unmarked, but with the plates and exotic antennae of a law enforcement vehicle—pulling slowly past the sliding doors and to a stop a bit farther along the drive's curb. Two uniformed officers emerged from the squad car and began to make their way toward the hotel entrance, while a third figure, in plainclothes, stepped out of the unmarked car.

John regarded me with the coolly satisfied gaze of a television cop who has trapped and conquered his quarry in time for the last commercial break. And I imagine that is exactly who he thought he was. "You are completely insane," I told him.

"Nope. I'm doing my job," he said.

The lobby doors slid open, and here came two uniformed police officers, along with a much older gentleman in a shirt and tie. I could see that the men in uniform were Martinez and O'Brien, the same two who had visited the branch that morning. "Officers," John called, raising his arm like a student who knows the answer, "we're over here."

O'Brien said something to the others before heading toward the lobby's front desk, and Martinez and the plainclothes officer headed in our direction. When they reached us, it was the older man who shook John's hand first. "So you're the fellow who called us? With the security team?"

"Yes," John said proudly. "I felt like this was something we should take care of as soon as possible."

The older man nodded, though with the raised eyebrows of someone who has yet to be convinced. "And you're the branch manager?" he said, turning to me.

"Yes."

"Well, I'm Detective Lou Buccholz," he said. "You may not remember me, but I handled a case that involved you a long time ago. A robbery maybe twenty-five years ago."

He was lying. He had to be lying. "I remember a detective named Buckle," I said. "But he was an older man."

He laughed. "My name is Buccholz. And I can assure you it was me, because I just looked at the report on the way over here."

"But you had gray hair, didn't you? You can't still be working for the police department."

"I went gray pretty early, so you're probably right that I was gray even then."

"How early?" I asked, incredulous. "How old were you?"

"Let's see," he said, rubbing his chin. "If that robbery was twenty-five years ago, I would have been thirty-nine."

"I could have sworn you were older."

He seemed amused, but I still couldn't shake the feeling that he should have been some kind of wizened ancient. He moved with perfect confidence as he pulled a pack of chewing gum from his shirt pocket, though, and his hands didn't tremble in any discernible way as he teased a stick of gum from the pack. And if it was true he was sixty-four, then his face was probably even less wrinkled than those of other men his age. When he looked at me, his eyes were clear and alert as he said, "But how old are *you*?"

"Now? Forty-nine."

He shook his head. "Forty-nine. Such an old man. Certainly one foot's in the grave already."

He laughed, and I managed to smile. Though it was also true that I hadn't the slightest idea where I would be taken next, or what kind of interrogation I was going to be subjected to there.

I'M SURE IT WAS a Sycora Park Suites energy-saving policy to leave the lights in the ballroom at their weakest setting when the place wasn't in use. The effect, however, was that as soon as I stepped into the room—Detective Buccholz had suggested I wait there for him while he consulted with the other officers—I felt as if I were either half conscious or under water. The profusion of tables that stretched off into the room's dim distance, each of them immaculately set and immaculately unattended, seemed tremendous, and the row of tables along the back wall, ready to hold the evening's buffet of dinner selections, looked impossibly long. Had we truly agreed to host this many souls? Would we really be providing this much food and drink? No wonder I'm broke, I thought. And why had I never noticed the unwavering beigeness of the place? The soft light, the silence, the muted tones—the space did not feel celebratory so much as funereal. It was as if I had stumbled into a wake at which I was the only attendee. And there was no body.

The door opened and I turned, expecting to see a representative of the law. But it was not the law. It was Catherine. "What are you doing here?" I said.

"I saw John in the lobby," she said. "So I knew something was up. Are you all right? You have a strange look on your face."

"It's nothing. Nonsense."

It was a lie. I actually had been thinking about how Miranda and I had, only a few years before, attended a funeral together in a room not unlike the one in which I sat. My mother's husband,

Eddie, had called one afternoon to tell me Carrie had tripped over a wooden planter box and, falling backward, hit her head against the surface of their concrete patio. She didn't lose consciousness, he said in amazement—he seemed still in shock himself as he spoke to me—but sat there with her hands on her head, complaining of pain throughout her skull that was so bad she didn't even want to open her eyes. When she hadn't been able to stand up, though, Eddie had called an ambulance. Carrie continued trading lucid conversation with him as they waited for the paramedics, he told me, and also as they rode in the back of the ambulance on the way to the hospital. By the time they made it there, though, he said, she had begun to fade. "She must have passed out while they were wheeling her inside," he said, "and they rushed her off into some room and then came back to tell me she had a cracked skull and her brain was bleeding, or there was bleeding on her brain—however they say it. And then not much later they said she wasn't doing well. No, they actually said she wasn't 'responding well.' And then I guess her body started shutting down, just kind of one system after another, and they couldn't do anything about it. And by the time I saw her again, she was already gone." I had for some reason thought Eddie was telling me a story of events that had occurred a day or two before. It wasn't until he was finished that I realized this had all happened within the last hour and a half, and that my mother had died only minutes before Eddie had called.

I told Miranda she had no obligation to attend the funeral of a grandmother who had visited her in person no more than once every four or five years, and who, because she lived thousands of miles away in the Florida Panhandle, may as well as have been on the moon, as far as I was concerned. But Miranda said she wanted to go, and so together we made the long trip to the small town my mother had called home for thirty years, and which I had never before bothered to visit. When we arrived at Carrie and Eddie's address, however, I was surprised by the appearance of the man who met us. I remembered Eddie as tall and gruff, but the man I shook hands with was at least two inches shorter than me, and seemed almost shy. Carrie had married Eddie when I was sixteen, after dating him for only six months, and I recalled him as someone who often told stories about the construction work he did for a living, though eventually I decided he probably liked that line of work because it allowed him to quit any job at any point, disappear for an indefinite period of time—hunting or fishing, supposedly—and then come back and either join up with a new job, or sometimes just rejoin the one he'd left. He was in his mid-sixties by the time of Carrie's death, though. The few times over the years that she had come to visit me, Eddie had stayed behind, so I hadn't seen him in person since he and Carrie had moved to Florida while I was in college. The only words I had traded with him in that quarter century had been the minimal pleasantries required to fill the interval between Eddie picking up the phone and his handing it to Carrie—never more than a minute or two of chitchat, rarely about anything other than the weather. Over the years, of course, I recognized that Carrie's decision to take a stab at marital happiness made perfect sense. She had been only thirty-three at the time she married Eddie—still young, and at what is now a perfectly normal age for a first marriage. And neither have I ever questioned my own decision to use college as an escape route from the dusty, barren town Carrie and I were stuck in. I found a university in the Pacific Northwest whose application packet featured photos of lush greenery and aesthetically pleasing mists—imagery I associated with tropical islands, really—and headed there with no intention of returning. And when Carrie told me a couple years later that she and Eddie were moving to Florida for what seemed to me an odd job opportunity—he was going to fix motorcycles in a shop where she could cover the reception desk, a situation that ended up lasting no more than six months for either of them—it bothered me not at all. Carrie and I went in different directions, probably for reasons no more substantial than that boys move away, and women remarry. We were both young, and went off to become new people. The place we had lived, the way we had lived: neither of us wanted that. It was just circumstance. I've always considered our escape from it a tremendous success for both of us.

When Miranda and I sat down in the small living room of the patio home Eddie and Carrie had been living in for the last decade, though—a side table held a photo of Miranda that was at least five years out of date—Eddie surprised me by claiming that he still worked construction. I don't possess the most voluble phone presence in the world, so Carrie and I spoke to each other only a couple times a year, for no more than half an hour each time, but I couldn't remember Carrie ever referring to Eddie's work life at all. I had assumed that hard labor wasn't something a man still did in his sixties, but although Eddie wore bifocals and had only a few wisps of hair left to comb across his scalp, his dark tan and the overdeveloped muscles in his forearms supported his claim. We spent a polite, formal day going through some of Carrie's things, but the only item I took—the only thing there that seemed to have any connection to me at all—was a box of old photos of Carrie and me in New Mexico, from when I was a child. The photos were almost comically devoid of content. We were often small within the frame, and behind us lay the flat, empty New Mexico landscape that I remembered stretching in every direction. The best example was probably a photo of the two of us on a dry winter day, standing on a dirt road outside of town. I looked no more than six years old, and the identity of the photographer was a mystery to me, as was any reason Carrie and I might have been outside of town. Had she been looking at houses? Had we been visiting someone? I had no memory of that day. And yet there we were.

The next surprise came when Carrie's casket was lowered into the ground the following day. Miranda and I—the granddaughter and the son—were both dry-eyed. Eddie, however, wept openly and unashamedly, and even leaned on women friends of Carrie's for support. At some point I recalled—out of nowhere, it seemed—that once, in an uncharacteristic or maybe just uncertain attempt at stepfatherhood, Eddie had asked if I wanted to go on a hunting trip with him. There was nothing less interesting to me at sixteen than stumbling through the cold woods with a gun, so I turned him down without a second thought. I probably also wanted to make clear my intention to shrug off the idea that Eddie was supposedly going to be a more permanent presence than the other boyfriends Carrie had had over the years, many of whom had been perfectly normal male representatives of our town, which meant that after dating Carrie for three to six months and realizing that anything longer-term would also involve the awkward, unathletic, science-fiction-reading boy that belonged to her—well, they moved on. After getting rejected, Eddie never invited me hunting again, and though at the time I felt this confirmed his dislike of me, I imagine it was actually my contempt for him that was perfectly clear. I may even have hurt his feelings. And there at my mother's funeral, as Eddie wept, I realized that my memories of him were either distortions or irrelevant, that I didn't know him at all, and that people and their lives are a mystery.

The next morning, Miranda and I stopped by the house before heading out of town, and Eddie hugged each of us tightly. He told us to take care of ourselves, that we would always be welcome in his home, and then continued to wave even as we pulled away in our rental car. When Miranda and I were settled in on our plane ride home a few hours later, she asked if I thought I would ever take Eddie up on his offer, and I told her I couldn't for the life of me think of any reason I would ever see him again. "How about because he was married to Grandma for almost thirty years?" she said. She was just out of college then, and had clearly picked up—from her professors, I assumed—the habit of phrasing her suggestions as if they were questions.

"But I don't really know him," I said. "He wasn't really a stepfather, and we're not friends."

"You could become friends," she suggested.

"I don't think I'm looking to be friends with old men in Florida. Are you?"

"No," she said, laughing. "I guess not."

"It's just you and me, kid," I had told her. And it had felt, in a way, just like the end of high school. Except that this time I wouldn't be going off alone to become someone new, but would be in the company of my daughter.

But where was Miranda at that moment, while I stood in the dim ballroom that was supposed to serve as her reception site, waiting for the detective to come in and ask whatever questions he intended to ask? She was on her way to Gina's gallery, they had told me, from where she would be delivered by Gina to Sandra. She was being passed along.

"So what's going on?" Catherine asked. "Why are you in this room, waiting to speak to the police again? Why is John acting so weird?" She was looking at me with an intensity that made it clear these were not rhetorical questions. She felt I was holding out on her.

"I guess they're upset I didn't tell them the guy who robbed you this morning robbed me once. But twenty-five years ago."

She looked confused. "And this is something you knew?"

"Pretty much. I was as sure of it as a person can be from looking at some photos."

"Why didn't you say so?"

"Because it's Saturday. It's my daughter's wedding day. Why doesn't anyone understand this? I'm completely baffled by the fact that everyone seems to think I owe it to the bank to sit around chatting with them on my daughter's wedding day. You know, if the bank wasn't open on Saturday, it wouldn't have been robbed today. Did they ever think of that?"

"You're angry about the fact that we're open on Saturdays?"

"I'm angry about how fucking insane it is that I cannot be left alone. I'm trying to find my daughter and talk to her on her wedding day. I want to talk to her. But the fact that I'm a branch manager, and I'm a branch manager Monday through Friday, and also on Saturday, even though I *took today off*, and I'm probably a branch manager on Sundays, too, so apparently I'm a branch manager all of the time—this allows the insane and stupid bank to stalk me every minute of every day, if it wants. This is exactly the can of worms I didn't want to open today. So yes, I didn't tell them. I thought maybe I would be left alone for one day. For one day of my life."

"I'm sorry. I wish we'd never been robbed. I wish there was some way I could have stopped it—"

"That's it," I said. "Right there. It's not your fault. You didn't do it. But you're starting to feel personally responsible for it. That's the trick that gets pulled on you. And what I have tried to say to them today is that we are not personally responsible for this robbery, we are not on the clock right now, so they can wait. They can wait until Monday. And do you see how it hasn't worked? Do you see how incredibly rude that kid out there is? He was hired by the bank. This is the person they chose to handle situations like this—that kid. And he does not deserve access to my life. He does not deserve to go through my finances and question me about the way I've handled my life. I hate the entire enterprise. And now you're not going to be working with me anymore, so I'm just going be coming in to a job I hate, and then going home. What's the point? You know who they're going to send to replace you, right? A kid. Someone getting ready to make exactly the same mistake I made with my life. Because nobody likes banks, and nobody likes the branch managers of banks. And they sure as hell don't trust them. So I'm sorry, but I don't know why you want to become one. It's stupid."

She smiled. "You're upset."

"Why are you smiling?"

"I'm sorry. I've just never seen you this way. I mean, it's not as bad as all that, is it?"

"I think it is."

"Well, it's true that you probably made things worse for yourself by not talking. But did you find Miranda?"

"No. Someone else did."

"Who?"

"I'm not sure." Realizing how true that statement was—how little I knew about any of what was going on—made me laugh, briefly. "Maybe everyone. But Gina and Sandra say they have everything under control now."

Catherine nodded. "So that can't be making you too happy, either."

"I wanted to talk to her. And what I've discovered is that she shares her life with them, but she doesn't share it with me."

"There are a lot of things going on for her today. I'm sure that if she needed you, she would have told you. You two are close."

Were we? I tried, inwardly, to summon a sense of our closeness. What came to mind were flashes—or maybe just impressions, really—of the time Miranda used to spend with me at the townhouse while she was still in high school. Those were quiet evenings of homework, or of the two of us sitting in the little townhouse living room, watching movies and eating popcorn. When it was Miranda's turn to pick the movie, she always chose similarly inane college romantic comedies, in which a dorky boy managed to impress a sorority girl, or a self-conscious girl ended up broadening the horizons of a blinkered nice guy. The movies weren't good—Miranda knew that as well as I did—and yet I remembered us laughing a lot. Laughing with and at those movies had felt like laughing with and at ourselves, and I may never have felt more comfortable laughing at myself at any other time or place in my life. I hadn't bought that townhouse until Miranda was halfway through her junior year, though, which meant that this mood I was summoning, this sense of closeness, was a situation that had existed only until Miranda went to college—no more than a year and a half. "You know," I told Catherine, "after we split up, Sandra used to complain that Miranda acted like she was on vacation when she was with me. The two of them fought constantly, and once Sandra actually said, 'We're throwing things at each other now.' She said she knew Miranda liked staying at my place mostly because it gave her a chance to get away from Sandra."

"I didn't get along with my mom when I was a teenager, either," Catherine said. "And I'm sure that was an especially hard time for all of you."

"But she never said or did anything like that to me. Maybe she *was* on vacation. She never talked about arguing with her mom, never complained about any rules, never argued about the custody schedule. You hear about kids struggling when their parents divorce, acting out or being defiant or whatever they call anger these days. But I always thought Miranda was happy."

"Maybe she was."

The empty tables, the silent dance floor: I did not want to be in that huge, dark room. "So why would she hide from me today?"

Catherine was peering at me again. "When was the last time you ate anything?"

"Probably breakfast."

"It's past four. You need to eat. You've seen videos of people fainting at weddings, right? You don't want that to be you. If you even make it that far."

I'm sure that by that little addendum, Catherine meant if I didn't faint from hunger before the wedding even began. My first thought, though, was that she meant if I lived that long.

The ballroom door opened again, and this time it actually was Detective Buccholz who stepped into the room. He held a thick file folder under his arm, and took a deep breath, as if preparing himself for some new level of conflict. "I'm sorry for the delay, but I think we can take care of this fairly quickly now," he said. "You must be the service manager, right?"

"Yes," Catherine said.

"Wonderful. You may go."

"You don't want to talk to me?"

"No."

"But I'm the one who was actually there during the robbery."

"I understand that. And now you may go."

Catherine eyed him with unhidden suspicion. "Do I have to? Can't I stay to help answer questions?"

"You are free to go," he repeated with the same precise courtesy as before. And opening the ballroom door as if to usher her out, he added: "Please."

She looked at me. The beige pantsuit she had been wearing all day remained spotless and unwrinkled, but when I realized, meeting her eyes, that the freckles I had noted on her face that morning had disappeared, I thought: When did she stop to put on makeup? And why do I never notice? Or why, today, am I so aware of this? "Give me a call when you're finished here," she said.

She walked out of the room at such a swift pace, and without even a nod in the detective's direction, that her compliance was clearly intended to insult. The detective, however, nodded politely as she passed, and then closed the door quietly behind her. When he returned to me, he even seemed amused. "She seems like an excellent employee," he said.

"Often," I said.

"So a few minutes ago, you were amazed at my age," he said. "But I'm a bit amazed, too. Because at my age, and with my years of experience in the department, I don't work weekends anymore. I should be at home right now, napping in front of a baseball game. But one guy's on vacation, and another is pretending to be sick, so here I am. And I'm confused, so what I'm going to ask is this: What the hell is going on? Why is that kid out there ruining my afternoon?"

By that point, of course, I felt I had figured out the best way to tell my side of the story. "He's playing junior policeman. And he seems to think it's his job to make everyone miserable. But the whole thing has nothing to do with me. I wasn't even there."

"Where were you?"

"I was at my ex-wife's house, getting ready for our daughter's wedding. Her wedding today. In a couple hours."

"And that's why you've been reluctant to spend time with John today."

"I spoke to him. This morning. But he's convinced that because this guy robbed me a long time ago there's some kind of deep connection between us, and if I sit down and look at old photos with him, it will result in a big breakthrough. He just will not accept that it has nothing to do with me. So regardless of what else happens, could you write somewhere in my file that I had more important things to worry about today, so I didn't particularly care about the bank, or its money, or who took it? But that this kid just will not accept that a coincidence isn't necessarily meaningful?"

He smiled. "I would be happy to do that for you, but there's a problem: I don't have a file on you. I'm not sure why you think I would."

"But you're holding something," I said. "What are you holding?"

"This," he said, raising the folder, "is a file we have on the guy who robbed your bank this morning. We have a file on *him*, because we keep track of crimes and the people who commit them. I'm not denying that you have better things to do today, or that you have a right to feel harassed. It's just that there's no place in the paperwork where we note whether an individual victim felt inconvenienced. Everyone feels inconvenienced."

His use of the term *victim* grated, but I let it pass. "But you must have notes on the first time this guy robbed me, right? You do write down the things people say?"

"Let's see," he said, setting the file on the nearest table and opening it up. There was such a profusion of pages and forms, of typed information and material taken down in various handwritings, and of photos of objects and places, that as the detective flipped through the pages, I could discern almost nothing at all. It wasn't until he was toward the bottom of the file that he said, "Here. This is my handwriting."

"Am I allowed to see this?"

"Probably not, so just tell people I looked at this in a very secure manner. But here it is." He paused, apparently reading through something, and then said, "So he asks you to give him money, you don't respond, he pistol-whips you, takes a bunch of money, and leaves."

"Right," I said. "That's it. So what are all of the rest of the pages in there?"

He began paging back through the papers and photos again. "I'm a little reluctant to tell you, because you're obviously very sensitive about your belief that your relationship to this case is just a coincidence."

"What do you mean? Are you saying he targeted me on purpose?"

He frowned, clearly trying to figure out how to explain something to me in simple terms. "You live in this guy's area," he said. "Or he lives in yours, depending on how you want to think about it. He robbed you twenty-five years ago—we got his prints that day—and then he was quiet for a few years. Then he robbed a bank out in Greenville, then he's quiet for a couple years before he's back here, but across town, where he hits a place for two thousand dollars. It's always the same: he walks in, robs a single teller, and gets out. Seven years later, over in Weaver, we have him hitting a grocery store branch for three thousand. A few years after that, he's in Clarkston, and it's a really good day for him, because he actually gets all of five thousand dollars." The detective flipped though several more pages, but too quickly to actually be reading them. "There are maybe half a dozen more in here, but they're just variations on the same theme. It looks like he only brought a gun a couple times, back in the beginning, and then after that he's had no visible weapon. And he left prints early on, but he hasn't left prints for a number of years now. So maybe he thinks he's getting away with this stuff."

"He's gotten smarter about it, at least."

"Only if you think committing federal offenses for no more than a few thousand dollars is smart. And only if he's naive enough to think this isn't going to catch up with him. We could get him *today.* It looks like your teller got a dye pack in with the money, so we know that two minutes after this guy left, there was an explosion of bright purple paint somewhere in the neighborhood."

"I'm sure he knows about dye packs."

"Of course he knows they *exist.* But the note he wrote today asked your teller to pretty please not give him one, and then she did anyway. So has he actually dealt with one of these things before? Did he have a plan for dealing with it? Two minutes is two minutes. And an exploding dye pack is often the first in a series of events that ends with someone in handcuffs."

"I guess. Though if he's gone twenty-five years without getting caught, I don't see why he couldn't go twenty-five more."

Buccholz looked at me as if I were a child. "You're thinking about this as if it's an on-off switch—as if succeeding once means you'll be able to get away with something forever. But I've been involved in law enforcement my whole life, and I can assure you that the rule is that the longer you try to get away with something, the higher the odds are that you're going to get caught. I don't see how this guy has managed to pull this off for twenty-five years, and I wouldn't be at all surprised if this is his last job. We have prints, a dye pack, photos and video, and we know he lives in the area. I'm not allowed to bet on whether or not we're going to catch someone, but if I were, I'd give this guy an over/under of twenty-four hours."

"He's gotten away with this for twenty-five years, but you think you'll catch him within the next twenty-four hours?"

"I don't think *I'll* catch him. I don't run very fast anymore, and I have no intention of chasing some guy and wrestling him to the ground. It's not personal. There are officers all over town keeping an eye out for him right now. His image has been forwarded to multiple jurisdictions and levels of law enforcement. I don't have to catch him personally. He will just, at some point, be caught."

"I see."

"That's why your belief that this is all a coincidence doesn't really hold. You've been a bank manager in this city for the last twenty-five years, and he's been robbing banks around here for the last twenty-five years, so it's not really a coincidence that he robbed you a second time. You two are in the same business. And that's pretty much the *opposite* of a coincidence." He closed the folder. "But statistical likelihoods are just my personal interest. What was it that was on *your* mind?"

"What do you mean?" I said. "Nothing is on my mind."

"You said you were worried about far more important things today. That's why you don't want to play games with the kid out there in the lobby, who, I will confidentially agree, seems like he's kind of an asshole."

"Right," I said. "My daughter is getting married today. And I wanted to talk to her."

"And you're being held up here?"

"Yes. I know where she's supposed to be right now, but if I want to catch her, I need to leave."

He shrugged. "You're aware that you're not under arrest, right? You're not being detained in any official way."

"What do you mean?"

"I mean we're just talking. And I think we both agree that the fact that we're even standing here in the same room is just the result of a misunderstanding. You're free to go."

"You don't have any other questions? I don't have to talk to the other officers?"

"I don't find you to be what we call a person of interest."

It was almost the nicest thing anyone had ever said to me. Either that, or my relief at finally finding someone who shared my opinion that there was no reason to question me—and who was simultaneously giving me permission to go collect my daughter—was so great that the gratitude I felt for the detective was out of all proportion to the event. The disinterest with which he regarded me probably had much more to do with boredom than generosity. And yet it was with the sense of having won some kind of prize that I said, "So I can just walk out?"

"I'm telling you that you may do that."

"Thank you," I said, starting toward the doors.

"Though, Paul?" he said. "If you want to avoid your young friend out there, you'll probably want to find another way out."

I looked around. Double doors to the kitchen were at the back of the room. And I assumed the kitchen would, at some point, open onto a loading dock or delivery entrance at the back of the building. I had an impulse to sprint immediately in that direction, but managed to resist it. "What will you tell everyone in the lobby?" I asked.

"I'll tell them you were cooperative and forthcoming, and that I'm confident you didn't have anything to do with it. If I'm the one who has to suggest to you to leave by the back door, it pretty much indicates you're not savvy enough to pull off a bank robbery. No offense."

"None taken," I said.

"But listen," he said as he turned to gather the contents of the Mooncalf file back into his folder: "May we never meet again."

It seemed like he meant it. "Yes," I said. "That would be nice."

III

Late on a Saturday afternoon in October of the year Miranda turned twenty-three, I decided to drive downtown and park across the street half a block from her apartment building. The breeze smelled of earth and apples, and autumn had begun to dab its brilliantine rust over the edges of things. Lawns lay damp and silver with the night's mist, leaves curled to yellow and orange, and the brick apartment buildings and old stone hotels that lined the streets downtown rose confidently into the clear afternoon sky. I tuned the radio to a ball game I mostly ignored, a sandwich and a magazine on the seat next to me. I felt faintly ridiculous, and yet also unable to stop myself. I wanted to know.

I'd thought I might be in for a long evening, but only a couple hours into the project the surveillance paid off, because here came Grant, walking toward Miranda's building from the other end of the block. I watched him make his way to the door of the building, press the intercom, and at the electronic buzz, pull the front door open and disappear inside. It was like watching a film projected on a screen: I felt no compulsion to take any kind of action. When they emerged a few minutes later, I started to slide down in my seat until I saw they were headed in the opposite direction, on foot. I hesitated a moment before I got out of the car and took a few uncertain steps, but it quickly became apparent they were paying little attention to their surroundings, and none at all to anything behind them. They were talking. It was dusk. Twin jet contrails flared pink against the scoured basin of sky as Grant and Miranda paused at an intersection, waiting to cross. I stepped into a doorway until they crossed, and then continued following, surprised at how naturally I assumed the role of the follower. This is my place, I thought. Just walking.

Though they were nearly a block ahead of me, I heard Miranda laugh. She sounded happy.

It didn't last long—a few more blocks, maybe. I watched them step into a restaurant I had never been to, but which I recognized. Like many of the places in that neighborhood, it was new, much talked about, and looked nice. It made sense: they both lived downtown, and they were eating downtown. This was their little world.

I didn't know what to do. I walked the streets aimlessly for a bit, killing time. Couples were headed to drinks, to dinner, or to see movies or shows. A sullen middle-aged panhandler, his dirty baseball cap pulled low, asked if I had a dollar to spare, and when I told him I was sorry, he muttered something inaudible, though the tone was clear. I asked him to repeat himself.

"I said you're going out to dinner, but you don't have a dollar?"

"Do you take credit cards?" I said.

He sneered. "Whatever."

"Because that's what I use. I don't have cash for you."

"Right. Your wallet's empty."

"I'm not going to give you a twenty-dollar bill."

"So go break it."

"How old are you?"

"Fuck off."

"Because if you haven't figured it out by now, I don't think you're going to."

"You're an asshole," he said. "People like you are born assholes."

"No," I said, "that's what you don't get. It takes work."

He flipped me off, and I laughed as I walked away. "I should kick your ass," he yelled after me, but I just kept walking, feeling the adrenaline in my veins as I made my way back to the restaurant. I stood across from the entrance, trying my best to see inside. It was a big place—part of yet another of the neighborhood's old warehouses—and there was no sign of Grant or Miranda through the front window. They should be seated by now, I thought. So I crossed the street and opened the door.

There was a burst of noise: voices, music, the clatter of plates. Pale muslin curtains twenty feet tall divided the immense room into multiple chambers. Leather settees lined the wall up front, filled with thin, well-dressed, chatty young people. Glowing light fixtures suspended from the high ceiling dotted the room, the shades shaped in the crazed geometries of Escher explosions or cubist suns. I'd read in the paper that the suave coach of the city's big college basketball team dined there regularly, as did other local celebrities: stage actors and actresses, jazz musicians, and politicians.

"Are you here for dinner?" the young hostess asked brightly.

"No," I said, nodding toward the bar. "Just a drink."

"Of course," she said. "Wherever you can find a place."

The bar was made of frosted glass and lit from within, so that everyone seated at it glowed as if they had been admitted to the cheerful afterlife. I managed to grab a spot when a couple stood to move into the dining room, and as I cautiously turned to follow their trek, I saw that seated on the far side of the room, maybe thirty yards off, were Grant and Miranda. Miranda's back was to me, but I could see her red blouse. She must have been speaking, because Grant was leaning forward with an attentive smile on his face, as if Miranda were quietly sharing a joke at the expense of someone nearby. I turned to the bar and ordered a vodka tonic from the hustling bartender while in the long mirror behind the bar—in the corner just above the pastis and ouzo—I found amid the confusion of faces and lights the small splash of scarlet that was Miranda's blouse. The little spot of color trembled as the room's din produced vibrations in the glass.

"Waiting for someone?" the bartender asked as he delivered my drink.

"No."

"Did you want to look at a menu?"

"Why not?" I said, peering again into the mirror. Beyond Miranda's red blouse, though, I saw only indistinct shadows, a darkness that shifted and rippled behind the shining bottles of liquor. I wondered what I intended to do. Confront them? No. But then how long did the surveiller need to surveil? I had my confirmation—nothing more was necessary. I had a fresh drink, though, and a menu in front of me. I watched the bartender shake a cocktail as if in a rage, though his face remained impassive. When he finished pouring and delivering the drink, he moved back down the bar. "Did you see anything?" he asked.

"You have ostrich on here," I said. "What does it taste like?"

"A lot of people like it. Have you ever had buffalo?"

"No."

"It tastes a lot like buffalo."

"How is that possible? One's a bird, the other's a what? A beast."

He shrugged. "I don't make 'em, I just serve 'em."

"I'll take the ostrich," I said. "Medium."

He took my menu and tossed it beneath the bar, as if it were just a cheap prop. For a few minutes, I actually enjoyed some anticipatory thoughts about ostrich, as well as some speculation on buffalo, instead of thinking about who was across the room. And then of course when I returned from my little mental flight and looked back into the mirror, the swatch of red was gone.

I turned. Their table was empty. So I turned even further, abandoning discretion as I wondered how they had slipped away. I had been distracted for no more than three or four minutes. Where could they have gone?

"She went home."

I spun back in the other direction, and there was Grant, standing five feet from me.

"You have no peripheral vision," he said.

Until that moment, I hadn't felt angry. Once he spoke, though—or maybe it was his tone—I felt the urge to spit. Instead, I concentrated on my drink. There were no open seats at the bar, though, so he ended up standing next to me, uncomfortably close. "This isn't a coincidence, is it?" he said.

We were surrounded by strangers, all of whom seemed to be

happily laughing and chatting. "That you're dating my daughter?" I said quietly.

"You followed us," he said. "I'm flattered."

"You shouldn't be."

"This is a bad way for this to happen. I wanted to tell you."

"So why didn't you?"

He shrugged. "Because when is the right time?"

Jesus. I could think of dozens of possible answers to that question. "There are thousands of women you could date in this city," I said.

"Not like her."

"Really? What about her is so unique?"

"You don't need me to answer that. You know how extraordinary she is."

"She's a receptionist at an art gallery."

"She's smart," he said. "And confident. With a great sense of humor."

"She's twenty-three."

"But with a tremendous ability to size people up, to see what's really going on."

"She's *my daughter*," I said. It seemed a fact so transcendent that it rendered anything else irrelevant. Miranda always had been, and always would be, my daughter. Before she was born—before *I* was born—and after both of us were dead, it would still be true. What could he possibly think he was doing?

"I guess I hoped you might be happy for us," he said.

"What a stupid thing to hope for," I said.

"She's an adult," he said. "And I didn't start it."

"You always start it. Everything about you is an attempt to attract women."

"You don't really know what you're talking about."

"Did you want another?" the bartender said. His tone seemed deliberately flat, as if he were aware of what he was interrupting.

"Yes," I said.

"Not for me," Grant said.

"You're not staying?" I said, but Grant didn't respond. I waited for the bartender to deliver my drink before I said, "How long?"

"A few weeks," he said.

I tried to process it, to place it into some version of reality, but I couldn't. "No."

"She asked me to get a drink after work."

"You could have said no."

"I did," he said. "I said it wasn't a good idea. But she asked me again two days later."

"You should have said no again."

"I did. She asked again."

I slammed my palm against the bar. "You should have said no forever."

He nodded. "I thought that, too. But then I couldn't figure out why."

I shook my head, stunned by how much I hated him. He couldn't figure out why? What was unclear to him? "Just end it," I said.

"Why?"

"Because I'm asking you to."

"What's between us is real," he said.

"Nothing with you is real," I said. "Everything is about appearances. You once told me everything is an interview. Remember?"

He seemed baffled. "No. I'm sorry. I don't remember every conversation we've ever had."

"You want to be with her because it will make you look good," I said. "That's the only reason you ever do anything. It's who you are."

"I'm surprised to find out how little you think of me. Though the idea that you could tell me who I am is completely preposterous."

"You're too complex for me?" I said. "Too incredibly subtle?"

"Subtle?" he said. "No. I'm too direct for you. When I want something, I pursue it."

"And you think I don't?"

"What have you ever wanted?"

"How about safety and security for my daughter?"

"She's hardly in danger," he said. "And I asked what *you* wanted, not what you've decided to demand of Miranda. When you say safety and security, I think what you mean is that you want an absence of conflict—for *yourself*. And that's nothing. It's not life."

"So I can't tell you who *you* are, but you can tell me about myself?"

"Sure, I'll tell you about yourself. What you're doing is right. You think I'll hurt your daughter, and you want to destroy anyone who might hurt her, because she's everything to you. But she's her own person now. And you have to be your own person, too."

"You must think I'm incredibly stupid," I said. "Do you really think you can feed me a line of conventional wisdom from some parenting guide and I'll be persuaded by it? You only ever have deep thoughts when you think they'll help you get what you want. You don't want me to let Miranda go because you think she needs to be her own person. You want me to let her go so she can belong to you."

"She's free to walk away from me if she wants."

"Like she was free to walk away from Ira?" I said.

He reacted as if mention of that name was some kind of disappointing but predictably underhanded move. "She was fifteen then."

"You're only right about one thing," I said. "Which is if you hurt my daughter, I will destroy you."

"As well you should," he said.

I had meant it as a real threat, but when I saw that Grant seemed not the slightest bit intimidated, I began to have the sinking feeling I have had so many times in my life: in the instant I am trying to be most forceful, I feel I am somehow losing my way. Because how was it that Grant was now agreeing with me? And how, by agreeing with me, did he seem to be strengthening his own position, rather than mine? I wanted to abandon words and thoughts and just grab him. But even in a blunt physical attack—even though I was taller than him and outweighed him—I felt confident he would withstand me. Fighting him was like fighting a wall: he was right in front of me, but there was no way to engage him. "You have to prove this to me," I said finally.

"What do you mean?" he said.

"You take this slowly. And you prove to me that this is real. For a long while."

"I understand." Only then did his gaze seem to turn inward—only then did I catch a glimpse of what might have been uncertainty.

"So what are you going to do now?" I asked.

"I'll see her again, if she wants."

The idiot. Did he not see he had already won? "I mean right now. Tonight."

"Oh," he said. "I told her I would call her after you and I talked. She was pretty upset."

"How gallant." I finished my drink while looking at the two of us in the mirror behind the bar. I had somehow become much older than Grant—I didn't like looking at myself next to him. "We're obviously not friends anymore," I said. "It would be completely impossible and ridiculous."

"Yes," he said quietly. "I suppose that's true." He turned to me and gathered himself as if to say something more, but seemed to change his mind. Without another word, he headed toward the door. I didn't turn to watch him, but followed his progress in the mirror's glass until he moved beyond the frame.

When I summoned the bartender a minute later to ask for another drink, I discovered my request wasn't necessary. He already had one ready for me.

EVERY SHIFT IN THE BREEZE, every creak of the half-open back door, every shuffle or sigh from the front room: each triggered the same little flourish of anxiety in me as I sat in Gina's office, waiting for Miranda. At first Gina kept up the pretense of doing work at her desk while I sat there, but she closed her laptop after only a few minutes, and now it was just the two of us sitting there, at loose ends. She didn't complain, but neither did she seem happy. Everyone wants a privileged position, and as the person who was to deliver the bride, she'd thought she had one. But now here I was, ruining it—and she had to make conversation, on top of it. "So Sandra said you're going to miss the photos," she said.

"We can take them after," I said. "The photographer has a plan."

She nodded, hesitating, and then plunged ahead. "And I suppose you know about her news?"

"Yes," I said.

"That's exciting, right?"

I shrugged.

"Are you angry I didn't tell you?"

"Why didn't you?"

"I didn't think it was my place. But you're not looking forward to being a grandfather?"

"Would you look forward to being a grandmother?"

"No," she said. "But isn't it different for men?"

"You mean death?"

She frowned, as if I were being rude. "It doesn't have to be death."

"That's what it's about, though."

"No. That's long off."

"Maybe," I said.

I heard the front door open and close then, followed by the faint press of steps. Gina went out into the gallery, and when I heard her say hello in a cheerful tone that implied familiarity, I stepped past the edge of the back wall prepared to see Miranda. The eyes that brightened with recognition at my appearance weren't hers, though. They were Grant's.

It may have been the first time he ever greeted me without smiling. All I got was a nod as he stepped past me to look into the back office. When he saw there was no one else there, though, he turned back, disappointed. "Someone is missing," he said.

"Yes," I said. "But her friend here says she's on her way."

He looked at Gina, then back at me, and it was then that we got the smile. "So we're all in the same place, waiting for the same person," he said. "How will we get to decide who gets to talk to her first?"

He asked the question in a tone so completely genuine that I assumed he was being ironic, though it's possible I was imagining strategy where there was none. "I don't think you're supposed to see her before the ceremony," I said. "It's bad luck."

"I'm just starting to think she might be looking for reassurance," he said.

I turned to Gina. "Is that what she needs?"

"I don't think she needs anything from either of you," she said. "But I don't know that my opinion carries much weight here."

"Of course it does," Grant said. "But I think a husband needs to be able to speak to his wife."

"You're not married yet," I said.

"Why do I feel like I'm in a competition here?" he said, still smiling.

"It's not a competition," I said. "You just can't see her now. You get to see her at the ceremony. And then for the rest of your life."

He looked at me as if trying to look *into* me, and I knew my gaze had probably gone flat and blank at that point. "I'm worried that you want to spirit her away," he said.

"No. I just want to speak to her," I said.

He continued to seem as if he were estimating something, though I wasn't sure what.

"You said you would prove it to me," I said. "That this was real."

"I think I've done that," he said.

I didn't. I had attached no concrete agenda to the demand and had set up no evaluative criteria, but still: all Grant had done was continue forward in the direction he'd already been going. He treated Miranda well, it seemed. And she fell further and further in love with him. It had been no great surprise when she stopped by my place early the previous fall to tell me the two of them were engaged. Grant hadn't asked for my consent, but I still managed to respond as if I were happy for her. Later that same evening, after Miranda had left—Sandra called. "I'm only going to say this once, and then never again," she said. "But I thought this was just something she needed to get out of her system. I honestly hoped he would do something stupid or horrible, and she would dump him and move on. Now I feel like she's announced that this disease is terminal."

"I should have stopped it," I said. "I made it too easy for him."

"No," she said, "I'm not going to blame you. I'm not going to blame anyone, because I can't. Because it will drive me crazy. I just need this one time to say how I feel about this. From here on I'm going to be positive, and I don't ever want to talk about it again. Do you understand that I can't talk about this, ever again? Because it will ruin my relationship with my daughter." She started to cry then. "I want my daughter to like me," she said between sobs. "But I hate what she is doing." And then she hung up. And she never did speak about it again. She never let any private conversation between the two of us—about Miranda, about the wedding, about anything—drift in the direction of her feelings. We were just planning a wedding—an event—and nothing more.

And yet there in the gallery, standing across from Grant, I thought: I should have asked him to perform a feat of which he was incapable. I should have named a price he could never pay. But what had I said? *We're obviously not friends anymore.* What did that matter? "Let me speak to her, Grant," I said. "She's my daughter."

He peered at me curiously, and then shrugged—and in doing so, his whole posture relaxed. "Maybe it is bad luck," he said.

"Maybe the groom shouldn't see the bride." He looked at Gina.

"She'll be there," she said.

And he turned to leave. I said nothing. Before opening the door, though, he stopped. "You know you don't get your money back on a lot of that stuff if there's not a wedding," he said.

"Have you ever known me to burn money?" I said.

"Yes," he said. "Once in a while. And with me, especially." But he pushed the door open anyway, headed out onto the street, and was gone.

"So do I have to go, too?" Gina said.

"No," I said. "I would never kick you out of your own place."

And it was then, finally, that I heard footsteps on gravel. Someone was in the alley behind the building. And when Miranda stepped around the back wall and stood there looking at us, still in her black T-shirt and khaki shorts, she looked perfectly dressed for a summer afternoon—if that afternoon weren't the one on which she was supposed to be getting ready for her wedding.

"Hi," she said. "Sorry if you've been waiting."

"It's okay," I said.

She tugged at the front of her shirt, ventilating, and stood at the edge of the office wall as if reluctant to actually step forward into the gallery. "Do you want to go for a walk?" she said.

"Your mom's expecting you at the hotel, you know," Gina said.

"I know," she said. "But I think there's time. Dad?"

"Yes," I said. "A walk sounds good."

MIRANDA AND I SET out a bit past four-thirty, at what was surely the hottest part of the day. We walked at first along the alley wall, taking advantage of the four or five feet of shade it cast across the gravel. After half a block, though, the alley ended, and we stepped onto the sidewalk and into the full-force blast of the sun.

"How are you wearing a suit today?" Miranda said. "You have to be boiling."

"I haven't had a chance to change."

"But why did you put it on in the first place?"

"I had to go to work."

She nodded as if that were a satisfactory answer. Above us, the sky held not the faintest shred of cloud—it radiated a blue so intense as to be almost sickening. The odors of asphalt and car exhaust hung in the air, and there was neither breeze, shade, nor shelter. Most drivers had their windows up in order to enjoy their air-conditioning, but a lone pickup with lowered windows treated us to a classic rock guitar solo that turned Doppler-shift sour as the vehicle passed. I felt a sheen of sweat rise over what felt like my entire body, but when I move to loosen my tie and undo the top button of my shirt, I realized I'd already done that, hours ago.

"They say it's the hottest day of the year," Miranda said brightly.

There was a beatific, unburdened quality to her smile—strange, I thought, less than an hour and a half from the scheduled start of her wedding. I walked forward at a steady clip, but Miranda altered her pace in accord with every little obstacle she discovered in her path, nimbly negotiating the cracks and crumbles of the old sidewalk by taking twice as many steps as me. Rather than taking a walk, she was choosing to *play* at taking a walk—but with perfect ease and without breaking a sweat. I had been called a string bean often enough as a kid, but any sense of myself as a dancer who might zig and zag around the cracks in a sidewalk had disappeared long ago. Before we had gone fifteen steps, I was dabbing at a trickle of sweat rolling from my temple. "So how have you been?" I said. "People have been looking for you."

A look of irritation replaced her smile. By mentioning the day's actual schedule, I had broken some kind of spell, it seemed. "I've been fine," she said. "Why were they looking for me?"

"I think you were supposed to be in certain places at certain times."

"They'll survive," she said, walking shoulder to shoulder with me until, at the end of the block, she leaned into me in order to turn me down another street. Amused by the rough affection of her technique, I asked where we were headed. "To see where everyone's going," she said.

"It's some kind of beer-drinking festival," I said.

Her eyes brightened. "Ooh," she said, quickening her pace and pulling me along by the arm. "Let's see what it looks like."

"Did you want to talk to me about something?" I said, resisting being hustled. "Or is this just a walk for our health?"

"What would I need to talk to you about?"

"You stuck me for the bill at lunch, for one."

"Oh, I know," she said, closing her eyes as if envisioning the event. "I'm sorry, Dad. I just couldn't talk right then."

"I suppose I wonder whether you're planning on attending your wedding today, too."

She pretended to think it over. "Will I get a decent table at the reception?"

"I think yours is supposed to be good. You might have to stand up and say something at some point, though."

"Shoot," she said. "I was hoping I could just have a good time. Now I have to make a speech?"

The lightness in her playacting seemed to bode well, or at least to suggest she understood there was more than one perspective on the day. And I always enjoyed playing her straight man—there was something tender about the way she trusted me to follow her. "A simple thanks will probably do," I said.

"As long as I don't have to say anything serious."

When we reached the end of the block, we came upon waist-high metal railings that blocked any further progress. Beyond the fence, one could see the chaos of the festival in full swing: an immense crowd filled the entire area, moving among and between tables set up along the perimeter of the streets. Aluminum kegs sat in ice-filled trash cans behind the tables, and the lines of tables extended in every direction, making it impossible to tell how many blocks the festival filled. Music carried from somewhere within, and napkins, wrappers, spilled food, and plastic cups covered the entire area. Squeezing my arm, Miranda flashed me a conspiratorial grin. "Let's go in," she said. "For just a few minutes."

"We have things to do," I said. "And I'm not dressed for this. I'll look ridiculous."

"So take your jacket off and carry it over your shoulder. Roll up your sleeves."

I gave her my sternest gaze. "We have places we need to be."

And with the same gaze, in the same low tone—like an audience member mocking a hypnotist—she said, "Five minutes, Dad."

The command was one I had used in her youth. When she didn't want to leave a playground, a birthday party, a roller-skating rink, or anything of the sort, I had always stated that same limit, in the same tone of voice. It had been more than a decade, though, since I'd said anything of the sort, and her sudden calling up of the phrase—and of the tone and facial expression—neutralized me to the point that I couldn't respond. And then she was leading me by the hand along the fence, toward an entrance manned by people uniformed in bright orange T-shirts covered with logos. "Miranda," I said.

"We'll just find out how much it costs," she said, continuing forward. "This is my dad," she told the woman in a floppy sun hat and oversized black sunglasses who sat at the table by the gate. "He wants to know how much it costs to go in."

"Five dollars to get in, one dollar per token, and each cup of beer costs two or three tokens, depending on the brewer," she announced.

Miranda looked at me. I shook my head, but that seemed to be the very response she wanted. "Two, please," she said firmly, pulling a twenty from her pocket. "And ten tokens." She handed the woman the bill, and the woman passed Miranda ten wooden nickels before stamping the backs of our hands. The stamp's image of a Tolkienesque sorcerer in a robe and pointed hat softened before my eyes as the ink bled into the reticulations of my skin.

"Can he leave his jacket here?" Miranda asked, pointing toward a cardboard box behind the woman that held an assortment of shirts, hats, and glasses.

"We don't have a coat check," the woman said. "That's the lost and found."

Miranda nodded, but when we stepped past the woman and into the festival, she circled behind me and tugged at the collar of my jacket until I obliged by slipping out of it. "The tie, too," she said, and I obediently removed it, then watched her stuff it into the jacket's inside pocket. While the woman manning the entry was engaged with the next customer, Miranda dropped my coat into the cardboard box. "No one's going to take it," she said, patting me on the back. She examined her palm with amazement. "You're soaked."

Of course I was. It was a hundred degrees, and I'd been wearing a suit and tie while she led me through city streets at a rapid clip. I could feel my shirt stuck to my skin all across and down my back. "I didn't dress to attend Brewfest," I said.

"Well," she said. "Roll up your sleeves."

I followed her order, but also furrowed my brow. "Five minutes, Miranda," I said sternly.

She laughed. We moved forward.

I was struck first by the tumult of voices and squeals and laughter, the sputtered hiss of valves dispensing beer, music from various distances and directions, suffering various degrees of distortion, and beneath it all the steady rumble and shuffle of shoes against pavement. By that hour, many of the tables were askew, with staffers and patrons who could no longer hide what a day of heat and alcohol had done to them. Some festivalgoers appeared, like us, to have just arrived, and therefore still to possess some composure, but that population was vastly outnumbered by those at other points on the sobriety scale. An energized group of braying college boys were pushing or jumping into one another in a ragged, sunburned way, spilling beer and mock-threatening one another with an enthusiasm frayed enough that one sensed the jousting could slip into actual violence, should one of them say the wrong thing, with the wrong shove, to another. There were also those whose energy was completely sapped: they shuffled slowly, stood in place, or sat on the curb, holding cups of beer they probably didn't want to drink, but from which they drank nevertheless. When Miranda moved to one of the nearest tables, I heard an eruption of applause and laughter behind me, but turned to find only a small group breaking up and moving off, and no evidence of what might have merited the cheer.

"This will make us feel better," Miranda said when she returned. "It cost three tokens, so it must be good." She handed me a bright red cup. I took a drink and discovered the beer to be surprisingly cold. I watched her take a modest little sip, but respond with a smile. "Isn't that good?" she said.

If she wasn't going to tell me, then what was there to talk about? I put my arm around her and pulled her next to me. "I wish we had more time," I said.

"Me too," she said.

We made our way farther along, toward a crowd of a dozen or so people gathered around a person who stood motionless before them, arms bent at the elbows and head canted at an odd, downward angle. The person was entirely covered—hat, sunglasses, face, and clothing—in metallic silver paint, and at first I took the angle of the performer's gaze to be the result of having entertained a child, until I remembered children weren't allowed in the festival. The man—if it was truly a man beneath that paint—ratcheted into motion then, twisting and raising his torso so that he was upright, then turning his head slowly in the direction of a young woman in shorts and a bikini top. She giggled nervously as the man raised his arms and brought his palms together and apart, miming applause. "Do you want a beer?" the woman asked loud enough for all of us to hear. When the robot responded with a slow, mechanized nod, she stepped forward and pressed her cup against his palm. His fingers curled with just enough force to make the cup buckle, a commitment to his role I noted with admiration. Then, through a series of agonizingly slow but transfixing movements, he lowered his neck, face forward, until his head extended from his body in a posture unnatural to any human beyond the confines of a yoga class. He raised his arm, adjusted his wrist to level the cup, and moved his hand toward his face, all through movements that seemed the product of gears rather than muscles. When he leveled the cup a last time and then brought it slowly and in a straight line to his lips, I knew, even before it happened, what the result would be. He brought the cup to his lips, tilted the bottom up—and never opened his mouth. Beer spilled from his lips, cascading to the pavement and rolling in a sudsy ribbon toward the curb. When the cup was empty, the man tilted his head in confusion, raising the cup to the mirrored lenses of his sunglasses to peer, baffled, within. Then, with a sudden and shockingly authentic mechanical convulsion, he flung his arm away from himself, releasing the cup so that it flew into the crowd. We gasped and laughed and cheered, and I noted the hint of a smile upon the robot's silvered lips. Was it a part of the act, I wondered, or a break in character? I couldn't tell—and then it was gone. He began to rotate his torso slowly in our direction, but I didn't want to be the next person pulled into the act, so I led Miranda away. "You see," she said. "This is fun."

"I see," I said.

"People should have fun. They should do what they want to do."

What was she talking about? Herself? Me? Somebody nearby was bellowing into a loudspeaker about a special offer, or a soon-to-start event, or maybe something else entirely—amplified into distortion, the speech was indecipherable. "What do *you* want to do?" I asked.

"Just walk," she said. "I just want to walk."

We wandered further through the festival, and when she looked at me again, the leaves of a streetside maple cast fluttering shadows across her face. A few more steps took us beyond those, though, and she raised her face to the sun, basking in the light as if it had only now appeared.

We came then to a long line of green bicycle racks filled with a chaos of frames, wheels, wires, and locks. A girl—she looked college-aged or recently graduated—stood there gripping the bar of the last bike rack to steady herself. Leaning forward, her eyes closed, she rested her head on her shoulder in an inebriated posture of either exhaustion or pain. There didn't appear to be anyone with her, and when Miranda asked if she was all right, the girl did not, at first, react. Then slowly, without managing to turn or acknowledge us, she shook her head. "Can I get you something?" Miranda said. "Some water? Or maybe someone who works here who can help you?" The girl could only shake her head silently, it seemed—when she tried to straighten and step from the bike rack, she wobbled, and we saw her tear-streaked cheeks and rolling, unfocused eyes. She closed them, seeking relief, but no sooner had she done so than she began to tilt dangerously backward. Miranda grabbed her quickly by the arm and helped her to the curb, where the two of them sat together, side by side.

I looked for a person of any authority in the area, but none was to be found. No one near the racks stood out as event staff, and neither did I see any police or security personnel. How a festival that centered on the consumption of alcohol could be almost entirely unsupervised was beyond me, but had there been a person in any official uniform there, I probably wouldn't have noticed the person I did, a man distinct at first only because he wore khaki chinos and, like me, a button-down dress shirt. He was walking toward a long row of green portable toilets that lined the opposite side of the street, and something about him struck me as familiar. I was maybe forty feet away, and had only an instant in which to look before he stepped into the toilet and closed the door, but it was all I needed. I'm seeing things, I thought. That cannot be him.

I had somehow finished my beer, and its presence in my empty stomach worked a dizzying effect in my head. I was standing in the sun, but I had stopped sweating, and my damp shirt felt cold against my body. Miranda was on the curb, rubbing the upset girl's back and speaking quietly to her. The girl nodded in response, and then her lips curled into another sob. Miranda looked up at me. "I think we need to find someone for her," she said.

The nearest tables were manned only by people pouring beer, and there was a line at each of them. Who was there to speak to? I looked back to the toilet the man had entered, but the door remained closed, so I stood there waiting. I wanted to see what he was going to do—and I suppose I wanted to see what I would do about it. When I turned back to Miranda, the girl had leaned away from her, head to the side. Quietly and with almost no movement, she vomited into the gutter. Miranda continued to rub her back and tell her it was okay, that she would feel better soon, while at the same time I turned to see the door I had been watching open again, and the man within stepped into the sunlight. The sleeves of his white dress shirt were rolled to above the elbow, and the shirt itself, in what I decided was an attempt to appear casual, remained untucked. The little pressureless faucets inside the portable toilets wouldn't have been much help cleaning purple ink from his hands, if that's what he'd had in mind, though it was also true that amid a crowd as tattooed, rubber-stamped, tanned, and sunburned as that one, probably no one would pay any attention to purple hands. The door of the toilet fell shut behind him with a hollow plastic thud as he hesitated, scanning his surroundings, and then walked in our direction. His hair was short and gray and his expression blank, save for his eyes, which looked as tired as they'd been in the photos I'd seen earlier in the day. When he reached the bike rack, he stopped no more than five feet from me. But his hands were clean.

Our eyes met, and he nodded. "How's it going?" he said politely. I hadn't heard Mooncalf's voice in twenty-five years—and even then, it hadn't been more than a couple sentences.

"Fine," I said. "Yourself?"

"I don't know," he said with a wry smile. "I may be finished for the day."

Amazing—he'd had a few! His light-banter tone, the way he leaned against the bike rack: he was going for casual, but I could tell that he, too, was steadying himself. "There's only so long you can get away with it, out here in the heat," I said. "A lot of people overdo it."

He offered only the same genial, almost goofy smile, which included an involuntary widening of his eyes that made him appear slightly dazed. All these years, I thought, and I catch you in an off moment. Was this a celebration? Or was it a professional strategy, the proper prescription for leavening the nerves and adrenaline after the event? And was he so meticulous as to have planned it ahead, to know that a quick place to blend in while coming down would be among the raggedly drunk and freshly sunburned masses downtown?

"They think they can have one more," I said. "And then it's even easier to say, Hell, why not another one? And before they know it, they're in a bad place."

"That's why I'm shutting it down," he said. "All these drunk kids are gonna be hurting in the morning."

I tried, quickly, to imagine a timeline. He shoves the bag of cash under his suit jacket, or maybe in the back of the waistband, and heads into the neighborhood, moving quickly between the empty buildings on his way to wherever his car is parked. He makes sure he hasn't been followed, then hops in, starts it up, and drives . . . home? Why not? The thing is over. The rest of his day is free.

But Amber gave him a dye pack. It would be explosive enough to blow the jacket right off his body, or explode the seams of his pants, if not to inject ink right into his skin. It would have soaked his entire back and legs, and probably injured him, as well.

This man next to me had a white shirt on. It was clean.

"What about you?" he said. "Are you done, too? Or are you just getting here?"

I believed it was him. The eyes, the hair, the voice—I believed it. And I thought, If you don't rob me twenty-five years ago, then Sandra doesn't see me as the wounded young man she can help. Even if Grant and Gina had still bothered to take me to Bristol's, I would have had no story to tell and no celebrity to trade on. So would any of my life have happened? Could I have been someone else? Someone other than the guy at the bank?

"Is there no one around?" It was Miranda's voice. She was still there, comforting the girl.

"I think it's last call," I told the man next to me. "I don't think we have a choice."

"That's good," he said. "Because it's true—I was thinking about getting one more. I guess they're protecting us from ourselves, huh?" With that, he pushed himself from the bike rack and began to walk away. "You have a good evening, now," he said, turning to look back at me one more time. And in that glance, and the tone of that last sentence, I thought I detected something. Had he recognized me?

Maybe I just wanted him to. Because he didn't alter his stride as he walked to the edge of the street, stepped onto a sidewalk next to a bordering fence, and made his way toward the nearest exit, half a block away. And I couldn't help it: I followed. Slowly, and from a distance, but still—I watched him walk toward the exit at what seemed to me a calculatedly normal pace, was close enough to see him move past the staff members still taking money from latecomers entering the festival as he slipped through the opening in the fence and continued on, past the stragglers milling outside. There were points at which people passed between us, but I caught sight of him again each time, and watched him walk at a brisk pace down the side street, away from the festival. A larger group of festivalgoers stepped in front of me at that point, and by the time they moved past—by the time I jogged around them, actually—he was most of the way down the block, passing quickly beneath storefront awnings. Parked cars blocked my view, but I thought I saw him—or part of him—once more. And then he was gone.

I approached one of the staff members sitting idly behind the ticket table, a young man whose face was hidden beneath a baseball hat and mirrored sunglasses. "I need some help," I told him. "There's a girl who's sick, and we don't see anyone with her."

"Here we go again," he said, sighing. But he rose dutifully, and followed as I led the way. And when we made our way back to where Miranda and the girl had been sitting, there they were, in the exact same spot. Just waiting.

WHY DID I EXPECT people would be there to meet us? The quaint childhood belief that your particular life is the main and only show never really goes away, I suppose. But not a soul noted our presence when Miranda and I stepped into the Sycora Park Suites. The fountain in the atrium ran at its relentless pace, the water cascading down through the tiers in a glossy white sheen of a piece with the light jazz playing on the lobby speakers and the ringing concussions created each time the lobby bartender set a rack of glassware on the bar. We encountered no one as we made our way around the atrium to where the elevator sat waiting for us, its glass panels glinting in the lobby lights like the facets of an oversized jewel. The door was open, and Miranda stepped in, but I hesitated. A hollow male laugh rang out from somewhere beyond or behind the front desk. *I could leave her now,* I thought. But Miranda said, "Come on. Take me up." So I stepped in, the doors closed, and the entire scene went silent. The fountain churned as we rose above it, and people moved through the lobby, but they were just mute images now, falling away.

"Is Mom angry?" Miranda asked. "Is the schedule ruined?"

"I don't think so," I said. "Most of the schedule didn't involve you."

"I missed the photos, though."

"There aren't wedding photos without a bride. They'll get them afterward."

As the elevator continued its ascent, it filled with the bright natural light that filtered down through the hotel's glass roof, and it was within that strange radiance that Miranda turned to me, looking surprised and a bit disappointed to discover that the world rolls forward just as easily in our absence as in our presence. "That's probably better, anyway," she said doubtfully.

"Your entrance will be more dramatic," I said.

"I guess people like it that way."

The elevator chimed softly, and we stepped out and headed down the hall. To our right ran the long row of room doors, and to our left, the half wall one could peer over to look into the abyss. We were only steps from Sandra's room when Miranda, as if remarking on nothing more than another of the day's mundane tasks, said, "So I wrote you a note."

"What do you mean?"

"I was thinking I might not give it to you," she said. "But I guess I wrote it for a reason." She pulled a folded envelope from her pocket and thrust it toward me.

"When did you write this?" I asked.

She shrugged. "This afternoon."

"Do I need to read it now?"

"No. Tomorrow, maybe, or the day after. It's not important."

She seemed unhappy with whatever was in the envelope, but we had reached the room by then. When Miranda knocked on the door, Sandra opened it immediately. She looked first at me, but without any recognition—as if she didn't even know who I was. When her eyes flicked to Miranda, though, she gasped. "Get in here. Where have you been?" she said, taking her daughter by the arm. I heard the voices of others within, but I never saw them, because the door was already swinging shut. "I was taking care of something," Miranda said, but by that point she, too, was only a voice. And with a metallic strike that echoed down the hall, the door closed, and I stood there alone.

I recall holding the brass handrail in the elevator to steady myself as it carried me to the lobby. My legs felt weak, but I put one foot in front of the other as I stepped from the elevator and tried to remember what it was I needed to do next. My tuxedo was in my car, but heading out into the heat seemed impossible.

Instead, I made my way to the middle of the lobby and sat on a park bench placed near the fountain, probably to further the atrium's pleasure dome effect. Something was off—I had stopped sweating during the Brewfest, but now that I was in the air-conditioned lobby, I felt warm again. A trickle of moisture gathered along my hairline, and I thought I might be sick. I told myself that simply couldn't happen in the hotel lobby on Miranda's wedding day. Once seated, though, I felt I no longer had the ability to move at all, and intending to spend a moment gathering myself, I closed my eyes.

The next thing I felt was a hand on my arm, gently shaking me. "Hey," I heard Catherine say. "Are you okay? Wake up."

I didn't know how long my eyes had been closed, but it seemed an effort to open them. I still felt as if I might be sick, and could not, in that state, say anything. All I was able to do was smile weakly and nod.

"What's wrong?" she asked. "Can you speak?"

I shook my head.

"Are you going to pass out?"

I managed, with great effort, to shrug.

"You should lie down."

I felt that if I did that, I might never get up again, so I shook my head.

"Stay here," she said.

I closed my eyes. When Catherine returned, it was with a glass of water in one hand and a plate with a sandwich and potato chips on it in the other. "Do you think you can eat?" she asked.

I drank some water and tried a bite of the sandwich. My body had shut down for a few minutes, it seemed, and now was starting slowly up again.

"Is everything okay?" she asked.

"Everyone's where they're supposed to be," I said, and took another bite from the sandwich. "This is good."

"You need it," she said. "But now that some of the color is returning to your face, I should tell you that I have news. They found the dye pack."

That stopped me. But then I thought, Every time I try to eat. So I took another bite and finished chewing before I said, "Where?"

"In a Dumpster behind the wine distributor," she said. "An employee was taking out the trash, and when he lifted the lid, everything inside was purple."

"It exploded in the Dumpster?"

"It sounds like it."

"Any money in there? Did he ditch the whole bag?"

"Annie said it was only the dye pack."

"Who is Annie?"

"The woman with security."

"Jesus. I completely forgot about the woman," I said.

I returned to my speculative version of the drama. Did he really have enough time to make it two blocks before the dye pack exploded? Did he sift through the money while he walked, moving fast, until he felt the one strap of bills that was different? But if that alley was where he stopped—whether surprised and angry, or pleased to find what he'd been looking for—it was true: he would have been only twenty yards from three or four Dumpsters, from piles of discarded boxes, and probably near one or two open truck beds, too. "He picked it out," I said.

"I guess so."

Regardless of whether it was luck or skill, I was astounded. It was a wonder. "He picked it out."

Catherine did not seem as impressed. "Can I make a personal observation?" she said.

"Sure," I said.

"You're kind of a mess. Where are you going to clean up?"

"I was planning on home."

"Do you know what time it is?"

"No. What time is it?"

"Too late for you to go home," she said. "Where are your clothes?"

"My tuxedo? In the car."

"Give me your keys," she said, extending her palm.

"What are you even doing here?" I said. "Why do you follow me?"

"I'm not following you. I have a room here."

"Why do you have a room? You live ten minutes from here."

"I don't want to worry about how much I should or shouldn't drink at the reception, or how late I should stay. It's easier to have a room."

I extricated the keys and dropped them into her palm. "How responsible of you," I said.

She handed me a plastic card—her room key. "It's 514. And you really need to clean up. You're pretty ripe. I'll bring your tuxedo up in a bit."

"Yes, ma'am," I said.

She turned, walked to the front of the lobby, and stepped out through the sliding doors. I sat there, eating my sandwich in silence. I drank more water. Could I stand and walk? Could I even make it up to this room? I stood. The world did not tilt. It was just there, waiting for me to navigate it. And as I made my way across the lobby, I thought: *It's alive!* I may even have smiled a bit at that, though I also realized I couldn't remember what happens in the story once the monster stands up. The next images that came to mind were of villagers and torches, as if there were no middle to the story at all. And I couldn't recall how the ending turned out, either. There was more than one version, I reminded myself. But no matter the version, he gets away, doesn't he?

WHEN I STEPPED OUT of the shower, I discovered my tuxedo and its attendant paraphernalia—including a plastic-looking pair of shoes and some cheap cuff links I didn't need—on the hanging bar next to the hotel room's door. There was no evidence of Catherine, though—I saw no suitcase or bag belonging to her, no papers on the table, no sign even of a moved chair or wrinkled bedspread. It was just an empty room that held me and two suits.

When I had the tuxedo on and had adjusted the cummerbund, straightened the tie, and squared the shoulders, I looked at myself in the bathroom's still-steamed mirror. I looked very much like myself again, I decided—the way people expected me to look. They would be pleased.

While hanging the jacket of my other suit, I removed two items from the pocket: the envelope Miranda had handed me on our way to Sandra's room, and the transfer form Catherine wanted me to sign. The envelope from Miranda wasn't sealed, and the note I removed from within was written on a couple sheets of yellow legal paper.

Dear Dad,

I don't know why I feel like I need to write you something. And since this is the third time I've tried to write this, I'm not going to let myself start correcting this one or throw it away, so it's probably going to be rough. On the other tries I started trying to explain things, or I was telling you what to do, and it just seemed ridiculous for me to be acting as if you didn't already know all the stuff I was explaining or that you would need me to tell you what to do. It sounded dumb, and it wasn't even what I wanted to say, so those didn't work. I give up on explaining anything. You know who I am. I don't have to explain myself. And like I told you a little while ago, the rest of it doesn't matter.

God. But I'm not going to throw this one away. Sorry!

There was this time that I was coming over to your house once. You knew I was coming over, I don't remember why. This was just a couple years ago. But when I walked up to the door, I could see you through the window next to the door. You were in the living room, but standing where I could see straight down the hall to you. I was just stepping up to the door, but you were standing down there, totally motionless, like you were looking at something on the wall, and I stopped before I came in, because I was trying to figure out what you were looking at. You had music on in the house. It must have been pretty loud, Dad, if I could hear it through the door! But then as I was watching, I saw you nod your head and dance for a few steps. You nodded like someone was talking to you, though I'm sure you were just responding to the words of the song, or maybe something in the music. But it was like someone was talking to you, and you were nodding, and then you did a little cha-cha. It was so cute, your little dance. And then you stopped and stood still, like you were listening again. And I knocked on the door as I put my key in, and then the weirdest thing happened, which was that by the time I turned the key and opened the door, you must have turned off the music. Because when I stepped inside the house, it was silent, and you were down there in the living room asking how I was doing, in your usual way. But whatever the music was, or even the fact that you had been listening to it, was just gone. I thought to ask what you'd been listening to, but I knew you would say it was nothing, or that you didn't know, or any of the things you usually say. We were supposed to go out to dinner or something, and you were ready, so we stood there chatting for a few minutes, and the whole time I was actually just hoping you would leave the room so I could sneak over and open up your CD player to find out what it was you liked so much. But you didn't leave the room, so I never got a chance to see what the music was. I never figured it out. You turned it off before I came in the door, as if you didn't think it was appropriate to be listening to music you liked while someone else was around.

This is not even what I wanted to write. And I didn't even write about that the other times I tried to write this letter. I don't know why I just wrote about that, or why I feel like I need to write a letter to you. But listen. Please know that you can come see me whenever you want. You don't have to be so formal or respectful or whatever. Maybe that's why I wrote about that. Sometimes you're too polite, I think. So please don't fade off into the distance from me because you think that's the respectful or polite thing to do, because I'm married or a big adult or whatever now. I want you to know that you can come over and talk to me whenever you want. And you can listen to whatever music you want. So what if things are changing? They're going to change even more, but that doesn't mean you have to start being more and more polite with me, or whatever it is that makes you turn your music off and never talk about yourself and, as far as I know, never do anything that would inconvenience anyone or cause anyone to think about you for more than two seconds. Don't do that with me. When you're polite and formal, sometimes it feels like you're acting like a stranger instead of my dad. I want you to be yourself. You don't have to stand quietly at the back of things because you're concerned you'll annoy someone or be embarrassing. You'll never annoy me or be embarrassing, or maybe I just want you to annoy me more often, and to be embarrassing more often. I want you to keep hanging around with me.

All right. This isn't what I was going to write at all, but it's just as good as anything else, probably. And I told myself I wouldn't throw this one away. You know everything else, and I have other things to do today. Knowing you, you're probably looking for me at this very moment. So I suppose I should let you find me.

Love,
Miranda

I put the letter back into the envelope, and returned it to the pocket of the jacket I'd placed on the hanger. She doesn't know what she's getting into, I thought. And how could she? She had never been married before, and neither had she been a mother. The nature of those experiences was just speculation for her. She couldn't know what married life with Grant would be like any more than anybody else could, and she certainly didn't know about raising a child. Becoming a mother would change her, just as the child's presence would change her life with Grant. It wasn't just her future that was uncertain, but who she would be in that future. I would love her no matter who she became, of course, but what was the source of this constant, unceasing desire women had to liberate me from something? Maybe that was the clearest sign Miranda was a woman now, equal to the others: she had joined them in telling me I needed to change. She should have consulted Sandra, Gina, and Catherine before telling me she wanted me to be annoying around her, or to embarrass myself. Was she aware what that meant? She had written this letter, for instance, and had walked with me through the festival, all while still not sharing with me the fact that she was pregnant. How was I to feel about that? My daughter was beautiful, but she was hiding something from me. I loved her more than anyone in the world—and she wasn't telling me something. What option did I have, other than to be quietly patient? That would be far better, at least, than telling her I understood she hoped today didn't mean good-bye, but that although I would of course continue to see and talk to her for the rest of my life, she was going to become a wife today, and a mother soon, and those offices would lay their not-insignificant claims on her. So today was, in many real and inescapable ways, indeed good-bye. Maybe she wished that wasn't true. I certainly did. I had no reasons for wanting time to move forward—the future, for me, seemed nothing but a consolation prize. Why pretend that I looked forward to age? No one in the world was as real to me as Miranda—as far as I was concerned, life went where she went. But as she had said in her letter, she had other things she needed to do now.

There was a knock at the room's door. When I opened it to find Catherine, I acted dismayed. "I was starting to think you weren't coming back," I said.

"Somebody seems much better," she said, stepping past me. I followed her out of the claustrophobic little entryway and into the room, watching her cast a surveying glance around the place. "Do you really think I would have left you in the state you were in without coming back?" she said.

"It wouldn't necessarily have surprised me."

"There, there," she said, giving me a little pat on the shoulder.

I unfolded the transfer request form I'd been holding and laid it on the little round table by the window. "Patronize me all you want," I said. "But the bank will still be a mess when you're gone. Where do I sign this?"

When she recognized what I was looking at, she seemed surprised. "I thought you said you wanted time to look it over."

"It's just a form," I said. "It doesn't merit reading. Where?"

She pointed to a line midway down the first page. I signed and flipped the form over, and she pointed to a line at the bottom of the second page. I signed, and handed her the form. "There you go," I said. "I officially consent and recommend you for open positions. Unofficially, I think it's a disaster."

"There are many capable service managers in the world," she said, stepping past me on her way back to the door. "You'll find someone."

I didn't follow her—I stayed where I was, looking out the room's large window. "Maybe. I suppose I'll miss you as a person, though, too. There's always that."

"As a person?" she said. "Does that mean personally?"

"It means not only as a coworker. I don't understand why you—"

"Stop," she said. "This isn't right."

She was behind me. I felt her fingers on the back of my neck, turning up my collar. "You can't see everything in the mirror," I said.

"Obviously not. And I'm not going anywhere, if that makes you feel better. If you miss me as a person, you can always call. My number is in your phone." She tugged at the collar, making further adjustments. I felt she was being a little rough. "This seems tight," she said. "Is it supposed to be this tight?"

"It's fine," I said. "But if today has taught me anything, it's that just because I have someone's number in my phone doesn't mean they'll actually answer when I call."

She turned my collar down and ran her index finger along the inside, smoothing it. And then I felt her hands on my shoulder as, before I even understood what she was doing, she kissed me on the back of the neck. "I will answer," she said.

I was stunned. Yes, I had been flirting with her all day—and maybe for years—but I had never *let on* that I was flirting with her. "That is entirely over the line," I said. "Now you *have* to transfer."

"Turn around."

I complied, and she looked me up and down with a critical eye. She stepped forward, straightened my bow tie, and kissed me on the cheek.

"Stop it," I said.

"There," she said. "You're fixed."

I shook my head. I wasn't done being outraged. I liked playing outraged.

"No. Don't," she said.

"Don't what?"

"Don't say anything. Don't ruin it. You're already late, so just go."

She was trying to be bold, but behind those freckles, I could see that she was blushing. I was probably blushing, too. We talked to customers, and to each other, every day. But Catherine and I were both quite shy, really. "I was just going to say thank you, Catherine," I said. "What did you think I was going to say? Something embarrassing?"

"Just go!" she said, opening the door and pushing me into the hall. It wasn't a mild push, either, but a shove, surprising in its force—she could probably have sent me right over the wall, had she wanted to.

THE FLORA IN THE Quad were in full bloom, the air heavy with the scent of grass and blossoms. The food and drink had restored the color to my face, and the change of clothes, though it consisted only of replacing one suit with another, had rendered me at least presentable. And I had made it, somehow, to the head of the concrete walk that ran down the center of the Quad. A black limousine entered from the opposite end, turned onto the curved drive, and crept slowly in my direction. Seated before me in the clean white chairs—half of them on one side of the walk, half on the other—were the assorted guests. And thirty yards away, waiting patiently with the pastor at the front of the crowd and wearing a tuxedo exactly like mine, stood Grant. It seemed far away, that end of the walk.

The sky was bright, and the sun hung lazily in the western half, as if determined to extend the day. As the limousine continued its slow journey around the Quad, though, I noticed that the sky to the east was already a deeper blue. The shift occurred somewhere overhead, I assumed. I felt outside of myself, as if watching silently while neither of us—the self standing and the self watching—was able to move or speak. When the limousine stopped at the head of the walk, the driver who emerged wore a black cap and dark glasses. I never saw his eyes, or even a distinguishing feature, as he opened the back door and Miranda stepped out. She, too, had been transformed, and much more dramatically than I. So much so, in fact, that at first it was difficult for me to recognize her. It was her, and it was not. This was not the way she dressed. It was not her makeup, not the way she wore her hair. But I suppose that is how people marry.

There were no flower girls or ring-bearing boys—she hadn't wanted them. It was just Miranda and I, standing there before the guests, all of whom had risen. She took hold of my arm, trembling. "I feel like I'm in a costume," she whispered.

I smiled, though it wasn't what I felt. What I felt was that it made no sense for me to walk down that aisle with her. The correct choreography would be for the bride to kiss her father, and then just walk away from him. She wasn't mine to give away.

But the musicians were already playing the march. There's still time, I thought. But I was wrong. Time was up. Miranda stepped forward.

Insights,
Interviews
& More . . .

Meet Dan DeWeese

I GREW UP ON A DIRT ROAD in the foothills of the Rocky Mountains, just west of Loveland, Colorado, during the 1970s and 1980s. I lived on what one might call "the first foothill": to the west were the undulating hills that form the doorsteps of the Rockies, and to the east were the unbroken plains that run from Northern Colorado through Nebraska, Iowa, and on into Illinois, where my maternal grandparents lived in Chicago.

The lack of intrusion from outside forces available to a child in those years, especially in a rural location before the introduction of the VHS tape, has been erased forever. Much of my childhood took place in that context, however, and I think fondly of it—my parents, sister, the 1970s in general—quite often. Even as a child, I had the freedom of being able to walk out the front door without anyone needing to ask where I was going, since there wasn't anywhere I *could* be going, other than outside to play. I rode a Denver Broncos Huffy bicycle both on and off the road, and raged, usually with tears, whenever the Broncos lost.

Loveland's newspaper, the *Reporter-Herald*, was an afternoon paper. I often grabbed it from the box by the road as I walked home from the school bus stop, and then read it, sometimes in its entirety, as soon as I walked into the house. What had happened in the world over twenty-four hours previously would, for the most part, still be news to me at four o'clock the next day, and my belief that the *Reporter-Herald* was both timely and authoritative remained intact throughout most of my childhood.

After high school, I was accepted into the production program of what was then called the Department of Cinema and Television at the University of Southern California. I was in South Central Los Angeles during the riots that followed the announcement of the verdict in the Rodney King case, as I was on the night of the North Ridge earthquake that collapsed apartment buildings and a section of Interstate 10. I lived and worked in Los Angeles long enough also to be there for the announcement of the verdict in the O.J. Simpson case, as well as for the day that two masked gunmen covered in body armor engaged in a protracted, post-bank-robbery automatic weapons shootout with Los Angeles police. These years were a unique education.

I returned to Colorado, this time to Fort Collins, where I studied literature and English education at Colorado State University, and taught as a student teacher at Fort Collins High School. I left Fort Collins for Portland, Oregon, but found no jobs available in the Portland Public School system. I showed up on the doorstep of a new journal called *Tin House*, but since I had no previous experience in publishing and was, as it were, a complete stranger, they had no open positions for me, either. Eventually, I took a job as a teller in a Wells Fargo branch.

I began to publish short fiction. Early stories appeared in *Missouri Review*, *New England Review*, and *Northwest Review*. Over the years, I went on to place work in places including *Pindeldyboz*, *Ascent*, *Washington Square*, and, yes, eventually, a few stories in *Tin House*. Foolishly, I also began work on a novel. After some years of work on that, I took the additionally imprudent step of founding *Propeller*, a quarterly magazine of art, literature, film, and culture, and Propeller Books, an independent literary press whose first book, *Nine Simple Patterns for Complicated Women*, is a collection of stories by Mary Rechner.

In 2011, this novel, *You Don't Love This Man*, was published by Harper Perennial.

The Sidelined Character

Paul, the main character in this novel, is not a typical main character. A detective trying to catch a criminal makes for a traditional main character, and likewise a criminal himself—a man of action, pulling off capers or on the run—often takes center stage. Many main characters in literature are people having florid breakdowns, because a person in the midst of a breakdown can engage in any number of impulsive, dangerous, or self-destructive acts which, when they occur in the pages of a novel rather than in real life, can be greatly entertaining. (In real life, they're usually less so.) There is also the illness-and-recovery narrative, of course, whose main character starts essentially where the florid-breakdown character ended, and whose story covers the character's journey back to health and happiness. And it's possible to string these kinds of characters together. Writers have gotten a lot of mileage out of a main character who starts as someone investigating or trying to get away with something, suffers a florid existential breakdown with episodes of diverting insanity, and then finds the road to redemption. The end.

A fellow writer once told me he was intrigued by how, in my novel, the voice of "a guy who is so sidelined" became so compelling to him. When I asked what he meant by "sidelined," he said that it was standard to read all sorts of things about a team's star or main players, but that there are always other players good enough to be on the team, but who rarely make it off the bench. Fans sometimes forget these players' names or that they're even on the team, even though the players are in practice every day, and then right there on the sidelines during every game. He said my novel was like reading the story of one of these players, and then realizing that you learn entirely different things about the team—and sometimes about the sport as a whole—when you hear about it from the sidelined guy.

I thought about this for a while. The first thing that occurred to me—and I was still following the sports metaphor here—is that a lot of players on the sidelines don't necessarily feel they actually *belong* on the sidelines. They believe that if they were given the opportunity to get in the game, they could have great success. For these players, using the word as a verb ("to be sidelined") makes sense, because they're not out of the game willingly—someone has put them there. Coaches, fans, and other players might disagree, of course, and suggest that the sideline is exactly where that player belongs. Controversies over who should be on the field and who should be on the bench are perpetual.

Then I thought about how strange it is that we don't read more stories about "sidelined" characters, because *everyone*, at some point, gets sidelined. People who were stars at one level find themselves struggling at the next, their previously effective skills and strategies no longer working. And even someone who has achieved success at the highest level, who has maintained the role of a team or organization's dynamic central character for years, has to accept less time in the spotlight as his or her career winds down. It doesn't matter who you are, how good you are, or what situations you have thrived in, and which you've struggled against—at some point, someone will tap you on the shoulder and point to the bench. You will be sidelined.

I think that because this moment is one we all fear and try to avoid, we don't often tell stories in which the central character is going through this crisis. A proper tragedy of dramatic Shakespearean proportions is almost easier: a confluence of events, combined with some fatal flaw in the main character, leads to a sudden downfall. Poison! Stabbings! Murders intentional and accidental! Yelling, screaming, gasping for air while commanding someone to *Remember me! Remember . . . argh . . . me . . . guh.*

Good fun.

Sidelined characters, on the other hand, have to keep right on living, even though they're often not even sure if they're in a comedy or a tragedy. They exist in an uncomfortable marginal space: on the team, but not often in the game. They have to mull over whether they've been unfairly sidelined, or whether the sideline is where they in fact belong. They might cry about the situation at times, and then at other times laugh. They may want fervently to be in the game, but then find that when their number is called, they experience a sense of dread. The sideline has become comfortable, and now that they're going into the game, they have to face the possibility of failure, and do so while knowing that one of the reasons they've been on the sideline in the first place is that they've made mistakes in games in the past. They may even feel the mistakes aren't their fault. Maybe if they were in the game more often, they would be able to relax a bit, and wouldn't make as many mistakes. Maybe the sideline has a spooky, dangerous power to turn great players *into* sideline players.

These doubts, crises, struggles, and examinations mean that though a story with the star character at the center of it can be quite rousing, there are actually many other fiendish little narratives that occur parallel to the star's story. And these other narratives, with their sidelined central characters, involve just as much love, desire, conflict, doubt, and struggle as any story. It's just that our eyes are often elsewhere, drawn to the dramas that are broadcast under the brightest lights. We know there are other players on the team, over there on the sidelines, but do we know their names? ▶

The Sidelined Character *(continued)*

Not always. Are they given an opportunity to tell their stories? Not as often.

So I suppose that word, if it *is* a word, is accurate: the main character of this story is a man who is sidelined. And this novel is what we hear when this man, who has spent the greater portion of his life standing quietly to the side, decides to start talking.

Author's Picks

Throughout the years I spent writing *You Don't Love This Man*, readers of drafts (pronounced: *my friends*) often asked to what degree I felt the main character was aware of how others see him. I was never able to answer this question definitively, but I will now claim this is mostly because I didn't want to say something like: "He is highly aware of how others see him, but he can't do anything about it, because he is almost entirely blind to how others see him."

I think most thinking and feeling human beings are trapped in that same nonsensical sentence, and I'm far from the first person to have written about it. The following are things I sometimes refer to when trying to explain to someone that I have a strong sense of self, but I have a hard time communicating it, because I haven't the slightest idea who I am.

***Blow-Up*, directed by Michelangelo Antonioni**
Antonioni's landmark depiction of the fact that the more closely we examine an image, the less clarity we have on what we see—or think we see—within its borders. It's not that we fail to see accurately, it's that each image is really just a smaller part of a larger, more complex image. And the reason we can't see the larger image with any clarity is that we're inside of it. It's the world.

***Late Spring*, directed by Yasujirô Ozu**
Ozu is a master of depicting situations in which characters feel compelled to say or go along with something socially acceptable, while simultaneously revealing the degrees, sometimes desperate, to which they wish they could refuse. Setsuko Hara smiles and smiles and smiles in this film, and it's a stunning, beautiful smile. It is also, often, a mask.

***Low*, David Bowie**
David Bowie, Brian Eno, Tony Visconti, Europe, the mid-1970s. The brilliance of this album isn't news. But in a world that often feels designed to reduce the opportunities for headspace, these artists crafted music—here and elsewhere—that created not only more opportunities for headspace, but offered brand-new flavors of it. My son was playing a cheap retro version of the old video game *Pole Position* the other day when a track from this album came on, and I started laughing. It was "Always Crashing in the Same Car."

***Solaris*, directed by Andrei Tarkovsky**
If you could live with your thoughts and memories instead of in the real world, would it be paradise or hell? Tarkovsky's answer, built atop the scaffolding of Stanislaw Lem's novel, only complicates the question, but in a way that feels moving and true. Late in the film, the sequence of weightlessness and a Bruegel painting breaks my heart, every time.

Author's Picks *(continued)*

***Eclipse*, by John Banville**
Here and elsewhere, Banville reveals his mastery at treading the line—he has expanded it into an entire territory, really—between what we call a "literary novel" (a suspicious redundancy) and that item named "the detective story." In addition to his crackling lexical energy, Banville's work hums along on the delightful paradox that "the literary" has always been that sound thrumming at the heart of the detective story, while the desire to make investigations has always been a motor that drives literature. So which is a subcategory of the other? Like Clint Eastwood in *A Fistful of Dollars*, Banville doesn't dissolve the two forces—he exploits them.

***The Friends of Eddie Coyle*, directed by Peter Yates**
A low-level, working-class con in Boston has gotten busted again, and now he's going to have to do time. Unfortunately, he happens to be married, with two kids, so he can't let that happen. He begins the game of acquiring, or crafting, information about fellow criminals, to offer the cops in exchange for his freedom. He believes he's good at this game. The degree to which we can see that this man is far from evil, but neither is he clever, is heartbreaking. This is 1970s filmmaking at its best, and with Robert Mitchum at the center of it, to boot. The film feels like a gift.

***Ways of Seeing*, by John Berger**
Now that we are ensconced in the info- and media-centric world of the great twenty-first century, this nonfiction book based on a series of television shows that aired on the BBC in the 1970s should be dated and obsolete. Berger won the Booker Prize for the fantastic novel *G.*, but every year, I watch students go home to read *Ways of Seeing*, and return a few days later surprised to discover that a slim little book, half of which is pictures, offers so many strategies for describing men, women, the images we make, and what we say about each other in those images.

***The Counterlife*, by Philip Roth**
The Counterlife is the tour de force of a mind—Roth's—that not only senses the manifold potentials bound up in any constellation of characters, but can then play those potentials out, with and against one another. Reading this novel is like watching a person play multiple games of chess simultaneously, and win them all. And here's the kicker: after that overheated description, it's also true to say that each section of this book reads fairly straightforwardly, and includes some good laughs.